Pigeon Post

ARTHUR RANSOME

A pigeon a day keeps the natives away
NANCY BLACKETT

PENGUIN BOOKS

Penguin Books Ltd, Harmondsworth, Middlesex, England
Penguin Books Australia Ltd, Ringwood, Victoria, Australia

—

First published by Jonathan Cape 1936
Published in Puffin Books 1969

—

Copyright © The Estate of Arthur Ransome, 1936

—

Made and printed in Great Britain by
Cox & Wyman Ltd,
London, Reading and Fakenham
Set in Monotype Caslon

TO
OSCAR GNOSSPELIUS

CONTENTS

CONTENTS

LIST OF ILLUSTRATIONS

LIST OF ILLUSTRATIONS

PUFFIN BOOKS

Editor: Kaye Webb

PS393

PIGEON POST

Titty and Roger stood on the end of the boat pier, coming home for the summer holidays, and watched the little white sail of the *Amazon* coming to meet them. They could see Dorothea holding the main sheet in both hands. They could see Dick's earnest face. They saw Peggy give him a sign. The little boat swung round, headed into the wind, and stopped at their feet. Roger knelt on the pier and grabbed her.

'Jolly well done,' he said.

'Hop aboard,' said Peggy. She was scribbling on a bit of paper. She rolled it up tight, opened a wicker basket, and brought out a pigeon. 'Come on,' she said. 'You slip the dispatch under the ring ... the rubber one.' Titty slipped in the tiny roll of paper.

'Off you go,' said Peggy, and the pigeon was circling above their heads, and then suddenly heading straight as an arrow for the Blacketts' house.

'I say,' said Titty. 'It can't be piracy or even war while we're camped in the garden. What's it going to be? It won't be North Pole again ...'

'Too jolly hot,' said Roger.

Peggy looked at them. 'Gold,' she said. 'Dick's a geologist and Nancy's turned him on to reading all Captain Flint's mining books.'

'There is plenty of excitement, a little danger, a quantity of hard thinking, planning and fun in connexion with a gold-mine. The ingenuity of this group of children is delightful and stimulating' – *The Times Literary Supplement*

'No other writer for children achieves his natural gaiety, his excitement; and with this story – romantic and yet surprisingly real – of children on a goldmining adventure, he is at his very best' – *News Chronicle*

THE LOOK-OUT

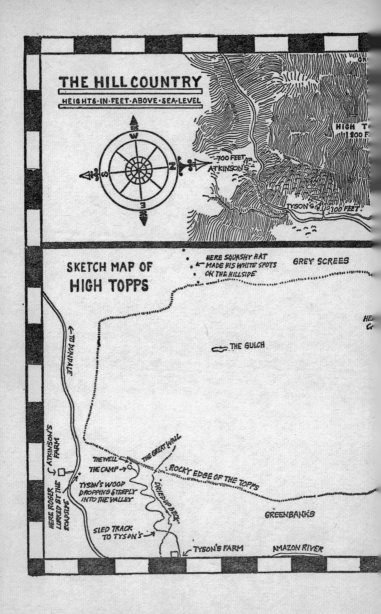

THE HILL COUNTRY
HEIGHTS · IN · FEET · ABOVE · SEA · LEVEL

HIGH T
1200 F

700 FEET
ATKINSON'S

TYSON'S ... 100 FEET.

SKETCH MAP OF
HIGH TOPPS

HERE SQUASHY HAT
MADE HIS WHITE SPOTS
ON THE HILLSIDE

GREY SCREES

HE
G

← OLD DUNDALE

THE GULCH

ATKINSON'S FARM

THE WELL
THE CAMP →
THE GREAT WALL

ROCKY EDGE OF THE TOPPS

HERE ROGER LURKED BY THE ROADSIDE

TYSON'S WOOD
DROPPING STEEPLY
INTO THE VALLEY

DRIED-UP BECK

GREENBANKS

SLED TRACK
TO TYSON'S

TYSON'S FARM

AMAZON RIVER

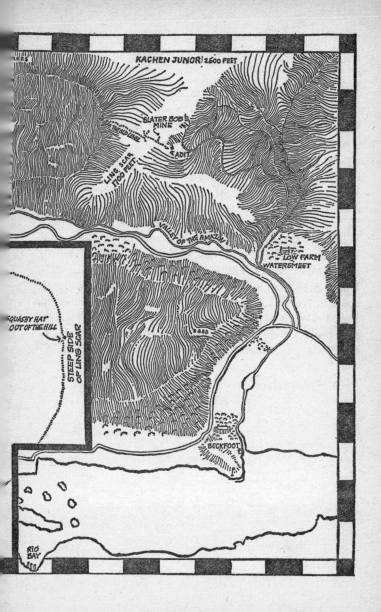

KACHEN JUNOR! 2600 FEET

SLATER BOB'S MINE

THE OLD LEVEL

LING SCAR 1700 FEET

ADIT

VALLEY OF THE AMAZON

LOW FARM
WATERSMEET

SQUASHY HAT OUT OF THE HILL

STEEP SIDE OF LING SCAR

BECKFOOT

RIO BAY

AUTHOR'S NOTE

I have often been asked how I came to write *Swallows and Amazons*. The answer is that it had its beginning long, long ago when, as children, my brother, my sisters and I spent most of our holidays on a farm at the south end of Coniston. We played in or on the lake or on the hills above it finding friends in the farmers and shepherds and charcoal-burners whose smoke rose from the coppice woods along the shore. We adored the place. Coming to it we used to run down to the lake, dip our hands in and wish, as if we had just seen the new moon. Going away from it we were half drowned in tears. While away from it, as children and as grown ups, we dreamt about it. No matter where I was, wandering about the world, I used at night to look for the North Star and, in my mind's eye, could see the beloved skyline of great hills beneath it. *Swallows and Amazons* grew out of those old memories. I could not help writing it. It almost wrote itself.

Haverthwaite, 19 May, 1958

CHAPTER 1

BEGINNING ALREADY

'HERE. . . . I say. . . . Yes. . . . That's me . . .'

Roger swallowed a bit of chocolate unsucked and unbitten. He and Titty leaned together from the doorway of the railway carriage. The train had stopped at the junction. There were ten miles more to go along the little branch line that led into the hills. Somewhere down the platform milk-cans were being shifted, making a loud clanging noise, so that, at first, they had not heard what the porter was calling out as he walked along the train, looking into one carriage after another. Now they heard it plainly.

'Mr Walker. . . . Mr Roger Walker. . . . Mr Walkerrr. . . .' The porter was going from door to door all down the train.

Roger jumped from the carriage while the porter was still two doors away.

'It's me,' he said. 'I'm Roger Walker.'

The porter looked at him.

'You, is it?' he said. 'Come along with me then. We've no time to lose, but they'll be a minute or two yet with them cans. Eh? Eh? . . . It's a basket for you. There was two, but one was for folk that come by the earlier train. We've to let fly before your train goes on. This way. We mun look sharp now. I've left it ready at end of t' platform.'

Titty was just getting out when a farmer's wife blocked the way making ready to get in.

'Here, my dear, you take a hold of this bag,' she said.

Titty took it and put it on the seat. The farmer's wife handed up one parcel after another and then climbed up herself.

'Losh! the heat,' she said, mopping her face and counting her parcels. 'This weather's enough to maze a body's brains. ... Three ... five ... and two's. ... Nay, that's nobbut six ...'

Titty, what with the farmer's wife and the clatter of the milk-cans, had not heard what the porter had said, but she saw him hurrying off and Roger running beside him. She looked at their own small suitcases and hesitated.

'Nay, nobody'll touch them,' said the farmer's wife.

'Thank you very much,' said Titty, jumped down, and ran after Roger and the porter.

'But what is it?' Roger was asking, cantering sideways and just dodging a milk-can that was in the way.

'Pigeon,' said the porter. 'Here you are now. Take this pencil. You've the book to sign.'

Roger, taking the pencil, signed his name in the place the porter showed him. Titty was already looking at the basket, a brown, varnished, wicker basket, lying on the platform. She read the label:

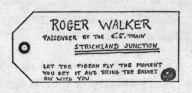

In a corner of the label, looking almost as if it were an official seal, was a small skull and crossbones done in blue pencil.

'It's Nancy,' cried Titty. 'She's beginning something already.'

'There's a live pigeon inside,' said Roger. 'Listen to it.'

'You've not got much time,' said the porter. 'Cut the

string there, and pull out the peg. All these small pigeon-baskets open the same way. Wait a minute. Best bring it beyond the roofing, so it gets a fair start in t' open.'

'Let it go?' said Titty. 'We'll never catch it again.'

The porter laughed.

'They've been sending one for me to fly for them every other day this last week. Name of Blackett, the folk sending 'em.'

'We're going to stay with them,' said Titty.

'Pigeon'll be there long before what you will.'

Roger had cut the string and pulled out the peg.

'I can see its eye,' he said.

They had walked nearly to the end of the platform, beyond the end of the station roof and were standing in the open air beside the engine.

'Let the door fall,' said the porter. 'Hold up the basket. . . . There she goes . . .'

The wicker door fell open. The shining bronze and grey head of the pigeon showed for a moment. Pink claws gripped the edge of the door. The basket was suddenly lighter, and Roger felt as if he himself had tossed the pigeon up into the air. It flew up above the roof, above the drifting white steam from the engine, and swung round in circles above the house tops, above the cricket ground, while the porter and Titty and Roger watched it. The engine-driver and the fireman leaned out from the footboard to see it too. Suddenly, when it was already no more than a circling grey speck, hard to see in the dazzling summer sky, the pigeon seemed to make up its mind and was off, north-west, straight into the sun, towards the blue hills of the lake country.

'I can still see it,' said Titty.

'I can't,' said Roger. 'Oh yes I can. . . . No. It's gone.'

'You'd better hurry back,' said the porter, and he nodded

to the engine driver, who nodded in return, as much as to promise not to start until they were in the train. The guard's whistle blew just as they reached the carriage.

'Look here,' said Roger to Titty as secretly as he could. 'Oughtn't we to give the porter something?'

Titty was already digging in her purse.

'That's all right,' said the porter. 'You keep it for pigeon food.'

'But it's not our pigeon,' said Titty.

'No matter,' said the porter, closed the door on them, and waved a friendly hand as the train pulled out.

'Thank you very much,' they shouted at him from the window.

'What was all to do?' said the farmer's wife, who had now counted all her parcels and was sitting in a corner of the carriage with her hands folded on her lap. 'Pigeon to loose? Now my son down in t' south, he's a great one for pigeons. Starts flying 'em when they're nobbut squeakers, he calls 'em. He flies 'em farther and farther, and before summer's out he's sending 'em up here to dad and me, and we loose 'em for him in t' morning and they've flown all t' length of England before dark.'

'Do you send messages by them?' asked Titty.

'Love from home,' said the farmer's wife. 'Aye. Dad's put that on a scrap of paper and tied it in the ring on a pigeon's leg before now.'

'I say,' said Roger. 'That's what Peggy meant when she wrote in her letter that they'd got something better than semaphore messages for this year.'

'Isn't it a good thing we were able to come?' said Titty. 'We might have had to wait at school.'

Roger leaned out of the window, with his eyes screwed up against the wind.

'I can't see a sign of that pigeon,' he said.

'It went off at such a lick,' said Titty. 'The train'll never catch it up.'

'Far to fly?' asked the farmer's wife.

'It's a house called Beckfoot at the other side of the lake.'

'Mrs Blackett's?'

'Do you know her?'

'Aye, and her daughters too, and her brother Mr Turner that's for ever gallivanting off to foreign parts . . .'

'We know him too,' said Roger. 'We call him. . . .' And he stopped short. There was no point in giving away Captain Flint's name to natives.

'You've been here before, likely,' said the farmer's wife.

'Oh yes,' said Titty. 'We always stay at Holly Howe . . . at least mother does . . . but Mrs Jackson's got visitors for the next two weeks. . . . Mrs Blackett's having us till then because mother didn't want Bridget to give us all whooping-cough.'

'We've come straight from school,' said Roger.

'Eh,' said the farmer's wife. 'I know all about you. You'll be the young folk that were camping on the island down the lake two years since when Mr Turner had his houseboat broke into. And you were here again last winter when the lake was froze over. But I thought there was four of you . . .'

'Five, with Bridget,' said Titty. 'John and Susan must be here already. It isn't so far from their schools.'

'And weren't you friends with the two at Mrs Dixon's?'

'Dick and Dorothea Callum,' said Titty. 'They won't be here for ages yet, because their father has to correct examination papers.'

*

It had been a long day's journey from the south, but the last few minutes of it were going like seconds. Already they were in the hill country where walls of loose stones divided field from field. Grey rocks showed through the withered grass. Grey and purple fells lifted to the skies. Titty and Roger hurried from side to side of the carriage, looking first out of one window and then out of another.

'Fair parched everything is,' said the farmer's wife. 'No rain for weeks and none coming, and no water in the becks. Folks are at their wits' ends in some parts to keep the beasts alive.'

'Hullo!' said Roger. 'There's been a fire.'

'More'n one,' said the farmer's wife.

The train was running through a cutting, the sides of which were black and burnt.

'Sparks from the engine?' said Roger.

'Aye,' said the farmer's wife. 'And where there's no engines there's visitors with motor-cars and matches and cigarettes and no more thought in their heads than a cheese has. It takes nobbut a spark to start a fire when all's bone dry for the kindling. Eh, and here we are. Yon's my farm . . .'

A farm-house, not unlike Holly Howe, flashed into sight and was gone. The farmer's wife jumped up and began collecting her parcels. The train came suddenly round a bend and began to slow up.

'There's the lake!' Titty and Roger cried together.

Far below them, beyond the smoking chimneys of a village, glittering water stretched between the hills. The train was stopping for the last time.

'The platform's on the other side,' said Roger.

'Who'll be there?' said Titty.

'Nobody,' said Roger.

But a red knitted cap was bobbing up and down among the people waiting on the platform. In another moment Nancy Blackett was at the door, and they were saying good-bye to the farmer's wife and struggling down with their suitcases.

'Here you are,' said Nancy. 'Hullo, Mrs Newby. Well,

Roger, did you get the pigeon all right? Did you let it fly? Mother and I had to start before it got home. She'll be here in a minute. Shopping. Gosh, I was nearly too late to meet you. You didn't forget the basket. Good. Good. Shiver my timbers but I'm jolly glad to see you. Come on. Let's get your boxes out of the van, and then we've got to go to the Parcels Office.'

Everybody in the world seemed to be talking at once, all round them, but presently their boxes came out of the van among the others, and Nancy, telling the porter to keep a look out for Mrs Blackett, was hurrying them along the platform.

'Is Captain Flint in the houseboat?' asked Roger.

'He's still in South America, isn't he?' said Titty.

'He ought to be here, but he isn't,' said Nancy. 'His mine wasn't any good and it serves him right, not being here in time for the beginning of the holidays. But he's on his way home. Some of his things have come already, but not the most important. At least it hadn't yesterday. It may be here today.'

She took them into the Parcels Office.

'You haven't a crate or a cage with something alive in it?' she asked the man behind the counter.

'Rabbits?' asked the man.

'The trouble is we don't exactly know.'

'Miss Blackett, isn't it?' said the man, running his finger down the columns of his book. 'No, Miss, there's nothing come for you. Not yet. Unless it's come by this train.'

'I've looked in the van already,' said Nancy. 'Look here, we'll be awfully busy tomorrow. So I won't be able to come across. But could you telephone if it comes?'

'Aye, Miss Blackett, I can do that.'

'But what is it?' asked Roger.

'It's called Timothy, anyway,' said Nancy.

'Another monkey?' said Roger.

21

LETTING FLY

'Or a parrot?' said Titty. 'He said he might be getting another.'

'Can't be either,' said Nancy, as they went back to the luggage. 'He said in the telegram that we could let it loose in his room. It can't be a monkey or a parrot. It must be something that can't do much damage and doesn't climb. Dick. . . .' Nancy checked herself and went on. 'We've been looking through the natural history books, and we're pretty sure it must be an armadillo. But we don't know. And we can't find out, because Uncle Jim is on his way home and we don't even know the name of his ship. Whatever it is, he must have sent it on in advance, or he wouldn't have telegraphed. . . . Hullo, here's mother.'

A smallish, ancient motor-car with badly dinted mudguards had driven into the station yard. Mrs Blackett, round, small, no taller than Nancy, was talking to the porter. She turned as they came up.

'Here you are,' she said. 'The last of the gang.'

'Except Timothy,' said Nancy. 'He's not here yet, but they're going to telephone the moment he arrives.'

'Yes, those two. . . .' Mrs Blackett was looking at their boxes. 'We'll have them both on the back. You've nothing else, have you, besides those suitcases? And how's your mother? And Bridget? Oh, I was forgetting you've come straight from school, too, and won't know any more than John or Susan.'

'We had a letter yesterday,' said Titty. 'Bridgie's only whooping about twice a day. So she's all right, and so's mother. At least she didn't say she wasn't.'

'Hop in,' said Mrs Blackett, when the boxes were strapped on the luggage grid. 'Thank you, Robert. You come in front with me, Titty. Don't anybody sit on my parcels. There are eggs in that basket, and tomatoes in the paper bag. Slam that door, Roger. Give it a push from inside to see it's properly shut. That's right, Nancy. . . . I'm glad your uncle didn't hear me get into those gears. . . . Yes, I've remembered to take the brake off . . .'

There was a fearful crash and rattle, and the little old car swung out of the station gates and turned sharp to the left.

'Don't we have to go round the head of the lake?' said Roger.

'You don't,' said Nancy. 'Not if young Sophocles flew straight.'

Titty, sitting in front by Mrs Blackett, looked round. 'Why did you call the pigeon Sophocles?' she asked.

'You may well wonder,' said Mrs Blackett.

'Oh, mother *do* look out for your steering,' said Nancy. 'You see, Uncle Jim gave us one, and called him Homer because he was a homing pigeon. And then when we got two more for company, we looked up Greek poets and found Sophocles and Sappho. And there you are. Phew! Mother. Lucky I caught the eggs . . .'

Their adventures had very nearly ended before they had properly begun.

'People ought not to go so fast,' said Mrs Blackett. She had braked the car so suddenly that Roger and Nancy had shot off the back seat and Titty had nearly bumped her nose on the windscreen. 'The roads are crowded with dangerous drivers. . . . It's hardly safe to be on them at all. All very well, Nancy. You can laugh as much as you like. People are most careless. Now then, I ought to have sounded my horn, if only I hadn't been listening to you . . .'

'Did you see who it was?' said Nancy. 'It was Colonel Jolys. He took off his hat. . . . No, don't try to turn round. He knows you didn't see him, and I gave him a grin anyway.'

'What's he got a trumpet for?' asked Roger.

'It's a hunting-horn,' said Titty.

'It isn't,' said Nancy. 'It's one of the old coach horns. He's been having a review of his fire-fighters. Didn't you see those brooms on long handles sticking up out of the back of his car?'

'It's the drought,' Mrs Blackett explained. 'We've had no rain for weeks, and if the fells should catch fire it would be a dreadful thing for everybody, and old Colonel Jolys has been organizing so that the moment there's a fire all the young men know where to go to be rushed off in motor-cars to help beat it out.'

'They sound coach horns,' said Nancy, 'and then see how soon they can start. Everybody who's got a motor-car is in it, and all the men. . . . Oh do look out, mother.'

Mrs Blackett, who had somehow got to the wrong side of the road, swerved back and straightened again. They were coming down the last steep drop into the little village that the Walkers and Blacketts called Rio. They turned the corner at the bottom. There was the sparkling water of the bay, with its landing-stages and its anchored yachts. Roger and Titty had seen it last in winter, frozen and covered with skaters. Mrs Blackett, with a screech of the brakes, pulled up. Nancy was out as the car stopped.

'Come on, you two,' she said, and Titty and Roger got out and followed her, wondering, along a wooden boat pier that seemed strangely high out of the water.

'What's happened to the lake?' said Roger. 'It used to be nearly up to the road.'

'No rain,' said Nancy, looking eagerly out beyond the islands. 'Half a minute. Yes, it's all right. Sophocles has got home. You stick here and wait for them . . .'

Already she was running back along the pier.

'I say,' cried Roger, staring after her. 'Mrs Blackett's turned round. Nancy's getting in. They're off. Hi! I say Titty! They've taken all our luggage!'

But Titty hardly heard him. Far away over the water, glittering in the evening sun, she had seen the white speck that had sent Nancy hurrying to the car. Two years had slipped back in a moment, and once again she was seeing for the first time the little white sail of the Amazon pirates.

Roger shook her by the arm.

'Titty,' he said, 'they've gone . . .'

Titty pointed to the little boat.

'It's all right,' she said. 'John and Susan and Peggy must be coming to fetch us across.'

CHAPTER 2

THE PLAN

TITTY and Roger stood on the end of the boat pier, looking
up the lake and across to the big hills and the proud peak of
Kanchenjunga that they had climbed the year before. Over
there was the Beckfoot promontory, hiding the Blacketts'
house, and between the promontory and the islands was the
little white sail of the *Amazon*. And then, as they watched,
they began to doubt. Who was sailing her? The little white
sail flapped in the wind. If that had happened once they would
have thought nothing of it. But it happened again and yet
again, and not only when the little boat was going about at
the end of a tack.

'Can't be John,' said Roger. 'Or even Susan. They'd
never let her shake like that. And Peggy's just as good as
John.'

The wind was blowing up the lake and the little boat was
beating down against it. A big lake steamer hid her for a
moment. Then she was gone behind an island. She turned
again and was slipping across towards the mouth of the bay.
And every now and then a long-drawn-out quivering of her
sail shocked the two experts watching from the pier.

'There's a red cap,' said Titty. 'That must be Peggy. But
it can't be her steering. I say, Roger, it's the D.'s. Peg's on
the middle thwart. Dorothea's hanging on to the mainsheet.
Dick's at the tiller. I saw the sunshine on his spectacles.
Three cheers. Mrs Blackett must be having them too.'

'But they didn't know anything about sailing.'

'They were learning on the Broads. Don't you remember?
Dot sent a postcard.'

'Let's wave,' said Titty. 'They can see us now.'

Peggy Blackett waved back to them. Dick and Dorothea were far too busy.

'They're not doing half badly,' said Roger. 'For beginners.'

The little boat came quickly nearer.

They could see Dorothea holding the mainsheet in both hands, watching Peggy for orders. They could see Dick's earnest face. They saw Peggy give him a sign. The little boat swung round, headed into the wind, and stopped at their feet. Roger knelt on the pier and grabbed her.

'Jolly well done,' he said. 'Hullo. You've got another pigeon.'

'Hop aboard,' said Peggy. 'And hang on to the pier. We've got to send her off with a message. What's the time?'

'My watch is bust,' said Roger. 'It always is.'

'Fourteen minutes past seven,' said Dick.

Peggy was scribbling on a bit of paper. She rolled it up tight, opened another wicker basket like the one that had been sent to meet them, and brought out a pigeon. 'Come on,' she said. 'You slip the dispatch under the ring . . . the rubber one.'

The pigeon had a metal ring on one leg and a rubber one on the other. Titty, with trembling fingers, trembling for fear of doing it wrong and making the pigeon uncomfortable, slipped in the tiny roll of paper.

'Off you go,' said Peggy, and the pigeon was circling above their heads, above the yachts in the bay, and was suddenly flying straight as an arrow for the distant promontory.

'Cast off,' cried Peggy, and in another moment they had left the pier and, with a fair wind to help them, were sailing up the lake after the pigeon.

'We didn't start to meet you till we got your message,' said Dorothea.

'What message?' said Roger.

'Sophocles,' said Dorothea.

'Which one is this?' said Titty.

'Sappho,' said Peggy. 'You watch the flagstaff on our promontory. They'll send the flag up as soon as Sappho's in.'

They were hardly clear of Rio Bay before Roger sang out, 'There's the flag.' Away up the lake, a flag, that at this distance looked plain black, was fluttering up the flagstaff on the Beckfoot promontory.

'Pretty quick,' said Peggy.

'It's as quick as a telegraph,' said Roger.

'Very nearly,' said Dick. 'On short distances like this.'

'There's Susan. . . . She's running away.'

'Gone back to camp,' said Peggy. 'They're busy with the tents. You know we're camping in the garden . . .'

'In the garden?' said Titty, rather sadly.

'Only till your mother comes to Holly Howe. You won't have *Swallow* till then, and we can't all eight of us cram into *Amazon*. So Wild Cat Island's no use. And anyhow, while mother's the only parent she wants to have us all within reach. She says she's too busy with paperhangers and plasterers to keep an eye on us if we camp too far from the house. It's not going to be as bad as it might be. We're going to do our own cooking. I say, did you know Susan's blued a birthday present on a mincing machine? To improve the pemmican.'

Titty cheered up. After all, it was only for a fortnight.

'Has Timothy come?' asked Dorothea.

'Not yet,' said Titty.

'We went to the Luggage Office to ask,' said Roger.

'I wish we knew when he was sent off,' said Peggy.

'Can I have a go at the tiller?' said Roger.

'Come on,' said Dick, and, for part of the voyage home, Titty and Roger took turns in the steering, just to make sure that they had not forgotten their ancient skill, while Peggy told them how the pigeons had been trained little by little to longer and longer flights, and Dorothea told them how she and Dick had been turned into able seamen on the Norfolk Broads. Soon they were near enough to the promontory to see the white skull and crossbones on the black flag.

'I say,' said Titty. 'It can't be piracy or even war while we're camped in the garden. What's it going to be? It won't be North Pole again . . .'

'Too jolly hot,' said Roger.

Peggy looked at them. 'Gold,' she said. 'Dick's a geologist and Nancy's turned him on to reading all Captain Flint's mining books, and tomorrow we're going right inside Kanchenjunga to talk to Slater Bob. He's an old miner, and mother says he knows where we ought to look for it.'

'Inside Kanchenjunga?' said Titty.

'With candles,' said Dorothea.

'Farther away from the point!' cried Peggy. 'We'll be aground.'

They gave the promontory a wide berth, and were presently sailing in towards the mouth of the Amazon river. They pulled up the centre-board and lowered the sail. Peggy took off her shoes and jumped overboard to pull the little boat over the shallows. She climbed in again. They rowed up the river between the beds of tall reeds, far higher above the water than usual, because very little water had been coming down the river during the drought.

'There's the boat-house,' cried Roger.

Beyond the boat-house, where the faded crest of the *Amazon* pirates was still to be seen, though it badly wanted repainting, was the old grey house of Beckfoot looking very strange with the ladders and scaffolding of the painters. On the lawn between the house and the river were a lot of white tents.

'Here they are!' That was John's voice, and there was John himself and Susan coming to the water's edge to meet them, and a moment later Nancy came racing round the corner of the house.

'Hullo,' said John and Susan.

'Hullo,' said Titty and Roger.

'Jolly good work with the pigeons,' said John.

'Where are the keys of your boxes?' said Susan. 'I'll get out just what you'll want in the camp.'

Term time was gone as if it had been wiped out. Real life was beginning again.

'Pretty good surprise, wasn't it?' said Nancy. 'I told mother not to let you know the D.'s were coming. Able-seamen both of them now. And with Roger promoted we'll have two able-seamen in each boat when your mother comes to Holly Howe and you have *Swallow* again. But we've got lots to do first. Did Peggy tell you? Lucky we've got Dick. He's geologist to the company . . .'

'What company?' asked Roger.

'Mining,' said Nancy.

'Supper in half an hour,' Mrs Blackett called from the house. 'You'll be ready by then. Supper in my camp tonight, not yours. I'll come to supper with you another day . . . to try Susan's minced pemmican.'

'Buck up,' said Nancy.

They had just time to look at their own tents, and at the camp fire, not on the lawn but in a little clearing among the bushes a few yards away.

'Now for the pigeon loft,' said Nancy.

They were raced across the lawn and round the house to the stableyard.

'Hullo,' said Peggy. 'There's that Squashy Hat again.'

A tall, thin man, in loose grey flannels, with a soft brown felt hat, was hesitating outside the garden gate. When he saw the eight of them pouring round the corner of the house he turned and went off up the road.

'That's the second time,' said Nancy. 'He was here yesterday, looking over the wall when we were putting up tents ready for the D.'s.'

'Visitors think gates and walls are just made for them to goggle over,' said Peggy. 'Here you are. Don't kick up too much row going up the ladder. That's the door they fly in at.'

They went up the ladder to see the pigeon loft, with its whitewashed sill for the pigeons to land on, and the little doorway with its swinging wires to let the pigeons come in and to keep them in when they had come. Nancy opened the big door for humans at the top of the ladder, and showed them the inner door of wire netting, and the big loft behind it, where Homer, Sophocles and Sappho were enjoying their evening meal, sipping water, and talking over the afternoon's flights.

'Look here, you *must* get your things changed,' said Susan, and they were rushed across the yard and upstairs in a house strangely dismantled, to get into camping clothes in a room crammed with all kinds of furniture wrapped up in dust sheets.

'Hurry up,' called Nancy from the hall, and they were rushed down again and into Captain Flint's study.

Captain Flint's study, close by the front door, seemed to be the only room in the house that was as they remembered it. There were the high bookshelves, the shelves of scientific apparatus, the glass-fronted cupboard of chemicals and the queer things hanging on the walls; spears, shields, a knobkerrie and the jawbone of a big fish. Even there, something was going on in the building line. Someone had been at work turning a packing-case into something rather like a rabbit hutch. On the table a big book of South American natural history was open at the coloured picture of an armadillo, and beside it was a slip of paper on which the careful Dick had noted down the usual size of such animals. This, no doubt, was as a guide in making a suitable place for Timothy to sleep in when he should arrive. Pinned to the mantelpiece, as if to let even his room know that he was coming, was the telegram, sent off from Pernambuco a week before, in which Captain Flint (Nancy's and Peggy's Uncle Jim) had announced that he was on his way.

THIS WILD GOOSE LAYS NO EGGS STARTING HOME BE KIND TO TIMOTHY GIVE HIM THE RUN OF MY ROOM   JIM

'Read that,' said Nancy. 'He's come another mucker. Wild goose means he was on a wild goose chase. And when he says "Lays no eggs," he means he hasn't found gold. That's what he went for.'

'You know,' said Peggy. 'The goose that lays the golden eggs. Well, this one didn't.'

'He might just as well have stayed at home,' said Nancy. 'And then he'd be in the houseboat and we could be making him walk the plank or anything else that turned up. The whole trouble is that he gets fidgets and goes off looking for things. Why shouldn't he look for things here? If we can find just a scrap of gold, then he'll stay at home instead of wasting our holidays by being too far away to be useful . . .'

The gong sounded in the empty hall.

They hurried into the carpetless dining-room to have their supper off a table made with the planks and trestles of the plasterers. Mrs Blackett served out good big helpings of mutton and green peas and potatoes, and everybody was too hungry to do much talking. Mrs Blackett herself talked all the time, of the papering and plastering and what not, and how the house must be ready before her brother came back, and how glad she was the Walkers and Callums had been able to come, and how much she was looking forward to seeing Mrs Walker and Bridget, when Bridget's whooping-cough should be over, and Mr and Mrs Callum, as soon as Mr Callum could get away from correcting examination papers. It was not till supper was nearly over that serious subjects were mentioned. 'And now,' said Mrs Blackett at last. 'How soon do you begin prospecting?'

'We're going to see Slater Bob tomorrow,' said Nancy.

'So long as you are all here to answer your names at night you can't get into much harm,' she said. 'I expect he'll tell you enough to keep you busy hunting all over the valley.'

'Is there really any gold?' said Roger.

'Slater Bob'll tell you there is,' said Mrs Blackett. 'He's been talking of gold ever since I was a little girl.'

It was really growing dark when they went out to the camp in the garden. The sun had gone down over the shoulder of Kanchenjunga, and the fiery sunset had dimmed and cooled to a pale green light behind the hills. A starry darkness closed down over the valley of the Amazon, and the silent little river, and the cluster of white tents on the lawn. The camp-fire among the bushes made the night seem darker than it was. They sat round it and talked, seeing each other's faces by the light of the flames. Bushes and tree trunks about them flickered into sight and out again as the flames leapt up or died. Everything seemed possible.

'It'll be the Swallows, Amazons and D.'s Mining Company,' said Nancy, and Titty started suddenly. She knew that Nancy had been talking for some time, but she had not heard what she was saying.

'When he sees what we've found, he'll never desert again,' Nancy went on.

Dorothea was still wide awake. She had not come a long railway journey that day. She spoke to Titty. 'Isn't it lovely?' she said. 'To think of him coming home and knowing nothing

34

about it. A failure. No gold. Nothing. Coming home alone. Even his faithful armadillo sent on ahead. And the boat moving through the tropical night. And Captain Flint walking up and down the deserted decks. Up and down, up and down. Thinking of failure. Not knowing that when he gets home, there'll be a gold mine at his very door.'

Titty looked away from the fire, and tried to see the outlines of the hills somewhere above them in the dark. She caught herself yawning. Tomorrow. . . . Her eyes blinked.

A sudden light showed through the bushes. Mrs Blackett's voice sounded across the garden. 'Time all you people were asleep. Titty and Roger must be nearly dead.'

'All right, mother,' called Nancy. 'We've a lot to do tomorrow,' she added, 'and we want to get up in the morning before the whole place is flooded with paperers and painters.'

'Come along,' said Susan.

She was already raking the embers together. Pocket torches flashed out. The eight prospectors left their camp-fire and went back to the lawn where the tents shone suddenly out of the darkness. Lanterns were lit for each tent. Frantic shadows swayed on the canvas as the prospectors struggled into sleeping-bags.

Presently the lanterns were blown out one by one.

Mrs Blackett's voice came again across the lawn.

'Everybody in bed? Good night. . . . Sleep well.'

'Good night. Good night.'

Titty lying in her sleeping-bag sniffed happily at the clean smell of the grass and canvas. She wriggled a hand out into the night to feel the dewy grass so near.

'Roger,' she whispered. 'Can you hear?'

'Yes,' said Roger from the next tent.

'This time last night we were still at school.'

'Well, we aren't now,' said Roger.

CHAPTER 3

CONSULTING SLATER BOB

WALKERS, Blacketts and Callums, Swallows, Amazons and D.'s, eight of them together, were nearly half-way up Kanchenjunga. They had set out in the Beckfoot rowing-boat, but had not been able to get far upstream because there was so little water in the river. So they had pulled its nose up a shingly beach and tied its painter to a hazel bush, and continued their journey on foot. All but Nancy carried knapsacks, with sandwiches and thermos flasks of tea. Peggy's knapsack held Nancy's provisions as well as her own, for on Nancy's shoulders, instead of a knapsack, was a pigeon-basket with Homer, Sappho and Sophocles inside. The expedition had followed their old track of the year before, past Low Farm, turning up from the Amazon beside the little beck, that usually came tumbling down to join the river but this year was no more than a trickle. They had come up out of the trees close by last year's half-way camp, and were following the cart-track up to the quarries. 'We may just as well use it,' Nancy had said. 'No point in pretending no one's ever been here, when we're going up to see Slater Bob.'

A great spur of Kanchenjunga, Ling Scar, rose above them to the left. They had been slowly climbing ever since they had left the river.

'There it is,' said Nancy at last, and pointed ahead of them, up the side of the Scar to a rampart of loose stones that rose out of the heather and bracken and scorched grass. 'All that stuff has come out of the inside of the hill.'

'Come on,' said Peggy. 'Buck up the able-seamen.'

But Susan stopped short. 'What's the time, John?' she

36

said. 'Ages after twelve o'clock. He'll be in the middle of his dinner if we go in now. We'd better have ours first.'

'Good idea,' said Roger.

'Oh well,' said Nancy. 'Everybody is a bit out of breath.'

Knapsacks were unslung and tired explorers flung themselves down on the heather at the side of the track. Nancy wriggled out of the straps by which the pigeon-basket had been fastened to her shoulders.

'I'll let them go now,' she said. 'No point in keeping them just for another few hundred yards. Come on, Roger, let's see you fly one. And you, Titty. I'll send Sappho off to show you how.'

She opened the basket, and put her hand in and caught the plump Sappho. A moment later, with a quick upward swing, she launched her into the air.

'Now then, Roger. Careful not to squeeze him.'

'Which is it I've got?'

'Homer. Off with him. That's right, Titty. Get hold of Sophocles. Don't wait, Roger.'

Homer and Sophocles were tossed into the air almost together. In a few seconds they were joined by Sappho, and circled high over the heads of the explorers.

'Mine's off,' said Roger.

'That's Sappho,' said Nancy.

'There goes Sophocles,' said Peggy. 'And old Homer.'

'I wonder which'll get home first,' said Roger.

'We can't tell,' said Nancy, 'unless someone sticks at home to watch the pigeon loft.'

'Couldn't they work some sort of signal?' said Dick.

'It's no good trying to teach pigeons to go and tap at windows,' said Nancy.

'But what about a bell?' said Dick, with sudden eagerness. 'I say, Peggy, how do those wires work when the pigeon flies home and pushes through them to get in?'

Out came pocket-book and pencil, and if it had not been for Dorothea reminding him about them, Dick would have had no time to eat his sandwiches. 'There ought to be a way of working it,' he said, putting his pocket-book almost unwillingly away, as Nancy jumped to her feet once more and empty thermos flasks were being stowed in the knapsacks.

'He's sure to have finished his dinner by now,' said Nancy, and the eight would-be prospectors took to the road again.

And then, just as they left the main track and began to climb up to the left towards that rampart of grey stones, they saw a man working his way down the ridge.

'Hullo,' said John, 'somebody's been climbing Kanchenjunga.'

'He's chosen a funny way to come down,' said Peggy.

Presently they saw that he, too, was making for those great piles of stones.

'I say,' said Nancy. 'I wonder if he is going to see Slater Bob.'

'Who's going to get there first?' said Roger.

It was going to be a very near thing. They had not got so far to go as the stranger, but they were working uphill, whereas he was scrambling down.

'Jib-booms and bobstays!' exclaimed Nancy suddenly. 'Do you see who it is?'

'It's that Squashy Hat again,' said Peggy.

'Who?' said Titty.

'You know. That man who was goggling over our gate.'

'You don't think he overheard any secrets?' said Dorothea.

Nancy stared at her. 'He couldn't,' she said, and then stopped. 'But that other time we caught him looking over the wall. He may have been there ages and heard all kinds of things. Hurry up. If he's going to be there, we shan't be able to ask Slater Bob about gold.'

But the stranger, it seemed, was as little anxious to meet

38

them as they were to meet him. He was slowing up. He stood still, watched for a moment, and presently sat down on the hillside.

'That's all right,' said Nancy. 'Come on. We'll easily hear if he comes in after us.'

A moment later they could see him no more. A scarred rock face rose above them. On either side were the great outworks of loose stones. A thin trickle of water ran along a winding gutter beside a narrow railway track. There was just room for them to step round a four-wheeled trolley. They passed a neat pile of the green slates with which the houses for miles round are roofed. Nancy put her head into a tumble-down shed.

'Not here,' she said. 'Bob must be inside.'

And then, turning a corner between the high walls built up on either side of them, they saw the narrow railway line disappear into a black hole in the rock.

'Hand out the candles, John,' said Nancy. 'One for everybody.'

John wriggled clear of his knapsack, opened it, and took out a bundle of eight brand-new candles that Nancy had wheedled out of cook.

'Are we going into that?' said Roger, looking doubtfully at Susan.

'We're all going in together,' said Titty. 'It'll be just like Peter Duck's cave in Swallowdale, only bigger.'

'Your cave in Swallowdale was probably an old working,' said Nancy. 'Uncle Jim said he thought it must be.'

'How far does it go in?' said Dick, peering through the entry into the darkness of the tunnel.

'Miles,' said Peggy. 'Out the other side of Ling Scar. Only the other end isn't safe. Here's your candle.'

'That's not the way to hold them,' said Nancy. 'Hold them miners' way, like this. Between your fingers. That's right. Palm up, wrist up, and fingers forward, so that your hand shields it from behind. Hold it low, so that the grease doesn't splash over you. Like this.'

'Better get inside before lighting up,' said John, who had had two matches blown out by little gusts of wind.

'And we'd better leave our shoes here,' said Nancy. 'It's called the Old Level, but it isn't as level as all that and there's one place where you have to paddle.'

'No adders?' said Roger.

'None in there.'

Eight pairs of shoes were left in a row outside the entrance to the level.

'Now then,' said Nancy. 'I'll go first. Only room for one at a time. Look here, Peg. You're the other one who knows it. You'd better come last, just in case.'

'In case of what?' whispered Roger.

Nobody answered him. One by one they went into the tunnel. Candles were lit.

'Everybody ready?' called Nancy, and her cheerful voice sounded strange and hollow though she was only a dozen yards into the hill.

They moved slowly forward in the narrow tunnel, each with a splash of candle-light.

'Hoo! ... Hoo! ... Hooo!' said Roger, listening to his own voice.

'Look,' said Dick. 'They must have blasted with gunpowder. You can see one side of the hole they bored for their charge.'

'Where?' said Roger. 'Oh, yes. I see it,' and he ran his finger along a smooth and narrow furrow in the rock.

'Get along,' said Peggy. 'Don't let's get left behind.'

'Look out for the water splash.'

A shout came from ahead.

'It's only about an inch deep.'

40

That was Susan's voice. They hurried on, and a moment later the lights far ahead of them disappeared. A faint glimmer on a damp wall of rock showed that the leaders had turned a corner.

'Let's run,' said Roger.

'No,' said Dick, but walked as fast as he could along the uneven damp ground between the narrow trolley lines. 'No good running if you can't see. You'll only catch a toe in a sleeper.'

Dorothea, Titty and Peggy hurried after them, their candles dribbling warm wax on their fingers.

'Why, it's nothing of a water splash,' said Roger, as he wriggled his toes in the puddle between the trolley lines.

'Dry summer,' said Dick. 'Perhaps it's deeper other times.'

'Last look at daylight,' said Peggy. 'That's the end of the straight bit.'

They looked back. The walls of the tunnel disappeared into darkness but, far away behind them, the entrance showed like a pinprick in a sheet of black paper.

'We must be right in the middle of the mountain,' said Titty.

'Not nearly yet,' said Peggy.

They turned the corner. That far away pinprick of light was gone. For a moment they saw a flicker ahead of them. It disappeared. The tunnel had twisted again, and John, Nancy and Susan were already out of sight. Just for a half second Titty hesitated. She looked back at Peggy. But Peggy was close behind her and showed no signs of stopping. Oh well, if Peggy did not mind it, Peggy who was afraid of thunderstorms, it must be all right. Titty looked down at her wavering candle. Was her hand shaky or was it not? Anyhow, everybody else's candle was flickering too.

'Listen,' said Dick.

Faint and far away they could hear a steady thudding noise.

'Slater Bob,' said Peggy. 'Good. He's there. I was a bit afraid he wasn't, with the trolley being left outside.'

Barefoot on rock and damp ground, they hurried on. Round another corner, and then another, and still the leaders were not in sight. The thudding noise ahead of them grew louder. It stopped, and began again on a different note.

'Doesn't sound like stone,' said Dick.

'Have you read *A Journey to the Centre of the Earth*?' Dorothea asked over her shoulder.

'About Hans Sterk and the hot water spouting out of the rock?' said Titty.

'About the mastodons,' said Dorothea. 'It's a whole herd of them, stamping.'

'Hurry up,' said Peggy.

At last, far ahead of them, they saw a group of shadowy figures with flickering candles held low.

The noise grew louder and louder. The tunnel opened out a little wider and higher at a sort of cross-roads where other tunnels joined it right and left.

'Nearly there now,' said Nancy. 'Had to wait for you, just in case Peggy forgot and you went straight on by mistake.'

'I'd remembered all right,' said Peggy.

'We might have gone on for ever,' said Dorothea.

'Might have been a job to find you,' said Nancy. 'Anyway, port your helm and head to starboard . . .'

Close together now, the whole party turned one by one into a tunnel that led to the right out of the main level. It twisted this way and that, and when they had gone forty or fifty yards along it, they were suddenly almost blinded by a bright light that made their candle-flames seem dim.

'Douse candles,' said Nancy, blowing out her own. 'So that they'll last out for the way back. We shan't want them now. Hullo, Bob. We've brought some friends . . .'

They were at the mouth of a lofty chamber in the rock.

The dazzling light of the acetylene lamp that hung from an iron spike driven into a crack in the rock, showed them a short, broad-shouldered old man leaning on a baulk of timber that he had been shaping with an axe. A ladder went up into the darkness overhead beside a wide smooth wall of green slate.

'Come in,' said Slater Bob. 'Come in and welcome. I'm nobbut shaping a two-three props to put where there's some gone a bit weak. Wouldn't do for me to be shut out. Not likely. Eh, Miss Nancy, but there's scarce room for t' lot o' ye. And no seats . . .'

'We don't want to sit down,' said Nancy. 'Look here, Bob, mother says you know something about gold in the fells, and we want to know where to look for it, if there is any really.'

'Gold,' said the old man, shading his eyes and looking at her through the dazzle of the light. 'Of course there's gold. There's everything in these fells if only a man know where. Slate for your roofs and slates for your schools and slate pencils too, though you don't use 'em as we did when I were young. And copper, too, for your kettles and your saucepans, though that new aluminy come in that soaks away wi' a drop o' soda and makes food taste funny to me. And you never know what you'll happen on. 'Twasn't slate they was wanting, the folk that cut this level. Copper they was after, and they got a fair doing of it too, out of yon pocket on far side of the level where you turned to come in here. They were still getting copper out o' that when I were a lad in the mines nigh sixty year since. And then they found no more and gave up, and I found the slate for myself just chipping about like. Slate's not copper, but it's right good stuff, and it'll keep my belly full and a fire o' nights, so long as folk build houses and set roofs on 'em to keep t' rain out . . .'

'But you don't burn slate,' said Roger almost to himself.

43

'Or eat it, you donk,' said Peggy.

Roger pretended he had not heard. As if he had not understood. And anyway, he had not meant to say it aloud. It was just a private joke that had come into his head. He slipped across and climbed a little way up the ladder and sat there.

'Yes, but what about gold?' said Nancy.

Slater Bob was not to be hurried.

'Copper and slate,' he said, 'and then there's black lead, graphite, they call it, for the wooden pencils. They think that's all gone, but there's more to find, for them that has eyes and a mind to 't. Five hundred year folk have been working these fells, and now they've all give up, all but me, more fools they, when it stands to reason there's more in t' fells nor ever come out. There was Queen Elizabeth had her Dutchies here, and a mort o' folk after that, scratting and scratting. And they're all dead and gone and the fells is here yet, and the scrattings on 'em nowt but a scar here and there, and the best of all still to find. An I'm not the only one to think so, mind ye. . . .' said Slater Bob. 'A gentleman was here only yesterday asking this and that . . .'

There was a sudden stir among his listeners.

'Not a man with a squashy hat?' said Nancy. 'I say, you didn't tell him anything about the gold, did you?'

'Nay, I didn't look at his hat. Ordinary hat it was, same as what gentlemen generally cover their heads wi'.'

'But you didn't tell him about the gold . . .'

'He didn't ask about it,' said Slater Bob. 'But the way he talked, I could see he knew a rare bit about mining.'

'He must have heard us planning,' said Peggy.

'Don't you tell him anything,' said Nancy. 'Not anything.'

Slater Bob looked at her.

'He said he'd be looking in again,' he said.

'He's just outside now,' said Nancy. 'We saw him. Just fend him off somehow. Don't tell him anything at all.'

44

'Well, of course, Miss Nancy, if it's like that . . . I never thought . . .'

'He's just spying round,' said Nancy. 'We caught him twice.'

'Well, I said nowt about gold to him, that's one thing,' said Slater Bob. 'And if he's that sort he'll get nowt out o' me, not if he asks his questions till crack o' doom.'

'And now about that gold,' said Nancy.

There was a moment's silence. The old miner looked queerly at his audience. Somewhere, far away in the level, there was the noise of a small stone dropping.

John looked at Nancy.

'Half a minute,' she said, listening. 'No. It's all right. Go ahead, Bob, but don't talk too loud.'

'But there's nowt to tell, Miss Nancy,' said the old man, 'nowt but what most folk knows.'

'We don't,' said Nancy.

'I can't tell more than what I know,' said Old Bob.

'Tell us all you can,' said Nancy.

'Well,' said Old Bob, screwing up his eyes and looking at the dazzling, hissing flame of the acetylene lamp. 'It was a young Government chap who found that gold. Just before the war begun. He'd been up here a week or two, looking round t' fells wi' his hammer and his compass and his maps and all. And when he come down in the evenings, he'd drop in every night to have a crack wi' Old Bob. There's none else living, he used to say, who knows more of the old mines. Not likely. My father was a miner before me, and his father before him, in the days when there was copper for all England going out o' these fells. Best part o' two weeks he'd been up above marking the old workings on his map, and then one day he comes in to me late at night. Near dark it was, and he'd had nowt to eat and nowt to drink, and he'd been up above scratting and scratting till he couldn't see his fingers. All of a dance, he

45

SLATER BOB TALKS OF GOLD

was. "Bob, my man," says he, "I've summat to show thee. Tak' a look at yon." And he brought his hand out of his pocket wi' a screw o' paper in it that he'd been holding for safety like. He opened that screw o' paper in the light o' my lamp. "Tak' a look at yon," he says, "and tell me if ye've seen owt like it."

'Well, I took a good look at it. And mind ye, yer mother's father took me wi' him when he went to Africa after that same stuff. I'm not easy fooled wi' metals and such. "Seen owt like it?" I says. "I have that, with the old queen's head on one side o't and Saint George a-sticking t' dragon on t' other," I says. He hadn't much, mind you, nobbut a pinch o' dust. Dust and a bit as big as a pin's head maybe. But it was t' colour of it.

'"I thowt ye'd know it," says he. "We'll be getting an assay o' this and be making our fortunes yet. Gold in t' fells. . . . That's a bit o' news to startle folk . . ."

'"They've been startled more'n a bit already today," says I. He'd come straight off t' fells to my cottage, and he'd seen nobody since morning. I give him t' newspaper, wi' t' news reet across t' front page, o' war begun and officers' leave stopped and the rest. "It'll blow over yet," he says, "but that'll tak me oop to London," he says, "and I'll be getting an assay of yon gold at t' same time." He was off next day by t' morning train. Reservist he was. He never come back, and that's all there is to it. But if you ask me, is there gold in t' fells, why, I says, "Aye, there is. Seeing's believing. And I've seen the stuff wi' my own eyes."'

'Yes,' said Nancy, 'but where was it he found it?'

'Ah, now,' said Slater Bob, 'if I'd knowed that, maybe I'd have gone looking for 't myself. And he tried to tell me, too. He'd his map he'd been making for Government, wi' numbers on it for the old levels, and adits and sinkings . . . numbers, mind ye, stead o' names like we call 'em, Grey Cap and

Slate Crop, and Brown's Dog, and Jimson's and Giftie and the rest. He showed me his map, but I couldn't make owt o' his numbers and arrows and all. He was to take me up to see the place when he come back. But he never did come back . . .'

'Yes, but which side of the valley was it?' said Nancy. 'If we only knew where to start looking it'd be quite enough.'

'Nay,' said the old man. 'It's not in this valley at all. It's away behind us, up yonder, t' other side o' t' Scar. He told me he found that stuff in a bit of a shallow bottom where folk had started a level and dropped it, up on High Topps . . .'

Nancy almost groaned. 'High Topps?' she said. 'But that's right over the other side of Ling Scar.'

'Aye,' said Slater Bob. 'On High Topps he found it. "By an old copper working," he said, "wi' heather growing along a fault in t' rock. Easy to find," he said, and he had it numbered on his map. But there's many a score of those old workings on High Topps, and every fault in t' rock makes a hold for heather. And then you might be standing on the very spot wi'out seeing what he saw.'

'Is it a long way?' asked John.

'Miles from Beckfoot,' said Nancy. 'Over the other side of this hill. We can't go prospecting up there and get back every night. Mother thought the gold was somewhere near.'

'Nay, it's on High Topps,' said the old man. 'The gold I'm telling of . . . not but what you might happen on it somewhere else. . . . No one knows yet nor ever will all that's hid in these fells.'

'If only it was a bit nearer home,' said Nancy. 'Oh well, I suppose we ought to be going back.'

Everybody could hear the disappointment in her voice.

'If you find it,' said the old man, 'I don't know but what I might give slates a rest. Give me metal every time.'

'We shan't be able to look for it just now,' said Nancy. 'But thank you very much for telling us about it.'

'Thank you very much,' said the others.

They lit their candles, said 'Good-bye,' and started along the tunnel, Peggy this time going first.

Dorothea was still thinking of the old man's story. 'He must have taken his map to the war with him,' she said, almost to herself, 'and then he was killed and someone found the map, and years afterwards, they'll guess what it means and come up here to look. ... Oh, I say ...' She stumbled, and her voice suddenly shrilled. 'Perhaps Squashy Hat has got the map and that's why he's here.'

'Gosh!' said Nancy. 'If he has, we've simply *got* to go there. There's no time to lose.'

She ran back.

'Look here, Bob,' she said. 'Don't you say anything about it to that snooper. He might go looking for it right away.'

'He'll get no forrader with me,' said the old man, and turned again to shaping his prop with his axe.

Nancy hurried after the others as fast as her guttering candle would let her.

*

'Is it all no good?' Roger was asking, his voice echoing in the tunnel.

'Don't talk,' said Nancy. 'Squashy Hat may be somewhere close to, and listening in the dark.'

Not another word was spoken on the way out. They hurried silently along. When they turned the last corner into the straight and saw the pin-point of light so far away in front of them, it was as if they could not make it grow bigger fast enough. Their candles were nearly done. The melting wax had not time to cool before it reached their fingers. Peggy, in front, blew hers out. The others did the same. They had no need of candles now. More and more clearly they could see the rugged sides of the tunnel. They came suddenly out into the sunshine among grey piles of stone and slate. Coming out like that into the light after being so long in the darkness inside the hill, they looked at each other as if they were seeing each other for the first time.

'Well, nobody's touched our shoes,' said Roger.

'Look here,' said Susan. 'You can get some of the dirt off by standing with your feet in the trickle. Don't put them all muddy into your shoes. Oh, Roger, *not* your handkerchief!'

'It's all right,' said Roger, finishing the drying of his feet. 'I haven't got a cold, so I shan't want to blow my nose or anything like that.'

'Hurry up,' said Nancy. 'We can get them clean afterwards. 'Let's just see if that man's still there.'

'Don't stare at him if he is,' said John. 'Just walk straight on as if you hadn't seen.'

Two minutes later they were leaving the outworks of the old mine, coming out between piles of rough stones and dropping down the track into the valley.

'He's there,' whispered Roger.

Up on the fellside above the entrance to the old level, the man with the squashy hat was sitting where they had seen him last.

'He's got a map,' said Titty.

'Perhaps it's *the* map,' said Dorothea.

'Don't let him see we've spotted him,' said John.

They walked steadily on till Nancy could bear it no longer.

'Somebody tie a shoelace,' she said. 'We must see what he's doing.'

Titty instantly limped, hopped once or twice, and stopped to untie a shoelace and tie it up again. 'He's coming down,' she said.

The others turned, as if to urge her to be quick. They could all see him, a tall, thin man in grey flannels, scrambling down through the bracken.

'He may not be going to the mine at all,' said Susan.

But at that moment they saw him reach the track and disappear among those great heaps of stones.

'He's gone in,' said Dorothea.

'He won't get much out of Slater Bob now,' said Nancy.

'He'll bump his head if he hasn't got a candle,' said Roger.

'Probably got one in his pocket,' said Dick.

'Not in his pocket,' said Susan. 'At least I shouldn't think so.'

'Look here,' said Nancy. 'We'll simply *have* to go and camp on High Topps.'

'Mother'll never let us,' said Peggy. 'She said we'd have to camp at Beckfoot as long as she was the only native. And when the other natives come everybody'll want to sail and go down to Wild Cat.'

'And then it'll be too late,' said Nancy. 'We've got to find it before Captain Flint comes home. And, anyway, we can't let Squashy Hat get in and find it first.'

'Do you think he's heard the story?' said Titty.

'Must have,' said Nancy. 'Look where he was coming from. Over the top of the Scar. He was coming from High Topps. He's begun looking already. And we're just hanging about. . . . Come on. When mother knows how awfully urgent it is. . . . And, anyway, it was partly her own idea. . . . Come on. Let's just see how soon we can get home.'

MINER'S WAY

CHAPTER 4

MRS BLACKETT MAKES
CONDITIONS

IT was no good trying to talk to Mrs Blackett until the paperers and plasterers had gone for the day. By that time the pigeons had been fed and Susan and Peggy had got the camp-fire going in the open space in the wood just off the lawn. Mrs Blackett was coming to join them at a meal, tea and supper combined, and the cooks were going to show how good a meal they could make with minced pemmican served hot with plenty of green peas out of a tin and potatoes they had dug for themselves in the kitchen garden. Meanwhile, Nancy and John were at work in the stable yard mending an old handcart. It was a good enough handcart except that one of its wheels kept coming off and one of its handles had been broken. By taking off the good wheel, at Dick's suggestion, they had found out what was wrong with the other, and the handcart was ready for use and was being run fast up and down the cobbled yard, to make sure that it would not come to pieces again, when Mrs Blackett, hearing the noise, came out to see what was happening.

'We've got to start trekking tomorrow,' said Nancy firmly. 'We've got to shift the whole camp up to High Topps.'

'But Ruth, I mean Nancy, you wild creature, whatever for? I thought it was all settled that you were to camp here and go prospecting for gold. Didn't you find Slater Bob?'

'Yes,' said Nancy. 'And the gold isn't here at all. It's up on High Topps. And there's someone else looking for it. We haven't got a minute to lose. It's too late to move tonight, but we'll get going first thing in the morning.'

'No,' said Mrs Blackett. 'Impossible altogether. Mrs Walker might not mind so very much, but there are the Callums.'

'What about Susan?' said Nancy. 'She'll look after them. Don't go and say "No" right away. Come along and see the others. Hi! John, do go and tell Susan mother's coming and everything's going to be all right.'

'I never said so,' said Mrs Blackett. 'Don't tell her anything of the sort.'

But John was gone. This was something between Nancy and her mother. He couldn't very well join in and say he wanted to get away from Mrs Blackett's garden. He slipped away through the house, putting his head in at Captain Flint's study door on the way. Dick was there, reading about gold in the Encyclopaedia. Dorothea was seated at the table taking the chance of scribbling down a few sentences in her story, *The Outlaw of the Broads*, that she had not had time to finish at school. Titty was looking at the picture of the armadillo.

'Come on,' said John. 'Come along to the camp. Nancy's begun persuading Mrs Blackett and they'll be there in two ticks.'

*

Mrs Blackett seemed to need a good deal of persuading. From the camp on the lawn, anxious watchers saw that neither Nancy nor her mother was in a hurry to join them. The two of them came round the corner of the house into the garden but they did not at once cross the lawn to the group of small white tents. Instead they walked up and down under those curtainless windows. Fragments of talk, sentences, half sentences, single words, floated across the garden. Mrs Blackett was explaining again and again why it was that, though she did not mind having six children not her own safely camped in her garden, she did not at all like the idea of letting them go camping miles away up on the fells where anything might happen to them and she would not be there to help. And then, whenever she got a chance, there came a loud, cheerful rush of persuasive talk from Nancy.

'As safe as houses. . . . Much safer in case of earthquakes and things. And anyway, now we know it's there, it wouldn't be much fun looking anywhere else. And you know we couldn't get home every evening. Not from High Topps. Cruelty to animals. We'd be on the road all day and never have any time there at all. Besides, it'd be much better if none of us were here while you're finishing up the papering and painting. Better for cook, I mean. And you know you're always saying Susan can be trusted to be sensible . . .'

That was all Nancy, but when she paused for breath, Mrs Blackett began again. 'It would be all very well if you were all Susans. There's only one Susan in the eight of you. It's the Dicks and Dots and Rogers I'd be worrying about . . .'

'Me?' whispered Roger indignantly.

'Shut up,' said Titty. 'They're coming.'

Mrs Blackett had turned suddenly off the path and was walking across the lawn to the tents. Nancy, with dancing eyes, as if she knew the victory was won, was close behind her.

'Where is Susan?' said Mrs Blackett. 'Oh, there you are.' She turned aside towards the camp-fire, from which Susan had just lifted a boiling kettle.

'It's no good trying to get any sense out of my harum-scarums,' said Mrs Blackett. 'Tell me, Susan, do you really want to go camping away up on High Topps instead of staying here?'

'Of course she does,' said Nancy.

'Pirates hold their peace,' said Mrs Blackett, 'long enough to let Susan answer for herself.'

'It's very nice here, of course,' said Susan.

Mrs Blackett laughed. 'So you do want to go?' she said.

'Only because of the gold,' said Susan.

'I'm sure there's just as much gold here as anywhere else,' said Mrs Blackett.

'Slater Bob said High Topps,' said Susan, 'and he told us just what to look for . . .'

'Well done, Susan,' said Nancy.

'But, of course, there may be other places.'

Nancy almost groaned.

'If only my brother were at home,' said Mrs Blackett.

'But the whole point of everything is to find the gold before he comes back,' said Nancy.

'It's to be a surprise for him,' said Dorothea.

'Or if you could only wait till your mothers are here to decide for themselves.'

'He'll be here before that,' said Nancy.

'And when they come we'll all be sailing,' said John.

'And somebody else is looking for it already,' said Titty.

'Not really,' said Mrs Blackett. 'Now, Susan. You tell me, what *would* your mother say?'

'She'd say all right if Roger went to bed at the proper time.'

'She'd tell us about gold-mining in Australia,' said Titty. 'She might even want to come too.'

'I dare say she would,' said Mrs Blackett. 'But that's just what I can't do with the house all upside down. And what about you?' she added, turning to Dick and Dorothea. 'What would Mrs Callum say?'

'She wouldn't mind if we promised to do what Susan told us,' said Dorothea.

'You see how it is, Susan. It all comes down to depending on you.'

'It's much safer than the island,' said Susan, and the others looked at her most gratefully. 'No night sailing or anything like that, even if we wanted. Nothing can go wrong.'

THE PIGEON LOFT

'If only it wasn't so far,' said Mrs Blackett.

'You've got Rattletrap,' said Nancy.

'And what about milk every day? It's not like the island, with Mrs Dixon just across the bay.'

'Atkinson's farm's close to High Topps,' said Nancy. 'You can see it on the map in Captain Flint's room. It's only just across the Dundale road.'

'And water?'

'There's the beck right on the Topps. We'll camp by the side of it, where the charcoal-burners were. Simply gorgeous, it's going to be.'

'Oh well,' said Mrs Blackett. 'But it's no good thinking I can keep coming up there to see you. One of you'll have to run down every day, to let me know no necks are broken or ankles twisted or anything like that.'

'What are the pigeons for?' said Nancy joyously.

'But I can't spend all day in the stableyard watching for a pigeon when I've five hundred thousand things to do and workmen in every room, and cook and me both run off our legs.'

Nancy looked sharply at Dick.

Dick, in spite of himself, turned a little pink. 'I think it would work,' he said. 'I think I could make the pigeon ring a bell when it came home.'

'That would settle it,' said Nancy.

'No it wouldn't,' said Mrs Blackett. 'Somebody would have to spend all day listening for the bell.'

'It wouldn't just ring and stop,' said Dick. 'The way I've planned it, it'll go on ringing and ringing till somebody comes and turns it off.'

Mrs Blackett, yielding, caught at a straw. 'If you can promise to send a pigeon home every day with a letter, and arrange for it to ring a bell that nobody can help hearing . . .'

'Dick'll do it,' said Nancy. 'That'll be a pigeon a day for

three days, and then one of us'll come home to bring them back. Well done, mother. A pigeon a day keeps the natives away. . . . We don't want to keep you away, of course. It's only to save you having to come.'

'Well, if Dick really can do it,' said Mrs Blackett doubt-fully. 'And if you can get milk at Atkinson's, and find a nice place with good water . . .'

'She's agreed,' shouted Nancy. 'Barbecued billygoats, mother, but I thought you were never going to.'

'I put all my trust in you, Susan,' said Mrs Blackett. 'And you, too, John,' she added. John grinned. It was kind of her to say it, but he knew she did not mean it. On questions of milk and drinking-water and getting able-seamen to bed in proper time, Susan was the one the natives trusted.

'We'll start the trek first thing in the morning,' said Nancy.

'No. No. No,' said her mother. 'You can't do that. Send out your pioneers and find the right place. Make sure about the milk from Atkinson's. They may be selling every drop they have with so many visitors about. And make sure of good water. You know what the becks are like and the Atkinsons may be short themselves. I can't have you simply setting out with nothing arranged. And Dick's got to turn your pigeons into bell-ringers or you can't go at all.'

'Oh well,' said Nancy. 'It won't really be a waste of time. John and Susan'll come and see for themselves and the others can be getting things ready. Someone's got to go to Rio to buy hammers. Torches, too, and a tremendous lot of stores.'

The rest of the evening passed quickly in feasting and planning.

'Not all mining camps have such good cooks,' said Mrs Blackett, sitting by the camp-fire after supper.

'The pemmican would have been better with a little chop-ped onion,' said Susan, 'but I didn't think of it in time.'

'I do hope I'm not doing wrong,' said Mrs Blackett, as at

58

last she left them, and they walked with her across the lawn
in the dusk and said their good nights at the garden door.

'You're doing exactly right,' said Nancy.

'I mean what I say about those pigeons,' said Mrs Blackett,
almost hopefully. 'They'll have to ring bells if I'm to agree to
your going.'

'They shall,' said Nancy.

'Don't sit up late.'

'Just till the flames die down.'

They walked slowly back to where the embers of the camp-
fire were glowing behind the bushes.

'You really think you can do it, Dick?' said Nancy.

Dick pulled his torch from his pocket and turned it on.
'I'll just go and make sure,' he said.

Very quietly they went into the stableyard. Dick climbed
the ladder to the pigeon-loft, leaned across and laid his torch
on the pigeons' landing-place, and felt the swinging wires.
There was a sudden fluttering in the loft.

'Phiu ... phiu ... phiu. ...' Peggy and Titty were
making noises to reassure the pigeons.

'I think it's all right,' said Dick. 'The wires are all
separate, aren't they? We'll have to fasten three or four of
them together.'

'What *are* you doing?' Mrs Blackett called from an upper
window.

'Just making sure about something,' said Nancy. 'Good
night, mother. We'll all go to bed right away.'

CHAPTER 5

PIONEERS AND STAY-AT-HOMES

LONG before Beckfoot was awake people were stirring in the camp. Nancy moved on tiptoe from tent to tent. Orders were given in whispers as if the old grey house itself had ears. Susan boiled a kettle at the fireplace among the bushes. Peggy laid wait in the road for the boy who brought the morning's milk from Low Farm. Dick and Dorothea, Titty and Roger woke to find smoke from the fire climbing through the morning mist, and Susan, John and Nancy beginning an early breakfast of tea and eggs and bread and butter. Another lot of eggs were being boiled hard and Peggy was cutting bread and butter sandwiches for the pioneers to carry in their packs. 'Don't make a noise,' whispered Nancy. 'Don't wake the house. Second thoughts are always worse, and you can't count on natives not to have them. Not even mother. The sooner we're off the better. Before she has time to change her mind. Hi, Peggy, you're the best hand with the pigeons. You go and catch them while we're getting the food down.'

The others hurried into their clothes.

'Look here, Dick,' said Nancy. 'The whole thing depends on you. It was only what you said about the pigeons that made her say she'd let us go. She'd ever so much rather have us roosting in the garden every night. We'll find a camp easily enough, but if you don't manage the pigeons' bell-ringing, it won't be any good.'

'And you know the things to buy in Rio,' said John. 'Hammers and new torches.'

'And goggles,' said Susan. 'Motor goggles will do. But you must have something if you're going to go chipping at rocks.'

'Don't send off the first pigeon too soon,' said Dick. 'Not till after twelve.'

'Are you going to send messages?' asked Titty.

'Of course,' said Nancy. 'It's a splendid chance.'

'Mother's moving about,' said Peggy, coming back with the pigeons in their basket. 'And cook's stoking up. You won't have long to wait now, Roger.'

'Shiver my timbers,' said Nancy. 'We ought to be stirring our stumps. We've ten thousand miles to go.'

They did not take the risk of going out by the stableyard and the gate, but slipped away in single file along the path through the wood and climbed the wall to get into the road. The others watched them out of sight.

*

The pioneers were well on their way when a gong sounded in the house. Peggy and Titty were tidying up in the camp, putting rugs and sleeping-bags to air. Roger was helping them, pointing out the things they had left undone. They hurried in to find Mrs Blackett already dealing out plates full of bacon and mushrooms along the bare trestle table in the dismantled dining-room.

'Good morning,' she said cheerfully. 'And where are the others?'

'Dick's gone to the stable,' said Dorothea, 'to look at the electric bell.'

'Oh dear, oh dear,' said Mrs Blackett. 'He isn't really going to try to do anything with it, is he? But where are John and Susan and Nancy?'

'They've started,' said Titty.

'The pioneers are on the march,' said Dorothea.

'Not without their breakfast?' said Mrs Blackett.

'They've had *their* breakfast,' said Roger, rather hungrily.

'They haven't *gone*?' said Mrs Blackett. 'I did want to see

Nancy. I've been thinking over that idea of your all going up on the fells to camp. There was something I wanted to say to her.'

'She was afraid there might be,' said Roger.

Mrs Blackett's mouth opened. For a moment no word came out of it. Roger, who had just made a very neat forkful of mushroom and toast, never saw how she looked at him. And then suddenly, she laughed aloud.

'My own fault,' she said. 'I ought to have got up in the middle of the night to make sure of that dreadful girl. What I wanted to say was, why couldn't we think of something else instead of gold-hunting, so that you wouldn't have to go so far away?'

Everybody looked at everybody else. How right Nancy had been.

'It was your idea, mother,' said Peggy.

'It was a dreadful mistake,' said Mrs Blackett. 'I never dreamed of Slater Bob sending you half across the country-side.'

'He couldn't help it if that's where the gold is,' said Titty.

'Oh well,' said Mrs Blackett. 'The Atkinsons may be sending all their milk to town, and I did say you couldn't go unless those pigeons rang bells, didn't I?'

'They're jolly well going to,' said Peggy, just as Dick came in.

'Can I use the electric bell there is in the stable under the pigeon-loft,' said Dick, 'and the wires that go across the yard?'

Mrs Blackett sighed. 'I suppose it would be unfair if I said you couldn't. Yes, you can do what you like with it. There's one thing about it,' she added hopefully, 'it hasn't worked for years.'

*

Soon after breakfast Peggy, Titty, Dorothea and Roger set

sail for Rio in the *Amazon*, leaving Dick to see what he could do with the bell. He had already taken it to bits and spread them on a sheet of newspaper on the bench in the old stable. Peggy had found him a large coil of insulated wire in Captain Flint's tool cupboard. It might almost have been left there on purpose. Dick had given Dorothea a list of things to buy, four yards of flex and some thin sheet copper. 'I'll never get the bell done if I come, too,' he had said, and Dorothea had promised to do her best. Dick watched the start, when Peggy took her shoes off to pull *Amazon* over the shallows. By the time she had hopped in again and *Amazon* was fairly sailing with Dorothea at the tiller, he was gone, and Titty, looking back, saw him disappear on the run, round the corner of the house. It was not going to be Dick's fault if things were not ready in time.

They tied up at one of the Rio boat piers and left *Amazon* in charge of a friendly boatman. Peggy wasted twopence by telephoning to the station to inquire for Timothy, but no livestock had come of any kind. Dorothea and Roger went off to buy the things for Dick, while the others were busy with the list of stores made out by Mrs Blackett. It was a good list, though when she had made it Mrs Blackett had been thinking that the camp would be no farther from home than Beckfoot lawn. Roger had looked through it while they were sailing across. Some people always forget things like chocolate in making out a list like that. But Mrs Blackett, after all, was Captain Flint's sister. Chocolate was in it, and oranges, bananas, tins of steak and kidney pie, tins of sardines, a large tin of squashed fly biscuits. It was a decidedly good list and Roger had had no criticisms to make. Then new torches had to be bought at the chemist's, and a new thermos flask in place of Roger's which had been broken. Then eight small hammers were bought at the ironmonger's and eight pairs of sun-goggles at the garage, and Titty, at the last moment, dashed into the stationer's and bought an enormous ball of string.

'Whatever for?' said Dorothea.

'Exploring tunnels like yesterday,' said Titty. 'Fasten one end of it, and unroll the other, so as not to get lost. You could feel your way out with it even if a bat had knocked your candle out and you hadn't any more matches.'

All four had parcels to carry, and the knapsacks on their backs, stuffed with tins, were heavy and uncomfortable before they came back to the boat pier, dumped their loads on the pier, stowed them in the *Amazon* and sailed for home.

*

Dick was hard at work. The morning had gone by at frightful speed. As far as he could see, nothing was wrong with that old bell but dirt and rust. But it took a long time to clean every bit of it, to get the rust off the gong and the verdigris off the brass terminals, to file the surfaces where they gripped the wires, and to get new bits of wire ready, with bright twisted ends to replace the old ones that he could not trust. Now he was putting it all together again. He was pretty sure he had thought of a way of turning the swinging wires of the pigeons' door into a bell-push, but that would not be much good if he had not got a bell for it to ring. He screwed the trembler into place, and adjusted it until the little hammer on the trembler did not quite touch the bell. But would it tremble? He looked it all over, and took the dry battery out of his pocket torch. He took two short bits of insulated wire and fixed one between the battery and one of the terminals. Holding his breath, he made contact with the other. Would it tremble, or would it not? A tiny spark flickered as the wire touched. The tremble shivered into life . . .

'Trrrrrrrrrrrrrrrrrrrr . . .'

And at that moment the provisioning party, who had

landed their cargo and dumped the stores in the camp, came running into the yard.

'Trrrrrrrrrr . . .'

'Oh, well done, Dick. It works,' cried Dorothea.

'Good,' said Titty, 'but are you sure it's loud enough?' The bell was certainly working, but would that faint tinkling purr catch the ears of busy natives?

'It's going to be a lot louder than that,' said Dick.

'Regular howling din, it ought to be,' said Peggy.

'Hurrah!' shouted Roger, paused for a moment to pull his new goggles out of his pocket, put them on, grinned horribly at Titty, and dashed off into the house to take the good news to Mrs Blackett.

Presently he came soberly back.

'What did she say,' said Peggy.

'She liked the goggles,' said Roger.

'Oh yes,' said Titty, 'but what about the bell?'

'She said, "Well done, Dick," and then she said, "It's clever of Dick to make the old thing work, but the point isn't whether Dick can ring it. The point is, can he make the pigeons ring it?"'

'You can, can't you, Dick?' said Dorothea.

'I don't know for certain,' said Dick. 'Not till I've tried. You got the flex all right? And what about the sheet copper? It's got to be fairly springy.'

Dorothea handed over her parcel. The others watched anxiously while Dick looked at the coil of flex and tried the thin copper with a careful finger.

'Is it all right?' said Titty.

'It feels all right,' said Dick.

'Are you going to use it now?'

'I must first see just what happens when a pigeon flies home,' said Dick. 'It all depends on how far they lift the wires.'

A gong sounded in the house.

'Grub,' said Roger.

'Gosh,' said Peggy. 'Dinner already.'

'I don't want any,' said Dick.

'But you must,' said Dorothea.

'The first pigeon may come any minute now, and I've simply got to see how it goes in.'

'All right,' said Peggy. 'We'll bring your rations out here.'

*

Mrs Blackett did not seem to mind. Dorothea took him out a plateful of cold beef and potatoes and cauliflower and a glass of the pirate grog that natives, who know no better, call lemonade.

'He wants the red book on mining,' she said, when she came back.

'Where is he?' asked Mrs Blackett.

'Sitting on the ladder by the pigeon loft,' said Dorothea. 'He can't do anything till a pigeon comes, and he says Nancy told him to dig out all he could about gold.'

'Oh well,' said Mrs Blackett, 'if he doesn't mind being worked so hard.'

'He likes it,' said Dorothea, and went off to get *Phillips on Metals* from Captain Flint's study, and to take it to the professor on the steps in the yard.

She came back just in time to hear Mrs Blackett say, 'That's all very well, Peggy, but you've forgotten one thing. What about Timothy? Who's going to look after him? What am I to do if the creature arrives and you are all away on High Topps? You haven't even finished the box to put him in at nights.'

'We'll get it done this afternoon,' said Peggy.

CHAPTER 6

NEWS FROM THE WILDERNESS

TITTY outside and Dick inside the pigeon-loft were waiting for the first of the returning pigeons. Dick was finding it hard to keep his mind on gold. He never had been able to think of two things at once. He laid *Phillips on Metals* aside and had yet another look at the pigeons' own front door. It was oblong, with a slide that closed either one half or the other. When the slide was pushed to the right the pigeons could go freely in or out. When it was pushed to the left it left an opening with a row of wires hung on a bar. A strip of wood on the threshold stopped them from swinging outwards, but a pigeon coming in could push through them, and as soon as it was inside they would fall back into place. Carefully, with a finger, Dick lifted two or three of the little swinging wires through which the pigeons had to push their way. They were very light. Everything would depend on the pigeons' strength and eagerness. Did they simply crash in, or did they feel their way in timidly, so that any little extra weight would stop them from wanting to come in at all? Titty was on the steps outside the loft, steep wooden steps up out of the old stableyard, keeping watch to warn Dick of the coming of the first pigeon. From there she could look out over the low buildings, and the shrubs and little trees beyond them to the hills on the farther side of the river, and, in the distance to the great mass of Kanchenjunga, brown and blue and purple, rising into the dazzling brightness of the summer sky. Somewhere up there, under the blazing sun, John, Susan and Nancy, pioneers, were exploring on behalf of the Company. Sounds of painters and plasterers at work, the moving of ladders and furniture, whistling and laughter, came from the house. But the noise of hammering and sawing came not from the house but from the camp in the garden, where Peggy and Roger were finishing the sleeping hutch for Timothy. Every now and then Dorothea came running into the yard to get more nails or screws from the old stable under the pigeon-loft where Captain Flint had a carpenter's bench.

Homer was in the yard before ever Titty saw him. Her eyes were almost blind with staring into the sky, trying to see a black speck that would come nearer and nearer, bigger and bigger, and turn at last into a pigeon. But she never saw how Homer came. Suddenly there was the fluttering of wings, and Homer was already in the yard, flying uncertainly from house roof to stable roof, puzzled, perhaps, by the sight of Titty sitting on the steps.

'Dick,' called Titty softly.

There was no answer.

The pigeon flew across towards the loft.

'Dick,' cried Titty, desperate. 'He's here.'

She heard a low murmur, 'Go and tell Peggy.'

The next moment Homer had lighted on the narrow shelf, stretched and closed his wings, and pushed his way in under the swinging wires which lifted to let him pass.

Titty slipped down the ladder and ran round the corner of the house to the camp on the green lawn.

'Peggy,' she shouted, 'one of the pigeons has come home.'

A saw was left sticking in the half-sawn plank that was going to be the armadillo's bedroom door. Roger dropped the hammer.

'Did Dick see it all right?' asked Dorothea.

'There'll be a message,' said Peggy.

'They may want us to come along at once,' said Roger.

All four of them ran to the stableyard. Peggy was first at the steps to the loft, the others close behind her.

'Got to go quiet now,' she said. 'Don't all barge in together. Sometimes they're a job to catch. Where's Dick?'

'In the loft,' said Titty.

Peggy gingerly opened the door and slipped in. The others waited on the steps.

In the loft Homer was enjoying his dinner, watching Dick out of one red-rimmed eye. Dick was still looking at the swinging wires through which the pigeon had pushed its way.

'It ought to be quite easy,' he said. 'If only we can make sure of a good contact when the wire is pushed up . . .'

'Eh, what's that?' said Peggy. 'Have you caught him?'

'Not yet,' said Dick. 'But he's got a message. Left leg.'

'Coo . . . coo,' murmured Peggy, and whistled the low pigeon call, 'Pheeu . . . phiu . . . phiu . . . phiu . . . phiu.'

Homer took a drink of water. Peggy caught him and took a tiny roll of paper from under the rubber ring on his left leg, let him go again, and Homer settled by the drinking-trough while Peggy carefully unrolled the message.

'Can we come in?' said Titty, just outside.

'Come along,' said Peggy. 'It's all right now.'

The others crowded into the loft. Peggy read aloud from the crinkled scrap of paper that tried to roll itself up again as she read:

'NO SUPPLIES FROM ATKINSON'S. OCCUPIED BY TREACHEROUS ENEMY.'

The signature was a skull, particularly grim.

'Bowlines and gaskets,' said Peggy, in the Nancy manner. 'That's pretty bad. The only other farm's right down in the bottom of the valley. Jolly long way to go for the milk.'

'Oh, I say,' said Roger.

'Shall we have to give it up?' said Dorothea.

'Nancy'll manage somehow,' said Titty.

'Come on,' said Peggy. 'Let's get our part done. We'll want the hutch for Timothy whether we go or not.'

'Well,' said Mrs Blackett, who had heard the rush to the stableyard and put her head out of the back door as they came down from the pigeon-loft.

'We've had a message from them,' said Titty.

'We can't get milk from Atkinson's,' said Peggy.

'I was afraid you might not be able to,' said Mrs Blackett, but she did not look particularly disappointed. 'And did the pigeon ring a bell?'

'I think the next one will,' said Dick.

'It may be no good even if it does,' said Dorothea.

'Will you want me to watch?' said Titty.

'No. It's all right now,' said Dick. 'I've seen how they come in. I've only got to make a bell-push for them.'

'Come on, Titty,' said Peggy. 'There's some painting to be done.'

*

Dick, who meant pigeons to ring bells no matter how melancholy were the messages they carried, knew now exactly what he had to do. Homer had shouldered through those swinging wires in the most encouraging way. There was going to be no difficulty about that. What he had to do was to make a little swinging trigger that would move with the wires as the pigeon pushed through and make contact between two strips of copper springy enough to grip and hold it till someone came to let it go. He did it, after two or three false starts, with the help of some stiff wire, a cork, a scrap of lead and the copper Dorothea had brought from Rio, which he cut with a pair of scissors borrowed from the unsuspecting cook. He worked as hard as he could to have it ready for the next pigeon, but by the time he had finished his pigeon bell-push and joined it up to the old wires across the stableyard, the afternoon was over and the workmen had gone for the day.

It was funny that second pigeon had not come. Good thing, though. He might yet have time to get the bell itself fixed up at the other end.

There was a sudden shouting in the yard.

'Ahoy!'

'How are you getting on?'

'Hasn't another pigeon come yet?'

The carpenters from the camp, their work done, were at the foot of the steps. Dick looked down, but hardly saw the finished sleeping-box for the armadillo, with a door to open and shut, and Timothy's name painted upon it. There wasn't a second to lose.

'Nearly done,' he said, and ran down the steps, picked up the bell and the coil of flex and bolted into the house. Lucky the batteries for the house-bells were close to the kitchen door. He had not any too much flex to spare. With trembling fingers, he connected up his bell and put it on a chair in the passage. Better than nothing. He was ready now, but in the stable he had seen a discarded, rusty tea-tray. That would be wanted too, before everything was quite as he had planned.

'No more news?' That was Mrs Blackett in the yard. 'Surely they'll have sent off another pigeon before now. Isn't it a blessing to have the place to ourselves and the workmen gone? Well, I must say, you've made a very handsome hutch, and those leather hinges to the door. . . . Peggy, you awful child, you haven't been cutting bits off your blue belt?'

Dick started to cross the yard. There might yet be time to fix that tea-tray.

'That belt was miles too long,' Peggy was saying.

Mrs Blackett flapped her hands in despair, and turned to Roger, who had taken Titty's place on the ladder and was finding his sun-goggles very useful in searching the sky for a pigeon. She was just going to say something to him, when

Roger shouted, 'Here he is,' and nearly fell off the ladder, pulling the goggles hurriedly off in order to see better as a pigeon swooped down into the yard.

'Don't frighten him,' said Peggy.

But Sophocles was startled only for a moment. He flew to the loft, waited on the ledge, looking down at the crowd of people in the yard, and then plunged in as if the swinging wires had not been there.

'Trrrrrrrrrrrrrrrrrrrr . . .'

Dick, who had stopped short as the pigeon flew down, smiled a slow, happy smile. The thing had worked. Sophocles had rung the bell.

'Trrrrrrrrrrrrrrr . . .'

'Well done, Dick!' 'What about that, mother?' 'He's done it.' Everyone was talking at once.

'Well, Dick, I must say it's very clever of you,' said Mrs Blackett.

'It'll go on ringing till you go to the loft and switch it off when you take the pigeon's message,' said Dick, watching the bell dithering as it lay loose on the chair.

'But do you think we'll hear it?' said Mrs Blackett, 'when we're racketing about and busy with other things.'

'It's going to be a lot louder than that,' said Dick.

'So we'll be able to go,' said Roger eagerly.

'Not if they can't get milk . . .'

'Come on, Dick,' said Peggy. 'And shut off the bell while I'm catching Sophocles.'

A moment later she was reading the second message:

'CRAWLING HOME MORE DEAD THAN ALIVE. BELLIES PINCHED. THROATS PARCHED. PLEASE PUT THE KETTLE ON.'

'Doesn't sound as if they had found a good water supply either,' said Mrs Blackett.

'It's just Nancy making it more exciting,' said Peggy. 'Come on. Let's get tea ready for them.'

'Can I borrow the step-ladder?' asked Dick, looking up at a beam that crossed the passage in a most convenient place.

'Anything you like,' said Mrs Blackett, and went off with the others to the camp in the garden, while Roger, much interested now that the bell was really working, stayed behind to help Dick.

It was a huge old tea-tray, and noisy if you only touched it. Dick punched a hole in the middle of it with a hammer and nail, and fastened the bell there. He punched two more holes, good big ones, and then, with Roger to help, put two screws through these holes and into the beam above the passage, not screwing them tight, but leaving them loose so that the whole tea-tray was free to rattle. Then he connected up the bell once more, put the step-ladder back in the hall where the plasterers had been using it, and took the tools back to the carpenter's bench.

'I'll just try it,' said Dick. 'They'll hear it everywhere.'

'Don't let's,' said Roger. 'Keep it till no one's expecting it. There's another pigeon to come yet.'

They joined the others by the camp-fire. Dorothea looked at Dick.

'Done?' she said.

'You wait,' said Roger, grinning.

There was a noise of cracking twigs in the wood, a noise of feet on dry leaves.

'Here they are,' cried Titty, and a moment later the pioneers trudged wearily into camp.

'What was it like?' said Roger. 'You haven't gone and found the gold already?'

'What about tea?' said Nancy. 'Our throats and tongues and skins are stiff with dust.'

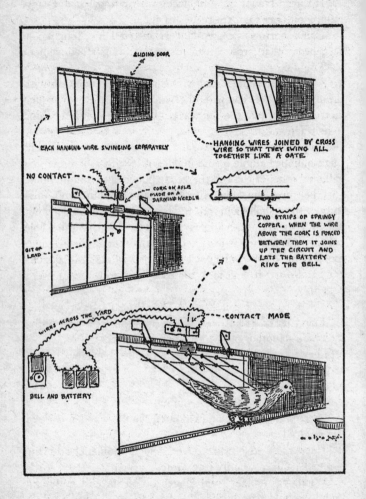

SLIDING DOOR

EACH HANGING WIRE SWINGING SEPARATELY

HANGING WIRES JOINED BY CROSS
WIRE SO THAT THEY SWING ALL
TOGETHER LIKE A GATE

NO CONTACT

CORK ON AXLE
MADE OF A
DARNING NEEDLE

TWO STRIPS OF SPRINGY
COPPER. WHEN THE WIRE
ABOVE THE CORK IS FORCED
BETWEEN THEM IT JOINS
UP THE CIRCUIT AND
LETS THE BATTERY
RING THE BELL

BIT OF
LEAD

WIRES ACROSS THE YARD

CONTACT MADE

BELL AND BATTERY

HOW DICK MADE THE PIGEONS RING A BELL

'Kettle's boiling,' said Peggy. 'Here you are, Susan, you'd better put the tea in yourself.'

'Quick, quick before we faint,' said Nancy.

'But do tell us what it was like,' said Dorothea.

'Grand Gobi isn't in it,' said Nancy. 'Not a drop of water anywhere. The beck by the old pitstead, where we meant to camp, is dry. We saw a dead sheep in it . . . at least in the place where it was. Vultures overhead . . .'

'A peregrine,' said John, who had caught the eager look in Dick's eyes.

'And what about Atkinson's?' said Mrs Blackett.

'Is it Squashy?' said Dorothea.

'Yes it is,' said Nancy. 'Well done, Peggy. Ow, I'd forgotten it'd be boiling. . . . And I haven't breath to blow it.'

'It *is* Squashy,' she went on. 'He's taken rooms at Atkinson's, so he'd be bound to find out everything we're doing. We'll have to keep away from there altogether. And I say, we know he's prospecting. There was a copy of the *Mining World* on Mrs Atkinson's window-sill.'

'Last week's,' said John. 'I saw the date.'

'Shove a little more milk in,' said Nancy, 'and then I'll be able to drink it.'

'But do go on,' said Dorothea. 'What did you do in the desert?'

'Walked and walked,' said Susan.

'Tightened our belts and staggered on,' said Nancy. 'There's no water for a camp. Not on the Topps, or even near the Topps. Up in the higher reaches the Amazon itself is only a trickle.'

'Never mind,' said Mrs Blackett. 'Worth while going up there just to find out for certain that that particular plan is no good.'

'No good,' exclaimed Nancy, spilling some of her tea.

'No good! But didn't you hear Squashy Hat is really a miner and lodging at Atkinson's? We can't let him have all the Topps to himself. Just think how sick Uncle Jim would be if Squashy found it. ... Of course we're going. What about the pigeons? ...'

'We got your two messages,' said Titty.

'Homer and Sophocles are back,' said Dorothea. 'And Dick has got the bell working. It wasn't done when Homer came, but Sophocles rang it like anything.'

'Not very loud,' said Mrs Blackett.

'But what about Sappho?' said Nancy. 'We sent her off second, ages before Sophocles.'

'She must have got lost on the way,' said Titty.

At that moment there came from the house the violent shrilling of a bell, a long jangling rattle and a resounding crash of broken crockery.

'Brrrrrrrrrrrrrrrr ...'

'What about that?' said Roger.

They started to their feet.

'Whatever was that smash?' said Mrs Blackett.

Nancy looked at Dick.

'It's Sappho coming home,' he said.

'Br!r!r!r!r!r!r!r!r! ...'

Tired as they were, the pioneers raced across the lawn with the stay-at-homes. The bell rang louder and louder. They turned into the yard. Cook was standing at the kitchen door with her hands to her ears.

'Br!r!r!r!r!r!r!r!r!r!r! ...'

'Where is it?' cried Nancy.

'In the passage,' said Roger.

As they went in, the noise was almost deafening. There, above their heads the bell was whirring, and the big tea-tray throbbing like a sounding-board. In the passage was a pile of broken plates.

'Lucky it wasn't the best service,' said cook. 'A noise like that, and me just crossing to the pantry . . .'

'Gosh!' said Nancy. 'Jib-booms and bobstays!'

'Br!r!r!r!r!r!r!r!r!r!r!r!r! . . .'

'Is *that* loud enough?' said Peggy, and ran after Dick up the steps to the pigeon-loft.

The bell suddenly stopped. Dick had turned it off from inside the loft. Peggy, who had caught the dawdling Sappho, came down again with a scrap of paper in her hand. Gloom showed in her face.

'Do read it aloud,' said Titty.

'It's the second message really,' said John, looking doubtfully at Mrs Blackett.

Peggy read it, while Nancy watched her with dancing eyes.

'WELLS DRY. BONES SCATTER THE DESERT. LIFE IMPOSSIBLE.'

'Well, that settles it,' said Mrs Blackett.

'No it doesn't,' said Nancy. 'We sent that off before going down to Mrs Tyson's. She says their pump's all right. And we can have all the milk we want. Only she wants to see you first about where we're to camp. She's in an awful stew about fires. And we promised you'd come tomorrow to talk to her.'

'But Mrs Tyson's right down in the valley,' said Mrs Blackett. 'You might just as well stay here.'

'Oh, mother, how can you?' said Nancy. 'Tyson's is miles nearer than here. It isn't like being on the wrong side of Ling Scar . . .'

'Oh dear, oh dear . . . ' said Mrs Blackett.

'What about those hammers?' said Nancy.

'We've got them,' said Titty.

'And gorgeous goggles,' said Roger, putting his on for her to see.

'Giminy,' said Nancy. 'Have you got a pair like that for me?'

'And we've got a splendid lot of stores,' said Roger.

'Good old mother,' said Nancy, and gave her mother a hard and dusty hug.

'And we've finished Timothy's sleeping-hutch,' said Peggy.

'Three cheers,' said Nancy. 'We'll start first thing in the morning. I wish my throat wasn't too dry to shout.'

'But Nancy . . .'

'Come along, mother,' said Nancy. 'That tea'll be just cold enough to drink.'

'And what about all that crockery?' said Mrs Blackett. 'If you're going to startle cook into dropping a trayful every day when your pigeon comes home, we shan't have a plate or a cup left at the end of a week.'

'Stop it out of our pocket money,' said Nancy.

'We'll all subscribe,' said Titty. 'There couldn't be a better cause.'

CHAPTER 7

TREK TO TYSON'S

In the morning they bathed in the river.

'It'll be the last chance,' said John.

'Except for anybody who comes to bring back the pigeons,' said Nancy. 'Somebody'll have to come every fourth day.'

'Poor beast,' said Roger.

'All right on a dromedary,' said Nancy. 'And we've got two.'

'Dromedaries?' said Roger.

'Bicycles,' said Nancy. 'Come on. I'll race you across the river and back.'

But, last chance though it was, nobody made the most of it. Nancy and John and Susan kept remembering things and reminding each other lest they should forget them later. Dick wanted a final look at the article on gold in the Encyclopaedia. Peggy wanted to make sure that Timothy had not arrived during the night, and was going to telephone to the railway station. Dorothea was a little worried lest she and Dick should not be able to pack their tents as neatly as the more experienced explorers. Titty, looking up at the hills and thinking of the long march before them, was eager to be already on the way. Roger had just been promised that he might go over the dromedaries with an oil-can and see that their tyres were pumped up. It was impossible just to swim and float in the morning sunshine as if nobody had anything else of which to think.

Ten minutes after breakfast was over, the camp was a wreck. Tents were being rolled up, tent-pegs gathered into bags, tent-ropes made up into neat hanks for easy stowage.

Susan was putting out the camp-fire in the bushes with kettlefuls of water brought from the river.

'Giminy,' said Nancy, looking at the lawn, all scarred with the marks of torn up tent-pegs. 'It's a good thing the G.A. isn't here to see that.'

'Lots worse than daisies,' said Roger.

'Never mind,' said Mrs Blackett. 'It'll have cured itself by the time we've got the house straight. But perhaps it is a good thing Aunt Maria can't see it now.'

They had hoped to get off right away, but the wrecking of the camp was only the beginning of getting ready. There were a hundred things to do. The handcart was waiting in the stableyard with the dromedaries, but it was very soon clear that the expedition had more baggage than it could carry. More and more things joined the waiting pile. A big wooden pigeon-cage, with wire netting in front and a slanting roof, was lifted up and made fast on the handcart with a loose end from the big coil of alpine rope. Bags of tick beans, Indian corn and maple peas for the pigeons were slung on underneath. Boxes of tinned foods joined the pigeon-cage. The handcart looked already as if it could hold no more while the big pile of baggage had hardly been touched. Every other minute one of the workmen came out of the house to ask Mrs Blackett this or that. And Mrs Blackett was going through a list with Susan and at the same time trying to answer not only the questions of the workmen but also those of the prospectors.

'What about our sleeping-bags?'

'Do the tents go on the handcart?'

'Can't we hang the cooking things on the dromedaries?'

'Titty, where's your ground-sheet? Oh, where *is* Titty?'

'She's in Captain Flint's room with Dick.'

'Where's Peggy's pillow?'

'Look here,' said Mrs Blackett. 'Don't all talk at once. You needn't carry anything you don't want. I've got to go up to see Mrs Tyson before you can begin to unpack, and I can take as much baggage as ever you like in Rattletrap.'

Nancy hesitated, and then made up her mind.

'That'll make things a lot easier,' she said. 'And after all, we *could* bring it all ourselves, but that would mean making two journeys, and we've no time to lose. It isn't as if it was just going to the North Pole or climbing Kanchenjunga or anything like that. It's serious business, with no pretence about it. We've got to find that gold before Captain Flint comes back, and he's on the way already.'

They pushed the old car out into the yard, and when they had crammed it with stores and bedding, things began to look a little more hopeful, though there was still plenty left to be carried by the dromedaries. By that time three parts of the morning were gone, and it was clear that there could be no hope of starting till after the midday meal.

Nancy dashed off to Captain Flint's room and found Dick busy copying out paragraphs from the Encyclopaedia into his notebook.

'Look here, Dick,' she began, and broke off.

'Good for you, Titty,' she said. 'That looks jolly fine.'

Titty, who felt that it was rather like desertion to go off without waiting for the arrival of Timothy, had hurriedly made some garlands of marigolds, and with red and blue pencil had drawn the letters of 'WELCOME HOME' on the lid of an old shoe-box, cut them out, strung them on cotton, and was now hanging them with the garlands on the front of the armadillo's sleeping-hutch.

'Look here, Dick,' said Nancy, glancing round the shelves of her uncle's room. 'Is there anything else we want for mining, besides the hammers?'

'I was thinking about that,' said Dick. 'If we do find gold, we'll have to crush it and pan it, and we'll want a crushing mill. He's got one, but it's a most awful weight.'

They looked at a big iron mortar and a huge pestle, the handle of which was bound with rags. Nancy lifted first the pestle, then the mortar itself.

'Jolly heavy,' she said. 'But we're sure to need them.'

They were carried out to the yard, and wedged on the handcart between two boxes.

'Gosh!' said Roger, when he saw them. 'What about pick-axes, too?'

'Borrow them,' said Nancy. 'But I bet no one's got a crushing mill but us.'

Things were looking a good deal more hopeful by the time cook called them in to eat cold mutton and salad in the dismantled dining-room.

'We're practically ready,' said Peggy.

'I'm glad of that,' said Mrs Blackett.

And soon after they had finished up a cold rice pudding and a lot of bananas and gone out for a last look round to see that nothing had been forgotten, Dorothea ran back into the house to tell Mrs Blackett that the expedition was starting.

John, who was taking first turn at pushing the handcart, had trundled it out into the road. Titty and Dorothea took the ends of the short tow ropes to help pull it along. Nancy and Peggy were holding the heads of the heavily laden dromedaries. Susan was still making fast some of the baggage. Dick bolted back to the study for Captain Flint's copy of *Phillips on Metals*. He came back with the red book.

'I'll take great care of it,' he said to Mrs Blackett.

'All right,' she said, 'so long as you keep it dry . . . and it doesn't look as if we're going to have any rain before next year,' she added, looking at the dusty road and up at the clear blazing sky.

'Half a minute,' said Nancy. 'Somebody take my drom. I've forgotten the blue beads.'

She gave her bicycle to Susan, and was gone. They could

82

hear her charging up the carpetless stairs. She was out again in a moment with two small necklaces of blue glass beads which she hung on the lamp-brackets of the dromedaries.

'Every camel in the East wears them,' she said, 'to keep off the evil eye, and our dromedaries will need them extra badly to save them from getting punctures.'

'How are we going to get them up the hills?' asked Roger, looking at the dromedaries, slung all over with baskets and bundles.

'You'll pull,' said Nancy. 'They always have a little donkey to lead the caravan.'

At the very last minute Peggy leant her dromedary against the wall, and raced up to the pigeon-loft for the tin of hemp and canary seed, a pinch of which was allowed to good pigeons for a treat.

They were off.

'Now, Susan,' said Mrs Blackett. 'I'm counting on you to look after them. . . . And, Nancy, I'll be coming along as soon as I can. Don't try to rush things with Mrs Tyson. Don't unpack anything till I've seen her and heard what she has to say. She may say she doesn't want to have you at all . . .'

'All right, mother. . . . We've promised.'

'About that bell,' said Dick. 'You do know how to turn it off when you catch the pigeon? You see if you don't, it'll ring until the batteries run down . . .'

'And until we are all driven mad,' said Mrs Blackett. 'Oh, yes. I won't forget. Pull down the swinging bit, and push the slide across till lunch-time next day. Then pull it back again, and wait with cotton-wool in both ears until the next pigeon rings the alarm . . .'

'You won't really need cotton-wool,' said Dick. 'But, of course, you could make it not so loud by muffling the bell with a cloth or something . . .'

'Never mind,' said Mrs Blackett. 'I was only joking. I shall want to hear it.'

'Good-bye, mother. Good-bye. Good-bye . . .'

The caravan moved off along the road. As they turned the corner where the fir trees hid the Beckfoot gate, they looked back for the last time, to see Mrs Blackett and cook who had run out at the last minute to see them go, waving their handkerchiefs. The next moment they could see them no more. The Swallows, Amazons and D.'s Mining Company was fairly on its way.

*

'I can't believe we're really off,' said Titty.

'If it wasn't for Susan, we wouldn't be,' said Nancy. 'Susan and Dick. . . . And the pigeons,' she added, looking at Homer, Sophocles and Sappho, balancing on their perches in the big cage as the handcart swayed along.

For the first half-mile it was easy going, but, when they had passed the place where the road round the head of the lake turned off over the bridge, things became more difficult. Their own road was narrow and winding, going up the valley close to the dried-up little river. Sometimes it almost touched the river bank, and then it would turn suddenly away to climb round a lump of rock only to drop steeply on the other side till it met the river once more. The handcart, with John pushing, Susan lending a hand, and Dorothea and Titty hauling in front, seemed light enough on level ground, but weighed as much as a steam-roller the moment it was going up-hill, and was inclined to get out of control as soon as it began to go down. It was the same with the dromedaries. The donkeys, Dick and Roger, had no sooner stopped pulling in front than they had to start holding back from behind.

Everybody, except John and Nancy, who had to mend it, was very glad when Peggy's dromedary, in spite of its blue beads, punctured its front tyre. This meant a rest, a small ration of chocolate, and the paddling of dusty feet in the shallow pools that were left among the stones of the river-bed.

The puncture was mended and they went on. The valley narrowed. Steep woods came down on the left of the road, and they passed the place where Titty had come down with the charcoal-burner the year before, to ride home on the end of a felled tree pulled by three huge horses.

'Let's go up and see if the wigwam's still there,' said Roger.

'It isn't,' said Nancy. 'At least, no charcoal-burners. They're miles away at the low end of the lake.'

On the right was the river, and on the farther side of it the fell, all rock and bracken, rose steeply into the sky.

'Greenbanks,' said Nancy. 'We were up there yesterday. High Topps ends just about there.'

'Couldn't we cross the river and go straight up?' said Roger.

'Got to get to Tyson's first,' said Peggy. 'I say, do pull back a bit. The beast's trying to run away.'

Beyond Greenbanks, the valley opened out a little, and there were fields on their left, looking brown and parched, with cows flicking flies with their tails. On their right the fellside was wooded, and the trees came right down to the river.

'How much farther?' said Roger.

'It's a good thing you didn't come yesterday,' said Susan. 'We did all this twice, and a lot more, besides exploring on the Topps looking for water.'

They were climbing all the time now, and nearing the head of the valley. There were waterfalls in the river, though hardly any water was coming down. Ahead of them, the

ON THE ROAD

woods seemed to stretch across from side to side, closing the valley with a green curtain.

'We're nearly there,' said John. 'Stick to it, Titty. Atkinson's is up at the top where the road goes through those woods. Tyson's farm is this side of them, down at the bottom.'

'It's such a pull,' said Roger.

'Let's have a chanty,' said John, and Titty, though she had not much breath, started 'Hanging Johnny', and the rest of them, shouting the chorus and stamping their feet on the road, felt handcart and dromedaries suddenly lighter.

> They call me Hanging Johnny,
> *Haul away, boys, Haul away.*
> They say I hangs for money,
> *So Hang, boys, Hang.*
>
> And first I hangs me mother;
> *Haul away, boys, Haul away.*
> Me sister and me brother
> *So Hang, boys, Hang.*
>
> And next I hangs me granny,
> *Haul away, boys, Haul away.*
> I hangs her up so canny,
> *So Hang, boys, Hang.*
>
> A rope, a beam and a ladder,
> *Haul away, boys, Haul away.*
> And I'll hang you all togedder,
> *So Hang, boys, Hang.*

Then they tried 'With one man, with two men, we mow the hay together,' but when they had got to 'ninety men and a hundred men' they gave it up and went back to 'Hanging Johnny'. They had gone through it for a second time, when

Titty felt that the chorus was somehow fading away. Nancy had stopped singing, and John, and now Susan. ... She stopped singing herself. What was it they were looking at? Were those chimneys, and a roof, under the wood at the other side of the river?

PESTLE·AND·MORTAR

CHAPTER 8

HIGH TOPPS

'HERE we are,' said Nancy. 'That's Tyson's.'

A narrow lane turned to the right out of the road, crossed the almost dry bed of the river by a small hump-backed stone bridge, and ended in the cobbled yard of a whitewashed farm-house. On one side of the yard was the house itself, with low windows and a porch with clematis climbing over it, a big cow-house with a barn above it, and an old pump with a shallow drinking-trough. On the other side was a wall of loose stones with a gate in it shutting in an orchard. Behind orchard and buildings a wood of oaks and birches and hazels, with here and there a pine, rose steeply up into the sky. Somewhere above the wood was High Topps, the workings of the old miners of long ago, and the precious metal they had come to find.

The handcart rattled over the bridge and across the hard cobbles of the yard. The dromedaries followed more quietly, though Roger felt it was only right that the journey should end on the run, and that the leading donkey should announce the arrival of the caravan with a loud triumphant bray.

Mrs Tyson came out of the porch just as Nancy was leaning her dromedary up against the orchard wall. Her arms were white to the elbows with flour, for she was busy baking, and she did not seem too pleased to find the farm-yard full of prospectors with their handcart and their laden dromedaries.

'And here you are,' she said. 'And where's Mrs Blackett? Goodness, there's a lot of you. There was only three yester-day. I don't know where we're going to put you all.'

'Mother's coming along.'

'You'll have told her what I said about fires,' said Mrs Tyson. 'And about there being no water up in the wood, with the beck run dry.'

'We told her everything,' said Nancy. 'It's all right. It's no good lighting fires where there isn't any water. And we're not going to unpack tents or anything till mother's been. Oh, hullo, Robin. . . .' A young man came out from behind the barn with a long pole and a bundle of brushwood at the top of it. He set it to lean against the wall of the barn with half a dozen others.

'That's Robin Tyson, Mrs Tyson's son,' Peggy explained to Dorothea.

'More fire-brooms,' said Roger.

'We'll likely need 'em,' said Robin.

'Have you joined Colonel Jolys' volunteers?' asked Nancy.

'No good to us,' said Mrs Tyson. 'However can we let them know if there's a fire? If owt catches here, we mun fight it ourselves. Before we'd get the word to the Colonel at head of the lake there'd be nowt left of our valley but ash and smoke.'

'If there's a fire we'll all help,' said Nancy.

'So long as you don't light it I'll be well pleased,' said Mrs Tyson.

'We won't do that,' said Roger indignantly.

'If I could be sure,' said Mrs Tyson. She looked up at the blue sky over the high wood behind the farm. 'Never a sign of rain,' she said. 'And it's weeks now the ground is cracking for it. Oh well,' she added, 'I've my baking to do whatever . . . and Mrs Blackett coming.'

'She won't be here just yet,' said Nancy. 'At least I shouldn't think so . . . not until the painters and paperers have gone. May we just leave our things here while we go up the wood to have a look at the Topps?'

'There's no carts stirring today,' said Mrs Tyson. 'Your things'll be out of the road again yon barn wall.'

'You'll want the pigeons out of the sun,' said Robin Tyson. 'Best wheel them into the barn.'

'Thank you very much,' said Titty, who had been trying to make a shady place for the pigeons by draping a bit of a groundsheet over their cage.

'Dump everything,' cried Nancy. 'Travel light. It's a bit of a pull to the top.'

The handcart was run into the barn, with the pigeons' cage upon it. Dromedaries leaned against the orchard wall. Knapsacks were slung off and piled in a heap.

'No need to carry anything,' said Peggy. 'Just a dash up the wood to have a squint at the goldfields.'

'Compass,' said John, digging one out of the outer pocket of his knapsack.

'And we'd better have the telescope,' said Titty.

'We might jolly well want it,' said Nancy. Already she was leaving the farmyard, and opening the gate into the wood.

The others crowded through.

'Shut the gate, someone,' said Nancy.

'Aye, aye, Sir,' said Roger.

It was pleasant to come into the shade of the woods after the long trek in blazing sunshine along the valley road. There seemed to be less dust in the air, and there was a clean smell of resin from the scattered pines, with their tall rough-scaled trunks, that towered among the short bushy hazels, the rowans, and the little oaks. A track wound upwards through the trees. Anybody could have told that it was very little used. Here and there were stony patches in it, where dried moss covered the stones. Here and there were little drifts of last year's leaves. Here and there under and near the big pine trees the path was soft and brown with fallen pine needles. The track was not wide enough for a cart, and probably it had been used only by sleds bringing bracken from the fells above.

'Is it wide enough for the handcart?' Peggy asked Susan. 'There won't be much room to spare.'

'We won't be taking it up there,' said Susan.

'Unless it rains and the beck fills,' said Nancy over her shoulder.

'Where *is* the beck?' said Titty, remembering the pleasant little stream up which she and Roger had explored together last summer when they had discovered Swallowdale and the cave they had called after Peter Duck. But in this wood there was no tinkling of falling water.

'Just crossing it,' said John, and a moment later a strip of shingle across the path and a deep furrow beside it showed where the beck had been.

'Stepping stones,' said Roger, and walked gaily across, stepping on the big stones that had been left there so that when the beck was flowing people crossing it could keep their feet dry.

'And no water,' said Dorothea.

The track climbed steeply upwards through the trees, sometimes leaving the stream, sometimes close to it, and then swinging away to one side and back again, in wide zigzags, to make the climbing easier. But this August of the drought it was not a stream but the dry bed where a stream had been. The expedition had been climbing for a long time before coming on a drop of water, and then, below what had once been a waterfall, they saw a tiny pool.

'Water! Water!' shouted Roger.

'Couldn't we camp here?' said Peggy.

'No good,' said John. 'It's only a bird-bath.'

'It's stagnant,' said Susan, 'or very nearly, and there isn't enough for any washing or cooking.'

A chattering jay blundered noisily away through the trees, when Titty pushed through the hazels to have a closer look.

They climbed on.

'How much farther?' said Roger, who had been growing less and less talkative as they climbed.

'Probably another hundred miles or so,' said Titty.

'Stick to it, Roger,' said Peggy. 'We're getting near the top.'

John and Nancy were hurrying ahead. Even Susan was walking faster than she had been. Dick, his eyes on the ground, and his hammer in his hand, was climbing doggedly away behind her.

'Do tell us what the Topps are really like,' said Dorothea.

'You'll see them in a minute or two,' said Peggy. 'It's years since I've been there.'

'Titty,' said Dorothea privately, 'about Squashy Hat. Is he really prospecting too, or is Nancy just thinking so, to make it more exciting?'

'If he knows about the gold,' panted Titty, 'he's sure to be prospecting. Anybody would be . . .'

'But if he doesn't know . . .?' said Dorothea.

'Hurry up!'

'We jolly well are,' said Roger grimly.

Suddenly the track divided into two. One path turned sharply left through the bushes. The other went on. The trees were thinning. Close before them was a thicket of brambles at the foot of a wide steep face of rock with heather clinging to it here and there. A grassy gully, clear of brambles, led to the top of the rock. Nancy, John and Susan were up there already. Dick, hammer in hand, was close below them.

'Come on,' said Peggy, and the rest of the prospectors ran, panting, after her, hearts pounding in their chests after the long climb. They dodged round the bramble thicket, raced up the green gully, and, a moment later, from the top of the rock, were looking out over the wild, broken moorland of the Topps.

*

'Well, what do you think of it?' said Nancy, waving her arms as if she had somehow herself conjured the whole of High Topps into existence.

Titty at first could hardly speak. That last run to the rock after the long climb from the valley had left her altogether out of breath. Spots swam before her eyes, but in spite of them she knew she was looking at a Klondyke, an Alaska, better than anything she had dreamed when they were talking of the goldfields in the camp at Beckfoot. Over there rose the great mass of Kanchenjunga. A huge arm stretched down from him towards the valley they had left, hiding all the Beckfoot country and the hills towards the head of the lake. A range of hills swept away to the south from the peak they had climbed the year before. Half circled by the hills there lay a wide plateau, broken with gullies, scarred with ridges of rock that rose out of a sea of heather and bracken, and close-cropped sun-dried grass. Away to the left the plateau sloped down and was crossed by a ribbon of white road. Behind the prospectors were Tyson's wood, and the deep valley of the Amazon out of which they had climbed.

'What's that native road?' Titty asked, when she had got her breath again.

'It goes over into Dundale,' said Nancy over her shoulder. 'It's the same road we trekked on coming to Tyson's.'

Roger was looking back down the smooth steep face of rock at the edge of the Topps.

'What a place for a knickerbockerbreaker,' he said.

'Landing in the brambles,' said Titty.

'I could stop myself,' said Roger.

'Don't try,' said Susan hurriedly. 'Who's going to darn you? Mrs Tyson isn't like Mary Swainson.'

'Well, if I mayn't slide down,' said Roger, 'isn't it my turn for the telescope?'

'Let him have the telescope,' said Susan.

'Here you are,' said John. 'Two minutes a turn. Every-body wants to have a look.'

'Where are the old workings?' asked Dick.

'All over the place,' said Nancy. 'You see Ling Scar? The big lump coming down from Kanchenjunga. That's the one we were inside when we went to see Slater Bob. The tunnel we were in is supposed to come out this side, but it isn't safe any longer. There are lots more along the ridge at the bottom, where the Topps begin. And there's a working in almost every bit of valley or rise all over High Topps. You know, just a hole, and a heap of scratchings outside it. You can see one from here. Over there. That black spot under those rocks . . .'

'Let's begin looking right away.'

'Oh look here, Captain Nancy,' said Susan. 'We simply can't. Mrs Blackett's coming, and we've tents to pitch and grub to cook. We ought to start down again almost at once.'

'First thing tomorrow then,' said Nancy.

'Where's the enemy?' said Titty.

'Squashy Hat? He's in the other farm. Where we ought to be getting our milk from really. It's the other side of the road, just below where it turns down through the woods. You can't quite see it from here. I wish you could. He's probably there now.'

'No, he isn't,' said Roger urgently. 'I'm looking at him now. Do be quiet.'

Roger was lying flat on his stomach, with his elbows dug into the ground, while he steadied the little telescope with both hands. One of his feet was kicking in the air. Its kicking meant 'Shut up, everybody!' but nobody knew the code because Roger himself had only that minute invented it.

Everybody, however, could see which way the telescope was pointing.

'Lurk!' said John suddenly, and the three other Swallows flung themselves flat on the ground.

'Lurk,' cried Nancy, and she and Dorothea and Peggy dropped together.

'Lurk! Lurk!' said Dorothea. 'Oh, Dick!'

Dick turned and saw that he alone was left standing. He understood, and crouched beside Dorothea.

'Sure it's him?' said John.

'Let's have that telescope,' said Nancy. 'It's him all right.'

About a mile away a grey figure was sitting on a rock.

'Got his back to us,' said Nancy. 'That's lucky. Look here, if he turns round he's bound to see us. We must get down into cover. Go on, Peggy. Reversing snake. You know. Quick. Wriggle away. Never mind getting your frock dirty, Dot. It'll get dirty anyway when we're prospecting . . . and everything's bone dry. It'll dust off. Well done, John.'

John, who had practised the reversing snake wriggle before, had been moving backwards over the ground from the moment he had seen that seated figure far away. He had slipped over the edge of the rockface and was hanging on there quite comfortably, able to look out, and able also at any moment to drop another few inches and be out of sight altogether. In another two minutes the whole expedition was in cover, some of them hanging, like John, along the upper edge of the steep rock face, and others crouching in the narrow gully where the old track came down the rock from High Topps into the wood.

'What's he doing?' said Roger.

'Just resting,' said Susan.

'Safest to lurk, anyway,' said Nancy. 'But he isn't just resting. Look. Look. He's got a map.'

'It may be only a newspaper.'

'Can't be,' said John.

Even without the telescope they could all see a sheet of something white in the hands of the solitary man out there in the middle of High Topps. The man was standing up now, looking at the white sheet in his hands, and then up at the hills.

'He's looking at a compass,' Nancy almost shouted. 'Won't you believe now? Go on. Take the telescope and see for yourself. Giminy. He's in the very middle of prospecting.'

One after another they looked through the little telescope and saw first, that the man was indeed Squashy Hat, and second, that he had put something on a rock, and kept looking at the map, then at the hills, then at the thing on the rock, and then back at the hills again.

'Well?' said Nancy.

'It looks jolly like it,' said John.

'I say,' almost groaned Titty. 'You don't think he's got the map Old Bob was talking about.'

Nancy thought for a moment.

'No,' she said at last. 'He wouldn't be looking so puzzled if he had. He'd be simply scooping the gold out. He's been up here three days at least. He was coming down the other side of that ridge the day we saw him go into Slater Bob's.'

'He's turned round,' whispered Dorothea.

Squashy Hat had folded up the map or whatever it was he was looking at. He had picked up the thing he had set on the rock and had put it in his pocket. He stood for a moment looking towards Kanchenjunga, then turned, and set off walking over the uneven ground.

'He's coming this way,' said Roger.

'He's seen us,' whispered Dorothea.

'Dead still, everybody,' said Nancy.

The distant figure was moving fast, now across bare rock, now knee-deep in bracken, now working along the sheep tracks through the heather.

'He hasn't seen anything,' said John.

'He's going down to the Dundale Road,' said Nancy.

'Going home to Atkinson's farm,' said Peggy.

They watched him till he struck the road, turned left along

it, and vanished where the road dipped towards the woods.

'Let's scout after him,' said Titty.

'We can't,' said Susan. 'Mrs Blackett'll be at Tyson's before we get down there.'

'Lucky beast he is,' said Nancy. 'Having his base camp right up here. . . . If only there was a drop of water in the beck. . . . You should just see the place I meant us to camp in . . .'

'Where is it?' said Titty.

'Here,' said Nancy. 'Close to the Topps. Better even than Atkinson's. Come along and have a look at it.'

She hurried down from the rock, dodged round the bramble thicket at the bottom of it, and pushed her way through the bushes.

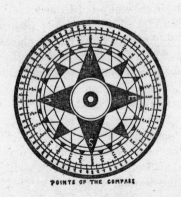

POINTS OF THE COMPASS

CHAPTER 9

TWO KINDS OF CAMPING PLACES

ONLY twenty or thirty yards below the steep rock face from the top of which they had been watching their rival, Nancy, followed by the others, came out from under the trees on a round piece of cleared ground.

'What a gorgeous place,' said Titty.

'It jolly well is,' said Nancy. 'This was the place I was thinking of, close to the Topps, close to Atkinson's, no time wasted anywhere, and if only it wasn't for the drought, there wouldn't be any dead sheep, and the beck would be full, and that puddle you saw where there used to be a waterfall would be a bathing pool big enough for a herd of hippopotamuses . . .'

'Not a herd,' said Dick doubtfully.

'Two or three little ones, anyway,' said Nancy.

John and Susan had seen the place the day before. Peggy had seen it long ago. Dick, Dorothea, Titty and Roger, were seeing it for the first time. It was a round level platform. Anybody could see that it had been levelled on purpose. One side of it had been built up from below. The other had been levelled by scooping away rock and earth out of the steep side of the hill. Not a tree was growing on it, though trees and bushes hedged it in so that people could have walked past it only a few yards away and not known that it was there. There were a few small bushes at the edge of it, and stumps of old trees just to be seen among the foxglove leaves, but most of the platform was bare of anything but dead leaves, and moss, with here and there a tuft of thin grass. At one side of it was something that looked at first like an untidy heap of larch poles.

99

'Someone's camped here before,' said Dorothea. 'Savages probably.'

'The very best kind of savages,' said Titty eagerly. 'They may be the very ones we knew.'

Roger was looking at the weathered, moss-covered larch-poles. 'I bet once upon a time it was a wigwam just like the one I slept in. I wonder if they had an adder in it, too.'

Dick and Dorothea looked at them with puzzled faces.

'It's an old charcoal-burners' pitstead,' said Nancy.

'You know,' said Peggy, 'where they had their piles of wood, and covered them up to burn slowly and turn into charcoal. These poles are what's left of the wigwam they lived in.'

'The ones we know are the Billies,' said Roger. 'Young Billy's about a hundred years old, and Old Billy is his father and even older.'

'There just couldn't be friendlier savages,' said Titty. 'They might almost have left the place specially for us.'

'They didn't really,' said Susan. 'Nobody's been charcoal-burning here for years. Look at the moss on those poles.'

'I know they didn't,' said Titty. 'But they might have. Look at the way Young Billy made a crutch for Roger. What I mean is, it's such a lovely place that you might almost think it was a present from them.'

'Hidden from everywhere,' said Dorothea.

'Ahoy! Nancy!'

John's voice sounded from above them. They looked up and saw him astride a branch at the top of a tall old ash that towered above the other trees at the side of the clearing.

'I can see Atkinson's from here,' he called down. 'I can see the garden, and those beehives, and the door. . . . Squashy Hat's just gone in. . . . And looking the other way I can see a lot of the Dundale road.'

'Gosh,' said Nancy. 'What a place it is. And a look-out post all ready for us.'

'And room for all our tents,' said Titty.

'And no danger of setting fire to anything,' said Peggy.

'Let's camp here, anyhow,' said Roger.

'We'll never find a better place,' said Titty.

'It's no good,' said Susan. 'We could manage all right if it was only getting milk from the valley every day. But we simply can't cart every drop of water.'

'We could go without washing,' said Roger. 'Unnecessary washing, I mean,' he added as he happened to catch Susan's eye.

'And anyway,' said Susan, 'we've got to camp where Mrs Tyson will let us.'

'When the charcoal-burners were here,' said Nancy, 'it can't have been a year like this. Oh, bother the drought. Well, you see why I wanted to come here. It's going to make it a lot harder for us, having to climb up from Tyson's every day . . .'

'And go back at night,' said Peggy.

'And Squashy Hat at Atkinson's, right on the edge of our goldfield . . .'

John came down from the tree.

'I'm going up,' said Nancy. 'I won't be a minute . . .'

'Oh come along, Nancy,' said Susan. 'We must get down to the farm. There's the baggage wagon to unpack, and the dromedaries and then all the stuff Mrs Blackett's bringing for us. And we'll make a gorgeous camp somewhere else . . .'

'Not like this one,' said Roger.

'What a camp it might have been,' said Titty.

'Might have been,' echoed Dorothea.

'Camp Might Have Been,' said Nancy. 'Jolly good name for it. Oh well, it can't be helped. Come on down and get our tents up, and we'll have breakfast early and be up here before Squashy Hat stops yawning and rubbing the sleep out of his eyes.'

'Which way?' said Roger.

'Through here,' said Nancy.

An old track partly bushed over, so that they had to hold the branches out of each other's way, led from the open pit-stead into the path by which they had climbed out of the valley. Susan and John, as soon as they were back on the path, set out at a steady jog-trot down the hill.

'Stir your stumps,' said Nancy, as she hurried after them.

*

The old track wound zigzagging to and fro down through the wood.

It had seemed a long climb, when, after the trek, they had left their baggage in the farmyard and gone on, travelling light, to have a look at the goldfields of High Topps. It seemed a great deal longer now, although instead of going up they were hurrying down. With every step now they were going further from the country they had to search. Every step now meant so much more time wasted at the beginning and end of every day. The sight of their rival had changed things for all of them. They had seen him, with a map, in the middle of the goldfields. There had been a doubt even in Nancy's mind. Squashy Hat might after all be no more than a casual visitor. It might have been just romantic curiosity that had brought him to Slater Bob's. Atkinson's farm might have been chosen as a lodging by someone not in the least interested in prospecting. But now, what doubt could there be? They had heard what Slater Bob had said. They had seen Squashy Hat waiting till they were out of the way and then going into the mine to talk to the old man. And now, each one of them had seen him messing about with a map in the very country they hoped to search.

'It'll be a race who finds it first,' said Dorothea.

'That's just it,' said Titty. She trotted on a few more steps before finishing what she had to say. 'And living up there he gets such a tremendous start.'

For a long time they jogged on down the winding track, clump, clump, down the straight bits, slowing up for the sharp turns, careful not to slip on the dry moss. Every time they came near the beck, or rather the place where once the beck had leapt sparkling from stone to stone, from waterfall to ferny pool, from pool to waterfall again, its dry bed reminded them of the perfect camp that might have been.

'Bother the drought,' said Roger.

'You can see there's been plenty of water,' said Dick. 'Look how green the ferns are even though there isn't a drop coming down the stream.'

'We'll never have a camp as good as that one,' said Dorothea.

'It's going to be an awful way to climb in the morning,' said Peggy.

They trotted on.

'And what about getting back to camp for dinner in the middle of the day?' said Roger.

'We'll have to carry it with us,' said Peggy. 'Susan and I'll have to cook it at the same time as breakfast.'

A shrill whistle sounded far below them in the wood.

'That's the mate's whistle,' said Titty.

'Coming. COMING!' they shouted.

They found the others waiting for them near the bottom. All three of them were close together, and there had been some kind of an argument. John was just winding it up.

'Look here, Nancy, Susan's right. It's no good thinking of a camp up there without a drop of water. Even if we hadn't promised.'

'And we may have a really good place down here,' said Susan.

*

As soon as they came back into the farmyard, they saw that Mrs Blackett had already been there. Someone had spread a tarpaulin on the ground. On it was a great pile of bedding and mattresses and rolled-up tents.

Mrs Tyson was looking at it. This time, somehow, she seemed much more pleased to see them. Perhaps Mrs Blackett had told her that they were a careful lot, not likely to set the fell on fire.

'Ah, here you are,' she said. 'Mrs Blackett didn't wait for you. She's a mort to do at home, so she said, so she was off again. But we've a grand place for you to camp. Here in the orchard, close by the house so you'll be handy if you want owt. And we've turned the old sow out, so she won't come tumbling your tents at night. And you'll find good water at yon pump across the yard, and plenty of it for all the drought. You'll be as well here as in your own house, better likely, with the workmen up and down with their papering and painting. You'll likely be putting yer tents up right away, I reckon. Mrs Blackett did say you'll be wanting to make a fire now and then. I don't hold with fires, but there's just one spot on the shingle by the bridge where there's no fear of owt catching. Things are that dry, you never know. And you'll be close by the house at night so that if you want owt, you've only to call and I'll hear you . . .'

She rattled on, friendly and kind, making them at home. And with every word she said their spirits sank deeper and deeper.

To be camped within hearing of the house and its natives, no matter how friendly. . . . To draw water from the farm pump instead of dipping it from lake or beck. . . . To have the tents not in a wood, or on the fell, or even in an ordinary field, but in an orchard, with apple and damson trees in their neat rows. . . . Why, Mrs Tyson was quite right, and they might almost as well be in the Beckfoot garden.

NICE AND HANDY TO THE HOUSE

Dick and Dorothea, perhaps, felt nothing of this, because, poor things, they hardly knew what camping was, but Roger and Titty looked at each other and then at John and Nancy and Susan and Peggy, waiting to see what their elders would have to say about it. Surely they would find some way out.

But no. The captains and mates pulled themselves together. Anybody who did not know them might easily have thought that they were very pleased. They followed Mrs Tyson into the orchard and said, 'Thank you,' almost as if they meant it, when she showed them the clear space along the wall where they could pitch their tents.

'You'll be tired after all that traipsing,' said Mrs Tyson. 'I'll be having supper ready for you in the parlour as soon as you've your tents fit up. And breakfast'll be at eight in the mornings . . . and your suppers at half past six.'

'But we'd rather do our own cooking,' began Susan, but Mrs Tyson would not listen to her.

'I've the table set out now,' she said, 'and the kettle's on the fire. So I'll be ready as soon as you are, as the saying is.'

There was nothing to be done about it. Mrs Tyson meant it all so kindly that even Nancy could not say no to her.

'And I was telling your mother I'll put you up some sandwiches each day, and with your flasks of tea you'll be able to picnic where you like. Well, well,' she broke off. 'I'll leave you to it. You'll be all right setting your tents up anywhere along under this wall.'

She went back to the farm-house.

The prospectors waited silently till she was gone.

'Barbecued billygoats,' said Captain Nancy, 'but this is pretty awful.'

CHAPTER 10

PROSPECTING

'PRETTY awful,' Nancy had called the new camp, with its row of tents along an orchard wall, and a pump handy, and meals ready-cooked in the farm-house. But, after all, it was nearer High Topps than the garden at home. From Beckfoot, prospecting would have been impossible. From Mrs Tyson's orchard, something could be done. They all knew that it had been a very near thing, getting leave to come at all. They were all tired, and by the time they had pitched the tents, and divided out the bedding, and had a bit of a wallow in what was left of the river, and a good hot high-tea or tea-supper in the farm-house, they were inclined to think that things might have been a great deal worse. They slept well, after they had grown accustomed to the irregular bumps of apples, dried up before their time, dropping from the trees. In the morning, even Nancy liked waking up in a strange place, though Mrs Tyson calling them in to breakfast did rather make it seem as if civilization was jogging the prospectors' elbows. And, of course, the pump in the farmyard was a bit of civilization, too, but able-seamen Dick and Roger did not on that account the less enjoy pumping cold water on each other's heads.

The trouble began when it came to starting for the gold-fields.

Mrs Tyson gave them porridge for breakfast as well as eggs and bacon, but all the time they were eating it the grandfather clock in the corner of the farm parlour reminded them with its loud ticking that they had no time to lose.

'Buck up, Roger,' said John.

'Pitch it in,' said Nancy. 'Giminy, we've seen him at it.

It isn't as if we didn't know he was there. It's been light for hours, and Squashy may be finding the place and staking his claim while we're just sitting here hogging.'

But the whole expedition was ready and waiting in the farmyard long before Mrs Tyson was ready to serve out the sandwiches and flasks of tea they were to take with them.

'If only we'd been doing our own cooking,' said Susan. But the one thing Mrs Tyson did not want them to do was to cook. She preferred to cook for them, and said so, and, after all, she might very well have told Mrs Blackett she would rather they stayed at home. They hung about anxiously, thinking of their lucky rival lodging almost within a stone's throw of the goldfields. Susan had a last look round the Swallows' tents, to see that all bedding was neatly folded, in case any stranger might come along. Dick sat in the farm porch for the sake of the shade, and had another look through *Phillips* on the forms of gold. Nancy and Peggy were in the kitchen helping Mrs Tyson (who could have managed better without them) by buttering slices of bread. The others were amusing themselves by giving hempseeds to Homer, Sophocles and Sappho. The method was to wet the tip of a finger by licking it, to put one hempseed on the wet fingertip, to poke the finger through the wire netting and to hold it steady, or as steady as possible, while a pigeon took it with a tickling peck.

'Who's going to take the first dispatch?' said Roger.

'Sappho,' said Titty.

'Why haven't you got her in the basket?' said John.

'The basket's all ready,' said Dorothea.

'I'm going to carry it,' said Roger.

'She's to stay with the others till the very last minute,' said Titty. 'Hey. Here they come.'

'Everybody collect a flask,' called Nancy. 'They're all in the porch. Susan's got the sandwiches. Come on. Where's that pigeon? Who's postman?'

'I am,' said Roger.

'Here you are then,' and she held out a scrap of thin paper. 'Don't go and lose it. If we had to send her back without a letter, mother'd be bound to think we meant her as an S O S. Now then, Titty. Let's see you catch her. . . . Oh no. Better not today. We're so awfully late already.'

In a moment Sappho, who did not seem to mind Nancy's firm clutch, was in the travelling-basket.

'Have you thought of what to say in the letter?' asked Dorothea.

'Found a ten-ton nugget of pure gold,' said Roger.

'Wouldn't it be lovely if we did?'

Sandwiches and thermos flasks were dealt out at last.

'Everybody got a hammer?' said Nancy.

'We're to be back for tea at half past six,' said Susan.

'Oh, look here,' said Nancy. 'It's as bad as being at school.'

'It can't be helped,' said Susan.

'Let's get started,' said John.

*

They climbed steadily up the path through the trees. It seemed even longer than it had the day before and the path was too steep for talking. Under the big rock face at the top of the wood they halted. Scouts, Nancy and John, went up the gully and disappeared, creeping low to the ground. The others waited by the bramble thicket below the rock. Dick was looking through his notes. For a few minutes nothing happened. There was a shout. Then Nancy appeared, standing up, on the top of the rock, which, by this time, they had agreed to call The Great Wall.

'All clear,' she said. 'Come on. We've got the Topps to ourselves.'

It was a funny thing, but you might almost have thought that she was disappointed.

'Perhaps he's hiding,' said Dorothea hopefully.

They hurried up the gully and looked out across the rolling, broken Topps, all heather, bracken, rock and close-cropped, dried-up grass, to the great mass of Kanchenjunga and the huge spur somewhere in the heart of which Slater Bob must be at work. The only living thing to be seen was John, who had raced across a hundred yards or so of open ground to climb a ridge of grey rock. He was signalling to them to come on.

'Not a sign of him,' said John, when the rest of the prospectors joined him.

'Let's begin at once,' said Nancy. 'Does everybody know what to look for?'

'Gold,' said Roger.

'Gummock,' said Peggy. 'Everybody knows that.'

Dick pulled out his pocket-book.

'Read it out, Professor.'

Dick found the right page.

'Sometimes gold is found in the form of dust. Sometimes in nuggets. Sometimes mixed with other minerals, particularly in quartz.'

'Why not in gallons,' said Roger. 'Two gallons one quart. Even pints wouldn't be bad.'

'Shut up,' said John.

'I looked up quartz,' said Dick gravely. 'It's a white, semi-opaque, crystalline substance.'

'People are keen on it for rockeries,' said Nancy. 'There's lots of it about.'

'What we've got to look for first,' said John, 'is an old working. Slater Bob said the gold was found in a dip by an old working, and we'll know it because of some heather in a crack in the rock.'

'There are dozens of old workings,' said Nancy. 'Some are just burrows. Some are caves. Some used to be caves and have got choked up. Some you can only tell by the lump outside where the turf has grown over the rubbish the old miners threw out.'

'Jolly easily miss the right one,' said John. 'High Topps is a whacking big place.'

They looked out over the rolling fell, all grey rock, and drab withered grass, and dusty bracken, with here and there a patch of purple heather.

'We'll work backwards and forwards in a long line,' said Nancy.

'Not too far apart,' said John.

'Right across the Topps to the foot of Grey Screes and back again. Strip by strip.'

'Like lawn-mowing,' said Titty.

They spread out, twenty or thirty yards apart, so that the eight of them, moving abreast, could search a strip of ground about two hundred yards wide. It would have been easy if the ground had been flat or all alike. But it was not. Some people found themselves going slowly over rocks and heather where anything might be discovered any minute. Other people galloped ahead over dry bent and dusty earth cracked in the August heat. The line was hardly straight for two minutes together. Nobody liked to hear the hammers of the others tapping on stone while they themselves might just as well be walking in a field.

Peggy, in the middle of the line, was the first to find one of the old workings. It must have been a very old one, perhaps one of those left by the Germans who came to these lake-country fells and mined copper in the time of Queen Elizabeth. It was not high enough to stand up in. Just a narrow hole that would have pleased a fox. All the others closed in to see it.

'No heather anywhere near,' said John.

They spread out again, and pretty soon a shout from Nancy

COMBING THE TOPPS

at the northern end of the line brought everybody running. She, too, had found an old working, this time a good-sized cave. There was no heather here, either, but it was too good a cave to pass by, and everybody went inside it and fingered the rough, chipped walls by the light of pocket torches. They even used Titty's ball of string, though there was no need, because Slater Bob had said that the working where the gold was found was not a deep one, and, anyhow, they were never out of sight of the entrance. Then, as they moved on, they came to a long, low ridge, where rocks stood up, bare of grass, and most inviting to the hammer. Everybody put on sun-goggles and did a little stone-breaking, and Dick, as geologist to the company, was shouted for by one after another of the prospectors to decide if this or that bit of stone was or was not valuable ore. At first people were inclined to keep specimens, just in case, and pockets and knapsacks grew heavier as the day went on, and then lighter again as hopes waned, and the specimens, no longer valued, were dropped by the way.

At last Susan, after a word with Peggy, blew three long blasts on her mate's whistle.

Everybody knew what that meant, and a few minutes later the line had closed in on itself, and the prospectors were wriggling out of the straps of their knapsacks, throwing themselves on the hot, dry ground, and opening thermos flasks and packets of Mrs Tyson's sandwiches.

'I say,' said Titty, as she put the pigeon's basket carefully on the ground. 'We forgot to bring a drink for Sappho. She won't like tea, and she'll be as thirsty as anybody.'

'We'll send her off now,' said Peggy. 'And there'll be some hope of her flying straight so as to have her drink when she gets home.'

'What shall I say?' said Roger, pulling out his bit of paper.

'ALL WELL,' began Nancy. 'PROSPECTING BEGUN. NO SIGNS OF HATED RIVAL. Mother'll be jolly pleased to hear that. She was a bit stewy, you know, for fear it might come to a battle.'

Roger wrote it down carefully, making his handwriting as small as he could.

'Shove in a skull,' said Nancy. 'Or let me. I know how they go with doing them all over the place.'

Skull and crossbones were duly added. The paper was rolled up till it was smaller than a match.

Titty and Roger were busy with the pigeon.

'Don't try holding her in one hand,' said Peggy.

'I've got her,' said Roger. 'But be quick with the message. She doesn't a bit like keeping still.'

The message was pushed under the rubber band. All was ready.

'Give her a good start,' said Peggy. 'Go on. Up into the air and away . . .'

'She's off . . .'

'News from the desert,' murmured Dorothea.

'Why doesn't she go?' said Roger.

'She's gone . . .'

The pigeon swung round and round above their heads, rising higher and higher till it hurt their eyes to watch her in that blazing sky. Suddenly she flew off, towards the valley of the Amazon, but so high that after the first two moments not even Roger could persuade himself that he could see her.

'I wonder whether cook'll drop a tray,' said Peggy, with a grin.

'Pity we can't be both ends at once,' said Nancy. 'I'd like to hear that bell go.'

With Sappho well on her way to a drink of cool water in the Beckfoot pigeon-loft, and a feast of pigeon meal, they settled down to their own dinner.

'Anybody who didn't know might easily think we were a picnic party,' said Peggy.

'Galoot,' said Nancy. 'How could anybody think anything else? No real camp. No real cooking. Susan's mincing-machine all wasted. Sandwiches in paper packets, some marked "beef" and some marked "jam". Of course it's a picnic.'

'They're not half bad sandwiches,' said Roger.

'Remember the pemmican in Swallowdale,' said Peggy.

'And the shark steaks when we were on Wild Cat,' said Titty.

'Hang the drought!' said Nancy. 'If we could only use the charcoal-burners' camp and be free of natives altogether.'

'There *is* one thing,' said Susan. 'No signs of Squashy Hat. And if he isn't prospecting, we aren't in such a hurry.'

Five minutes later she herself was the first to see him.

They had eaten their sandwiches and drunk the hot tea out of the thermos flasks, hot tea which, in spite of its hotness, is the most refreshing of drinks on hot days. Peggy had surprised everybody by serving out a ration of chocolate from a secret store of her own ... 'only just in time,' as Roger pointed out, because it was on the point of melting and pouring away out of the paper in which it was wrapped. It was time to go on with the search. Nancy had jumped to her feet to shame the general laziness. Roger was pretending to be asleep. Dick was looking towards Kanchenjunga, thinking of rock-faults and geological strata and likely places for mineral deposits. Titty and Dorothea were cramming the wrappings from the sandwiches into the outer pockets of their knapsacks. Susan had already slung her knapsack on her back and was looking across the Topps towards the Great Wall and Tyson's wood, when she saw something moving in the bracken. Someone was coming up towards the goldfields from the Dundale road.

CHAPTER II

FENDING OFF THE ENEMY

'Lurk!' said Susan.

Nancy dropped as if she had been clubbed.

'Dick!' said Dorothea. 'Lie down!'

'It's Squashy Hat,' hissed Titty.

'Oh, all right,' said Dick, and lay down, while Nancy wriggled like a snake towards a largish tussock of rank grass. All the others were flattening themselves to the ground.

'He's coming up from Atkinson's,' said Peggy.

'It's him all right,' said John.

'What are we going to do now?' asked Dorothea, looking eagerly at the wriggling Nancy.

'Probably hide,' said Titty.

'He may have been watching us all day,' said Roger.

Nancy, under cover of the tussock, raised herself inch by inch to look out.

'We can't let him come up here,' she said.

'We can't stop him,' said John.

'Of course we can,' said Nancy. 'If he's looking for our gold he won't want us to see him find it. He won't want us to see even where he's looking. He won't go anywhere where he sees us, at least, he won't if he's after the gold. If he isn't, it doesn't matter either way. We've got to be all over the place. We'll soon see if he's prospecting or not.'

'He's opening his map,' said Susan, who alone had never stirred. 'He's sitting down.'

'Back to us,' said Nancy. 'What luck. Clear off, everybody. We mustn't all be in a bunch. Go on. Get as far as you can towards him without being seen. Spread out and be doing something. Do anything. Look for white heather. There isn't any, but it doesn't matter. Look for birds . . .'

'Or lizards,' said Dick.

'Why not caterpillars?' said Roger.

'Caterpillars'll do very well,' said Nancy. 'There are those big velvety ones in the heather.'

'What shall I do?' asked Dorothea.

'You and Titty can go for a walk,' said Nancy. 'But walk the right way and be well away from the rest of us before you start.'

'You mustn't let him think we're doing it on purpose,' said Susan. 'He may not be a rival at all. And if he talks to you, Roger, you're to remember that these are the holidays and he isn't a schoolmaster . . .'

'I don't know what you mean,' said Roger.

'Oh yes, you do,' said John. 'No secret cheekiness. That's what she means. And you jolly well know it.'

'Everybody as polite as pie,' said Peggy.

'No talking if you can help it,' said Susan.

'Don't waste time,' said Nancy. 'I'm off. Get away as quick as you can. . . . Spread right out. . . . So that whichever way he goes there'll be somebody . . .'

'Come on, Dot,' said Titty.

'What about our knapsacks?'

'Mine's got an orange in it for later on,' said Roger.

'Better take them,' said Susan. 'I'll take the empty pigeon-basket.'

John went one way, Nancy another, followed by Peggy. Susan, bending low, was creeping directly towards the ridge where Squashy Hat was sitting with his back to her, looking at his map. Nancy's plans were all very well, but Squashy Hat was a stranger, and if there was any talking to be done, she would rather do it herself. Titty or Roger might go and say something to him that would be difficult to explain. Dick and

Roger were running side by side towards a big patch of waist-deep heather, their eyes on the enemy, ready at any moment to stop and be looking for caterpillars if he showed a sign of turning round. Dorothea and Titty were alone.

'If we creep along behind these rocks we're all right,' said Dorothea. 'And once we get into the bracken we can crawl along as far as we like.'

They set off. John, Susan, Roger and Dick had vanished altogether. Now and then they caught glimpses of the red woolly caps of Nancy and Peggy.

'They always forget those caps,' said Titty. 'Anybody can see them miles away.'

But presently they were in tall bracken and could see nobody at all. They crawled, bending low, so that anybody looking at the bracken would have thought that a sheep was pushing its way through beneath the waving fronds.

'Sure we're going the right way?' said Dorothea.

'Yes,' said Titty. 'Look at Kanchenjunga. We can't go wrong, or at least not very, if we keep him behind our right shoulders.'

They could not move fast, and they were both very hot and out of breath when Titty stopped short in the bracken.

'I'm going to stand up and have a look,' she said.

'Shall I, too?' said Dorothea.

'Half a second,' said Titty.

Cautiously she lifted her head. They were on the top of a low bracken-covered ridge. A couple of hundred yards off she could see Squashy Hat.

'Now's your chance,' she whispered. 'He's looking the other way!'

Squashy Hat, tall, thin, with stooping shoulders, was looking at his map again. He was standing up on a pile of rocks that rose out of the heather. From this small height he was looking across High Topps towards the place where the woods dropped down from it into the valley of the Amazon. Titty and Dorothea looked that way, too, wondering what had become of Dick, Roger, John and Susan.

Squashy Hat swung slowly round. They both dropped to their knees in the tall bracken.

'I'm going to have another look,' said Titty, at last. 'I simply must get up. There's an old bracken stalk running into my knee. . . . Hullo. He's off. He'll be running into one of them any minute.'

Dorothea rose, too.

Squashy Hat, the folded map in his hands, was walking, long-legged, through the heather.

'Look, look. There's Susan.'

Somehow or other, out of nowhere in particular, Susan had appeared. She was standing in the heather, with her back to Squashy Hat, and nobody could have guessed for a moment that she knew that he was there.

'He's seen her.'

'Guilty conscience,' said Titty. 'I thought so. He *is* looking for the gold and doesn't want us to know it.'

Squashy Hat had stopped short, changed course, and was swerving away to the right. They could see that now and then he glanced at Susan, who, for her part, was sauntering as well as anybody can saunter in heather.

'He's going to get round beyond her,' said Dorothea.

They watched for minutes that seemed hours.

Suddenly Squashy Hat checked again.

'He's seen somebody else,' said Titty. 'Good. Good. I was afraid nobody could have got there in time. But I can't see who it is.'

'On that rock,' said Dorothea. 'Something moving.'

Just for a moment, far away, they caught sight of John on a far-away clump of rocks, looking at the summit of Kanchen-junga through the telescope.

Squashy Hat turned uncertainly and came wandering back. He left Susan well on his right, and then, as if by accident, changed course again to go up on High Topps between the sauntering Susan and the patch of deep bracken from which Titty and Dorothea were watching him.

'Ought we to go that way to frighten him off?' asked Dorothea.

'Perhaps we ought,' said Titty. 'Or one of us. I'll go. Somebody ought to be here in case he comes this way.'

She hesitated a moment, and then was glad she had not started.

Suddenly, in the heather right in the path that Squashy Hat was taking, they saw a small boy, and heard an eager yell.

'Hi! Dick. I've got a beauty!' That was Roger shouting.

'Is it a fox-moth larva?' came Dick's answer. And they caught the sparkle of the sunshine on his spectacles.

Squashy Hat changed his course again and came walking almost directly towards Titty and Dorothea. He took off his squashy hat and wiped his face with a handkerchief. Then he put his hat on again and came steadily on, along a well-trodden sheep track. He was fanning himself with his folded map, and looking very bothered.

He was close to them when they heard him talking to himself. 'Straordinary thing,' he was saying. 'Never would have thought it. . . . Whole place seething with children. . . . Oh, I beg your pardon.' He had suddenly seen Dorothea and Titty pushing their way through the bracken only a yard or two away.

He was off again, moving along the edge of the Topps not very far above the Dundale road from which he had come. Then he seemed to think better of it, and turned right once more, as if to strike up into the heart of the wilderness. But there, right in his path, suddenly appeared a girl with a red knitted cap, making a very good show of using her red cap as a butterfly net in an unsuccessful chase of a white butterfly. And far away beyond the entomologist they could see another red cap. What Nancy was doing, they could not see. But she was there, for a few minutes later they saw Squashy Hat swerve off once more, and this time he seemed to have made up his mind that there were too many people about for whatever he had meant to do, for he held right on along the edge of the Topps, and did not bear north again until he was climbing the lower slopes of Grey Screes.

One by one the prospectors came together once more.

'Well done, everybody,' said Nancy. 'And you saw the way he shied. Anybody could tell he was up to no good.'

'What's he doing now?' said Roger.

Nobody could quite make out, even with the telescope. Squashy Hat seemed to be busy with something high on the side of Grey Screes about opposite the middle of the Topps. Through the telescope they could see that he was climbing among the rocks, but he seemed to spend a long time in one place, and once or twice people thought they had heard the faint click, click of a distant hammer.

'Bet he's just gone up there to be able to see where we're prospecting,' said Nancy.

'Well, there's no need to show him,' said John.

'He won't stay up there for ever,' said Nancy.

But Squashy Hat seemed to be in no hurry. The afternoon slipped away, while the prospectors lay in the heather and watched their rival. They looked at two or more of the old workings, not in the least likely ones, because there was no heather anywhere near. They did quite a lot of stone-breaking, but found nothing that Dick thought was anything like the proper colour to be gold. But, with Squashy Hat up there on the hillside above them, they did no more of the regular combing of the wilderness.

At last they saw him turn back. Instead of coming straight

across the Topps, he came down by the way he had gone up, which showed clearly that he had had his eye on the eight who were watching him. He came down to the Dundale road and then strode steadily along it.

'Going back to Atkinson's,' said Nancy.

'To have his tea,' said Roger, and Susan looked at her watch.

'We're going to be late,' she said.

'Oh, look here,' said Nancy. 'Now's our chance. Let's spread out again and search another strip. Don't be a Great-Aunt.'

'We're late already,' said Susan.

John agreed with Susan.

'We've done him for today, anyhow,' said Titty.

'But we've done hardly anything ourselves,' said Nancy. 'And we never will get anything done while he's at Atkinson's, close to the Topps, and we're right down in the bottom of the valley. If only the beck wasn't dry and we could camp up here, we could be looking for gold before he gets up, and after he clears off to hog his ill-earned grub.'

They went slowly back across the Topps to the Great Wall and Tyson's wood. They went down the gully, past the bramble thicket, and not even Susan objected when, instead of going straight down the path, they turned through the bushes to have another melancholy look at the old pitstead of the charcoal-burners. Nobody could have dreamed of a finer place for their camp, with its clear patch of levelled ground where the charcoal-burners had had their fire, and the trees all round it to give shade, and the old ash that might have been specially planted to allow a sentinel to look out over the tops of the other trees and to see what the enemy might be doing at the farm on the farther side of the Dundale Road.

'If only there was a drop of water,' said Peggy.

'But there isn't,' said John, 'and no hope of any.'

'Oh well,' said Nancy at last. 'Come on. Down to Tyson's. Supper in the parlour. Bed in the dormitory. You can't call that beastly orchard anything else.'

Mrs Tyson was waiting for them when they came home.

'This won't do, Miss Nancy,' she said. 'You're more'n an hour late, and the chops I'd on for you'll be pretty near cinders.'

CHAPTER 12

POT OF PAINT

THEY were still at breakfast next day when a motor-car drew up in the farmyard with a squeak of brakes and the sudden scrape of locked wheels on the stones.

'It's mother!' cried Nancy, and jumped up. 'I bet it means Timothy's at the station.'

They ran out into the yard. But Mrs Blackett had not come to announce the arrival of the armadillo.

'Good morning,' she said. 'No. Nothing's come. But look here, Nancy, you've got to do something about your Post Office. Hours of delivery . . . most irregular. . . . Not fair on the public to ring them up at dawn . . .'

'Dawn?'

'Five o'clock this morning, Dick's horrible invention began to do its worst. We did our best to sleep through it, but couldn't. In the end I had to get up and go down to the pigeon loft. It's very pleasant out of doors at that time of the morning, but I'd rather have had my sleep out all the same.'

'But we sent the pigeon off quite early,' said Roger.

'The bell began at five o'clock this morning.'

'It was that wretched Sappho,' said Nancy.

'Perhaps we'd given her too much to eat,' said Peggy.

'I did give her some hemp,' said Titty.

'Hemp!' said Nancy. 'You must never give them hemp *before* a flight. But I expect she'd have dawdled, anyway.'

'Oh, Sappho! Sappho!' said Titty, who was looking into the basket that Mrs Blackett had brought with her.

'Sappho, indeed,' said Mrs Blackett. 'Just idling about and then waking people up at five o'clock.'

'Good,' said Roger. 'You've brought her back. So we've three pigeons in hand.'

'Two and a half,' said Mrs Blackett. 'I don't think Sappho ought to count.'

'She always was undependable,' said Nancy.

'Well, don't use her if you don't have to. The other two were always better, weren't they? . . . Ah, how do you do, Mrs Tyson. I hope they're not giving you too much trouble . . .'

'So long as there's no fires, I won't complain. Fires is what I'm afraid of, with no water coming down the becks and all as dry as tinder. But if they could be more on time at night. . . . With the farm to run and all, I can't be waiting about keeping meals ready. . . .' And with that, Mrs Tyson made room in the doorway for Mrs Blackett and they went into the farm-house for a little private talk, leaving the indignant and bothered prospectors in the farmyard.

'Did you hear that?' said Nancy. 'And it isn't as if we'd lit any. The mates haven't even had a chance of boiling a kettle. And if only she'd let us do our own cooking, it wouldn't matter to her how late we were.'

'It's jolly unfair,' said Roger.

'Look here, mother,' said Nancy, when Mrs Blackett came out again, 'couldn't you persuade her to let us cook? It's simply awful having to start home ages before we're ready.'

But Mrs Blackett would not even try. 'It would be all very well,' she said, 'if there was water anywhere else. But there isn't, and Mrs Tyson might easily say she wouldn't have you here at all. I wouldn't blame her if she did. And as for starting home early, just think how much earlier you'd have to start if you had to come all the way home to Beckfoot. No. I'm afraid you'll have to make the best of it. And do, please, try to be in time for meals.'

'If it rains and the beck on the Topps fills up again, it'd be all right for us to camp up there.'

'I suppose it would,' said Mrs Blackett. 'But it doesn't look much like rain. Well, good luck to you. I'm glad you saw nothing of your rival . . .'

'But we did. Almost as soon as we'd sent off Sappho. He was charging about all over the place. But we fended him off . . .'

'Oh, Nancy!' said her mother, and looked at Susan.

'It was quite all right,' said Titty. 'He went away of his own accord.'

'I'm glad of that,' said Mrs Blackett. 'But don't go and get into trouble with strangers. Better keep out of his way.'

Already she was sitting in the driving-seat and racing the engine. 'And now,' she said, 'I must hurry back to my plasterers and painters. You needn't send a pigeon today. But I'll expect one tomorrow. Homer or Sophocles. Not Sappho, *if* you please.' Rattletrap leapt forward. Mrs Blackett waved a hand, clutched at the wheel with it, missed the gate-post by an inch, and was gone.

'Homer and Sophocles ought to give Sappho a talking to,' said Dorothea.

'They'll have a chance today,' said Titty, as she opened the door of the basket and let Sappho join the other pigeons in the big cage.

*

It was perhaps two hours later, but to Roger, lying in the bracken at the roadside, just opposite the gate to Atkinson Ground, it seemed much more like four. The expedition had been split in half. 'We can't keep out of his way,' Nancy had said, 'if we don't know where he is.' When, after waiting a long time for their sandwiches and thermos flasks, they had at last climbed the wood and come out on the Topps above the

Great Wall, they had seen no signs of their rival. John had pointed out that he might have gone off the other way, and it had been decided that Peggy must lead a scouting expedition, while John, Susan, Nancy and Dick went on with the combing of the Topps. Everybody knew that Dick was too absentminded for scouting, and, as a geologist, he was needed by the prospectors. Nancy would have liked to go scouting down to Atkinson's herself, but Peggy was the only one of the more experienced scouts who had not been at Mrs Atkinson's when the pioneers had first learnt that Squashy Hat was lodging there. It would never have done if Mrs Atkinson had recognized them and told Squashy Hat who they were. So Peggy had planted Dorothea with a whistle in a good place well above the Dundale Road, Titty at the point where the road dived down below the wood, and Roger opposite Atkinson's gate, while she herself had crept through the trees to the Atkinsons' garden and seen Squashy Hat smoking an after-breakfast pipe. She had come back and signalled this news to Roger. He had signalled it to Titty. She had signalled it to Dorothea, and Dorothea, after whistling to attract their attention, had signalled on the single letter 'Q' to let the prospectors know that they could work in peace for the enemy was safely in his earth. Then Peggy had once more gone down through the trees into the enemy's country, and Roger, for a very long time indeed, had been lying on his stomach looking out across the road between the stalks of the bracken. Fern-like fronds of bracken shaded his head, but the sun scorched his back and two flies seemed to be taking turns in settling on his nose. They were small and black, but, he thought, very brainy for their size. Again and again he had waited with hand poised ready to bat them when they perched. Again and again he had been too late and batted his nose from which a fly had flown just as his hand came down. It was too hot, and batting his nose made him hotter.

Besides, he ought to be keeping still, and he changed his plan and let the flies have things their own way and showed how an Indian would behave, stirring not at all, while a fly with cool, sticky, tiny feet, moved up his nose, down it, circled its tip, and walked slowly up one side of it. By squinting he could almost see it, not properly, but bigger than it really was, close under his eye.

How long had Peggy been in sight? Hang that fly. Far down the cart track leading through the trees to Atkinson's, was a huge old oak tree. Roger could see its wide trunk, just where the cart track bent and disappeared. Only a moment ago, he could have sworn, there was no one there. And yet. . . . How long had he been squinting at that fly? . . . Now, clear enough, he could see Peggy, with her back to the tree, facing him, with one hand outstretched, and the other lifted, pointing just about at two o'clock. Q for Squashy Hat. . . . And then. . . . Yes. . . . Down went her left hand and up went her right . . . straight above her head. D . . . Danger. Squashy must be leaving the farm. He must be close by. Peggy had dropped flat to the ground in front of that old oak, and was wriggling back into the bushes. She was gone.

Roger, flies forgotten, turned and snaked away from the screen of bracken to a holly bush, behind which it would be safe to stand. From there he looked up the road along the edge of the wood. Was Titty on the look out for him. She was. You could count on her for that. QD. . . . Roger saw her repeat his signal and vanish to signal it on to Dorothea. A moment later, faint and distant, he heard Dorothea's whistle. Far out on the Topps the prospectors knew that Squashy Hat was on the move before ever he had left Atkinson's wood. Good work. Jolly good work. Indians themselves couldn't have sent the message quicker. And Roger crawled back to his post among the bracken and watched.

Yes. There he was. Roger, peeping through the bracken

stalks, looking across the road, saw him coming up the Atkinsons' cart track. Thin, long-legged, Squashy Hat was swinging along between the ruts. He was close to the gate. He was coming out on the road. He was on the road, within a foot or two of the silent watcher in the bracken. How loud his feet sounded. Hobnailed boots, thought Roger. All the Swallows and Amazons had rubber soles, because, as John had said when he was smaller than Roger was now, 'You never know when you may get a chance of going aboard somebody's boat.' Rubber soles were good for scouting too. Clump, clump, clump, the hobnails rang on the hard road, and between the clumps the sharp tap of an iron-shod walking-stick. Squashy Hat did not seem to mind how much noise he made. Roger shifted a little to see the better. What was he carrying in the other hand? A milk can? And he had a haversack over one shoulder. Roger wondered whether haversacks that swung at your side were as good as knapsacks that bumped up and down on your back. And there was his hammer, slung in a ring at the side of his haversack. Anybody could see he was a prospector. And talk about squashy hats! Roger had never seen a squashier.

And where was Peggy? Roger looked again down the cart track into Atkinson's wood. Why didn't she come along? Nothing to wait for after the enemy had left. Roger expected to see her come out from among the trees. But there was no sign of her. And Squashy Hat would be out of sight in a moment. He was moving with a long, easy stride, not hurrying, but getting fast over the ground. Going up-hill, too, thought Roger. . . . What would happen next? And suddenly he drew in his breath so sharply that it almost turned into a yelp.

Someone, something, had clutched him by the ankle.

'Shut up,' hissed Peggy. 'You'll give us all away. It's only me, you blessed gummock.'

'But I never saw you cross the road,' said Roger. 'How did you do it?'

'Just walked,' said Peggy. 'I Indianed a bit so as to get to the road a bit below the gate. Then I only had to wait till I could hear old Squashy pounding up the hill. Then I slipped across and Indianed along this side just for practice.'

'I didn't mind, really,' said Roger.

'Lucky he didn't hear you,' said Peggy. 'I say. Did you see what he's carrying?'

'Milk-can,' said Roger.

'It isn't,' said Peggy. 'It's the rummest thing. I had a good look at it over the wall, while he was waiting for Mrs Atkinson to bring him out his sandwiches. It's a pot of white paint.'

'Whatever for?'

'I don't know. Come on and report to Nancy. We'll pick up the others on the way. See if we can snake up to Titty without her spotting us. Come on. The main thing is not to touch anything that can make a noise. I'll go first. You keep close behind and stop dead if you see me stop . . .'

*

The prospectors on the Topps had been hard at work, though you cannot search as wide a strip of ground with a comb of only four teeth as you can with one of eight. They had been into two or three old workings, but had found none that looked at all like the place the old miner had described. They were well out in the wilderness when Dorothea's whistle brought work to an end. They looked back towards Tyson's wood. There she was, and there could be no mistake about the signal. A moment later she had vanished.

'Good for her,' said Nancy to herself, and waved to the others.

The four of them came together on a rocky hillock and waited. It seemed a long time before they caught sight of Squashy Hat coming along the Dundale road.

'Sure it's him?' said John.

'Of course it is,' said Nancy. 'Nobody else walks like that. Perfect ostrich.'

'I can't see Dot,' said Dick, 'or any of the others.'

'They'll be snaking,' said Nancy.

'There's one thing,' said Susan at last. 'If we can't see them, I don't suppose he can.'

Nancy looked at John. Just the faintest ghost of a grin showed on both their faces. It was not fear of a rival prospector that was bothering Susan. Hers was an almost native fear lest this grown-up stranger should guess that he was being used for scouting practice by Titty and Roger. She did not worry so much about Peggy and Dorothea. They, after all, had mothers who perhaps would not mind. But she knew that her own mother, away in the South with the whooping Bridget, would much rather Titty and Roger fell down, or caught colds, or got dirty all over, than that anybody should even think they were letting themselves be rude. John looked at Nancy, and Nancy looked at John. They both knew Susan very well.

'There they are,' said Susan. 'It doesn't matter if he does see them now.'

The scouts had made good use of every bit of cover, and they were already on the Topps and well away from the Dundale road. Nancy waved to them, and they came on at a steady trot. Squashy Hat was making no attempt to come up into the country from which yesterday he had been so successfully fended off. He was sticking to the road. He disappeared now and then where the road dipped, but did not leave it until he was near the other side of the Topps, when they saw him climbing along the steep side of Grey Screes.

The scouts, breathless and terribly hot, dropped on the ground beside the prospectors.

'He's got a pot of paint,' panted Peggy.

'He didn't see any of us,' said Roger.

'White paint,' said Titty. 'It's a new tin. I was only two yards from the road when he went by.'

'Oh, rot,' said Nancy. 'It's probably something to drink.'

'I thought it might be a milk-can,' said Roger.

'It's paint,' said Peggy. 'I read the label on it.'

'He must be up to something jolly rum,' said Nancy.

'Perhaps he isn't prospecting at all,' said Susan hopefully.

'He's got his hammer,' said Roger.

'Anyway,' said Nancy, 'so long as he's up there, we can see him. No danger of being surprised. We may as well get on with the work.'

'What about our knapsacks?' said Roger. 'Won't it be easier to carry the grub if it's inside.'

'It *is* inside,' said Susan. 'Sandwiches and a thermos in each knapsack.'

'Inside *us*, I meant,' said Roger.

'That's not a bad idea,' said Nancy. 'And then we can travel light, and come back to collect the baggage on the way home.'

*

All afternoon a long line of prospectors worked across the Topps and back again making sure they missed nothing on two wide strips of that desolate country. All afternoon Squashy Hat was moving slowly about on the steep slopes of Grey Screes. For a long time even Nancy began to doubt whether he was indeed prospecting. Why, when the gold was some-where on the Topps, should Squashy Hat clamber about those rocky slopes? But late in the afternoon they heard him. They were all together after looking at an old working, when, perhaps because for a moment no one was talking, they heard a faint, a very faint click far away.

'Listen!' 'Listen!' 'Sh!' Everybody was asking for quiet from everybody else. They heard the click again. From far away, up the steep hillside, the sound carried in the windless air.

Dick had the telescope.

'I can see him tapping,' he said. 'Look here. I'll drop my hand next time I see him tap. ... Now ...' His hand dropped, and a moment later that faint metallic click was heard by all of them.

'He's prospecting, all right,' said Nancy.

'But what on earth did he want the white paint for?' said John.

Time went on, and Susan, remembering what had been said that morning, began to be worried about getting back to Mrs Tyson's. They worked across to the hillock where they had left their knapsacks, and then moved slowly on towards the Great Wall and Tyson's wood.

'We simply *must* be in time tonight,' said Susan.

'We can't go while he's still on the prowl,' said Nancy.

'He's coming down,' said John.

And then there was a sudden yell from Roger, who was taking a turn with the telescope, and at first had failed to find him.

'We told you it was white paint. We told you it was white paint. Look what he's done!'

The telescope was passed from hand to hand. Squashy Hat was indeed coming fast down the mountain-side, but up there, where he had been during the afternoon, he had left his mark. Everybody could see it when he knew where to look for it . . . a round staring splash of white among the grey rocks.

'But what's it for?'

'It may be just a trick,' said Nancy. 'To make us think he's up to something there when he's really busy somewhere else.'

Even Susan forgot Mrs Tyson and the time, while looking at that white spot, like a target, painted in that impossible place, and at the painter, Squashy Hat, who was hurrying down towards the road.

'Perhaps he's coming down now because he's seen us clearing off,' said Peggy.

'Let's not go,' said Titty.

'Let's pretend to,' said Nancy. 'We can see if he goes home if someone goes up that tree by the old pitstead. Gosh, it is awful that we've got to go down to Tyson's and leave him with the whole Topps to himself.'

They went down the gully in the rock, past the bramble thicket into the clearing the charcoal-burners had left. It looked even better than it had the day before. John climbed to the topmost branches of the old ash tree, from which he could see Atkinson's farm and long stretches of the Dundale road.

'Can you see him?' said Nancy.

'He's walking jolly fast,' said John.

'Come along,' said Susan. 'We're late already.'

'We must make sure he goes home,' said Nancy.

'Go on,' said John, from the tree-top. 'I'll catch you up.'

Susan started slowly on, but stopped. What was the good of getting back before anybody else?

Every now and then, when Squashy Hat was hidden by a dip in the road, there was a new alarm lest, now that they had gone, he should secretly turn up again towards the Topps. But he came steadily on, and, at last, the look-out announced that he had been seen at Atkinson's. The look-out, a little ashamed now, slid down the tree and hurried after Susan.

'We simply couldn't have gone without making sure,' said Nancy.

They went down the path at a quick, desperate trot.

An angry bell sounded down in the valley below them.

'Where's Dick?' cried Dot suddenly.

'Dick!' shouted John.

'Coming!' His voice sounded from far above them. They slowed up a little to wait for him, though that bell went on ringing.

'Hurry up,' called Dorothea.

He caught them up at the bottom of the wood. In his hand was something like a blade of grass. He threw it away as they ran through the gate.

Mrs Tyson was standing outside the farm porch, and the bell was in her hand.

'It's not a bit of good my trying to keep things hot for you,' she said.

'We're awfully sorry,' said Susan. 'We did try . . .'

'It isn't only once,' said Mrs Tyson. 'It's every day . . .'

Roger wanted to say that they had been there only two days, but he thought better not.

The prospectors sat down to supper in deep gloom.

CHAPTER 13

CAN'T ANYBODY DOWSE?

THEY had nearly finished the rice and stewed prunes that came at the end of that melancholy meal when Dick came out with a surprising sentence.

'You know,' he said, 'I do believe there *is* water up there.'

'In the beck?' said Nancy, 'but the beck's gone dry.'

'Just behind the place where the charcoal-burners had their fires,' said Dick.

Everybody stared at him.

'He doesn't really mean it,' said Titty sadly.

'But he does,' said Dorothea. 'Don't you, Dick?'

'Well, I found a lot of those green rushes,' said Dick, 'the ones that you peel and they look like soapsuds inside. And the man who came to my school last term to look for water said those rushes were the surest sign there was . . .'

'What?' said Nancy. 'A dowser? I wish we had one. There used to be one in the village, and long ago he found water for Beckfoot. Before we were born. But he's gone away now.'

'The man who came to the school called himself a water diviner,' said Dick. 'They ran short of water in the playground, and he found a spring for them. But he probably knew it was there.'

'Did you see him do it?' said John.

Nancy was leaning eagerly forward. She had pushed her plate impatiently away. 'What did you see him do?' she asked.

'He had a forked stick,' said Dick. 'Hazel. He held one end in each hand, and then he walked about until the stick began to twist. At least he said it did. And they found water there all right. They dug, and it came bubbling up only a few feet down.'

'How did he hold the stick?'

There was something in Nancy's voice that stopped Titty's last spoonful of prune juice just as she was lifting it. Nancy, she knew in a moment, was off on some new idea.

'Like this,' said Dick. 'In both hands. He made me hold it, but nothing happened. He made us all take turns holding it.'

'And did it happen with any of you?'

'One man said it did. But I don't see how it could.'

'Come on,' said Nancy. 'It won't be dark for another hour. Hazel, you said. There are lots at the bottom of the wood. Giminy. If it worked with him why shouldn't it work with one of us? I bet it will. Come on, Peggy. Buck up, you Swallows. Roger doesn't want a second helping.'

'No, thank you,' said Roger, when Susan looked at him.

Titty swallowed that last spoonful of juice.

They crowded into the passage and out through the farm door. Just by the gate into the wood Nancy found what she wanted.

'What about this,' she said, cutting a forked branch of hazel and slashing off the smaller twigs from it.

'The branches weren't as long as that,' said Dick.

'Well, get it just right,' said Nancy, busy with her knife. 'Will that do?'

'That's what it looked like.'

'Now then,' said Nancy. 'How do I hold it?'

'No,' said Dick. 'The man had his knuckles underneath, fingers on the top, and the ends of the stick came out between his fingers and his thumb.'

'Where's some water?' said Nancy. 'We ought to try where we know there really is some.'

'There's none coming down the beck,' said Peggy.

'What about the pump?' said John. 'There must be a spring somewhere near it, to keep it going in spite of the drought.'

'What's going to happen?' said Roger.

'Water divining,' said Titty.

Nancy was walking slowly down the yard towards the pump by the barn. She was holding the forked hazel twig, one branch in each hand, and with bent head, watching the twig, hardly lifting her feet from the ground, was moving slowly along. Dick was close beside her. So was John. Peggy was walking backwards in front of her. Dorothea was watching Dick.

'What ought it to do?' said Nancy.

'The water diviner said it dipped every time he came near water.'

'Does it feel like dipping?' asked Peggy.

'Not yet, you gummock,' said Nancy. 'It's still a long way from the pump.'

She moved a little faster.

'I'm bound to come over the spring if I go right round the pump.'

She came to the pump. She squeezed past between the pump and the wall of the old barn. She walked all round it.

'Perhaps it only works with running water,' she said. 'Pump a bit, somebody, so that the water's moving.'

John worked the handle up and down. A stream of water gushed from the spout and splashed into the trough below it.

Nancy walked round again.

'It doesn't budge,' said Nancy. 'Come on, John. You have a try. We'll all try. If only one of us could do it, we could find our own wells and camp wherever we wanted.'

'If there was water underneath,' said Dick.

Nancy put out her tongue at the professor, and gave the twig to John. She began pumping.

'Not too hard,' said Susan. 'Mrs Tyson says there's no water to spare, even in the well.'

'You've got hold of it all wrong,' said Nancy. 'Here, Titty. You pump. Get your fingers on the top, John.'

Titty worked the squeaking pump handle gently up and down so that a trickle of water and no more dribbled out of the spout.

John, shown by Dick and Nancy how to hold the twig, walked round the pump. The stick showed no signs of moving.

'Come on, Susan. You next,' said Nancy.

'What's that jam jar for?' asked Titty, but Roger was already slinking away with it towards the gate into the orchard. No one else had noticed him.

Susan tried, and after her Peggy. Then Dick, though he said he didn't really believe in it. Then Dorothea, who in spite of Dick's unbelief, desperately hoped it would work with her. It did not.

Roger was waiting for his turn. Three or four times he made Dick show him just how the twig had been held by the water diviner.

'I believe it's going to work,' he said. He skipped quickly round the pump.

'Well?' said Nancy.

Roger was moving sideways across the yard.

'Where are you off to?' said Nancy.

'It seems to tell me where to go,' said Roger, moving a little faster.

'Don't be a little owl, Roger,' said John.

'Aye, aye, Sir,' said Roger, hurrying towards the gate.

'Hi!' said Captain Nancy. 'Bring it back. There's no water there . . .'

'Yes, there is,' cried Roger. 'Look at it. Wagging like billy-ho.'

The stick wagged up and down like a pump handle and wagged sideways like the tail of a dog, while Roger held it over some rank dock leaves close by the orchard gate.

Nancy grabbed at him. He dodged her, dropped the stick, bent down and lifted a broken jam-pot full of water from under the leaves where he had hidden it.

'Who said there was no water?' he laughed, darting out of reach.

'I'll shiver your timbers for you,' said Nancy, laughing in spite of her disappointment. 'Oh well, if it doesn't work it doesn't.'

'Titty hasn't tried,' said Peggy.

'Here you are,' said Nancy. 'Don't play the goat like Roger. If only it worked with one of us, everything would be all right.'

Titty took the stick. Nancy put her hands in the right position for her. The others were already losing interest. Even Peggy, who had wanted her to try, did not wait to see what happened, but began talking to Susan about carrying water up the hill in milk cans. 'We'd want too much,' Titty heard Susan say. 'Washing, and washing up, and cooking and teeth and, anyway, we wouldn't be allowed . . .'

'Go on,' said Nancy, with hope still in her voice. 'Close to the pump . . .'

And at that moment Titty almost stumbled. . . . It couldn't be the stick itself pressing against the soft flesh at the base of her thumbs. She pulled herself together. Silly to be startled like that. And anyhow nothing could have happened. Why, Dick himself had said that nothing could.

'Half a minute,' said Captain Nancy eagerly. 'Didn't it give a sort of jerk just now?'

Titty looked round miserably. 'It can't have,' she said.

'There it is again,' said Nancy. 'Look here. Come back a yard or two and go over that bit again.'

Everybody was alert now, and watching.

'What happened?' said Roger. 'I didn't see.'

'Slowly . . .' said Nancy.

Titty's eyes were swimming. She saw the ground of the yard at her feet through a mist. Something queer was happening that she could neither help nor hinder. The stick was more than a bit of wood in her hands. It was coming alive. If only she could drop it, and be free from it. But there was Captain Nancy's voice, talking, close to her and yet far away. 'Go on, Titty. Go it, Able-seaman. Or is it just your hand shaking?' Suddenly, a yard or so from the pump, there could be doubt no longer. The ends of the stick were lifting her thumbs. She fought against them, trying as hard as she could to hold them still. But the fork of the stick was dipping, dipping. Nothing could stop it. Her hands turned in spite of her. 'Titty! Titty!' They were all talking to her at once. The next moment the stick had twisted clean out of her hands. It lay on the ground, just a forked hazel twig with the green showing through the bark where Nancy's knife had trimmed it. Titty, the dowser, startled more than she could bear, and shaking with sobs, had bolted up into the wood.

Steps sounded behind her.

'It's all right, Titty,' Susan was saying. 'Never mind. It's over now, anyway.'

'Sorry,' sobbed Titty. 'Awfully sorry. I didn't mean to . . .'

'All right, Titty. . . . All right. . . . Steady on.'

Somehow or other she must stop this silly trembling, she, an able-seaman, an explorer, a mining prospector. She stood still and caught hold of a branch, hardly seeing it. Suddenly she saw it was a hazel branch. She let go of it as if it had burnt her.

'Come on, Titty.' Susan was patting her shoulder.

'Just a minute or two,' said Titty, swallowing hard. 'I'm coming back. . . . But. . . . Oh, Susan. . . . *Not* to do it again.'

'No, no,' said Susan. 'They won't even ask you.'

Susan was right. After that first moment of horrified astonishment at Titty's tears there had been eager talk. There had been more experiments with the hazel twig, but it had not stirred in any of their hands. Still, some of them, at least, were sure they had seen the thing happen. And then John, who had started to run after Titty and stopped short, thinking it better to leave her to Susan, had had a private word with Nancy.

'Giminy, I wish it had been me it had happened with,' said Nancy.

'We've got a geologist in the expedition,' Peggy was saying as Titty and Susan came down out of the wood. 'And now our own dowser. . . . At least . . .'

'Shut up,' Titty heard Nancy say.

Dick was holding the hazel twig, looking at the cut ends of the fork. 'I don't see why it should,' he was saying. 'There's nothing to make it twist. It can't have, really. She must have just thought it did.'

'Look here,' said Nancy, suddenly and loudly. 'What about a wallow in what's left of the river? We'll have to buck up before it's too dark to find the wettest bits.'

Five minutes later Titty and Nancy were lying side by side in one of the pools of the river. The river had sunk so low that they could not get properly under water.

'Beastly shallow,' said Nancy, splashing with hands and feet and pretending not to be aground.

'Hardly fin-room for a minnow,' said Titty gratefully.

Not one single word was said to her about what happened when she held the hazel twig.

THE DIVINING ROD

CHAPTER 14

DESPERATION

NOT a word was said to Titty about dowsing, but next morning, tents were still being tidied when she noticed that Nancy had disappeared.

'Where's Captain Nancy?' she asked.

'Gone on,' said Peggy, and at that moment they all heard a very loud but very bad copy of an owl call from high in the wood where Nancy was already climbing.

'I'm ready,' said Titty, 'except for the provisions.'

'So'm I,' said Dick.

'Nancy's forgotten her hammer,' said Peggy. 'And she's gone without waiting for her grub.'

'I'll take it,' said Titty.

'Better start, anybody who's ready,' said Susan. 'We'll catch you up. Go ahead, Titty. Then you won't have to hurry later on. Roger, your toothbrush is quite dry . . .'

'Well, I was just going to use it,' said Roger.

'I must just finish my diary,' said Dorothea.

'Come on, Dick,' said Titty.

'Leave your flasks,' said Susan. 'We can't fill them till Mrs Tyson's ready with the tea.'

Dick and Titty hurried off into the wood.

They climbed fast at first, hoping to catch up Nancy. They called to her once or twice but got no answer. Even in the shade of the trees it was very hot and they were both out of breath before they had got half-way up the winding path to the Topps. They had passed the place where the path crossed the dry bed of the beck when Titty stopped short.

'Let's just rest half a second,' she said. 'It's no good thinking we can catch her.'

'We'll have a look at the pool,' said Dick.

They turned aside through the trees to the shrinking puddle that in other years had been a deep little pool in the stream that had come leaping down, waterfall after waterfall, from High Topps to the valley below. It was small and stagnant, but on a hot day even to look at a puddle is better than nothing and the ferns that hung over it were cool and green.

'It's gone down a bit even since we came,' said Titty. 'Somebody's been drinking at it. Natives, perhaps . . .'

'Animals,' said Dick. 'Very small ones. Look at the tracks.'

He flung himself down and peered through his spectacles at faint muddy prints on the white stones. Some small animal had wet its feet and brought them damp and muddy from the pool, leaving its footprints on the stones. The mud had dried at once. A breath of wind would have swept the little dusty marks away for ever.

'What is it?' said Titty. 'No Timothies here.'

'Can't be a stoat or a weasel,' said Dick. 'Toes too near together. I've got a book with lots of tracks in it, and the stoat's toes spread out wide. Not like these. I wish I could see where he went. But the ground's so dry there are no tracks to be seen . . .'

'Not even Captain Nancy's,' said Titty, and with that they left the little pool and hurried on up the track after the leader of the expedition.

'Yes there is,' said Dick suddenly, stopping short.

'Is what?' asked Titty.

'Spoor,' said Dick. 'You can see someone's been this way. Cutting sticks.' He pointed at some new cut twigs lying on the ground.

'She may have been laying a pattern,' said Titty. 'You

know, to show which way she went. But the sticks aren't crossing.'

'Here's some more,' said Dick. 'She's just been chopping as she went along.'

'Let's trail her,' said Titty, 'for practice.'

They climbed on with their eyes on the path.

'Hullo! Here she's dropped a whole stick.'

Dick picked up a twig about a foot long. Titty found another not unlike it, the end of it showing the marks of a knife.

They went on.

'Now she's hacking away at another,' said Titty. Scraps of thin bark and bits of twig and chopped-off leaves littered the path.

'Making arrows?' said Dick. 'She did once, didn't she?'

'That was last year,' said Titty. 'For sending messages. This year we're all together. She can't be thinking of shooting at Squashy.'

'Listen,' said Dick.

They were near the top of the wood. Another bend of the winding path would bring them to the place where the old charcoal-burners' track turned off into the bushes.

'I can hear her,' said Titty.

'Shall I shout?' said Dick.

'Not when we're trailing her,' said Titty. 'We ought to creep on feet like cats.'

They heard cheerful shouting far away below them in the wood.

'The others are coming,' whispered Dick.

'She's at Might Have Been,' said Titty. 'Probably up the look-out tree.'

They crept away through the bushes till they came to the tall ash. But no sentinel was up there above their heads. They came to the edge of the old pitstead. There was no one there.

And then, suddenly, they caught a glimpse of her under the trees between the pitstead and the Great Wall. They dodged silently nearer, round the edge of the clearing. Nancy, with bent head, seemed to be walking to and fro, looking at the ground.

'I know what she's doing,' said Dick suddenly. 'She's . . .' But he did not finish his sentence. 'Is anything the matter?' he asked, seeing Titty's face.

They could both see Nancy now.

She was walking slowly about with a forked hazel stick in her hands. First one way and then another she walked, bending low, holding the point of the fork before her over the short tufts of green rushes.

'But it didn't work with her,' said Dick. 'Only with you. . . . If it did work. Did it, or was it just because . . .?'

'Don't talk about it,' said Titty desperately.

And just then they saw Nancy, giving up all hope of dowsing, suddenly jerk herself upright and toss the forked hazel away into the bushes. She put her hands to her mouth and gave an owl call far too cheerful to be really like an owl's. A moment later she had disappeared, and they could hear her scrambling up the Great Wall. The owl call came again.

Dick tried to answer.

'Hullo!' Nancy's voice came through the trees. 'Where are you? Come along.'

Other owl calls, good and bad, sounded in the wood.

'They're all coming,' said Dick, as he started forward.

'Don't say anything about what she was doing,' said Titty urgently.

'All right,' said Dick, and they ran through the trees, along the edge of the bramble thicket, and up the gully in the rock to find Nancy, shading her eyes with her hands, looking out over the Topps.

'I KNOW WHAT SHE'S DOING'

'Well,' said Nancy. 'He isn't there yet. Awful climb from the bottom, isn't it?'

They threw themselves down on the top of the rock, already hot from the sun, and a moment later Dick had forgotten dowsing, mining, and everything else in watching a small, brown lizard dodging in and out along a crack in the stone.

Titty could not forget. She was still remembering what she had seen, when the rest of the Mining Company came out from the trees below the rock. John, Susan, Peggy, Dorothea . . .

'Come along, Roger,' called Susan.

Roger, lagging behind the others, came into sight carrying the pigeon basket, and Titty felt worse than ever.

'Sorry, Rogie,' she cried out. 'It was my turn to bring the pigeon. I forgot all about it. I say, did you bring the right one? Sophocles is the one for today.'

'He weighs two tons more than Homer,' said Roger.

'Let's have him now,' said Titty, and she ran down the gully and took the pigeon basket. 'Oh, Rogie, I am most awfully sorry.'

'It's quite all right,' said Roger.

But, for Titty that day, everything was all wrong. She could not get the dowsing out of her mind. What if they failed? What if the time came to leave and they had found nothing, and instead of going off knowing that at least they had done the best that could be done, they would have to go knowing that if only she, Titty, had been a little different, the expedition might not have been chained to the Tysons' pump? She could hardly bear to look at the others. Nobody was worrying her about it, and even that made things seem worse. She wished that nobody had ever thought of trying an experiment with a hazel twig.

The experiment had somehow changed things for everybody. It was all right to sleep in a solemn row of tents under the orchard wall, and to be in time for meals in the farm, so long as this was the very best that could be done. But now, it was almost as if someone had half opened a door and shut it in their faces.

'Is Squashy in sight?' she heard John ask.

'No,' said Nancy. 'But he may be behind a ridge or something.'

Even Nancy's voice had lost its cheerful ring. Her owl-call had sounded cheerful enough, but owl-calls are not like talking. The most cheerful person can make a melancholy owlcall, and the most melancholy person can tuwhit tuwhooooooo as if everything was as right as it possibly could be.

Scouts were sent down to Atkinson's, but somehow even scouting was not what it had been. Prospecting went on rather half-heartedly. Near the middle of the day Squashy Hat was seen high up on Grey Screes, but nobody had seen him going there, and he might have been there all morning. Nancy's signal calling in the scouts was not understood by Dorothea, and in the end John went back over the Topps to explain, and had to go down into Atkinson's wood to find Peggy, who had found a good watching post by the garden wall and was still thinking that Squashy Hat was in the house.

'He must have set out long before we posted our scouts,' said Nancy, and Titty knew that everybody was thinking that if only they had been able to camp in the old charcoal-burners' pitstead close to the edge of the Topps such a thing need never have happened.

Sophocles carried a dull message. . . . 'ALL WELL. LOVE.' . . . Nancy had not even the heart to put a skull and crossbones on it.

Only once did anything stir the melancholy of the day, and that was when the day was nearly over.

'He's painted another white spot,' said Roger suddenly, just as the prospectors were starting home.

There it was, a great splash of white on the grey rock, a little way below the first.

'Well, we can't do anything about it tonight,' said Susan.

'Or in the morning,' said Nancy, 'not if he's going to be there before we get up.'

'It's awful not being able to cook,' said Susan. 'We can't even start until Mrs Tyson lets us have breakfast.'

They marched home almost in silence.

Tonight nobody wanted to turn aside to have another look at the old pitstead. Titty, as she passed it, looked the other way. She was still seeing Captain Nancy walking desperately up and down with the forked stick and at last throwing it into the bushes. She knew that Nancy had been hoping that, after all, the divining rod would work with her as it had seemed to work with Titty. . . . If indeed it had worked. Titty had begun to feel doubtful about it herself, though, when she thought of it, she could almost feel the ends of the twig twisting in her hands. What if the whole expedition was going to peter out and come to nothing because of their having to camp in a place that could hardly be called a camp . . . at least not a camp like Swallowdale or Wild Cat? Why even the Beckfoot garden was better. What if Captain Flint were to come home? . . . 'Well, and what have you been up to?' he would say, and they would have to answer, 'Nothing.' . . . No nugget of gold. . . . Nothing. . . . And then he would hear how a perfect stranger had nipped in before them. . . . Titty could hardly bear the thought. And there was Might Have Been, the perfect camping place, with the cleared platform for the pitching of their tents, and the Great Wall handy to look out over the Topps, and the Look-out Tree even handier to let a sentinel keep an eye on Atkinson's. If only the beck had not run dry. Suppose Dick was right about those tufts of dark green rushes. Suppose the water were there all the time needing only to be found. Suppose the hazel twig would work with her and she could find it if she chose to try. Suppose the expedition had its own water diviner, and the water diviner, just at the very moment of real need, was refusing to help them.

Titty walked a little faster.

For the first time the prospectors were back at Tyson's in time for supper.

'That's right,' said Mrs Tyson. 'Better for everybody. Keep it up if you can, Miss Nancy. You've had a good day, I reckon, and home early to end up well.'

There was talk of other holidays during the meal, of sailing, of battles on sea and land, of stories made up by lantern-light in the cabin of an old wherry in Norfolk, of fishing for trout that other summer when the becks had been full of water. But no one had the heart to talk of mining. Nobody could have guessed that this was the evening meal of a company of gold seekers.

'What's the matter, Titty?' asked Susan privately, noticing that all through supper Titty had not said a word.

'I'm quite all right,' said Titty.

After supper she slipped out.

'Where's Titty?' said someone a little later.

'Giving fresh water to the pigeons, probably,' said someone else.

But Titty, her lips firmly together, was once more climbing the steep track up Tyson's wood.

THE DIVINING ROD

CHAPTER 15

TITTY MAKES UP HER MIND
TO IT

THERE was plenty of light in the sky but the wood was in shadow and it was almost dusk under the trees. Titty climbed the steep path, bending forward, hurrying, her lips pressed together, moving as quietly and quickly as she could, and listening all the time for a call from the farm below her. She knew very well what she meant to do, but she did not want the others to guess. She must try the thing again. . . . But not with anyone to see. It would be too dreadful if the others were watching and at the last moment she could not bring herself to touch the twig. So for the first ten minutes she climbed fast but set down her feet as softly as she could, and listened, almost as if she were an escaping prisoner.

It would have been fun to take Dorothea with her, or Roger, or Dick, just for the escaping, but not for the work she had to do. For that she did not want a single one of them. Whatever happened when it came to the point, she would find it a good deal easier if she were alone.

After ten minutes' climbing she stopped to take breath. A good thing there had not been much regular prospecting that day. A good thing, too, that it was the cool of the evening. She listened. From far away down the valley she heard the mooing of a cow. A sheep-dog was barking. Hens were fussing loudly in the Tysons' farmyard. She could just see a bit of the grey slate roof far below her. It looked as if she could almost drop a stone on it. But no one was calling 'Titty!' That was all right, and she set off again.

It was growing darker very quickly. The glow in the sky

over Swallowdale and the fells on the other side of the valley was climbing higher, and the dusk was coming up after it over the eastern hills. Just for a moment it felt a little queer to be alone there in the darkening wood. And then there was a sudden disturbance of leaves and presently the long 'Tuwho-oooooooooooooo' of an owl. Real owl, thought Titty, not an owl-call, and she remembered a night when she had been alone on Wild Cat Island, and an owl had called like that and everything had turned out right just when it seemed to be going wrong. It was a good omen.

She passed the place where, that morning, she and Dick had found those tiny footprints round the lingering puddle of the dried-up stream. It was too dark now to see if it would still be possible to track Nancy by the scraps of hazel twig she had left behind her. Her hands opened and shut as she wondered whether after all she could make herself take Nancy's hazel fork into her fingers.

She must. She must.

'Steady,' she said to herself. 'And don't be a gummock. No point in getting out of breath.' Thinking about Nancy's forked hazel she had almost broken into a run. She slowed down again.

She had reached the top of the wood and the turning through the bushes to the old pitstead of the charcoal-burners when she heard a quick rustling of dried leaves and twigs. Something small was coming down to meet her. She pulled out her torch, but did not light it. The thing, whatever it was, was on the path close above her. She stood perfectly still. There it was. A rabbit? No. She knew now what it was that had left the muddy prints by the pool half-way down the hill. Steadily trotting down the path, now and then lifting its head to sniff, a hedgehog came hurrying in the dusk. He seemed to know that something strange was about, but he looked for things of his own height, and never saw Titty, towering above him. He passed close to her feet, carelessly, noisily hurrying down the path as if the wood belonged to him.

'He wants water, too,' said Titty to herself. 'And he's got to go down the hill for it, just like us. He'd be jolly glad if I did find any near the top.'

She let the hedgehog get well below her, so as not to startle him, and then went on to the camp that might have been. There was more light in the open space that the charcoal-burners had cleared. Titty knew just where Nancy had thrown her forked twig in the morning. Nancy would be sure to cut the right twig. It would be better to try with that instead of looking for another.

She found the twig at once and picked it up by the point of the fork, putting off to the very last minute the holding of those two ends in her hands. But perhaps it would not work, anyway.

Titty swallowed once or twice. No one was here to see. No one would know if, after all, she could not bring herself to do it.

'Oh, come on,' she said to herself. 'You've got to. Better get it over.'

She turned the twig round and took the two ends, one in each hand just as Nancy had shown her by Mrs Tyson's pump. She found herself breathing very fast.

'Duffer,' she said firmly. 'You can just drop it if you want.'

She began walking to and fro across the level platform of the old fire spot. Nothing happened.

'Idiot,' she said. 'It won't be here, anyway.'

She left the platform and went in among the trees, looking in the dim light for Dick's green rushes. She found a tuft of them. Still nothing happened.

'It's all right,' she said to herself. 'You can't do it. It was only accident the other night. Nothing to be afraid of anyway. And you've tried. So it isn't your fault . . .'

And then she nearly dropped the twig. There it was, that tickling. Faint. Not like that other night at Tyson's. But the same thing. The twig was trying to move.

For a long time she stood where she was, somehow not daring to stir. Then she took a step or two, and the stick was as dead as ever.

'This is silly,' she said, and stepped back to the place where she had been and felt the stick press against the balls of her thumbs just as it had before.

'Well, it can't bite you,' said Titty, and made herself walk to and fro, in and out among the bushes and low trees at the edge of the wood just as she had on the open platform of Might Have Been.

The twig was moving again. Again it stopped. Again it twitched in her fingers.

'There *is* water here,' said Titty to herself. 'There must be. Unless it's all rot, like Dick thought.'

She walked slowly on. The twig was pulling harder and harder. She wanted to throw it down, but, somehow, by herself, she was not as frightened of it as she had been when, all unexpectedly, she had felt it for the first time. No one was watching her now, for one thing. She had won her battle the moment she had brought herself to hold the twig again. Now, already, she was almost eagerly feeling the pulling of the twig. When it weakened she moved back until she felt it strengthen. Then again she walked on. It was like looking for something hidden, while someone, who knew where it was, called out hot or cold as she moved nearer to or farther from the hiding place.

Suddenly, as she came nearer the Great Wall, the twisting of the twig became more violent. Here was a shallow dip in the ground between two rocks, and, yes, there was another tuft of those rushes in the bottom of it. She walked in between the rocks and it was just as it had been in the farmyard at Tyson's. The stick seemed to leap in her hands. The ends of it pressed against her thumbs, while the point of the fork dipped towards the ground, bending the branches, twisting her hands round with them, and at last almost springing out of her fingers.

'It's here,' said Titty. 'I've found it.' She had no longer any doubts. Dick was wrong. This was nothing of her imagining. No imagining could make the hazel twig twist her hands until they hurt. She was no longer afraid. This was a secret between her and the twig. Whatever the reason might be, the thing worked. She was as sure that there was water there, just where she was standing, as she was that it was late and getting dark and that Susan would be very cross with her if she were not at Tyson's at bed-time. She laid the hazel twig on the ground exactly where she was standing, and then set off through the trees. She came out on the charcoal-burners' platform. 'Might Have Been,' she said to herself. 'It'll be Can Be after all.'

It had grown much darker, and every now and then she found herself leaving the path. She listened for the hedgehog, but could not hear him. She tried to find the place where she and Dick had turned aside to the little pool left by the dried-up beck. But she had missed it in the dark, and dared not turn back. Well, tomorrow, perhaps, the hedgehog would not have to come so far for his evening drink. She lit her torch and hurried down the path.

'Titty! Ahoy!'

That was Nancy's voice below her in the wood.

'Coming,' she shouted. 'Ahoy!'

*

Susan and John were talking things over on the bridge. Roger was with them, flipping small stones and bits of dried moss over the parapet on the stones of the river bed. Every now and then there was a faint splash when a stone happened to fall in a place where there was still a little water. It was like tossing up with a penny. A splash counted as 'Heads'. No splash meant 'Tails.' Roger was trying to get three splashes running. A little way below the bridge, in the shallow pool that was the best they had been able to find for a bathing place, Peggy, Dick and Dorothea were paddling or rather kicking their feet in the water, very soothing to tired feet after a long day's prospecting in the upland wilderness.

Up in the wood Nancy was calling.

'Titty. . . . Ahoy!'

Titty had somehow disappeared, and Nancy, who thought she had seen her go through the gate into the wood, had gone off to look for her.

John and Susan listened.

'It's all very well,' said John, 'Nancy pretending she doesn't really mind. We should, if it was Peggy who could dowse and didn't. If only it had been you or me instead of poor old Titty.'

'It's no good,' said Susan. 'You know what Titty's like. She gets so stirred up by things. I thought she was going to be ill last night.'

'I know,' said John. 'But it does seem so awful when it's one of us, and with the whole expedition being messed up because of not being able to camp on the Topps.'

'Everything would be different if only we could,' said Susan, 'but we can't ask Titty to try it again.'

'Three splashes running,' said Roger.

But neither the captain nor the mate was listening.

'The Amazons'll be thinking we let them down,' said John.

'There's nothing we can do about it,' said Susan. 'And anyhow she very likely couldn't find water even if she did have a shot at it.'

'It's the not trying that's so awful,' said John.

'Three splashes running,' said Roger. 'Didn't you hear? Three splashes running. Something good's going to happen.'

'There she is,' said Susan.

Far away up in the woods an answering 'Ahoy' came through the dusk. They heard Nancy's 'Ahoy, Ahoy . . . oy' again.

'What's she been doing up there?' said Susan.

'Just getting away from all of us,' said John. 'I bet she's pretty wretched about it herself.'

'Well,' said Susan. 'Let's get the lanterns lit in the tents. It's about time people went to bed . . .'

Five minutes later the tents were glowing dimly in the dusk. Every now and then the flash of an electric torch showed where Nancy and Titty were coming down the wood.

'Ahoy,' shouted Peggy, who hated going to bed alone in the tent she shared with Nancy. 'Hurry up!'

And then suddenly came the sound of running feet and Nancy raced into the farmyard, through the orchard gate and into the bunch of prospectors who were just making up their minds to skin their clothes off and burrow down into their sleeping-bags.

'Swallows for ever!' she was shouting. 'Titty's done it. All by herself. She's done it after all . . .'

'But what? . . . what?' everybody was asking at once.

'What?' cried Nancy. 'The only thing that matters, of course. She's been dowsing. She's been up the wood again to

Might Have Been. She's found a spring, by Dick's rushes. Just where we wanted it . . .'

Titty, suddenly very tired, came after her into the orchard.

John grabbed her with one hand and kept patting her shoulder with the other. It was too dark to see his face but she knew how pleased he was.

'Well done, Titty,' he was saying. 'Well done. Jolly well done.'

'How did you do it?' said Peggy.

'Did you see any water?' said Dorothea.

'Of course she didn't,' said Nancy.

'We may not be able to get at it,' said John.

'Barbecued billygoats,' said Nancy. 'If it's there, we'll get at it all right if we have to dig through to Australia.'

Bit by bit the whole story came out, how Nancy had cut a forked stick in the morning and tried in vain, how she had been seen by Dick and Titty, how Titty had gone up the wood after supper, how, up there, close behind the pitstead, she had tried with the stick that Nancy had cut, and how, just by those clumps of rushes that Dick had noticed, the stick had twisted in her hands again.

'Was it very horrible?' said Dorothea.

'Not really,' said Titty honestly. 'Not after the first moment.'

'Did it really twist of itself?' said Dick.

'Of course it did,' said Nancy. 'Well done, old Titty. Three cheers for the Able-seaman. You've saved the whole thing. We'll be nearer the Topps even than Squashy himself. Once a day somebody'll come down for milk, and all the rest of the time all the rest of us'll be prospecting like anything . . .'

The tents, lit by their lanterns, were glowing brighter and brighter along the orchard wall as the dark closed down over the valley.

Nancy, Peggy, and John were eagerly talking of what

would be needed in the way of picks and spades for well-digging. In one tent a shadow humped itself and straightened. One lantern was blown out.

'Quiet,' said Susan. 'Titty's asleep already.'

'I'm not,' Titty was just going to say, but the words would not come and a moment later they would not have been true.

The others settled down for the night. Talk died. Lanterns went out one by one. There was dark in the orchard. There were no lights downstairs in the farm. A candle flickered behind a bedroom window. It went out like the lanterns of the camp.

The prospectors called 'Good night' from tent to tent, softly, so as not to wake the sleeping dowser, but much more cheerfully than on any night since they had left Beckfoot.

Suddenly Roger remembered something.

'Didn't I tell you?' he called out. 'Didn't I tell you something good was going to happen, when I got three splashes running?'

No one answered.

'Pigs,' said Roger, and settled himself to sleep.

THE DIVINING ROD

CHAPTER 16

SINKING THE WELL

In the morning there were doubts.

Titty woke to hear people talking outside her tent.

'You know it may be just Titty,' Susan was saying, 'and she won't like it if we go up with spades and it turns out to be all Peter Duck.'

'Um.' That was Nancy's voice. 'Bet you anything she tried it last night. Couldn't you see what a dither she was in?'

And afterwards, when breakfast was over, and the prospectors were nearly ready to start, John came to Titty and asked her privately, 'I say, Titty. What about taking spades? We don't want to cart them up there for nothing.'

'I'll carry a spade,' said Titty.

'Anyway, she thinks she did,' said John to Nancy as they went off to see what they could borrow from Mrs Tyson.

'Spades?' said Mrs Tyson. 'You're not going digging in the orchard, now are you?'

'Oh no,' said Nancy.

'Up in the wood,' said John.

'Better see what Robin can do for you,' said Mrs Tyson. Robin Tyson, Mrs Tyson's grown-up son, who managed the farm, found them a couple of spades. He also hoped they were not going to dig in the orchard, and laughed when he heard they meant to dig in the wood.

'You won't do much with a spade, I reckon,' he said. 'It's a crowbar's what you want. More stones than earth you'll find.'

'Can we take a crowbar?' asked John.

'Bit of a weight,' said Robin Tyson. 'Best let me carry it up the wood for you.'

'Oh no,' said Nancy. 'We'll manage, two of us. Thank you very much all the same.' The very last thing anybody wanted was to have natives butting helpfully in, especially in such a business as well-sinking where, after all, there might be no water.

In the end, they took two ordinary spades, a small gardening spade of Mrs Tyson's, which they found in the lean-to behind the beehives, and an enormous crowbar which John and Nancy carried between them.

'Which pigeon?' said Roger.

'One we can count on,' said Nancy. 'There may be some tremendous news.'

'I'm taking Homer,' said Titty, and set off knapsack on back, the small spade over her shoulder and Homer in the travelling-basket in her free hand. Would there be tremendous news or would there not? Waiting in the yard another minute was more than she could bear.

Dorothea ran after her and caught her up. They climbed the steep winding path together.

'It will be lovely if you've found a spring,' said Dorothea.

'But what if I haven't?' said Titty. 'We can't tell till they've tried.'

'I'm going to put it in a story,' said Dorothea. 'Different, of course. I'm making you a boy, and you do that business with the stick all by yourself and you've got a spade with you and you start digging. It's at night, and the moon rises through the clouds, and all of a sudden you've dug deep enough and the water comes spouting up into the moonlight . . .'

'Go on,' said Titty. 'What happened next?'

'I'm not quite sure yet,' said Dorothea.

*

Hot and breathless, the prospectors came at last to the place where the track divided. They pushed through the overgrown path under the tall ash tree and out into the open pitstead of the charcoal-burners.

'Where's the stick?' said Nancy.

Titty, with all the others close behind her, hurried across the clearing, and in among the bushes and small trees that grew between it and the steep rock face that marked the edge of High Topps.

'It's through here, somewhere,' she said. 'There were two rocks, and a clump of rushes growing in a dip.'

'Here's a clump of rushes,' said Dick.

'Not those,' said Titty. 'That's where I tried first and nothing happened.'

Today, somehow, Titty felt altogether different about the hazel twig. The first time she had held it, it had startled her most horribly. The second time, by herself in the dusk, she had had a hard fight to bring herself to try. But now the trial had been made. She was ready to try again. She wanted to convince the doubters. She wanted to be sure herself that she had not gone through that struggle for nothing. They must find water now. They simply *must*.

'There's the stick,' she cried. 'It's all right. It's just where I left it. At least I think so.'

Nancy picked it up, and held it in dowsing fashion.

'Go on, Titty,' she said. 'Try it again. It doesn't give a wriggle with me.'

John and Susan looked with surprise to see Titty almost eagerly take the stick. Dick was watching to see exactly how her fingers gripped it. Dorothea was watching her face. Peggy and Roger were looking at the ground almost as if they expected the water to come shooting up.

'I'll start a bit on one side,' said Titty. 'Nothing happened last night when I was here. . . . It was when I began to get near those rushes. ... It's beginning. ... It's pulling.'

'Look here, Titty, you're making it do it yourself.'

'I'm not,' said Titty.

'Keep quiet,' said John.

'It's going right down. ... Look at it,' said Peggy.

'Does it hurt?' asked Dorothea.

'Don't bother her,' said Nancy.

'This is the place,' said Titty. 'I simply can't hold it any more.' And as she spoke the forked stick sprang free and dropped almost at her feet.

'Mark the place all round,' said Nancy. 'With the crowbar. Go on, John. Oh well, the spade'll do. Let's get going.' She flung off her knapsack, grabbed one of the big spades and drove it as hard as she could into the ground almost before John and Peggy had finished scraping a line all round Titty and the stick. The spade went in about an inch and a half before being brought up hard by a stone.

'Good thing we brought that crowbar,' said John. 'Look out for your feet, everybody.'

The crowbar had a sharpened end, and John brought it down point first into the ground. Again and again he brought it stabbing down, loosening earth and small stones.

'Who's got the little spade?' said Nancy. 'Let's clear that bit while John's jabbing up some more.'

'Let me,' said Roger, and lifted the first spadeful of loosened stuff.

Dry as the earth was, it was hard work breaking it up, because it was so full of stones. John drove in the crowbar here and there to make work easier for the spades. Then Nancy took over the crowbar, and Peggy jumped to save her toes.

'Look out,' said Peggy.

'Sorry,' said Nancy. 'I didn't mean to come so near.'

Presently the crowbar rang on something that sounded and felt like solid rock.

'We're done,' said Nancy.

'We can't get through rock without a drill,' said Dick.

'Let's have another jab,' said John.

He drove in the pointed end of the crowbar now in one place and now in another. At last it went in rather farther than usual and without the sharp ring of striking rock.

'I've got to the edge of it,' said John.

He began wriggling the crowbar in the hole it had made.

'It's not solid rock,' he said. 'I can feel the thing shifting.'

A few minutes of hard work with spades and fingers cleared the earth from the top of a huge stone. John worked the crowbar in at one side of it and swung sideways with all his strength. Nancy added her weight to his.

'It's moving! It's moving!'

'Shove the spades in to hold it,' said John.

Spades were shoved in. The crowbar was shifted to another place and driven in once more.

'Now then!' said Nancy.

'Beef!' cried Roger.

The stone was lifting. One more terrific heave loosened it altogether. It rose up on end, was grabbed by half a dozen hands, and a moment later was pulled clear of the deep, smooth socket it had filled so long.

'That earth's wet,' said Dick.

'Water! Water at last!' cried Dorothea.

There was no water, but everybody could see that the bottom of the hole out of which they had lugged the stone was dark and damp. Nancy dropped on her knees and felt it with her hand.

'She's got it all right,' she shouted. 'Good for the dowser! Well done, Titty! Come on. We've only got to dig deep enough. Nothing else matters! No prospecting today . . .'

And then, for the first time that day, they remembered Squashy Hat. Roger and Peggy were sent up the gully to the top of the rock. Far away on Grey Screes they could see that splash of white paint among the rocks. But there was no sign of the rival. John handed over the crowbar to Nancy and shinned up the old ash tree to the look-out branch and reported that Squashy Hat was walking up and down, smoking, in the Atkinsons' garden.

'Somebody'd better go down there to keep watch,' said Nancy. 'Somebody who can be spared from the digging.'

'Dorothea,' said Peggy.

'I'll go, too,' said Titty, and seeing the surprise in Nancy's eyes, added, 'I'd like to, really. I'll come back again later on.'

'Well,' said Nancy, 'there aren't enough spades to go round and you'll be much more useful there.'

*

Titty and Dorothea went off with their knapsacks along the edge of the wood and down to Roger's lair in the bracken opposite the gate where the cart track to Atkinson's left the Dundale road.

'I'll tell you what,' said Dorothea. 'I've got *The Outlaw of the Broads* in my knapsack, and I'll read you some of that to take your mind off the digging.'

And so, while Titty lay in the bracken, looking across the road and down the cart track among the trees, watching for Squashy Hat, Dorothea lay beside her, propped on her elbows above her exercise books, and read in a voice little above a whisper how the Outlaw of the Broads hid in the reeds and slipped down river under the very noses of his enemies.

'The reeds shivered and parted. . . . The outlaw's boat nosed her way stealthily into the moonlit river. . . . The coast was beautifully clear but only just . . .'

Titty listened sometimes with half, sometimes with three-quarters and sometimes with the whole of her mind when the tremble in Dorothea's voice showed that she was getting near an exciting moment. But she found it hard to forget the furious digging that was going on under the trees at the top of Tyson's wood. What was happening up there? How deep had they dug? Had they been held up by solid rock? She had seen the damp earth with her own eyes. Would that be all? Perhaps everywhere it was damp if you got below the surface. Or would they really find water? What was that story the friendliest of all natives used to tell about the blackfellows in the Australian bush who found water by magic in the year of the great drought when the sheep were dying by thousands on the sheep stations? Here, too, there was a dead sheep, and the hedgehog from the bramble thicket had to go half-way down to the valley to drink in the stagnant puddle left from the dried-up beck.

The morning was over when the sight of Squashy Hat coming up the cart track brought the reading to a sudden stop. But he was not going prospecting. He turned down the road instead of going up towards the Topps. They watched him out of sight.

'We ought to let them know,' said Titty. 'And one of us ought to stop here in case he comes back. Look here, Dot, do you mind if I go? I simply must see how deep they've got.'

Dorothea did not mind at all. 'All right,' she said. 'There's a bit just coming that wants rewriting. I'll get it done so that it'll be all right to read by the time you come back. It's no good reading aloud when you have to keep changing things in your head as you go along.'

*

Titty came back along the edge of the Topps. The well-sinkers seemed strangely quiet. She listened for the ring of the crowbar on a stone. There was not a sound. They were not even talking. For one dreadful minute she thought the dowsing had been a failure after all. She came down the gully and through the trees below the rock. What were they doing, all in a bunch together? A great pile of stones and earth showed that they had dug a long way down before giving up. Had they done all that for nothing?

'Hullo, Titty,' cried Nancy. 'Come and look. You've done it all right.'

'We've got the first mug of water,' said Peggy. 'Pretty thick, but it's settling down. Dick's dropped a white stone in and you can see it already.'

'It's a spring,' said John. 'And you found it. Come on, Nancy. We've only got to keep on digging. Keep the stones separate. We'll want them later.'

'Let her have a look,' said Nancy.

They made room for her, and Titty, staring into the mug, saw a brown liquid, and looking closer saw that the top half inch of it was almost clear.

She found herself, most oddly, biting hard at her own lips and feeling a strange hotness in her eyes.

She made her report.

'Good,' said Nancy. 'He's wasting his last chance. We'll be camping up here tomorrow. Barbecued billygoats, but won't he be sick when he finds we're on the Topps before him and after him and all the time.'

Nancy hesitated, but only for a moment.

'Do you think Mrs Tyson will let us?' said Susan.

'Where's that pigeon?' she said. 'We'll send him off at once.'

'What are you going to say?' asked Roger, pulling out a stump of pencil and a slip of paper cut to the right size.

Nancy put the paper on a stone, sucked the pencil and wrote:

ALL WELL. TITTY FOUND WATER BY THE TOPPS. SHIFTING CAMP TOMORROW. PLEASE COME AND TALK TO MRS TYSON. AND BRING THE PIGEONS. S's, A's and D's for ever.

THE FIRST MUG OF WATER

'How's that?' she said, handing it round. It was approved and as Titty set off along the Topps to join Dorothea, Homer, tossed into the air from the top of the rock, was already flying to Beckfoot with the news.

*

'How lovely,' said Dorothea as Titty dropped beside her in the bracken, and told her that they had found water or at least mud. 'I knew it was going to be all right. And I've altered that last chapter altogether. I'll have to begin reading from a little before the place where I left off. You won't mind, will you?'

'Susan says it's time for grub,' said Titty.

'All right,' said Dorothea. 'We'll get it over. It always spoils a story if you have to keep stopping.'

The afternoon slipped by in literary criticism. No novelist ever had a happier audience. 'It's a simply splendid story,' said Titty, when Dorothea had read to the end of her notebooks, and explained what was still to come, and had gone back to the first chapter to remind Titty of the little bits that were going to be important later on.

By the time Squashy Hat had come back, walking slowly up the road, as if he were a little footsore, and had turned through the gate at Atkinson's, it was already late in the day, and the scouts went back together.

'I was just going to send Roger for you,' said Susan.

'What do you think of it?' said John. 'Solid rock at the bottom. We couldn't get any deeper.'

All the mess of digging had disappeared. The pile of stones painfully dug out had been built into a low wall guarding the well on three sides. On the fourth side three big stones made steps so that people could go comfortably down to fill kettle or bucket.

'Oh, Titty!' said Dorothea. 'And look at the water.'

'I say,' said Titty. 'It's miles better than I ever thought it could be.'

'Your well,' said Nancy. 'Down it goes on the map. If ever anybody earned a place on a map it's you. Titty's Well. And people will be jolly grateful for ever. At least they ought to be. And to us, too, for digging. It's been an awful sweat.'

Dick had cut notches on a stick to measure the depth of the water in the rocky hole.

'Just as deep as it was before,' he said. 'And we've thrown lots of it away to get rid of the mud.'

'Bubbling up all the time,' said Roger.

'Jolly good water,' said Nancy, sipping the water that had been clearing all afternoon in the mug. 'Better than at home. This is water worth drinking.'

The others, urged by Susan, put off their first tastes until tomorrow.

'What about starting down,' she said. 'We can't do any more until it settles.'

'Don't want to do any more,' said Nancy. 'Giminy, I'm stiff all over.'

'So am I,' said John.

'Dick,' said Titty. 'I wonder if the hedgehog'll come and drink tonight.'

'Let's wait and see,' said Dorothea.

'He'll be stirring any time now,' said Dick.

But, for once, Nancy agreed with Susan.

'Come on,' she said. 'We'd better hurry. We've simply *got* to get Mrs Tyson in a good temper.'

They hurried down to the farm, took turns to wash under the pump, and were in time for Mrs Tyson's supper. Nancy chose her moment while Mrs Tyson was dealing round large plates of macaroni cheese, to break the news.

'We're moving tomorrow,' she said. 'We've found water

in the top of the wood. You won't have to cook for us any more.'

Mrs Tyson did not believe her.

'There's never a drop of water up there but the beck, and that's dry.'

'We've got a spring of our own,' said Nancy.

'You must have your joke, Miss Nancy,' said Mrs Tyson.

'It isn't a joke,' said Nancy. 'It's a proper well. Mother's coming in the morning on purpose to see it.'

'Eh,' said Mrs Tyson. 'I'm glad your mother's coming. She'll talk sense. But you'd no call to bring her chasing up the valley for nothing, and her in a scrow with her papering and painting, and the house thrutched up with the plumbers and all, and your uncle coming home, and only twenty-four hours in a day when all's said and done.'

Supper was a joyful meal, and soon after it everybody was glad to go early to bed.

'Last night in the dormitory!' Nancy called out exultantly by way of saying good night.

'What if Mrs Blackett says No?' That was John's voice.

'Mother'll never say No when she sees a well like that.'

Titty, already in her sleeping-bag, clenched her hands as if to feel again the strange pulling of the hazel twig. Was it worth while, that struggle of hers? A million, million times. She could not make out now how it was that she had ever been afraid.

CHAPTER 17

SHIFTING CAMP

WHEN Mrs Tyson called them in for breakfast not a tent was standing in the orchard dormitory. A row of paler patches on the ground close under the wall showed where they had been. Some of the tents were already folded up and packed on the handcart. Others were being knelt on to make them stow a little flatter. John was overhauling the Alpine rope. Susan was going through the stores they had so far had no chance of using. Knapsacks were being stuffed to bursting point.

'What's gone with you, Miss Nancy?' said Mrs Tyson. 'You'll never be carting all this up the wood to bring it down again. For bring it again you will. I can't have you up there with no water, and cooking, too. The bent'll flare like hair in a candle if you get a spark in it. Eh me, and what you want up there these hot days I can't see. You'd be better off playing in the bottom. . . . There's no cooler place than our orchard, without it's the dairy.'

'We've got plenty of water up there now,' said Nancy.

'You mun tell me a better one nor that,' said Mrs Tyson. 'And you aren't going up the wood before your mother comes, are you?'

But that was exactly what Nancy had in mind.

The moment breakfast was over, the last of the tents was put on the handcart. The big pigeon cage, in which Sappho the undependable was travelling alone, was planted on the top of them, and roped down. Knapsacks for which there was no room on the handcart were slung underneath it. Susan and Peggy pushed. John and Nancy hauled from in front, with ropes over their shoulders. The shifting of the camp had begun.

'We'll do our best to get back before mother comes,' said Nancy to the four able-seamen, who were to wait for Mrs Blackett. 'But we must get some of the tents up to make it look like a camp already. Don't let her get talking to Mrs Tyson and deciding things in a hurry. And whatever happens don't let her bolt before we're back. Puncture her tyres . . . anything you like . . . but keep her here. She may easily put her foot down the wrong way if she doesn't see the well and doesn't know what a beauty of a camp it's going to be.'

The handcart wobbled out of the gate. The able-seamen followed, and watched their elders get it round the first sharp corner in the steep path up the wood.

'There's only just room for it,' said Dick.

'Fine big donks,' said Roger.

'Donk yourself,' said Peggy over her shoulder. 'You wait till it comes to lugging up the dromedaries.'

The able-seamen went back to the orchard and arranged all that was left, ready for the next journey. They led the dromedaries out of the barn, propped them against the wall, and slung bundles of sleeping-bags across saddles and carriers.

'We can't do any more without the knapsacks,' said Dick.

'Let's go and meet her,' said Dorothea.

They left the orchard and went through the farmyard, across the little bridge, and sauntered slowly down the road above the dried-up Amazon. They took their shoes off and paddled where the water came just over their ankles in what had once been a deep pool. Their minds were far away. Nancy had seemed fairly confident, but what if Mrs Blackett took a native view of things? What if the well had dried up? What if Mrs Tyson refused to be persuaded?

'Listen,' said Titty at last, and began putting her shoes on.

Far away down the valley they could hear the clatter and clang of old Rattletrap.

'It's Mrs Blackett,' said Dorothea.

They had just time to get their shoes on and scramble up to the road.

'Here she comes,' said Roger, and round the corner came the ancient motor-car. Mrs Blackett jammed the brakes on hard and it stopped with a squawk as the locked wheels scraped on the road.

'Hullo,' she said. 'Where are the others? Hop in if you can find room. Take the pigeon basket on your knee. . . . And get your feet up on the top of those cases. I've brought you three dozen bottles of ginger pop. But where's Nancy?'

'They've all gone up to the new camp,' said Dorothea.

'You haven't really found water, have you?'

'It may have dried up by now,' said Titty.

'There was lots yesterday,' said Dorothea.

'Has Timothy come?' asked Roger.

'No,' said Mrs Blackett. 'I inquired at the station only yesterday. And no letter from my brother. Funny. He may be nearly home by now, and we don't even know the name of his ship. Hold tight, everybody. Sorry. The thing always does start with such a jerk.'

Everybody bumped backwards as old Rattletrap leapt uneasily forward with a sudden clash of gears.

'Perhaps if you let them in slowly,' said Dick.

'It always stops if I do. I don't believe I'll ever get in the way of it.'

She drove on, swerved sharply to the right over the narrow bridge and stopped in the farmyard.

'I'd better turn while I'm about it,' she said, when they had clambered out. Dick and Roger, Titty and Dorothea kept watch and shouted to let her know when anything looked like touching as she worked the car round in a series of short dashes to and fro across the cobbled yard.

'Oh well,' she said, as she stalled the engine and got out and looked round the car. 'That front mudguard was dented already several times. And that one at the back's always unlucky. There's no real harm done.'

'Don't go in to see her till they come back,' said Titty urgently.

'Nancy'll be here any minute,' said Dorothea.

But Mrs Tyson was in the porch and Mrs Blackett had seen her and they went into the farm together.

'They're just coming,' said Roger. 'I can hear the hand-cart bucketing down.'

But it was too late. A council of the natives had begun. When the captains and mates came racing into the yard with the handcart, they saw Rattletrap and the four able-seamen alone.

'Giminy!' said Nancy. 'You haven't let her go in.'

'We did our best to stop her,' said Dorothea.

But just then Mrs Blackett came out and they heard Mrs Tyson talking to her. 'Of course, Mrs Blackett, it's for you to say.' Good. Oh good. Nothing was settled yet.

'What's all this, you savage creatures,' said Mrs Blackett, kissing Nancy and Peggy, 'about moving your camp up to the Topps? And Mrs Tyson says you were so comfortable here.'

'We were. . . . We are,' said Nancy, getting between her mother and the porch. 'Too comfortable,' she added, in a hollow whisper, making saucer eyes at the same time. 'But it's not only that. We've got to be nearer our work. And you said we could if there was any water. Just wait till you've seen Titty's well. And we'll be much less bother to Mrs Tyson. And Susan's just bursting to do some cooking. Aren't you, Susan. And . . . Oh, anyway . . . come along and see it . . .'

'Where is it?'

'By the old pitstead. Just where we want to be. On the edge of High Topps.'

'Climb right up there?' said Mrs Blackett. 'I'll be dead half way . . .'

'Oh no you won't,' said Nancy. 'Look here. We've got the handcart. We'll easily run you up, all pulling together.'

'If I must, I must,' said her mother. 'But not on the handcart, thank you. You must let me go my own pace.'

'We won't be going fast,' said Peggy. 'We've another load to take up.'

'She's brought cases and cases of grog,' said Roger.

'Well done, mother!' said Nancy.

'You're never going to take all those bottles up there only to bring them down again.' Mrs Blackett was talking almost like Mrs Tyson.

'We won't have to bring them down,' said Nancy. 'Not till they're empty. Just you wait till you've seen the camp.'

*

Titty herself was surprised to see how much had already been done, when Mrs Blackett and the laden dromedaries, each with a pulling donkey on a rope ahead, and the handcart, with the cases of ginger pop, and all the rest of the baggage and stores, with Homer and Sophocles in the travelling-basket roped on the top, came through the bushes into the old clearing left by the charcoal-burners. She had last seen it as a bare platform among the trees at the top of the wood. It was now a camp. Susan had built her usual stone fireplace in the middle of the pitstead, and five of the tents were up, all facing towards the fireplace and well shaded by the trees.

'Well, I must say, it is rather charming,' said Mrs Blackett, who was very out of breath after the long climb. 'And you've got a lovely cool place for the pigeons,' she added.

'It's simply miles better than that orchard,' said Nancy.

UPHILL WORK

'It wasn't like a camp at all, being down there. This is the best we've ever had except Wild Cat Island.'

'But where's your water?' said her mother.

'Come and look,' said Nancy, and led the way through the trees at the back of the camp, when Titty had another surprise.

The stone-built walls of the well looked already quite old. Somebody had put a lot of moss in the crevices between the stones and wetted it to give it a chance. In that hot weather, just to see damp green moss was refreshing, and, as for the well itself . . . the mud had settled and the little pool was sparkling clear.

'Do you mean to say you made it?' said Mrs Blackett.

'It took all yesterday,' said Susan.

'And there was nothing here before?'

'Jolly stony ground,' said Roger.

'And Titty found the water with a divining rod?'

Mrs Blackett did not ask to be shown how it was done. Perhaps, while she was climbing up the wood, she had heard something from Nancy about that first experiment by the Tysons' pump.

'Well, Titty,' she said. 'You'll make your fortune if you want to, going about conjuring wells out of dry ground for anybody who wants them.'

'This is the Great Wall,' said Nancy, leading the way past the bramble thicket to the foot of the rock, 'and we go up this private gully . . . not private for you . . . and then we can see out over the Topps.'

'Funny,' said Mrs Blackett, looking out over that wild country, at the great mass of Kanchenjunga rising on the farther side of it, at the curving ridge of the mountain that shut it in from the north, at the rolling fells to the south and west. 'Funny. It must be a hundred years since I was up here last . . .'

Dick looked at her with serious doubt.

'Yes,' she said. 'There were no things like that when I was up here last. Rattletrap and all his kind had hardly been invented.'

She was looking away to the south, where a short length of the Dundale road showed white and dusty, climbing over the fells. A motor-car was drawn up there, and little specks of colour at the roadside showed where the motorists were resting on the scorched, drab grass. The specks vanished. They were getting into the motor-car which presently moved off and was gone.

'And Atkinson Ground is just round the corner, isn't it?' Mrs Blackett was saying. 'Much nearer for you to get your milk from.'

'But we can't,' said Nancy. 'There's someone . . .'

'Oh yes,' laughed Mrs Blackett. 'Your hated rival. Some harmless visitor, I expect. I don't suppose he knows the part you've cast him for . . .'

'You wouldn't say that if you'd seen him messing about on the Topps,' said Nancy, 'and painting white spots up on the Screes.'

'Oh well,' said her mother. 'If he's busy up there you won't be in each other's way. But don't go and play any tricks on him. Remember he isn't your long-suffering uncle.'

They had been some ten minutes on the top of the Great Wall, and had found a comfortable seat for Mrs Blackett in the heather, when Dick, who had been looking for a lizard and had decided that no lizard was likely to show himself with so many people about, began looking far away in hopes of seeing a hawk or buzzard, and suddenly asked, 'I say, Titty, have you got the telescope?'

'I have,' said John.

'Where that motor-car was, along the Dundale road,' said Dick. 'Is that smoke?'

'You've got very good eyes in spite of your spectacles,' said Mrs Blackett. 'If you can see anything over there.'

'I can see all right with spectacles. It's only without them I can't,' said Dick, 'or when they get a bit damp.'

'He's right,' said John. 'Have a look, Nancy.'

'Some muttonhead visitor's been chucking matches about,' said Nancy.

'I'll race you.'

She dropped the telescope in her mother's lap, and was off. John went racing after her.

'May I look?' said Roger, picking up the telescope.

'John's catching her up,' said Titty.

'Nancy's still ahead,' said Dorothea.

'I can see the smoke quite plainly,' said Roger.

Mrs Blackett jumped to her feet. 'I don't wonder all the farmers are nervous,' she said. 'You know that was the real reason Mrs Tyson wanted to keep you under her eye. They're all terrified of a fire this weather. And a fire gets started so easily. If Dick hadn't happened to look that way . . .'

'They've got there,' said Roger. 'Dancing on it . . .'

'May I look?' said Dorothea.

Everybody looked in turn. There was no more smoke to be seen, but John and Nancy close together, stamping on the ground. At last they started back, looking over their shoulders now and again for fear some spark they had not noticed might be still alive in the dry turf.

'Good job you spotted that,' said John, when they came back to the rock.

'Well done both of you,' said Mrs Blackett. 'I'll tell Mrs Tyson on my way home. Who knows where that might have ended? I'll tell her she can sleep the easier for having you up here to keep an eye lifting for things like that. Only, whatever you do, don't set fire to the place yourselves.'

'Mother,' said Nancy indignantly, 'have we ever?'

'No, I must admit, you haven't. And the old pitstead's a pretty safe place for a camp. If only everybody made fire-places as good as Susan's, we might get through the drought without ever giving old Colonel Jolys a chance.'

'He'd be awfully disappointed,' said Peggy.

'I suppose he would,' said her mother, 'but other people would be very pleased. You've no idea what a fire can do. I remember when we were children seeing the hills on the other side of the lake ablaze. You know where you had your igloo last winter . . . up above there it started, and killed every tree for seven miles each way, and left three farm-houses burnt out. I don't wonder Mrs Tyson's nervous. People were lucky to get away with their lives.'

'Do tell us all about it,' said Dorothea.

They took Mrs Blackett half-way down the wood.

She would let them come no farther.

'You've got your camp to get going. And you've been up and down twice already. No, no. You run back. I'll put in a good word for you with Mrs Tyson.'

'I never really thought she'd agree,' said Susan, as they came back to the clearing.

'She wouldn't if it hadn't been for Titty's well,' said Nancy.

'And the putting out of the fire,' said Titty.

'It all helped,' said Nancy. 'She'll use that to calm down Mrs Tyson.'

'What about having fire-brooms of our own?' said John.

'Why not?' said Nancy. 'If that doesn't please Mrs Tyson, nothing will.'

There was no prospecting done that day. John began making the fire-brooms at once, and, as Nancy said, nobody can make a camp in a minute and a half. After those dreadful nights in the orchard dormitory, with civilization at their very elbows, they wanted to make this camp a good one. They pitched the rest of the tents, Roger's and Titty's, with the others at the edge of the clearing, and slung the store tent between a couple of young pine trees. They made a cool cellar for the ginger pop under an elder bush. They built supports to keep the pigeon cage off the ground. Susan and Peggy, cooks once more in their own right, demanded fire-wood. All hands were turned on to gather fallen branches and bring them into camp, where they were broken up and piled in a stack. John and Nancy made big brushwood brooms and bound them with string to strong young ash-poles. Susan had built the best fireplace of her life in the middle of the clearing, well out of the way of overhanging trees, and the fire-brooms came in useful at once in sweeping the ground all round the fireplace clear of the dead leaves that might so easily have been lit by a chance spark.

'They're better fire-brooms than they've got at Tyson's,' said Titty.

'Let's make a fire in the grass somewhere . . . just a little one . . . to see how quickly we can put it out,' said Roger.

'Not until there's been some rain,' said John, who had been hankering after the same thing himself. 'One spark when it's as dry as this and we'd have the whole Topps ablaze.'

'Stack them like they do at Tyson's,' said Nancy, and the eight fire-brooms were piled together, with the handles on the ground, and all eight brooms meeting at the top.

'Like a stork's nest,' said Dorothea.

'On eight legs,' said Dick.

In the middle of the day they were glad enough of Mrs Tyson's sandwiches, but towards evening Susan lit the camp-fire in the new fireplace. John and Nancy were just thinking of tossing up to see who was to go down to Tyson's for milk when heavy steps sounded on the path and Robin Tyson came tramping into the clearing. Mrs Tyson had heard what Mrs Blackett had to say about Titty's well, and had agreed to let them camp there, but she had sent Robin up the wood to see for himself. He had brought a can of milk with him.

'And mother says you've nobbut to ask if you want owt.'

'Thank you very much,' said Susan.

Robin Tyson looked curiously round.

'And where's this water of yours?' he said.

'Here you are,' said Nancy. 'Come along and look.'

And Robin Tyson followed her out of the camp and in among the trees between the old pitstead and the Great Wall. There she showed him Titty's Well, where, at that very moment, Peggy was dipping water to fill the big kettle.

Robin dipped his finger in the well, and licked it.

'Nay, that's queer,' he said. 'Good water, too, and all these years I've niver known it was there.'

'But it wasn't,' said Nancy.

Robin looked at her, and at the others, Roger, Peggy, Dorothea and John, who had come to see what he thought of it.

'Stands to reason it was there,' he said.

'Well, of course it was,' said Nancy, 'but we had to dig for it. Titty found the place with a hazel twig, dowsing.'

Robin looked as if he thought there was no point in arguing with Nancy.

'Well, it's good water,' he said. 'Mother was feared you were lapping from yon beck. Beck's not healthy, nor won't be till we get rain and a big spate.'

He dipped his finger and tasted the water again.

'Good night to you all,' he said, and went off. For a long time they could hear his heavy boots on the stony track going down the wood.

Back in the camp, the fire was blazing heartily. A saucepan was sizzling at one side of the fireplace. Susan and Peggy slung the big black kettle on its cross-pole and lowered it carefully into the flames.

'Plain pemmican for the first night,' said Susan.

'When?' said Roger.

'Not till the kettle boils.'

'Oh,' said Roger.

'Rather be at Tyson's?' said Nancy.

'Jolly well not,' said Roger. 'I say, it's a long time since anybody's had a squint at Squashy Hat.'

'May as well,' said Nancy, 'but he wasn't there when I looked last.'

A scouting party went up the edge of the Topps. Roger was first up the gully in the rock. He looked across to Grey Screes.

'He's jolly well been there,' he cried.

'How do you know?' said Nancy. 'Oh gosh! what on earth *can* he be up to?'

Dusk was falling, but even in the twilight they could see that up there on Grey Screes Squashy Hat had been at work again. There had been two of those white spots. There were now three.

'Blow supper,' said Roger. 'Let's start at once.'

'Too late,' said John. 'We'd have to take a lantern and we'd be seen for miles.'

'Now you see the good of camping up here,' said Nancy. 'No waiting for Mrs Tyson tomorrow. We'll start at dawn and go up Grey Screes and find out what he's doing and be down again while Squashy Hat's still snoring in his feather bed.'

They went back to the new camp, where in the dusk the camp-fire burned more and more cheerfully.

'Tea's nearly ready,' said Susan.

'Mister Mate,' said Nancy. 'That Squashy's gone and painted another spot. We've got to see what it's all about. John and I are going to start at dawn, and we'll have to take Dick too, to see what it is Squashy's hammering at. I don't believe he's found anything, but we'd better make sure.'

'Dick'll have to get early to bed,' said Susan.

'We all will,' said Nancy.

But for the first time those holidays they were camping in the wilderness in a camp of their own, free from even the friendliest of natives. Plain pemmican, followed by bread and marmalade and apples, was perhaps not quite so good as Mrs Tyson's farm-house suppers, but somehow it seemed much better worth eating, washed down with tea of Susan's brewing made with water from their own well. 'What about songs?' said Nancy, throwing the core of her last apple into the fire. They sang their old favourites, 'Spanish Ladies' and 'Hanging Johnny' and a dozen others, while the firelight flickered on the trunks of the trees and the half-circle of pale tents. After the songs they sat on, listening to an owl below them in the valley, and the crackle of their fire, and watching the smoke climbing above them into the starry sky. White spots or no white spots, good resolutions went for nothing. It was late indeed when at last they had snuggled down into their sleeping-bags and blown out their lanterns for the night.

CHAPTER 18

THE WHITE SPOTS

It was late indeed and the sun was pouring down on the tents before they woke again. It was already too late to be worth while starting before breakfast. John raced down to Tyson's for the morning milk because he could do it quicker than anybody else. Breakfast was pitched in at high speed. Squashy Hat might be stirring now at any minute, and when John, Nancy and the professor hurried out across the Topps a scouting party was told off to watch Atkinson's farm and to give warning the moment the enemy was on the move.

*

'But what's it for?' said Nancy.

They were looking at a great patch of white paint on the face of a rock a long way up the steep slopes of Grey Screes. There seemed to be no reason for it at all. Here was nothing but craggy hillside, hard to climb, with no signs of old workings of any kind. Up here, they were high above the Topps. The country they had left spread below them like a map. They could even see glimpses of the distant lake, and the farther hills, and High Greenland where, in the Christmas holidays, Dick had rescued a crag-fast sheep. But they had not climbed so high only to look at views. John scratched the white paint with his fingernail.

'It's just ordinary paint,' he said.

'Come on,' said Nancy. 'Let's go on and have a look at another.'

They climbed, sometimes on hands and knees on the rocks, sometimes skirting round a bit of crag too steep to climb. They came, breathless, to the second of the white patches. Standing beside it, they could see another higher still.

'Well, it beats me,' said Nancy.

'Found anything, Professor?' said John. Dick was digging at something with a knife and looking very worried.

'He's been hammering at this stuff,' he said, 'but I can't think why.'

A little above the big round splash of paint there was a wide crack in the rock full of what looked like rust and ashes, brown, reddish and black. Here, and nowhere else, were marks of a hammer. Bits of the stuff were lying loose. It looked as if someone had been trying to clean out the crack.

'What is it?' said John.

'Iron, I should think,' said Dick, 'with that rusty stuff, but I don't know.' He had pulled the mineralogy book from his knapsack, but found no help in it.

John and Nancy attacked the stuff with their hammers.

'It's just dirt,' said Nancy.

'It can't be that,' said John. 'Let's go up to the top one.'

They climbed again, and came to the first and highest of the white patches. And here, too, there seemed to be no reason for it, unless it was that near this patch also was what looked like an old crack in the rock, six or seven inches across, full of this same reddish dirt.

'He's been doing a good deal of hammering at this one,' said John.

'Trying to sink a well,' laughed Nancy, poking the handle of her hammer into a deep hole in the dirt. There were chips of grey rock round it as if someone had been using hammer and chisel. Small scraps of reddish dirt were scattered about.

'Let's go down again to the bottom one and see if there's any of the same stuff there,' said John.

'Right,' said Nancy. 'That'll settle it. But, I say, Professor, are you sure about the stuff?'

'Not really,' said Dick, 'but it looks like rust. And, anyhow, it isn't gold.'

They raced downhill, leaping, running, sliding, pulling up short and going carefully sideways down the steepest bits until they came to the lowest of the white paint splashes.

'Here it is,' said John. 'Just the same as up above.'

They were looking at another crack in the rock full of red dirt exactly like the stuff they had been looking at. Here, too, were marks of Squashy Hat's hammer and chisel. Dick picked up bits of the stuff one after another.

'I don't believe they're worth anything at all,' he said.

'Hullo, here's his paint-pot,' said Nancy.

They all three had a good look at the paint-pot, as if that could answer questions. But it answered none. It was an ordinary tin of paint with a wire handle for carrying, and a press-in lid. It was labelled 'Household Paint. White. For indoor or outdoor use.'

'I wonder if it's the same crack going all the way up the hill,' said Dick. 'Each bit points about the same way, and there's a lot of grass and loose stones. Perhaps if we could clear it away we'd find it was all one crack.'

Dick, in that moment, had come very near the truth, but none of them knew it, and Dick himself presently threw the idea way. He was still looking at bits of the reddish stuff that had been chipped from the crack. 'He can't really be interested in that rubbish,' he said.

'Got it,' said Nancy. 'Galoots we are. Gummocks. Mutton-headed gummocks. Of course he isn't. He's only pretending. He's guessed that Slater Bob has told us something he hasn't told him. He comes up here just to have an excuse for watching us. From here he can see everything in High Topps. That's it. You know, he didn't start coming up here till after we'd begun prospecting.'

She stopped suddenly, looking at John's face which had turned the colour of an over-ripe tomato.

'What's the matter?'

She turned to see what he was staring at.

Fifty yards away on the hillside Squashy Hat himself was standing, with his back towards them, looking away into the distance as if he did not know they were there.

Nancy's mouth fell open. She still had the stranger's can of white paint in her hands. She put it hurriedly down in the place where she had found it.

'He was looking this way when I first saw him,' whispered John, who was feeling almost as if he had been caught in somebody else's garden.

'I'm sure it's only iron,' said Dick, who had been scraping away at a bit with his pocket-knife.

'Shut up!' hissed Nancy. 'Look!'

'Let's ask him what the stuff is,' said Dick.

'We can't,' said Nancy. 'We've got to get out. Come on. Don't look his way.'

Dick looked at John, but John, too, was all for getting out, as quickly as possible, without actually running away. After all, not one of them knew Squashy Hat. And even if he was a rival, and trying to find the gold that they were after, it was not very pleasant to be caught examining his can of paint and looking at the places where he had been busy with his hammer. Mother was the friendliest and most understanding of all natives, but this was not a thing of which she could be expected to approve.

Silently, and not exactly hurrying, but not dawdling either, they went down Grey Screes and across High Topps to the camp.

They did not once look back at the Screes. Squashy Hat may have been looking at them or he may not, but both John and Nancy felt his eyes on their backs. Dick, thinking of the

AS IF HE DID NOT KNOW THEY WERE THERE

red dirt, had other troubles. He cheered up, however, on the way.

'Perhaps he didn't know what it was himself,' he said at last.

'He was only using it for an excuse to be up there spying on us,' said Nancy. 'The white spots are all part of his villainy. What he wants is to keep an eye on us, and to be ready to jump our claim the moment we find the gold. We were quite right to go and look. Even Susan would say so. But I don't know what our scouts were doing not to warn us he was coming.'

Half-way across the Topps they met Roger, Peggy, Titty and Dorothea hurrying to meet them.

'Did he say anything?' asked Dorothea.

'What happened?' asked Titty.

'You're a fine lot of scouts,' said Nancy bitterly. 'Letting us get caught like that. Why didn't you signal?'

'We did,' said Peggy.

'Like windmills,' said Roger, 'for hours and hours, but it wasn't any good because you never looked at us.'

'I suppose we can't have done,' said Nancy, rather sheepishly for her.

Back in the camp, where Susan had made scrambled eggs for them on a huge scale, breaking sixteen eggs one after another into the frying-pan, a council was held. Whatever happened everybody was to keep clear of Squashy Hat. Susan was very firm on that, and John and Nancy, after the morning's experience, seemed almost as native as Susan.

'But he didn't really say anything,' said Dorothea.

'It was just as bad as if he had,' said John.

'Perhaps worse,' said Susan.

'Perhaps we ought to stop prospecting except when he isn't there.'

'If we do,' said Nancy, 'he'll know we've found out that

his scratchings and blobs of white paint are just to hide that
he's watching to find out where Slater Bob told us to look.'

'Nancy's right,' said Captain John. 'We've got to go on
just as if we hadn't found him out.'

'We haven't really,' said Dick.

Sophocles was sent off soon after dinner. The message sent
with him said nothing about Squashy Hat.

NEW CAMP COULDN'T BE BETTER. AND YOU JUST TRY
OUR COOKING, SUSAN'S I MEAN.

The skull with which the message was signed was grinning
so cheerfully that nobody could have guessed how near things
had come to being very awkward.

That afternoon a long line of prospectors combed the
Topps as if there was no Squashy Hat busy on the hillside
above them. And Squashy Hat, for his part, went on with his
work as if there were no prospectors looking up every now
and then to see what he was doing. He even added yet another
white spot to the others, a little way below the third. He left
Grey Screes and went home while the prospectors were still
on the Topps. It seemed almost as if he did not care what
they might be doing.

There was no need now to get down to Tyson's farm for
supper, and the combing went on till dusk. Peggy was sent
off first to run down for more milk. Susan followed her to get
the fire going and to cook the supper. The others went on till
they could hardly see.

After supper Nancy and John marked the map that they
had made, putting black dots to show the old workings they
had found, and rough shading over the strips of country
that had been combed. The shaded part seemed very small
when they remembered how many days had gone.

'You know we did more the first day than we've ever done
since,' said Nancy.

'Well, we've had to have somebody keeping an eye on him,' said John.

'And then there was the well to dig and shifting camp,' said Nancy.

'How many more days have we got?' said Titty.

'Nobody knows,' said Nancy. 'Anyway we jolly well will get up early tomorrow, and we'll search about two hundred square miles.'

'Combing?' said Roger. 'I don't believe it's any good. Marching along in a row we'll never find it. It may be in the part we won't get at till it's time to go. If it's there at all.'

'We jolly well know it's there,' said Nancy. 'We're bound to find it if we go on. If we start just dashing about all over the place we may miss it altogether.'

CHAPTER 19

ROGER ALONE

'Squashy's gone.'

'Not really?' Titty, from the foot of the ash tree, was looking up at Captain Nancy who was high in its branches and looking out.

'He has,' Nancy called down. 'He's gone off down the road. We'll have the Topps to ourselves again.'

Titty ran back into the camp.

'Nancy says he's gone down the road . . .'

'Let's get breakfast over quick,' said John, who had just got back from Tyson's with the morning milk.

A moment later Nancy slid down the last few feet of the look-out tree and rubbed the green lichen stain from her knees. Twenty minutes after that, the eight of them were already spreading out in a long line and beginning a new day's combing of the Topps. With Squashy Hat gone the other way, down the road, perhaps, indeed, round the head of the lake to Rio, they meant to take their chance and cover all the ground they could.

But, for one reason or another, it was a duller morning's work than usual. They found only two old workings to look at, and neither of them even looked as if it might be the one of which Slater Bob had spoken. Both tunnels were in a broken-down state, and John and Nancy let none of the younger ones go inside. Titty's ball of string was left unused. Roger grew more and more bored. Even Titty began to think it a pity there was no scouting to be done. Dorothea now and then looked regretfully towards the white splashes on the hillside. What sort of a story was it when it was without a villain?

Dick alone, for whom, at the moment, nothing mattered but different kinds of stones, kept his hammer busy and was happy.

At noon they were back again at the near side of the Topps. This was according to plan, and they ate their midday dinner, pemmican (cold), apples, bunloaf and marmalade, and a bottle of ginger-beer (grog) apiece, in the shade of the trees. They sent off Sappho early, to give her plenty of time to get home. The message was cheerful: 'ALL GOING WELL.' Roger thought it much too cheerful considering there was more than half the Topps still to be searched.

In the afternoon they started again on another strip of country, and worked their way across to the foot of the Screes. There was a little more interest this time, because they had several stony ridges to cross, and little valleys and ravines in the Topps, where they found heather and grey rock together. But though this seemed very hopeful, they found no signs of old workings, and when, towards evening, after moving north so as to cover fresh ground, they started to work back again towards the valley of the Amazon, Roger was almost in a state of mutiny.

They were not half-way across the Topps when he invented a private game. He looked right and left along the line of prospectors. Nobody was as hopeful as in the morning, and the line was not as straight as it had been. Some lagged, others were going too fast, and the line curled this way and that among heather and bracken and rock as they made their way slowly home. Still, a line there was, and Roger thought that it would be rather good practice for scouting if he were to try to get from one end of it to the other without being seen. Nancy, whose eyes were sharpest, was luckily on his left. All the others were on his right. He took a good look across country. There were John, Titty, Dorothea, Peggy, Dick and Susan. He noted things likely to be useful, a patch of rocks, a gully, and, best of all, a wide stretch of bracken, not twenty yards ahead of him and stretching away over the Topps, nearly as far as the rocky ridge over which Dorothea was scrambling on her hands and knees.

Roger waited at the edge of the bracken. Nobody was looking his way. Now was the chance. Good. There was an old sheep track through the bracken. Roger looked round once more, and, a moment later, supposing people had happened to look that way, they would have seen nothing but a slight stirring of the bracken tops.

He had passed behind both John and Titty and lay at the edge of the bracken, peering out to see what had become of Dorothea. There she was, close to him. Roger lay perfectly still. Almost he had come out in front of her, when even Dorothea would have seen him. She had left the rocks and was walking slowly across some open ground, talking aloud. Perhaps she, too, was getting a little tired of prospecting. 'The outlaw saw his chance, and, hidden by the dusk, passed unseen within a stone's throw ... within an arrow-shot – no ... passed between his enemies so close that they might have touched him.' Just for a moment Roger thought that Dorothea had discovered him and was talking like this to let him know she knew what he was doing. Then he remembered *The Out-law of the Broads* and knew that Dorothea, while prospecting with the others, was also busy on a chapter of her book.

From where he lay, no one else was in sight. He let Dorothea get a little farther from him, and then, low to the ground, slipped behind the rocks she had just crossed. Here he rested in a good place from which he could look out and see what all the others were doing. He had Peggy, Dick and Susan still to pass. That ought to be easy enough, he thought, once he had worked across this rocky bit and got into the heather. All three of them were prospecting hard. He watched them for some time. Not one of them ever looked back. They were going steadily ahead.

Roger looked round towards the others, Dorothea, Titty, John and Nancy. He could keep this lump of rocks between himself and them nearly all the way to the heather. He set out once more, dashed across a bit of open ground and lay low for a moment to take his breath and listen. No, Peggy had not seen him. There she was, pushing her way through some bracken, in a hurry to get to the next stony patch where there might be a chance of finding something. Roger was on his feet again, and slipped over another twenty yards to lie behind a rock. Then came a long awkward bit where he could not safely even lift his head. He crawled, flat on his stomach on the dried-up grass. This was real stalking. Much better fun than prospecting. He wished Titty was in it too. Hullo. What were Dick and Susan doing? Had they found something? They had stopped and were close together, looking at some rocks. Bother them. How could a stalking Indian slip past behind them if instead of moving forward they just stuck in one place. Roger waited. And still Dick and Susan did not move. Roger's patience gave out. Of course, it was taking an awful risk, but once he could get into the heather he might manage to get across in front of their very noses without being seen.

He was in the heather, worming his way along an old sheep track. The heather, already showing purple, had all but over-grown the track, so that Roger, crawling on his stomach, had to push his way through. There was a steady buzz of bees at the opening flowers. A twisted root of heather in the track reminded Roger of the adders that all this time he had for-gotten. Well, it was no good thinking of banging with a stick, because he had not got one, and anyway the one thing an Indian must not do is to make a noise.

Roger made up his mind not to put his hand anywhere without first making sure that he was not going to put it on a sleeping snake.

He met no snake, but was watching for one so carefully that he forgot his stalking and everything else, and was startled almost into squeaking when right in his face, not a yard in front of him, an old cock grouse got up, with a whirring of wings like the sudden running down of a gigantic clock and a loud 'Go back! Go back! Go back!' as it flew away over the heather. It was more like an explosion than a bird. Roger half jumped up, bit his tongue most painfully, and dropped to the ground again just in time. He heard Dick's voice.

'Something startled that grouse. Did you see what it was? It couldn't be a dog.'

Dick's voice seemed to come from a little to the right and in front of him. Voices carried so well on that clear still day. Roger would have given a good-sized bit of chocolate to know just how far ahead of him Dick was. But he dared not lift his head above the heather. Dick had noticed the grouse and must be looking at the very place. It would be just like him to come through the heather to find out what it was that had made the grouse get up. The only thing to do was to hurry on without shaking the heather and to hope that there were no more grouse.

The sheep track did not run straight, and five minutes later Roger was wishing he had a compass. 'At least,' he said to himself, 'not exactly a compass so much as a periscope, so that I could poke it up out of the heather and look round without being seen.'

And then, suddenly, the heather came to an end, and Roger, on all fours, found himself looking out over a hollow in the moor. The rocks dropped sharply away beneath him to a grass-covered bottom. On the other side of it rocks rose again. Beyond the hollow he could see far away to the edge of the Topps, and the Great Wall, and the uppermost branches of the Look-out Tree above the hidden camp.

Steps sounded, and the noise of people pushing through the deep heather not twenty yards behind him. It was no good waiting until they trod on him. Roger began working down to the bottom of the hollow, holding on by the heather that grew in the cracks of the rocks. At any moment the other prospectors might be looking down upon him from above. Half-way down he slipped. As he fell, he rolled over, caught at a clump of heather, and found himself hanging from it, a foot from the ground. Small stones clattered by. He let go of the heather and dropped and found himself looking into a dark three-cornered hole in the rock. This was better than anything he could have hoped. He crouched in the mouth of the hole, and looked up, to see nothing but rock and the heather from which he had been swinging. The heather had sprung back. No one looking down from the top could see him. . . .

He was only just in time.

'Did you hear that?' Dick was asking. 'Why, hullo, here's another of those ravines.'

'This is the one we saw this morning,' said Susan. 'We've been here. We've got too far to the right. My fault, calling you over to look at those stones. Look. We've got much too far from Peggy. Push away to the left. No good going over the same ground again . . .'

'Aye, aye, Sir.' That was Dick's voice, close above him, and Roger grinned to hear Dick talk in the manner of ship's boys and able-seamen.

They were working through the heather away to the left, and presently would be able to see the whole length of the gully. Roger pulled his torch out of the stern pocket of his shorts. What sort of a hole was this that he had found just when he needed it? He flashed the torch into the darkness. He saw at once that it was one of the old workings, and a very old one. Inside the hole there was a tunnel that opened after a few yards into a small cave, much like Peter Duck's cave in Swallowdale. It went no farther. That was why no one had noticed it this morning. Most of the old workings were easily found because of the lump outside them, often covered with turf, but still unnatural, built up out of the waste stuff that the old miners had brought out of the rock. This working had been abandoned almost at once, the little pile thrown out had been scattered about the bottom of the gully, or maybe taken away and used for walling a sheepfold. There had been nothing left outside to show that the entrance was more than a dark shadow under overhanging rocks.

Roger, with torch lit, moved on tiptoe about the inner cave. He was safe here. Susan and Dick could walk right past without suspecting. No one would ever guess how he had managed to vanish so completely. He crept back to the mouth of the cave and listened.

From somewhere far away on the left, he heard a faint 'Ahoy!'

'Ahoy! Ahoy!' Susan and Dick were answering. Yes, they had passed the end of the gully. There was nothing in those 'Ahoys' that meant anything to interest Roger. Nobody had noticed he had gone, or there would have been a different note in Susan's voice. Nothing had been found or there would have been a different note in Dick's or Peggy's. These were the 'Ahoys' of disheartened prospectors, just calling to each other for company's sake in the wilderness. No use showing himself just yet, or they would not realize what a gorgeous bit of Indianing he had done. No use appearing before anybody had missed him.

He went back into the cave to think out a really good use for it. It was a pity Titty was not here, but, after all, if she had been, it would have been her discovery as much as his. And it was just about time, Roger thought, that he ought to begin discovering things for himself. He flashed his torch over the rocky ceiling and chipped sides. Hundreds of years ago people had been working here. He thought of Slater Bob, all alone in the middle of Ling Scar, working away by himself. It was easy to pretend that the few yards to the mouth of the cave were really half a mile or even more. A little light came in from outside. That could not be helped. 'Oh, well,' said Roger to himself, 'that could be from one of those big lamps somewhere just round the corner.' Rather a good thing, on the whole, because it let him save his torch, now that his eyes were growing accustomed to the darkness. What about doing a little mining now that he was here? Slater Bob did not just sit in the middle of the hill doing nothing. Roger pulled out his goggles, put them on, and struck the wall of the cave a smart blow with his hammer. The noise was much greater than he had expected, though the stone did not even chip. Would they have heard that noise outside? He waited a minute or two, listening. Then he tried again. Then, with his torch, he began looking round the walls for a place to hit where he might have some chance of breaking off a bit of stone. Not much fun in hammering a rock when nothing happens. At the extreme inside of the cave he found a crack running not quite straight up and down, but very nearly so. Holding the torch in his left hand, he hit out with the hammer in his right. A bit of rock flaked away.

'Not quite so hard here,' said Roger to himself, and took another whack or two up and down the crack. More rock came away. 'Slater Bob's pretty strong,' said Roger, and let fly again. Rock was falling round his hand in small bits. He saw another crack close by the first. Had it been there before or had he made it? This was real quarrying. He hit away at the rock between the two cracks, and stepped back with a squeak. A bit of rock as big as a Latin dictionary had come loose. Roger jumped clear as it dropped, but a smaller bit that came with it hit his ankle.

ROGER IN THE MINE

'Ow,' said Roger, and bent to rub the place.

That was enough. He would leave quarrying to Slater Bob. And then, as he stooped and rubbed his ankle, and shone his torch on it to see if the skin was broken, which it was not, he caught a sudden glint from among the stones at his feet.

He tore off his goggles to make sure. It could not be, and yet. . . . He picked up a scrap of rock and took it to the daylight at the mouth of his cave. He came back and peered into the place from which the big lump had fallen. He pushed his torch in there to get a better look. He turned to get out of the cave and to go shouting across the Topps after the others. But no. There would be plenty of time for that. After all that combing of theirs. . . . Let them wait. . . . There was plenty of life in his torch yet. All thoughts of Slater Bob forgotten, torch in one hand and hammer in the other, Roger set to work in earnest. Chips of stone flipped him on the cheek. He put the goggles on again to save his eyes. Nothing else mattered. In there, in the hole that he had made, was something that was going to come out, or Roger Walker, gold-miner, would know the reason why.

CHAPTER 20

WHAT'S BECOME OF HIM?

IF it had been earlier in the day somebody would have noticed at once that there was a gap in the line and that one of the prospectors was missing. But the day had been long and very hot, and by the end of the afternoon even Nancy was not as strict as she had been. Again and again the line had been broken when somebody had found something or other and all the others had come together to see what it was. It had never been anything worth looking at, from the mining point of view, and the prospectors had spread out again to go on with the combing of the Topps, feeling more and more disheartened. They had come to spreading out anyhow, in no particular order, so that each time people had different next-door neighbours. When Roger slipped into hiding he had been next to Nancy, but when Nancy next looked that way and called out to John it never occurred to either that there ought to have been someone else between the two of them. It was growing late, and they were back at the side of the Topps above the valley of the Amazon, and Nancy had at last agreed that they had done enough, when the discovery was made. They had come to the place where they had dumped their knapsacks after the midday meal. One by one they stiffly twisted their arms through the straps, ready for the short walk home along the edge of the moorland. The pile of knapsacks grew smaller, until of all the eight only one was left.

'Hullo! Where's Roger?' said Titty.

'Roger!'

'Roger, ahoy!'

'Come on. Don't start lurking. We're going home,' said Peggy.

'Grub!' shouted John. 'Hurry up!'

But no tousled head of Roger bobbed up from behind rock or heather or bracken. There was not a sign of him to be seen.

'He's just sloped,' said John.

'He's a bit tired of prospecting,' said Susan.

'Poor old Rogie,' said John, by way of apology to Nancy, 'He's always in a hurry, you know ... getting out the oars the moment the wind drops.'

'I know what he's done,' said Peggy. 'I bet he's gone scouting down to the bracken opposite Atkinson's gate, to see Squashy come prancing home.'

All day there had been no sign of Squashy Hat on the Topps. Again and again the prospectors had looked up to the white painted patches on the rocks of Grey Screes, expecting to see their rival, and listening for the tapping of his hammer. Except for the creaking flight of a family of wild swans far overhead, and the occasional protests of startled grouse, they might have been the only living things in that deserted wilderness. This had been good from the prospecting point of view, but, as the prospecting had been unsuccessful and duller than usual because no longer new and, in spite of Nancy's faith, becoming less and less hopeful, they had almost been sorry that Squashy Hat had not been there. Roger was not the only one who felt that a little scouting, Indianing and signalling would have been a happy change. No one felt much inclined to blame him.

They all hailed together, 'Roger, Ahoy – oy – oy – oy!'
There was no answer.

'He wouldn't hear with the wood between us,' said John.

'Specially if he's snuggling down in the lurking-place,' said Peggy. 'I'll go and dig him out ...'

'Come on, John,' said Nancy. 'Let's go, too. He may have

spotted Squashy up to something or other. Come on, Susan. Let's all go.'

But they had been on their feet all that hot day, and Susan, though tired enough already, knew that they were again short of milk and that it was her turn to go down to the farm. John and the two Amazons ran on together, at a steady trot, along the edge of the Topps, close above the wood, disappearing when they dropped down to the Dundale road.

The main body of prospectors were just reaching the Great Wall, and were turning down the gully into the wood when they saw them coming back. . . . Nancy, John, Peggy . . .

'They haven't got him,' said Dorothea.

'He'll be coming along behind,' said Susan, but just then they saw the three stop and heard 'Roger, Ahoy!' called out again into the summer evening.

Susan looked back over the rolling desert of the Topps.

'Botheration,' she said. 'He ought not to start games right at the end of the day.'

They waited.

'He's not there,' said John, 'unless he's simply being a goat.'

'We went right down to Atkinson's,' said Peggy.

'We had a look at Squashy,' said Nancy. 'He's got back and we saw him light his pipe, sitting on the bench in the garden.'

'But what about Roger?' said Susan.

'In the camp, probably.'

Titty, Dorothea and Dick raced off together, down the gully, past the bramble thicket, in among the bushes, past Titty's well and into the camp.

'Hey! Roger!' called Titty.

'He may be croodling to the pigeons,' said Dorothea.

'He isn't,' said Dick. 'I went there first to see.'

'He isn't in his tent,' said Titty.

'I know what he's done,' said Dorothea, just as Susan and the others came into camp. 'He's run on down to get the milk from Mrs Tyson.'

'He did say he was going to one day,' said Titty.

'Oh well, that's all right,' said Susan, relieved, and then, a moment later, 'He hasn't taken the milk-can.'

'Just like Roger,' said Nancy. 'Mrs Tyson'll lend him another.'

'I'm going down to meet him,' said Susan. 'Look here, Peggy. You'll get on with the supper. It's awfully late already.'

'Fried cannon balls,' said Peggy. 'There'll still be time to do them if you're going down after Roger.'

'John, give her a hand with the mincing,' said Susan, and, taking the milk-can, hurried off through the trees.

Fried cannon balls were an improved form of pemmican. John opened a tin of corned beef while Nancy was stirring up the fire to do its duty, and Peggy, with reverent fingers, was putting Susan's mincing machine together. The corned beef, a couple of onions and some stale bread saved by thrifty cooks were put through the machine, and then mixed together in a pudding bowl with a raw egg and the little that was left of the morning's milk. The mixture was rolled into balls, by Titty and Dorothea, who happened to have the cleanest hands. Butter was melted in the frying-pan, and then a skilful circular motion, close above the flames, gave the cannon balls a chance of being browned on all sides. This was very hot work, and the prospectors did it in short shifts, those who were resting anxiously watching the one in charge of the heavy frying-pan, because a slip, or twist of a weak wrist had been known to send all eight cannon balls together headlong into the fire.

The cannon balls were nearly ready when they heard Susan calling 'Roger' below them in the wood.

They looked at each other with horror.

'But wherever *can* he be?' said Nancy, almost angrily.

The next minute Susan panted into camp with the milk. She had come up the steep path out of the valley just about as fast as she could. They could see at once that she was very worried.

'Mrs Tyson's never seen him,' she said. She almost choked on her words. 'He must be still on the Topps . . . or anywhere. . . . He may have gone and twisted an ankle like he did last year. . . . He may have gone into one of the old workings. . . . Roger!' she called out desperately. 'Come along. Supper. Nobody's cross with you!'

'He may be stuck in a mine,' said Dorothea, her eyes widening, 'shouting and shouting, and no one to answer.' She was divided between pity for Roger and the awful thrill of the mess into which he might have got.

'Starving,' said Titty, with tears in her eyes, and for once nobody laughed at the thought of Roger's hunger.

'And it'll be pitch dark in another few minutes,' said Susan.

'Come on, John,' said Nancy, pulling herself together. 'No time to lose. Nothing else for it. We've got to go up again and find him. Dick, Titty and Dorothea stay here in camp. We four'll go and look for him. Better take lanterns. Where's that Alpine rope? . . .'

And just then the pale red glimmer of a dying torch showed between the trees and Roger walked into camp.

*

Pity and fear for him were gone in a moment.

'Miserable little idiot,' said John.

'Where have you been?' said Susan.

'Hullo,' said Roger, seeing what was in the frying-pan that Peggy was holding. 'Cannon balls. I'm jolly glad I wasn't late.'

'Shiver my timbers,' said Nancy. 'If you were a ship's boy in *my* ship . . . *or* an able-seaman.'

He came slowly towards them, keeping one hand behind his back.

'What have you done to your hand?' said Susan.

'Nothing,' said Roger.

'Why are you hiding it?'

'Got something in it,' said Roger.

He faced the whole indignant company and held out a large lump of white quartz.

'Gold,' he said simply. 'Look at it and see.'

Nancy grabbed the stone.

'The other side,' said Roger.

'Golly,' said Nancy. 'Hi! Look at this, John. Where's Dick? Come on, Professor! Is it or isn't it?'

Everybody was crowding round. Heads, shoulders, bumped together. Nancy gave the stone to John.

'Come on, Dick,' said John.

Dick pushed his spectacles straight. His hands shook a little as John pushed the lump of quartz into them.

Everybody had caught a glimpse now of the crack in the white sparkling stone, the brown earth in the crack, and in the earth, and on either side of it shining specks of yellow.

'It must be,' cried Dorothea.

'Of course it is,' said Titty.

'It's the right colour,' said the Professor.

'Hurrah!' cried Peggy. 'We've done it after all.'

'Yes, but where's the place,' cried Nancy. 'Come on. We'll want these lanterns after all. We must stake our claim before Squashy finds it too.'

'I couldn't find the way there in the dark,' said Roger, looking at the cannon balls.

Nancy's face fell.

'It's all right,' said John. 'No moon. Squashy couldn't find it either.'

'They've got to have their suppers,' said Susan.

'Oh well,' said Nancy regretfully. But even she could see that it was no good going stumbling about the Topps in the dark. She gave up the idea. 'Squashy'll be having his supper, too. . . . But not a celebration feast. Come on. Those cannon balls are cooked. Kettle's boiling. Let's get at it. Flowing bowls! . . . Oh, well done, Roger!'

Roger grinned, but looked a little doubtfully at Susan.

Two minutes later supper had begun. The night closed down and shut them in with their camp-fire. They bit into their cannon balls and asked questions. Roger bit into his and answered, but did not tell too much.

'But just where is it?' Nancy asked.

Roger finished his mouthful before speaking, with a politeness that was almost maddening. He wanted time to think. He had found the place, and tomorrow he would show it them, but he wasn't going to tell them exactly where it was and have them all dashing in ahead of him.

'You turn to the right after a bit,' he said, 'and then there's a clump of dead grass, and a bit to the left and then a bit straight and a bit to the right again, and then you go down a bit after going up, and you leave a patch of bracken on the port hand, and a brownish rock to starboard . . .'

'Oh shut up, Roger,' said John. 'Don't play the donk.'

'Well, she asked me,' said Roger, and took another largish bite of cannon ball.

'But is there a lot of it, or just this bit?' said Susan.

'Is it in an old working?'

'Was there any heather?'

Roger, when he was again free to speak, told them that it was in just such an old working as Slater Bob had described, that the heather was there, and that there was lots more gold where the first lump came from.

Titty listened to him and watched him.

'It's all right,' she said at last. 'He really has found it. Good old Rogie.'

More than that he would not say, but it was enough. As the meal went on, and empty stomachs were filled, the realization of what had happened sank deeper and deeper. Somewhere above them, out there in the blackness of the night . . . out there in the wilderness they had searched so long . . . the gold was waiting for them, after all. . . . And Roger, sitting there with his mouth full, had seen it and touched it and brought some away and knew the very place where it was. People kept getting up from the fire and sitting down again. The lump of quartz was passed from hand to hand. Dick, cramming in the last of his cannon ball, scrambled into his tent to get the metallurgy book. Dorothea, forgetting for once *The Outlaw of the Broads*, murmured to herself.

'Walking up and down on deck,' she murmured. 'Up and down. . . . Up and down . . .'

'As glum as anything,' said Titty. 'If only we knew the name of his ship to send him a telegram . . . or, just think, if only a pigeon came flying to perch on the mast with the news . . .'

Even John could hardly keep still.

Nancy went stamping round in the dark, spilling the tea out of her mug, and talking to herself. 'Shiver my timbers! . . . Done it after all! . . . Barbecued billygoats! . . . Giminy! . . . Golly! . . . Forty million thousand pieces of eight!'

'You'll get your hair on fire if you don't look out,' said Susan. 'Look out . . . Dick!'

And Dick, who had not heard at first what she was saying, moved just an inch or two farther from the flames still reading *Phillips* on gold by the flickering light of the camp-fire, looking first at the page where the letters seemed to dance before his eyes, and then at those glittering specks on the white quartz.

'Go to bed, everybody,' cried Nancy suddenly. 'Now. At once. We've got to get our claim staked the moment it's light enough to see.'

PESTLE·AND·MORTAR

CHAPTER 21

STAKING THEIR CLAIM

'Show a leg, my hearties!'

Nancy woke the camp with a cheerful shout. The prospectors leapt to life. Everybody was awake and busy by the time she was half-way down to Tyson's with the milk-can. She astonished Mrs Tyson by reaching the door of the dairy almost before the milk was brought in. By the time she was back at the camp, all faces had been washed, teeth cleaned, beds made and tents tidied. The kettle was already boiling. Breakfast was the quickest meal they had ever eaten. They even used cold water to cool their tea because it was too hot to drink. Peggy took her apple up the ash tree and reported that Squashy Hat must be still in bed. John, between mouthfuls, sharpened a stout stick. If there was a claim to be staked it was just as well to have things ready. It was no good thinking there were sticks to cut on the Topps. Nancy watched him for a moment, and said, 'We'll want a good-sized bit of paper.' Dorothea dived back into her tent and came out with an exercise book.

'Will this do?' she asked.

Nancy looked at it and saw *The Outlaw of the Broads* printed on the cover.

'It's all right,' said Dorothea. 'There's nothing inside this volume yet.'

'Look here, Dot,' said Nancy. 'We'll get you another in Rio . . .' and then she hesitated. After all, Roger was Roger. 'I won't tear any leaves out now,' she said, 'but bring it along, just in case it's needed.'

Today even Susan was ready to put off washing up until a

little later, and the whole expedition set out across the Topps.

Roger, for once the leader, was the least hurried of the party. The others kept pressing round him, as if the nearer they kept to him the sooner they would see the place for themselves.

'Can you see it now?' asked Nancy.

'It's beyond those rocks.'

'Which rocks?'

'Those.'

'But there are rocks all over the place.'

'It's beyond the ones I'm looking at.'

'Oh go on, Rogie,' said Titty. 'Do tell us what to look for.'

'There's nothing to see till we get there,' said Roger, and kept steadily on at his own pace.

Presently he walked a little slower, and then stopped, and looked about him.

'Don't say you've gone and forgotten where it is,' said Peggy.

Roger grinned.

'Don't be a donk,' said John. Both he and Titty had seen that grin and known that Roger had fished for Peggy and caught her.

'Well, I might have forgotten,' said Roger. 'It was jolly dark before I got home.'

They walked on over that rolling, rocky country, which had changed in the night for all of them. It was no longer a country to be searched by long, laborious combing, with everybody out in a row. Roger had almost come to hate it by the time he had given up being a tooth in the comb and begun a little Indian work of his own. Today it seemed altogether different even to him. Gold had been found, and he had found it. No more combing for anybody. The only thing they had to do was to gather up the nuggets. Or was there more to do?

The others were cross-questioning Dick as they walked along, and Dick was showing Nancy a paragraph in the metallurgy book.

'Crushing and panning,' she was saying. 'We'll have to do that anyhow, to get the gold by itself. Jolly good thing we brought Captain Flint's crushing mill.'

'It won't be an ingot even then.'

'A nugget,' said Titty.

'Of course not,' said Nancy. 'Gold dust.'

'And what then?'

'Slater Bob'll show us how to make it into ingots. We must have at least one ready for Captain Flint.'

'We might make him a pair of gold earrings,' said Titty. 'Like Black Jake had in *Peter Duck*.'

'He'd never wear them,' said Peggy doubtfully.

'A good big shiny blob to hang on his watch chain,' said Nancy.

'And enough to make a gold collar for Timothy,' said Dorothea.

There was a sudden melancholy pause.

'If he isn't dead,' said Peggy at last.

'It's weeks since that telegram came,' said Nancy grimly, and then suddenly shaking off her momentary gloom, 'Oh well, if he's dead he's probably been dead ages, and been sunk to the bottom of the sea.'

'Wrapped in a Union Jack,' said Dorothea.

'Suffered a sea change,' murmured Titty, 'rich and rare . . . probably coral . . .'

'Anyway we can't do anything about it,' said Nancy. 'And the gold'll console Uncle Jim a bit, or it jolly well ought to. . . . Though you can get awfully fond of things like armadilloes. . . . Oh giminy. . . . It can't be helped. Look here, Roger, how far now?'

'Nearly there,' said Roger.

'But we've searched every bit of this.'

'I know,' said Roger.

A minute or two later he stopped short, looking down into the narrow little valley.

'But we've been here,' said John.

'I told you you had,' said Roger. 'But it's here all the same.'

'It's the place you said was just like Swallowdale,' said Dorothea to Titty.

'So it is,' said Titty. 'Only there's no beck, and no cave.'

'There's a cave all right,' said Roger.

At his first glance he had almost doubted whether this was indeed the place. Just for one moment he had had a panicky fear that he had brought them to the wrong valley, that he had found his cave only to lose it. Then he saw the place where he had slid down on the farther side, the heather with which he had broken his fall, the dark shadow below it.

'Here it is,' he said.

'But where?' said Nancy.

'Don't be a donk,' said John. 'Where is it?'

Roger was scrambling down into the ravine. He thought of wandering round and seeing how long it would take them to find the hole, but decided it wasn't really safe. Nancy had been waiting long enough already. So he walked straight across the ravine, and before he was half-way across the others had seen it. There was a general rush. John and Nancy jostled in the hole.

'In there?' said Peggy.

'Roger, you didn't go in,' said Susan.

'Jolly lucky I did,' said Roger.

'Look! Dick's got a bit,' said Dorothea.

'I must have dropped it coming out,' said Roger.

'Hurry up, Susan,' said Peggy.

'Oh, look here,' said Roger. 'Play fair. I found it,' and he shot into the opening after Susan.

The cave left by the miners of long ago seemed a good deal smaller now, with eight prospectors bumping about inside it and seven torches sending bright round patches of light over its rough hewn walls and roof. It had seemed quite large the day before to Roger, alone in it, with a single torch with which he could not light up more than a small bit of it at a time.

'It's the smallest of all the ones we've seen,' said Peggy.

'So long as it's the right one,' said Nancy. 'But look here, Roger, where is that quartz?'

'Perhaps there was only that one bit,' said John.

'You've got to hammer for it,' said Roger. 'I didn't see any till I did.'

Torch after torch flashed on the rocky wall at which he was pointing. There was a general shout. On the ground under the wall were chippings of quartz and a lump or two of grey stone, and above the chippings they could all see that it was as if two rocks had been pressed together sideways to make a sandwich with a thin layer of quartz as the potted meat between them. The crack ran almost straight up and down, and in it, beside the white gleam of the quartz under the light of the torches, there was the yellow sparkle of metal.

'Giminy,' cried Nancy. 'He's found it all right. Look out, John, with that hammer. Let's get a fair whack at it.'

In the general rattle of hammers up and down the narrow vein it was lucky nobody got hurt. Bits of stone and quartz were flying in all directions.

'Do take care,' said Susan. 'Put your goggles on. . . . If a bit gets in somebody's eye!'

'That's my nose,' said Roger.

'Sorry,' said Peggy.

'There's gold on almost every bit,' said Dorothea.

'Quartz is jolly hard stone,' said Titty.

'So is Peggy's elbow,' said Roger, very tenderly feeling his nose. 'Not broken,' he admitted, 'but it easily might have been.'

'Look here,' said John after a few more minutes of hammering. 'This is a waste of time. We ought to be using dynamite.'

'Oh good,' said Roger.

'Captain Flint's got some gunpowder,' said Peggy.

But for once Nancy was not for going to extremes.

'Captain Flint'll do the dynamiting,' she said. 'He'll simply love it. And we'll all help. But it's no good wasting any of the blowing up and all that before he comes. It's that that's going to keep him at home. He didn't like us letting off that firework on the roof of his houseboat, but he likes blasting as much as anybody . . .'

Susan was much relieved. 'Fireworks are all very well,' she said, 'but dynamite . . .'

John was a little disappointed.

'We don't need it,' said Nancy. 'The more blasting we leave him to do, the better he'll be pleased. All we've got to do is to show him there's something worth blasting for . . .'

'There'll be no holding him,' said Peggy, 'as soon as he sees this.'

'Well, it's no good just batting at it,' said John. 'Waste of time. We want chisels. . . . And what about the crushing and panning?'

'We'll want a bucket for water,' said Dick. 'And something shallow for the panning.'

'Frying-pan's the very thing,' said Nancy.

'I'll go to Tyson's for chisels,' said John.

'A bucket for water . . . the crushing mill . . . frying-pan. . . . Don't let's waste another minute,' said Nancy.

They hurried out into the ravine, tore off their goggles, and stood blinking in the sunshine, comparing the golden, glittering specks on different bits of quartz.

'Slip up and scout, somebody,' said Nancy.

Roger was already climbing up. He stopped well above their heads. One foot kicked in the air.

'He's seen Squashy,' said Titty.

'He's just going up on the Screes,' Roger whispered hoarsely.

'Pretending,' said Titty, 'and then he'll jump our claim the moment we're gone.'

'Golly,' said Nancy, 'and we haven't staked it yet. Dot, we'll have to use that paper.' She pulled her blue pencil from her pocket.

Dorothea tore a page from her exercise book. 'Won't you put the book under it to write on?' she said.

Roger came sliding down to see.

Nancy, pressing the exercise book against the face of the rock, wrote in big capital letters.

S.A.D. MINING COMPANY.

'What does it mean?' said Roger.

'Swallows, Amazons and D.'s Mining Company, you bone-headed young galoot.'

'But why sad?' asked Roger, skipping hurriedly out of reach.

Nancy laughed and scrumpled that leaf up.

'Sorry, Dot,' she said, 'I'll have to take another, just in case there are more donks about.'

On the second leaf she wrote 'S.A.D.M.C.' and waited, blue pencil in air.

'Trespassers will be prosecuted,' murmured Roger.

'It isn't trespassers that matter,' said Titty. 'It's jumpers. If Squashy tried to jump our claim . . .'

'We'd jolly well kill him,' said Nancy.

'Well, let's say so,' said Roger.

But both John and Susan were against this.

'It's no use threatening something you can't do,' said John.

'Don't say what we'll do,' said Susan.

'What about "All rights reserved"?' suggested Dorothea.

But Nancy was busy again with her blue pencil.

'How about that?' she said at last, and held up the notice she had finished.

S.A.D.M.C.

THIS GULCH IS CLAIMED

JUMPERS BEWARE

BY ORDER

S.A.D.M.C.

'Jolly good,' said John. 'We don't want to worry ordinary decent people, only jumpers. No one will know what it means unless he's someone we want to frighten off. And he won't know what on earth is going to happen to him. Far better than saying he'll be hanged or anything like that . . .'

'Things worse than death,' Dorothea tasted the words with relish.

'So long as he thinks it's something pretty unpleasant,' said Titty.

John began working a hole in the ground with the point of his stake.

'Not there,' said Nancy. 'Much too near. We've claimed the whole gulch. Supposing he does come snooping along there's no need to show him the way into our mine. He may never see it. You know, we never spotted it ourselves first time.'

John used a stone to drive the stake into the ground in the middle of the little valley. He split the top of it with a knife and wedged in the notice.

'Three cheers for Golden Gulch,' said Nancy. 'Not too loud. ... Come on now and get the things. No need for everybody to come. The able-seamen stay on guard. We'll do the carting.'

The captains and mates climbed the side of the Gulch and were gone.

'I'll just make sure what he says about crushing,' said Dick, and settled down to frantic study of *Phillips on Metals*.

'Let's get some more of the gold,' said Dorothea.

Titty and Roger followed her back into the mine.

'Gosh,' said Titty. 'What a blessing you found it.'

'No more combing, anyhow,' said Roger.

CHAPTER 22

CRUSHING AND PANNING

A HEAVILY laden party of prospectors came back from the camp. John carried a bucket full of water, very difficult not to spill on the uneven ground of the Topps. With his free hand he steadied a pole on his shoulder. Nancy, who was also carrying the big hurricane lantern, had the other end of the pole. Captain Flint's heavy pestle and mortar swung from the middle of it. Peggy staggered along with a brilliantly cleaned frying-pan and a knapsack in which were eight bottles of ginger pop. John had been down to the farm and borrowed a big cold chisel from Robin Tyson. Susan was carrying the kettle and a knapsack full of food for the day, a huge supply of thick potted meat sandwiches and a lot of apples.

'You should just have seen Captain Nancy cleaning up the frying-pan,' said Peggy, as the able-seamen met them in the gulch.

'Not Nancy,' said Titty.

'Got to have it clean,' said Nancy, and Titty understood how Nancy had suddenly come to take an interest in washing up. There was all the difference in the world between a pan that was to be used for gold-mining and one that was used only for scrambled eggs.

'We've got a bit more gold,' said Roger. 'But you can't do much with only a hammer.'

'Let's get at it with the chisel,' said John.

*

The hurricane lantern swung from an ancient iron peg left in the rock of the cave by the miners of long ago and dwindled with rust till it was hardly thicker than a nail. John, his eyes protected by motor goggles, was at work at the vein with hammer and chisel. Nancy, also wearing her goggles, was sitting on a rock just outside the door and crushing with the pestle and mortar. In the bottom of the mortar she had put a large lump of quartz. She had tried one way of crushing and

then another and had found that the best was the simplest. Holding the pestle with both hands she lifted it and brought it down only an inch or two on the quartz in the bottom of the mortar that rested on the ground between her knees. Lift, drop. Lift, drop. Thud. ... Thud. ... Thud.

'It's breaking up,' said Dick.

'Smaller and smaller,' said Titty.

'Let me try,' said Roger.

Thud. ... Thud. ... Thud. ... Not a real thundering bang, of the kind Nancy would have liked. A dull scrunching thud. Again and again and again.

'Perhaps somebody sat on that very stone,' said Dorothea, 'and did the same a hundred years ago.'

'Look here,' said Roger. 'Who found the gold? You ought to let me do some of the crushing.'

Nancy's lips were tight together now. She was getting hotter and hotter.

'Try if you like,' she said at last. 'Two and a half minutes. . . . Don't believe you'll last a second longer.'

'I'll do it till it's powdered,' said Roger.

'It's got to be very fine powder,' said Dick. 'Fine enough almost to float . . .'

'Come on and try,' said Nancy.

'You time me, Dick,' said Roger, putting his goggles on and taking Nancy's place.

At the second or third blow he looked a little surprised.

'It's quite easy,' he said, but hardly sounded as if he meant it.

'Half a minute,' said Dick, looking at his watch.

'Oh look here,' said Roger. 'It must be more than that.'

'Don't stop crushing while you talk,' said Nancy.

'But he said it was only half a minute. . . .' Roger clenched his teeth and went on with the work. . . . Up with the heavy pestle and down again. Up and down. Up and down. Thud. Thud. Thud.

'One minute,' said Dick.

'Minute and a half to go,' said Nancy.

'Stick to it, Rogie,' said Titty. 'You've nearly done another half minute.'

Roger tried not banging quite so fast.

'Minute and a half,' said Dick.

'One more minute,' said Titty.

Roger, very red in the face, pounded on. Thud. Thud. Thud.

'Good man, Roger,' said Nancy. 'I didn't really think you'd last so long.'

'Two minutes,' said Dick.

Roger's eyes bulged behind his goggles, but a faint grin began to show on his face. He was going to be able to do it. Thud. . . . Thud. . . . Thud. . . . He quickened up the pace. Thud. Thud. Thud. He was looking at Dick. Thud. Thud. Thud. Thud. . .

'Two and a half minutes,' said Dick, and Roger dropped the pestle, rolled off the stone he had been sitting on and lay panting on the ground.

'Somebody else's turn,' he said, with what breath he had left.

'You did jolly well,' said Nancy.

After that Dick and Titty and Dorothea had a go at the crushing. Then John came out from the mine with some more good bits of quartz in which there were quite large splashes that glinted gold in the sunlight.

'Don't put them in yet,' said Dick. 'Let's get one lot really fine enough for panning.'

'It's going to take a good long time,' said Nancy.

John took on for a bit, talking at first but soon content to pound away in silence.

'It's getting pretty powdery,' said Roger, looking into the mortar a few minutes later.

'Take care, Roger!' said Susan.

'That bit did hit me on the forehead,' said Roger.

'It might have got your eye. You shouldn't have taken your goggles off.'

'Don't try to shove your nose into it,' said John. 'Here you are, Susan. You have a go. How fine does it really have to be, Professor?'

'The book doesn't say,' said Dick. 'But it can't be too fine. It all depends on gravity. Gold's heavier than stone. We've got to get it into particles, and then the gold particles'll go to the bottom when we're doing the panning. If the particles aren't very fine they'll all go to the bottom at once instead of the lighter ones hanging about in the water.'

'This lot must be pretty nearly done,' said Nancy, when everybody had had another go with the heavy pestle. There were no lumps left in the bottom of the mortar, and a fine dust, that seemed to be growing paler and paler, spirted round the pestle in little puffs of grey smoke.

'Let's try the panning,' said John. 'We may as well find out whether it works at all.'

'Do we pour the water on the powder or the other way round?' said Nancy.

'Water first,' said Dick, 'and properly they have a machine to keep the water on the joggle.'

'We'll do our own joggling,' said John. 'Look out, Nancy, don't fill the frying-pan too full.'

Titty, Dorothea and Peggy came out just in time to see the panning begin. John was holding the frying-pan half full of water. Nancy took a pinch of the fine dust from the bottom of the mortar and dropped it on the top of the water, where it spread over the surface.

'Good. Good,' said Dick. 'It's fine enough. Now joggle.'

John began a quick wriggling motion, so that the water in the frying-pan broke into little pointed waves. 'Ow. Sorry,' he said. 'It's jolly hard not to splash.'

'Anything going to the bottom?' Nancy was trying to see what was happening but this was impossible while the frying-pan was being kept on the joggle by John.

'Oughtn't the gold to have gone through by now?' asked John.

Dick was hunting in the book. He found the place. 'It doesn't say how long it takes,' he said. 'But anyhow, they use a stream to wash away all the light stuff and leave the gold behind. I should think you ought to throw the top lot away . . .'

'It'll mean an awful lot of water,' said Susan.

JOGGLING THE PAN

'If we had an empty pemmican tin we could pour it into that, and let the stuff settle, and use the water again,' said Dick.

'Anyway, we can spare this lot,' said Nancy. 'Chuck it away and let's have a look at the gold.'

'Carefully,' said Peggy. 'Don't let it wash the gold away, too.'

John let the dirty water and the scum that was still on the surface flow away over the edge of the frying-pan. Heads crowded closer to see what was left.

'But it's all gone,' said Roger, and turned to look at the small grey puddle on the ground.

'No, it hasn't,' said Nancy. 'You can see the glint of it.'

There certainly was just a trace of something at the bottom of the frying-pan.

'Drop more water,' said John.

Susan poured it out. John swilled the frying-pan round with it, so that all the dust that was left in it was gathered together. He stirred it up, and joggled it again.

'Try now,' said Nancy.

John poured off the water. Along the edge at one side of the pan there was certainly something left.

'It may be only shining because it's wet,' said Titty, remembering the pearls dived for long ago in the water by Wild Cat Island, gleaming pale jewels that turned to dull pebbles as soon as they had dried in the sun.

'It's the real thing,' said Captain Nancy. 'Anyway, it'll be dry in a minute in this sun.'

'Spread it on a bit of paper,' said Susan.

'Who's got any?' said Nancy.

The blank volume of *The Outlaw of the Broads* lost another page. The sediment, glittering yellow, was spread on it with the point of a knife.

'I think we ought to wash that lot again,' said Dick.

'Giminy,' said Nancy. 'We can't. If we do, there won't be any left at all.'

Crushing and panning was going to be much harder work than anybody expected. Turns with the huge pestle were made shorter and shorter. One minute each was enough for Roger and Dick, Titty and Dorothea, but every minute helped to rest the tired muscles of the others. Dick suggested taking that first tiny pinch of gold dust to show Slater Bob, but the actual mining of the quartz was going on so well now, with the help of Robin Tyson's cold chisel as well as the hammers, that it seemed a pity not to crush and pan until they had a bag of gold worth looking at.

They rested for dinner and, crawling up the side of the gulch and using the telescope, saw that Squashy Hat, high on the hillside above them, was sitting on a rock and resting, too. After dinner and grog ('The only thing against these bottles,' said Roger, 'is that they aren't big enough inside'), they remembered the pigeon that was to go to Beckfoot.

'What will she say when she hears we've found it?' said Peggy.

'I wish we had a code,' said Nancy. 'But it's no good expecting her to read a semaphore picture when she's busy with paperers and plasterers. And, anyhow, it'd take too long to draw.'

Dorothea looked puzzled for a moment.

'Code,' said Titty, 'in case somebody else got hold of it.'

'Somebody might shoot the pigeon,' said Roger.

'Some horrid ally of Squashy's,' said Titty.

'We'll put it so that she'll know and no one else,' said Nancy. She carefully tore a narrow slip from the bit of paper on which lay that tiny pile of golden dust. For a moment she sucked the pencil she had borrowed from Dick. She wrote. 'What about this?' she said. 'ROGER FOUND IT. TONS AND TONS.'

'But there isn't really much,' said Dick.

'Not already panned,' said Nancy. 'But there will be. Look at the lumps waiting to be crushed, and anybody can see we could go on mining it for ever.' She scribbled, 'LOVE FROM THE S.A.D.M.C.', and finished by drawing the usual crossbones and a skull that was grinning from ear to ear.

'Who's going to send it off?' she asked.

'I am,' said Roger, 'and I'll take the kettle for more water.'

'Don't you want to do some more crushing?'

'Later on,' said Roger. 'But I think I ought to send the pigeon off first. Come on, Dick. Let's both go.'

But Dick was far too much worried about the right methods of panning to think of anything else. Titty, Dorothea and Roger went back to the camp together, where Homer, alone in the big cage, was waiting his turn to fly.

Titty caught him and held him gently while Roger slipped the message under the rubber ring on his leg. They put him in one of the small travelling-baskets and carried him out on the Topps so that he should get a clear start. Roger took him in both hands.

'It's the best news you've ever carried,' said Dorothea.

'Now then,' said Titty, and Roger flung him up into the air.

The pigeon flew far across the Topps before beginning to rise. Then, making a wide circle in the air, he came back high over their heads, higher, higher.

'Hullo,' said Roger, 'there's another pigeon ... higher still.'

'Rogie,' cried Titty. 'It's a hawk!'

Far, far above the soaring Homer, they could all see a tiny speck in that brilliant sky that almost blinded them. A tiny black speck, dropping, dropping, nearer ... hovering ... dropping again, while Homer the pigeon climbed through the air to meet it.

'Homer! Homer! it's a hawk!' Roger shouted.

'It'll get him,' cried Titty.

'It's probably a hawk of Squashy Hat's. He's been waiting on purpose, hooded, on a gloved wrist,' said Dorothea, 'and Squashy's flown him at our Homer.'

'Can't we do anything?' said Titty. 'Hey! Hey!' she shouted and waved her arms frantically to frighten the hawk.

But now it seemed that Homer had seen his danger. He was climbing no longer, but coming down again, in queer zigzag flights. The hawk suddenly dropped like a stone.

'He's got him!' sobbed Titty.

'Missed him,' shouted Roger. 'Well dodged.'

The hawk was rising again, flying above the pigeon who was now not far above the ground. The two birds were close together. The hawk swooped. Homer seemed to slip sideways in the air and, a second later, had plunged into the green tops of the trees.

'Done him!' shouted Roger.

'But the hawk's gone after him,' said Titty.

'He hasn't got him,' said Roger. 'Look!'

And they saw the hawk rise again above the trees, hover for a while, and at last swing away and up until they lost sight of it against that blinding sky.

'Squashy Hat must be feeling pretty desperate to try a horrid trick like that,' said Dorothea.

'What if Homer stays in the wood?' said Titty. 'We haven't got another pigeon to send.'

'Better ask Nancy and Peggy,' said Dorothea. 'Let's go back to the gulch. Dick'll be wanting a fresh lot of water by now.'

They went back to the camp and visited the pigeon cage, half expecting to see a fluttered Homer waiting about outside. But he was not there.

'Dodging along through the trees,' said Roger. 'Good old Homer.'

They filled the kettle at Titty's well and, taking turns to carry it, set out once more for the gulch. Long before they reached it, they could hear the 'thud, thud, thud' of the crushing mill.

'Squashy Hat's simply bound to hear it, too,' said Dorothea.

'Hey,' said Titty, as they came down the steep side of the gulch. 'Hey,' she called, to make herself heard through the steady thudding of the pestle. 'Squashy'll hear you. Won't he come to see what you're doing? It's a terrific noise . . .'

Nancy stopped pounding, and then they could hear, thin as if far away, the ring of hammer on chisel inside the mine, where John and Peggy were getting out more quartz. Dick and Susan were busy panning, joggling the frying-pan.

'Can't be helped,' said Nancy. 'And we've plenty of scouts. It wouldn't take a minute to hide everything away in the mine. Besides he'll never try jumping when we're all here. It's afterwards there's a danger. He might come snooping along before there's anyone about.'

'He's just tried to catch Homer,' said Dorothea. 'He loosed a falcon from his wrist . . .'

'We didn't exactly see him do it,' said Titty. 'But we saw the hawk come down on Homer the moment he'd started . . .'

'He didn't get him?' Nancy started up.

'No,' said Roger. 'Homer did some jolly good dodging and got into the trees. Then the hawk went back.'

'Will Homer get to Beckfoot all right?' said Titty.

'Oh yes,' said Nancy. 'He'll be a bit late, that's all. The same thing happened once before. Perhaps it's the same hawk . . .'

'Not Squashy's,' said Dorothea, with disappointment.

'Why not?' said Nancy. 'Yes. It's just the sort of thing he would do. What's Squashy up to now?'

Even Nancy was glad to stop crushing. She climbed with them up the side of the gulch and looked up the hillside. There was Squashy Hat, and there, above him, were the white splashes he had painted on the rocks.

'Fetch John,' said Nancy suddenly. 'Giminy. . . . This is serious.'

Roger was gone. Sliding and stumbling down the steep side of the gulch he shouted into the mine. 'Quick. Quick. John. Nancy wants you . . .'

John came hurrying out. Peggy was close behind him. Susan and Dick were already scrambling up to join Nancy.

'What is it?' said John.

'The white spots,' said Nancy. 'Gummocks we were not to notice it before. They're in a straight line . . .'

'Like leading lights,' said John. 'So they are.'

'But, barbecued billygoats!' cried Nancy. 'Can't you *see*? They're pointing exactly HERE.'

It was true. All the white spots were in line with each other, and that line, if carried on down the hill and across the Topps, would touch Golden Gulch.

'And each new one he does is a bit nearer,' said John.

'He's a lot nearer now than the bottom white splash,' said Titty.

'And exactly in a line with all the others,' said Dick.

'He's painting another now,' cried Dorothea.

They could all see a white patch growing even as they watched. Squashy Hat straightened himself. They saw him stoop once more. 'Hiding the paint-pot,' said Nancy. They saw him look up the hillside at those other splashes, and then, turning round, look long and carefully over the Topps.

Then, as if his work was done for the day, he picked up his coat, flung it over one shoulder and went striding off, coming down the hillside and working across towards the Dundale road. There, where he had been, another white glaring splash of paint brought the line he was marking another three or four hundred yards nearer to the gulch.

'That settles it,' said John. 'I'm going to sleep here tonight.'

'Let's all stay,' said Roger.

'Watch and watch,' said Titty.

'What about the camp?' said Susan. 'And water? And milk and everything?'

'Someone ought to be here,' said John.

'I will,' said Nancy.

'Oh no,' said Peggy, who hated sleeping in a tent alone.

'There isn't any thunder,' said Nancy.

'There might be,' said Peggy.

'Well, I'm going to stop, anyhow,' said Roger. 'I found it.'

'It's only for two nights,' said John. 'If we pan a good lot by tomorrow night, we'll take it to Slater Bob next day, and once he's in it, too, Squashy'll be done for.'

'Tents?' asked Susan, and Roger knew she had given way.

'No need,' said John. 'Sleeping-bags . . .'

That night Golden Gulch was never unguarded. When they went back to the camp for supper, Nancy and John took turns in keeping watch from the top of the look-out tree. After supper, John and Roger, each with a sleeping-bag rolled up and stowed in his knapsack, went off again into the dusk. The others watched them and, long after they had lost sight of those dim figures, waited on the top of the Great Wall staring out over the Topps.

At last, when dark had fallen and Susan was telling them it was time to be in bed, they saw the distant flashing of a torch.

'Something's happened,' said Dorothea.

'Signalling from Mars,' said Dick. 'Do you remember?'

'Shut up,' said Nancy. 'It's a message. Who's got a torch

with some life in it? Flash back. . . . Three flashes, so they'll know we're watching.'

Peggy flashed her torch.

Out there in the darkness the flashing began again. Longs and shorts. Shorts and longs. Nancy was reading the flashes and saying the letters out loud.

'G . . . O . . . O . . . D . . . end of word . . . N . . . I . . . G . . . H . . . T . . .'

'Go on, Peggy. Flash back "Good night" to them.'

There was a pause. Flashing began once more from out on the moor.

'Y . . . O . . . H . . . O . . . end of word.'

'That's Roger.' Everybody laughed. There were no more flashes.

'John's made him go to bed,' said Susan.

'Come on,' said Nancy. 'John's jolly well right. I'm nearly dead anyway with all that crushing. And another day of it tomorrow.'

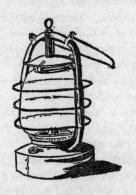

CHAPTER 23

JACK-IN-THE-BOX

ROGER woke early. It had been too late the night before to make a really good heather bed and, though he was by now well accustomed to sleeping in his tent, sleeping in the open was a little different, and the sun on his face and an ache in his hip-bone worked better than any alarm clock. He looked at John, but John was sleeping with his head in the crook of his arm. He tried to go to sleep again and failed, and so lay there, planning his day. More crushing and panning. Well, he supposed it couldn't be helped, but it was almost a pity there wasn't something else to find. At last he crawled out of his sleeping-bag and had a look round the gulch. There had been no visitors in the night. There were none in sight this morning. Only on the long slope of the Screes there were the white splashes marking how Squashy Hat had been coming nearer and nearer. He looked across towards Tyson's wood. No. Yes. A wisp of pale smoke, and then a steady stream poured straight up into the air above the trees.

'Hi! John,' shouted Roger. 'Time to get up. Susan's started making breakfast.'

John yawned and stretched himself, sat up, kicked free from his bag, and then, turning it inside out, spread it in the sun. Roger, watching him, did the same. Yawning and sleepy-eyed they set out across the Topps.

'No one came,' said Roger.

'He might have if we hadn't been there,' said John.

'What do we do today?'

'Crush and pan.'

'All of us?'

237

'Nancy's going to Beckfoot for the pigeons. And we'll want scouts out, of course.'

'I'll scout,' said Roger.

'Hullo! Swallows ahoy!' Nancy was hailing them from the top of the Great Wall.

'Hullo!'

'News!' shouted Nancy.

She came to meet them with a letter in her hand.

'It's from mother. Susan got it when she went down for the milk. Mother's sent the pigeons back, so no one need go to Beckfoot today.'

'Oh, good,' said Roger. 'So Homer did dodge the hawk and get home.'

'Jolly late, she says. But that's not the news. A huge crate of stuff has come for Uncle Jim. No Timothy. . . . But he may turn up any day if he was sent off at the same time. And mother says she thinks Uncle Jim must be nearly home. We haven't a minute to lose.'

'If we go it all day we'll have panned enough by tonight,' said John. 'We'll take it to Slater Bob tomorrow to get it made into an ingot.'

*

Breakfast was eaten in a hurry. John and Nancy took turns in keeping a look out from the tree, but today, at least, Squashy Hat was not getting up early. After breakfast everybody went to the gulch. Yesterday's work did not more than half fill a small tin that had once held cocoa.

'Isn't it enough?' said Dick, dipping a finger in the golden dust and watching it sparkle in the sunlight. 'What about taking it to Slater Bob now, to let him test it and make sure.'

But John and Nancy had made up their minds. They wanted to take the old man enough gold dust to make a respectable ingot. They meant to fill the cocoa tin to the brim.

The day's work began. John, Nancy, Susan and Peggy were mining, crushing and panning. Dick, Dorothea, Roger and Titty were posted in good lurking places to give warning if Squashy Hat came anywhere near. It would never do to have him sneaking up to the gulch and finding the miners actually busy with the gold. For some time the work went steadily on, and then Squashy Hat was sighted, coming up from the Dundale road. A signal was passed to the gulch. Just in case, work stopped, and everything was hidden in the mine. The scouts, lying in the bracken, watched the enemy go by. Today, instead of going up the Screes to his white spots, he marched straight across the Topps to Ling Scar, the long ridge that came down from Kanchenjunga towards the valley of the Amazon. The scouts watched him climbing up and up until at last he disappeared over the sky line. They signalled 'All clear'. A hand waved from the heather at the edge of the gulch. A minute or two later they heard the dull thud, thud, thud of the crushing mill begin once more.

'They're all right for a bit, anyhow,' said Roger, who had plans of his own. 'What about looking for diamonds? In one of the other workings.'

'Better report at headquarters first,' said Dorothea, and the four scouts went dutifully back.

'Good,' said Captain Nancy, resting from the crushing for a moment as she listened to what they had to say. 'Walking? Was he going somewhere or just mooching about?'

'He walked straight ahead,' said Dick.

'And jolly fast,' said Roger.

'Just as if he was keeping an appointment,' said Dorothea.

'Oh well,' said Nancy. 'He won't get anything out of Slater Bob.'

The scouts waited a moment. Were they wanted for any-thing else? Nancy started again banging away with the pestle. Susan came out of the mine with a new lot of quartz.

'Come on,' said Roger.

'Where are you off to?' asked Susan.

'Going diamond-mining,' said Roger.

'Who is?'

'I've got a letter to finish,' said Titty.

'Dick and Dot are coming, anyhow,' said Roger.

'All right,' said Nancy. 'Scout at the same time. Keep an eye lifting for him when he comes back. We may have to head him off.'

'Aye, aye, Sir,' said Roger, joyfully.

'What do you want Titty's string for?' said Susan.

'To find our way out,' said Roger.

'But you mustn't go into the old workings,' said Susan.

'Oh, I say,' said Roger. 'Then how can we find the diamonds?'

'Well, you mustn't go into any John and I haven't been in. Even Nancy says that lots of them aren't safe.'

'There are those two caves we were in the other day,' said John, coming out of the mine. 'They're safe enough. You can explore them as much as you like. I say, Nancy, what about this bit? Pretty good, isn't it?'

'The best yet,' said Nancy.

'I can take the string then,' said Roger. 'And look here, Titty, do let me have your torch, I used mine right up finding the gold.'

*

The morning slipped away. Susan and Peggy had tossed up who should make dinner. The winner was to be the cook. Susan had called 'Heads' and so it had been, and she had left the others still working away in the gulch and gone back to the camp, where she found Titty, who had finished one letter, to Daddy in China, and was busy on another to Mother and the whooping Bridget. Susan put the kettle on. That morning in going down for the milk she had borrowed a saucepan secretly from Mrs Tyson. The others, thinking that all the cooking things were being used for panning in the gulch were expecting the poorest kind of dinner, and Susan was going to give them a surprise. She was hotting up two tinned steak and kidney puddings, and a lot of new potatoes and some French beans. Titty wrote slowly on. She had already told the best of natives that they were all very well and that they had found gold and that Captain Flint was going to be most awfully pleased. . . . 'But the armadillo's never come, and Dorothea thinks he was probably buried at sea. Roger was the one who found the gold. I found water with a forked stick. It was horrid at first but I didn't mind it the second time. Did you ever try doing it? How is Bridget? Do come quick. Now we've found the gold we're going to let a real miner make it into an ingot. We'll be ready to go to Wild Cat Island as soon as Captain Flint comes. But we can't till he does because we have to guard the mine. Much love. Your loving Titty. Roger would send his love but he is diamond-mining. Much love. I mean it. Titty.'

'Dinner's nearly ready,' said Susan at last. 'Better go and signal to Roger and the D.'s and between us we'll carry it across to the gulch . . .'

*

Diamond-mining had not been a great success.

Roger, Dick and Dorothea, a little tired of exploring caves that had been explored already, were resting in the heather on the northern side of the Topps, where Ling Scar, that steep spur of Kanchenjunga, rose above them like a wall.

Roger was winding the end of the string round the ball

which had slipped and unrolled a few yards of itself. It had not been of much use after all. Exploring those old caves could have been done without a string. Not one of them was more than a few yards deep.

'It isn't really fair,' said Roger. 'I'd never have found the gold if I hadn't gone into that mine in the gulch without waiting for anybody else.'

Dick said nothing. He was lying on his back, with his hands over his spectacled eyes, looking up through his fingers into the blazing sky. He had tried using goggles but found them too uncomfortable when he had to wear spectacles as well. Somewhere up there was a hawk, perhaps the same hawk that had swooped at Homer ... a black speck ... there it was again ... or had it gone? ... the sky was so bright that his eyes watered and he closed them, and it was as if a warm red curtain shut out everything ... he remembered the circulation of the blood and began wondering if each drop of blood ran the whole way round and how long it took. ..

Dorothea agreed with Roger. Coming along the edge of the Topps under Ling Scar, they had seen hole after hole in the side of the ridge, and each one had looked more promising than the last. And it was such waste to leave them unexplored when you had a ball of string waiting to be unrolled and far better than any trail of crumbs like those dropped by Hansel and Gretel. And what if the three of them should really find something. If gold, why not diamonds? In any case it seemed a pity not to look. At the same time she understood Susan's feelings.

'She can't do the cooking and keep an eye on us. .... And she knows the others are all too busy.'

'If only I hadn't found the gold we'd still be looking for it,' said Roger.

'Wouldn't it be awful?' said Dorothea. 'Nancy says there's

no time to spare as it is. And there isn't. He'll be coming any day . . .'

'So'll mother and Bridget,' said Roger, seeing a new light. 'And then there'll be blasting . . . and we'll go to the island . . . and have a battle with the houseboat. I'll swim you round the island. Or from the island to the shore. That's farther. Can you swim?'

'Of course he can,' said Dorothea. 'Why, last holidays when he fell overboard . . .'

The words faded into silence.

'Dick,' she whispered.

Roger had seen what she had seen and was lying flat as a snake against a rock. Dick opened one spectacled eye and found Dorothea's face close to his own. The look on it was enough to keep him quiet. In a moment, he too had seen.

Not thirty yards away from them, where the dried mosses of the Topps ended like a sea against the barrier of the ridge, Squashy Hat stood blinking in the sunlight beside some rocks. He took off his squashy hat and brushed it with his sleeve. Then he took off his coat and looked at it, dusting away some dirt that he saw there. It was clear that he had not the slightest suspicion that he was not alone. But how had he come there? There had been no one there a moment before. They had themselves seen him go over the ridge early in the day. Even during their hunting for diamonds they had never forgotten that they were scouts as well.

The sight of Squashy Hat or anyone else walking on the Topps would have caught their attention at once. And here he was, close to them. If he had come down the ridge they must have seen him, and he must have seen them, but anybody could tell that he did not know they were there. They crouched behind a rock and watched.

Squashy Hat looked round over the Topps, as if to choose

SQUASHY HAT COMES OUT OF THE HILL

his direction, and then set off at his usual steady long-legged march.

'Oughtn't we to head him off?' said Dorothea.

'He isn't going near the gulch,' said Roger.

'But how did he get here?' said Dick.

They watched the tall, lanky figure striding over the mosses and then, like Indians, wormed their way towards the place where they had first seen him.

There, among the rocks, they found a hole hardly higher than one of themselves. They stared through it into the darkness but could see nothing because of the bright sunshine outside.

'It's a mine,' said Roger.

'He must have been hiding in it,' said Dorothea.

'But we saw him go over the ridge,' said Roger.

'We'd have seen him if he went in here,' said Dick. 'There must be another way in.'

'Jolly good snakework,' said Roger. 'If he got here without us spotting him. . . . I say, it's quite a decent tunnel inside.'

He had pulled out the torch Titty had lent him and was flashing it into the hole. Dick and Dorothea peered past him.

'It must have had a bigger opening once,' said Dick.

'Half a minute,' said Roger, backing hurriedly. 'I'd better fasten the end of the string.'

'Oh! but look here, Roger, ought we?' said Dorothea. 'Susan said . . .'

'Squashy's lots older than John or Susan,' said Roger. 'Susan said we weren't to explore any hole where she and John hadn't been, so as to be sure it was safe. Well, he's older than both of them put together, and he's a native, too. It's perfectly absolutely certain this one's all right. . . . And here's a bit of heather that'll just do . . .'

He squatted on the ground and tied the end of his string to

the brown stringy stem of the heather. Then, letting the ball unroll as he moved, he went back into the tunnel.

'Come on, Dick,' he said. 'Somebody else must hold a torch. It takes two hands to look after this string.'

'It must be all right,' said Dick. 'We've only just seen him come out.'

'Just a little way,' said Dorothea.

A moment later all three of them had disappeared into the side of the hill. Once inside, they stopped to look out from the darkness of the tunnel across the sunlit Topps. Squashy Hat was walking steadily away.

'Oughtn't somebody to watch him?' said Dorothea.

'He isn't going anywhere near the gulch,' said Roger. 'Come on. This is a bigger cave than ours. We might find anything.'

'How did you find the gold in ours?' said Dorothea.

'Oh, just banging about with a hammer,' said Roger. 'Come on. Let's go a bit further in. Look out for the string.'

'It isn't as dry as ours,' said Dick, who was looking carefully at a damp, shiny place on one wall. . . . 'Probably because ours is only shallow and this one goes into the hill itself.'

'Well, we mustn't go very far, anyway,' said Dorothea, 'but do let's find something.' Already she saw their proud return, opening their hands to show the treasure they had found. Probably not gold . . . but something else. . . . Silver would hardly be worth while. . . . Diamonds? Why not? Underground, in a place like this, they might find anything.

'Do look out for the string,' said Roger. 'If you tread on it and bust it we won't find our way back.'

'But we can see the light at the opening,' said Dick.

'I can't now,' said Roger. 'The tunnel twists a bit. . . . Where's your torch? I say, this is real exploring . . .'

'Not too far,' said Dorothea.

'Hullo,' said Dick, who was tapping with his hammer. 'Wood. They've been propping it up a bit . . .'

'Or a hiding place,' said Dorothea. 'They may have hid all sorts of things behind the wood.'

'Propping it up,' said Dick. 'It's been a bit crumbly. You can see here. There's only just room to squeeze past . . .'

'Perhaps that's the end,' said Dorothea hopefully.

'It isn't,' said Dick. 'It gets bigger and goes on again.'

'You wriggle through, Dot,' said Roger. 'Or I will, and you take the string for a moment. Don't go and tread on it again.'

They climbed over the loose stuff that had half choked the passage and threw the light from their torches this way and that over the solid stone walls.

'Hooo . . . Hoooo,' said Roger, making his voice hollow to match the tunnel. 'I say, we're going to come to the end of the string pretty soon.'

'We'll have to turn back then, anyhow,' said Dorothea.

*

It was just about now that Titty, who had seen them lurking in the heather far away, and had herself taken cover to watch Squashy Hat, looked for them again and could not see them. She had her message for them, from Susan, and had to find them. And now they had vanished altogether. Good scout-work, of course, but, at this moment, rather a nuisance.

PESTLE·AND·MORTAR

CHAPTER 24

BURIED ALIVE

TITTY was sure she had seen them over there under Ling Scar, the long spur of Kanchenjunga that was like an arm flung round the northern side of High Topps. She had caught sight of Squashy Hat first, striding towards her over the rough ground, 'late for dinner at Atkinson Ground', she had guessed. She had watched him carefully, to make sure he was not going too near Golden Gulch, in which case she would have had to dash across in front of him to warn the prospectors. Then, when she looked again for Dick, Roger and Dorothea, she could not see a sign of them. They had been lurking behind some rocks, so as not to be seen by Squashy Hat. That she had understood. But he was a long way this side of them by now. There was no friendly bracken patch over there in which they could be snaking along unseen. They had not had time to move very far, and Titty brought the telescope to bear on one group of rocks after another, looking for a hat, a hand, a leg, no matter what, that should betray their hiding place.

'Jolly good Indianing,' said Titty to herself, and then, as she had a message to give, and it was no good signalling at people you couldn't see, she set off at a run across the dried-up mosses.

*

This surely was the place where she had seen them last. That was the face of rock they had been looking at. Why, there were the marks of their hammers. She looked carefully round. And there were the remains of three sucked oranges carefully pushed away to be tidy in among the roots of the heather. 'They ought to have brought them back to the camp to burn,' thought Titty. 'But they may have pushed them in there just for the time.' But where were they? She looked back across High Topps. Squashy Hat was already nearing the Dundale Road hurrying home to his dinner. She called out, not too loud.

'Ahoy!'

She listened.

'Ahoy, you idiots,' she called again. 'Grub! Susan says you're to come.'

What was that? Was somebody answering? But where from?

Titty glanced at one after another of the black holes along the foot of the Scar. After what Susan had said, surely nobody would have gone into one of the old workings even to hide from Squashy. And then, suddenly, she saw a tuft of heather jerk. It was a windless day. Perhaps there was a weasel in the heather. Very quietly Titty moved towards it. It jerked again, and this time she saw the string stretched from the heather and disappearing into a tunnel.

'Roger!' she called.

Dick and Dorothea were different. Perhaps it was all right for them, but what Susan would say if she knew that Roger had gone into one of the unexplored workings, Titty did not like to think.

'Roger!' she called again.

The string jerked, but there was no other reply. If all three of them were in there and talking, they would probably never hear her. What dreadful bad luck that she had lent Roger her torch. He must be brought out at once. Titty took hold of the string and gave it a pull. There was a faint jerk at the other end of it. She did not pull it again. What if it were to break on a sharp edge of rock, and the others were to be left

249

without it. Titty looked round again from the mouth of the hole. There was nobody in sight except Squashy, just disappearing as he dropped down from the Topps to the Dundale road. No sign of Susan. No sign of the miners at Golden Gulch. There was no one to whom she could signal. And, anyhow, it would be better to get Roger out before ever John or Susan, specially Susan, knew that he had gone in.

Titty took the string lightly in her fingers and set out stoutly into the darkness.

For the first few yards she could see well enough. It was odd, coming in from the dried-up fell, to feel her feet on mud, or at least on ground that was sticky. She remembered going with the others to see Slater Bob, and the puddles in the tunnel, and the trickle of water at the side of the narrow trolleyway. But it grew darker very quickly, and it was not at all pleasant, feeling along the rough surface of the rock, and letting her fingers slip gently along the string.

'Hi! Stop! Roger!' she called.

'Hullo!' There was an answer. Quite near. But why was there no light? She was sure Dick and Dot had taken their torches when they set out, and she had given her own to Roger.

'Hullo!' she called back. 'Where are you?'

'Hullo!' came the answer again. More like Dorothea than Roger.

'Ow!' She bumped into something right in front of her. Rough, damp wood. There was a rattle of small stones and loose earth.

Titty stood still. At least she had matches. She pulled out her box and struck a match. She saw that she was at a sort of kink in the tunnel, which turned sharply right, and then left again. It had been roughly timbered at the bend, many, many years ago, and above her head were bending planks, resting at the sides on upright timbers. Earth and small stones were

'THEY'VE GONE IN!'

dropping through the spaces between the overhead planks, and some of the supporting timbers seemed to have slipped, so that the tunnel was already very narrow, and to get round the bend she had to creep over a pile of stones and earth. Just the very sort of tunnel that Susan had been afraid of. Just the sort of place that even Captain Nancy had said was not particularly safe. She must get Roger out of it at once.

'Roger,' she called. 'Wait a minute. Don't go any farther.'

'Hullo!'

There they were, close to. She saw the string leading round the corner, just as her match went out, burning the tips of her fingers. A moment later, in the darkness, she saw the glimmer of light on the wall, and then, creeping on, she saw, not far ahead of her, the shadowy figures and the electric torches of the exploring three.

Again she bumped into one of the old timbers at the side of the tunnel. Again something seemed to give, and a shower of small stuff came down on her head from between the old planks with which miners long since dead had roofed in their narrow alleyway.

'Roger!' she called. 'Stop! You've got to come out at once. Susan said we weren't to go anywhere in the workings unless she or John had been in first to make sure it was all right.'

'But it *is* all right,' said Roger. 'Squashy Hat came out of this hole himself, and he's bigger than either of them.'

'But it's all falling to bits,' said Titty. 'Listen. It's still trickling down where I bumped into the side. Just listen to it. You're to come back at once. Come on. Look here. Are you an AB or aren't you? The captains'll be awfully mad. As well as Susan . . .'

'Out of the very bowels of the earth he came,' said Dorothea, as much to herself as to the others.

'He just bobbed up like an earthworm,' said Roger, 'and brushed his old hat and off he went.'

'But listen,' said Titty.

Dick was flashing his torch over the sides of the tunnel which, here, were solid rock, without any supporting timbers. Everything here was solid enough. But from behind them, at that kink in the tunnel, where the roof had been shored up with wooden props, and the planks were bulging overhead, came again the noise of falling earth.

'It was quite all right when we came through,' said Roger.

'But listen to it,' said Titty. 'Come on. We've got to get out quick.'

There was the noise of a heavier stone falling in the tunnel behind them, the creak of splitting wood, again that noise of trickling earth, suddenly growing louder, louder. There was another creak, and then a dull rumble and a crash, followed by little noises of stone on stone, falling gradually away into silence.

Roger and Dorothea flashed their torches on each other's faces. Dick was already hurrying back towards the place where the noise had been. Titty grabbed Roger by the arm, and herself started back along the tunnel.

'Look out,' said Roger. 'Look out for the string. Don't get it tangled in your feet.'

'We can't get out this way,' said Dick quietly. 'Those old timbers must have slipped and the tunnel's blocked.'

'Shut in,' said Dorothea.

'But we've got to get out,' said Titty.

'Can't we climb over?' said Roger.

'Buried alive,' said Dorothea.

Their torches showed a mass of loose earth and stones with here and there the end of a rotten timber sticking out of it. The tunnel was blocked. The ancient roofing had given way and a tremendous weight of stuff had come down with it.

'More'll come down if we try climbing over,' said Titty.

'They'll come and dig us out,' said Dorothea. 'They'll find the string just going into nothing but earth.' She was looking at the string at her feet, disappearing under the fallen stuff that blocked the tunnel.

Titty's voice rose suddenly higher. 'But they mustn't!' she said. 'They mustn't. Susan'll think Roger's dead. We've got to dig through it ourselves ... quick ... quick, before they guess what's happened.'

'Look out,' said Dick. 'These timbers are giving, too. Get away. Get back to where it's all rock.'

They scuttered back along the tunnel.

'I say, I'm awfully sorry, Titty,' said Roger.

'Well, we'd better go on,' said Dick calmly. 'We'll be able to get out where Squashy Hat got in. He didn't get in here ...'

Dick's words somehow surprised everybody. With the mouth of the tunnel being suddenly closed behind them, the others had forgotten that they could still go forward even if they could not go back.

'Come on,' said Titty. 'As quick as ever we can. Susan'll be looking for us almost at once. She'd sent me to bring you home for grub.'

Roger tugged at the string. It was no good. He pulled it with all his force, and the string broke. Titty knew just what the searchers would find, the little clump of heather, the string leading from it into the hill, and then vanishing under such a weight of earth and rock as might take days to shift. If once they saw that, nothing could save them from thinking that Roger and the D.'s and Titty herself were buried underneath it.

'Oh, don't waste time,' she cried. 'Come on. Don't bother about winding up the string.'

'We may want it,' said Dick, who was no longer absent-minded. Just as when they found the cragfast sheep in the winter holidays, he seemed to be thinking of everything at once and to know what to do.

'Don't waste the torches,' he said. 'Just in case. Put yours out, Dot, and yours, Roger. We'll use mine up first. We must have one to make sure of the footmarks.'

'Footmarks?'

'Squashy Hat's,' said Dick. 'I was looking at them just before we heard you shout. It's damp on the ground, and they're as clear as can be. . . . Not here . . .'

'We've all been trampling round like buffalo,' said Titty, almost laughing with relief.

'Here you are,' said Dick. 'This is as far as we got. And there are the marks of Squashy's boots.'

Titty looked at them in the light of Dick's torch held close to the ground. Large boots, his had been, with climbing-nails round the edges of the soles.

'You couldn't have better hoofmarks,' she said.

'Lots of them,' said Dick, 'and all pointing one way. He's been through more than once. We've only got to follow them and we're bound to come out somewhere.'

PESTLE·AND·MORTAR

CHAPTER 25

HURRYING MOLES

It was not too easy to move in single file along the tunnel by the light of a single torch, but they knew that Dick was right. Torches lasted a long time when you just flashed them on and off, but they faded away very quickly if you kept them lit and tried to read by them or anything like that. With only three good torches they could not afford to waste light. Who could tell how long the tunnel might be?

Dick went first, stooping low, lighting up the big footprints clearly marked on the damp floor of the tunnel. Year after year had gone by with no one passing that way. Dust had fallen and turned to mud, and now there were the big footprints, heel and toe, heel and toe, made by Squashy. This was easier tracking than when Dick and Titty had tried to follow Nancy's footsteps up the dry path through the wood.

After Dick came Roger and Dorothea, looking forward into the darkness over the stooping Dick, and seeing the rocky sides and roof of the tunnel, lit up here and there from the torch that Dick was holding only a foot above the ground as he looked from footprint to footprint. Titty came last, but all three of them were as near Dick and his light as they well could get, and Titty was urging him to get on a little quicker.

'She's sure to come to look for us,' she said. 'Do hurry up. Never mind the footprints. So long as the tunnel doesn't divide we must be going right.'

'All the footprints head this way so far,' said Dick.

'Then get on,' said Titty.

Dick hurried on. At least, he did not examine each separate footprint, but walked forward, content to see that the footprints were there. On and on he walked, the others close behind him. The tunnel was narrow, but its walls and roof were rock.

'It's all right,' he said quietly, 'so long as there's no more timbering. Nobody would bother to put wood unless they were afraid of something falling.'

He flashed the dimming torch on walls and roof.

'Squashy must have got in somewhere,' he said.

Suddenly there was a check. Titty felt that something was different. They were walking on hard rock. Dick bent again.

'No more footprints,' he said.

'Do let's get along,' said Titty.

'Let's have a better torch,' said Dick. 'Come on, Roger, the one you've got isn't bad. You come in front, and we'll give mine a rest. It's nearly dead.'

Roger changed places with Dick, and galloped eagerly forward. Suddenly he stopped.

'What are we going to do now?' he asked.

The tunnel opened into a vault where four or five other tunnels met. They all seemed about the same size, and not one of them was exactly opposite the tunnel through which they had come.

Roger waved his torch round.

'Stop,' said Dick. 'Where did we come out? We mustn't move till we know.'

'This one,' said Titty.

'Look here,' said Dick. 'You just stand where you are so that we shan't get muddled.'

'Awful if we tried to get back the same way,' said Dorothea.

'I'm going to try along each tunnel till I find more foot-prints,' said Dick.

'Take the string,' said Roger.

'Good idea,' said Dick.

'Can't we both go?' said Roger.

'No,' said Titty. 'You're no good at tracks, and Dick is.'

'You look after the end of the string,' said Dick. 'And look here. Let me have the good torch. You take mine for now.'

He was off, creeping along with Roger's torch, searching the floor of one of the tunnels. For a moment or two Titty, standing in the mouth of the tunnel through which they had come, could see him shadowed by the light. Then his tunnel bent, and the three in the vault were left in absolute darkness.

Roger switched on Dick's torch. There was no life left in it. It made a feeble red glow, but even that was better than nothing.

'Don't let go of the end of the string, Rogie,' said Titty.

'Can't,' said Roger. 'I've got it twisted round my finger.'

'He's coming back,' said Dorothea.

A glimmer, faint at first, grew brighter, and then the torch shone out, as Dick turned the corner and came straight towards them, coiling the string as he came.

'Not a sign of anything there,' he said. 'I'll try the next.'

'Squashy simply must have come through one of them,' said Dorothea. She spoke in a very low voice, listening all the time to the steps of Dick going away down the second tunnel.

'It's going to be all right,' said Roger, to himself as much as to Dorothea.

'It's the time that matters,' said Titty. 'He's coming back again. . . . No good?'

'I went the full length of the string,' said Dick, 'and the ground was quite sticky enough to show if anybody'd been there. It'll probably be this one. One of these two must be the main tunnel. They're both about opposite ours. You haven't moved, have you?'

'Not an inch,' said Titty.

The next moment they were startled by a cheerful shout

from Dick that echoed hollowly in the vault as if it came from all the tunnels at once.

'Come on,' he shouted. 'Got them again.'

'Can I go in front?' said Roger.

'Better let Dick do it,' said Titty.

'Oh well,' said Roger. 'Anyway, I'll carry the string.'

The small procession hurried on. For a long time there was no talking.

'It must go right through the hill,' said Dorothea at last.

'It'll come out on the other side where the quarries are,' said Roger.

'But that's miles and miles,' said Titty. 'And we've got to get back.'

'Will the torches last?' said Roger. Their second torch was already growing dim.

'There's still mine,' said Dorothea.

'I say,' said Titty. 'Perhaps this is the Old Level. Nancy did say it's supposed to go right through. Perhaps Squashy was talking to Slater Bob and came back this way.'

'We must be more than half through,' said Dick.

They stumbled along as well as they could.

'It's a pity this didn't happen when all our torches were new,' said Roger.

'Let's have yours, Dot. We'd better give Roger's a rest. It may buck up a bit if we do . . .'

Dick stopped and gave Roger back his torch. Dorothea held out hers.

'It's not much better,' she said. 'I went and used it the night before last, putting down something I'd forgotten till I woke up in the dark.'

'Better than either of the others,' said Dick.

'Listen!' said Titty sharply.

'Falling in somewhere else,' said Dorothea.

'No. Somebody's at work,' said Titty.

'Bet it's Slater Bob,' said Roger.

'Come on,' said Titty.

Two minutes later they stopped short. A new noise sounded close by, a deep hollow rumbling and clattering like a goods wagon banging over the points in a railway siding. A light suddenly appeared, and a small loaded trolley swung round out of a side tunnel and rattled away ahead of them with a man trotting behind it.

'Slater Bob,' cried Roger. 'I knew it was. That must be the tunnel from his slate mine. We're nearly out.'

'Don't shout,' said Titty, just in time. They were safe now, and she could think of other things. 'Look here,' she said. 'We must find out first if Squashy was talking to him.'

In another minute they had reached the place where the side tunnel from Slater Bob's quarry joined the Old Level.

'Doesn't it seem ages since we were here?' said Dorothea.

'He's been here,' said Dick. 'Squashy Hat's footprints come across out of the side tunnel. They wouldn't if he'd been walking straight through.'

'Is Slater Bob a friend or an enemy?' asked Dorothea.

'That's just it,' said Titty. 'We don't know. Anyway, hurry up now. We've got an awful climb before we get back.'

They all but ran along the Old Level, but could not really go fast, because of tumbling over the sleepers of the little trolley rails. They came to the turn in the level and, there, a bright pinprick in the darkness far ahead of them, they could see daylight at the entrance.

'Saved,' said Dorothea.

'Not if Susan's found that string,' said Titty.

'She may have found it and sent off Sophocles for help to dig us out,' said Dorothea.

'Awful,' said Titty. 'Do buck up, Roger . . .'

And then, at last, breathless, blinded by the sudden sun-

shine, the hurrying moles found themselves staggering about
under the open sky.

*

'And where are you come from?'

A broad-shouldered old man, with huge hands that hung
below his knees, was looking at them from beside the trolley
that he had begun to unload. It was the old miner, Slater
Bob.

They blinked back at him.

'Were ye hiding when I come out wi' trolley? I never saw
nowt . . . nor heard nowt.'

'We've come right through from High Topps,' said Roger,
and was going on to tell the whole story when he saw Titty
looking at him.

'Ye've not come right through the level?'

'We couldn't help it,' said Dick.

Titty looked at Dick. Was it safe to say anything at all.

'We've got to rush back,' said Titty. 'The others won't
know where we are.'

'Yon end's not fit,' said the old miner. 'Ye haven't left
them in t' level? Miss Nancy ought to know yon end's not
safe.'

'They're all right,' said Titty. 'They can't get in. A lot
of rock's tumbled down.'

'By gum,' said the old man. 'Born lucky, some folk. But
what were you doing in t' level at all?'

'We saw someone come out,' said Roger, 'so we knew it
was all right.'

'Aw reet for t' likes o' him. Why, he's a miner. Been mining up and down since he was so high. Diamond mines an' all.
It'll take more'n t' Owd Level to kill t' likes of him. Why,
he's as good a miner as I am. He was telling me only this
morning he'd like to put some new timbering along at far

end. And now it's come down. Lucky you're not under it . . .'

'Has he been through before?' asked Roger.

'Aye,' said the old man. 'More'n once, when he's been having a crack with me. And what are you doing on High Topps? You can tell Miss Nancy from me she should know better than to let you folk into t' levels.'

Titty began picking her way through the slate heaps. Who knew what Roger would say next. One thing was clear. Squashy Hat had somehow got on the right side of Slater Bob, and it was not safe to say anything at all. And anyway, there wasn't a minute to lose. It might be rude to dash away, but there were Susan and Nancy and John and Peggy on the other side of the hill not knowing what had become of them. If they had found that scrap of string leading into the tunnel, they would be thinking the very worst.

'We've simply got to go,' she said. 'Good-bye. We didn't mean to come through the level when we started . . .'

'So long's no harm's done,' said the old man. 'It's been ready to fall long since. And Mr Stedding'll mostly come over the fell.'

'The man with the squashy hat?' asked Dorothea.

'Nay, there's nowt wrong wi' his hat,' said Slater Bob. 'And the mining that man's done, it's a pleasure to hear him . . .'

'Good-bye,' called Titty.

'Good-bye,' called the others.

'We'll come out on High Topps if we go straight over?' asked Dick.

'Aye,' said the old man. 'Ye can't miss t' way. But you'd find it easier walking by t' road.'

'No time,' said Titty. 'We've simply got to rush.'

'Good-day to you,' called the old man, and turned again to lift huge slabs of slate in his great hands, taking them from his trolley, and setting them down with others waiting to be worked.

*

'You heard what he said?' whispered Titty, as they got clear of the loose stones by the opening of the level, and were climbing up the rocky slopes above it. 'You heard. He's in with Squashy Hat. And Nancy was going to ask him to help. I was afraid every minute you were going to tell him we'd found the gold.'

'I wasn't,' said Roger.

'Are you sure we're going all right?' asked Dorothea.

'So long as we're going straight up,' said Titty. 'And with Kanchenjunga over there.'

'But is he?' said Dorothea. 'We can't see the top of him.'

'It's all right,' said Titty.

'If only we had a compass,' said Roger.

'You can get lost even with one,' said Titty. 'Remember that fog on the way back to Swallowdale.'

Dick stopped and pulled out his watch. 'There is a way,' he said. 'I found it in a book last term. You point the hour hand at the sun, and then half-way between the hour and twelve o'clock is south . . . or north . . .'

'South,' said Titty, looking at the watch which Dick held in the palm of his hand. 'It can't be anything else. But where's High Topps?'

'Pretty well south, too,' said Dick.

'We're all right. But do hurry up.'

They climbed as fast as they could. Titty felt her want of breath almost hurting her. The sweat off Dick's forehead kept dripping on the glasses of his spectacles. Roger was bending forward and helping himself up with his hands. Dorothea was panting to herself, not out aloud, though the words seemed to drum in her ears. 'The next bit'll be the top. The next bit'll be the top.'

'Stick to it, Dot,' said Dick, trying to wipe his spectacles without stopping his climb.

'Go it, Rogie,' said Titty. 'Remember poor old Susie.'

'Poor old hen,' said Roger, and then he remembered that it was mostly his fault that they had gone into the level, and added, 'I don't really mean she's a hen.'

'So long as we aren't too late,' said Titty, and then for a long time, they climbed without another word.

At last, tired nearly out, they came to the top of the ridge. There, away to the right, rose the peak of Kanchenjunga. Away to the left were the Swallowdale fells on the farther side of the valley of the Amazon. But, though they were on the highest point of the ridge, they could not see down on High Topps. The ridge itself was wide, and they had to struggle across another hundred yards or so, of rock and heather, before they could see more than the corner of the wood by the Great Wall and a short white curling strip of the far away Dundale road. Then, at last, they could look down on the mining country.

'But where are they?' said Roger.

'They've dashed off to get help,' said Dorothea.

'Oh, no . . . no,' said Titty. Nothing could be worse than that.

'There's the gulch, anyway,' said Dick. 'And nobody there.'

They ran down a slope and up the other side, where a steep bit of rock let them look down the side of Ling Scar to the place where Roger, Dick and Dorothea had seen Squashy Hat come out of the hill, dust his old coat and stride away.

'There they are,' cried Roger.

'Yell. Yell,' said Titty. 'They're coming to the hole. They can't have seen it yet. Or have they? Wave anything you've got. Why haven't you got a handkerchief, Roger? Now you see what happens when you go off without one.'

Their throats were dry. It was as if their mouths were full of dust. The best shout they could raise was weak and short.

'Coo . . . eeee,' cried Titty, as her mother, that friendliest of all natives, had taught her long ago. But the sound seemed to carry no way. She might have been talking to Roger or Dick, near enough almost to touch.

'Ahoy . . .' shouted Roger, but had not breath to make the 'hoy' draw out to anything better than a croak.

'Come on,' said Titty. 'It's downhill. . . . But look out how you go. Don't go and twist another ankle.'

'They've seen us,' Dorothea whispered hoarsely.

Far away below on High Topps, the four figures of the elders had suddenly stopped moving.

'Give me your handkerchief,' said Titty. 'Oh, if only we had two sticks.'

Titty scrambled to the top of a big rock, and, with a hand-kerchief in each hand, waved her arms round and round. Yes. Down on High Topps, they were looking. She put her left hand behind her back, and held her right arm out and slanting downwards. Then she held her left arm slanting up and her right slanting down. She did it again, and then whirled both hands to show that she had finished a word.

Dick was struggling for his pocket-book.

'What's she said so far?' he asked, in a whisper, as he found the page where, in the Christmas holidays, Nancy had drawn the semaphore code for him.

'A . . . L . . . L All,' said Roger.

'W . . . E . . .,' said Dick, looking out the letters as Titty made them, 'L . . . L . . . Well.'

'What are they doing?' said Roger. 'Susan's turned round and she's walking away.'

'She's jolly mad,' said Titty.

'And John's beckoning,' said Dorothea. 'And Peggy's gone after Susan to bring her back.'

'Look out. Nancy's going to signal. Ow. She's using Morse and going an awful lick.'

Nancy was flicking a handkerchief to and fro, sometimes in a wide sweep from side to side, sometimes in a short flick above her head. Dick and Dorothea gave up all hope of reading her longs and shorts, but Titty and Roger read the letters out one by one.

'P . . . U . . . D . . . D . . . I . . . N . . . G.'

'Pudding,' said Roger. 'They've kept some for us.'

'She hasn't finished the word,' said Dick.

Titty was reading steadily on. 'H . . . E . . . A . . . D . . . S . . . End of word. Puddingheads . . .'

Puddingheads? Well, they had expected to be called worse things than that. All four of them felt rather better. If only Susan wasn't going to be too native. They ran, jumped, tumbled, climbed, slipped, and ran again, as they rushed down the ridge.

*

'Look here, Titty,' said Susan, who had been brought back and was waiting for them with the others. 'You ought to have had more sense. Taking them away up the fell like that when you knew it was dinner-time.'

'But she didn't,' said Dorothea.

'Yes, she did,' said Susan. 'I told her to bring you back at once. And that's hours and hours ago.'

'She didn't take us over the top,' said Roger.

'She only brought us back that way,' said Dick.

Not twenty yards away was the dark entrance to the Old Level, and do what they would, Dorothea and Titty could not keep their eyes from straying to that clump of heather just in front of it. Nancy's eyes followed theirs.

'It was my fault,' said Roger. 'We didn't mean to. Not at first. But we've been right through . . .'

'Through what?'

'Giminy,' cried Nancy suddenly. 'Look at this. . . . You don't mean to say you've been THROUGH? . . .'

'It's the Old Level,' said Peggy.

Susan turned on Roger. 'You promised you would never go into any of the mines unless John or I had gone in first and said it was all right . . .'

'Yes, but Squashy Hat's a native and older than you, and we saw him coming out,' said Roger. 'So we knew it was all right. And we went in, and then Titty came to fetch us back.'

'Then why didn't you come?'

'We couldn't,' said Titty. 'But it was quite all right. And we went on and on and came out at Slater Bob's quarry. It's no good going in now, John . . .'

But John, torch in hand, was following the string into the tunnel.

'Do you mean you got right through to Slater Bob's?' said Nancy. 'Why, he told me this end was all timbered and rotten and not safe. We'll go through now. We'll go through right away. We've got a grand lot of gold dust. It'll save a whole day. The sooner we get him to make the ingot the better. Look here. I'll race back to the gulch for the dust. And we'll want the lantern, too . . .'

'But we can't,' said Titty. 'Slater Bob's not on our side any more. He's in with Squashy Hat. . . . He's been seeing him again and again. . . . He admitted it, didn't he, Dot? It isn't safe to tell him anything. I was in a stew all the time for fear he would ask us about the gold . . .'

Nancy, who had been on the point of galloping off, stopped short.

'You didn't tell him?' she said.

'Not a word,' said Titty. 'But he told us Squashy knew everything about mining, and you could see by the way he said it whose side he was on.'

'Well, that busts everything,' said Nancy. 'No wonder Squashy's been spying on us and creeping nearer and nearer. And think of telling him when he'd promised he wouldn't. You simply can't trust natives when they get together.'

'What are we to do?' said Dorothea.

'Can't we make an ingot ourselves?' said Nancy.

She looked at Dick.

Just then John came back out of the tunnel. He had a cut end of string in his hand and was coiling it up. He unfastened the other end of the string from the clump of heather. His face had gone quite white, and he looked queerly at Titty and Roger.

'Come on,' Peggy was saying. 'Let's all go into the tunnel, anyway.'

'There's nothing to see,' said John. 'Not now . . .'

Nancy glanced at John. What was the matter with him?

'Get Susan away,' whispered John, for Nancy alone. 'Don't let her go in . . .'

Just for one moment Nancy hesitated. Then her clear voice rang out again.

'No good going through to the enemy,' she said. 'Waste of time. No good talking to Slater Bob if he and Squashy are allies against us. Look here, Professor, how do they get an ingot out of the raw stuff? . . . Come on, Susan . . .'

John and Nancy were already moving away from the rocks where the tunnel came out of the hill. The others moved with them. Only Peggy hung back for a moment, wanting to explore the end of the tunnel, but got such a look from Nancy that, though she did not know the reason, she gave it up and hurried after them.

'Roger, what *are* you doing?' said Susan suddenly.

'Tightening my belt,' said Roger. 'We've had nothing to eat since breakfast.'

'Nobody's had any, thanks to you people,' said John.

'It's all spoilt and gone cold and greasy by now,' said Susan.

'I bet it's jolly good,' said Roger.

'Let's go and eat it, anyhow,' said John.

They hurried across the Topps, talking less of the passage through the mountain than of the treachery of Slater Bob in making friends with the enemy in spite of all his promises.

'Susan,' said Titty suddenly, as they came near the Great Wall, 'has the pigeon gone? You haven't told Mrs Blackett about anyone being lost? . . .'

'We were just going to,' said Susan.

'How awful,' said Titty.

'We ought to send him off at once,' said Nancy.

And before they settled down to eat the dinner that Susan had cooked for them so long ago, Sophocles was flying on his way.

No one could have guessed from the message he carried how very different a message might have been sent a little earlier.

'We must tell mother not to let out to anybody we've found gold,' said Nancy. 'She might easily meet Slater Bob.'

So the message ran:

KEEP OUR SECRET EVEN FROM VENERABLE SLATERS. THIS IS IMPORTANT. ALL WELL. NO TIME FOR MORE. S.A.D.M.C.

CHAPTER 26

'WE'VE GOT TO DO IT ALL OURSELVES'

In the ordinary way nobody much likes steak-and-kidney pudding that has been boiled at one o'clock, emptied out of its tins at two, and eaten all cold and greasy at six. But today the starving prospectors' only thought seemed to be that they could have done with a little more of it. People were seen to scrape up even the grease with bits of bread, to eat those bits of bread as if they enjoyed them, and to lick their fingers afterwards. The beans were rather sad and flabby, but Susan hotted up the potatoes again while the pudding was being eaten. They made a separate course, and it was found that ginger beer had a very good effect in clearing off the film of grease which had coated everybody's tongue.

They had eaten the potatoes and were well into the apple course (two Newtown pippins apiece) before they could forget their hunger and turn to serious talk.

'Well,' said Nancy. 'We've got to manage without getting any help from Slater Bob. Everybody agreed?'

Dick was wiping his spectacles. At the time, when he had heard the way Slater Bob spoke of Squashy Hat, he had agreed with Titty. But now he was not so sure. There was so much he wanted to ask.

'Couldn't we go and see him without telling him everything?' he said.

'But we don't want to,' said Nancy. 'Not with him and Squashy being blood brothers and all that.'

'But perhaps they aren't,' said Dick.

'Of course they are,' said Titty. 'You heard what Slater Bob said.'

'Couldn't we manage to show our stuff to Slater Bob without telling him just where we found it?'

'But why?'

'Just to make sure,' said Dick.

'Oh look here,' said Nancy. 'Squashy knows exactly where we've been, and if we go and show Bob what we've found, they'll put their horrid heads together and they'll both know what we've found and where we've found it, and our claim'll be jumped before Uncle Jim knows we've staked it.'

'It isn't as if we really knew,' said Dick. 'And with Slater Bob knowing all about it. . . . He'd tell us just what to do.'

'Isn't it all in the book?' said Nancy.

Dick looked at the red book from which, indeed, he had hardly been parted since the expedition began. He had read the chapters on gold mining again and again, but a few words of advice from a real miner would be worth a lot of reading. There was all that stuff about assaying and chemical tests. There was a chapter on iron smelting that he thought might help, but there was nothing in the book about turning gold dust into ingots.

John, for once, was more inclined to agree with Dick than with Nancy.

'If they're really working together,' he said, 'why doesn't Squashy come along to the gulch to see what we're doing?'

'He's getting nearer every day,' said Nancy. 'He'd have been in it, all right, if it wasn't for us being always there.'

Captain John jumped to his feet.

'There's been nobody on guard for ages!'

'And we left the gold dust in the mine,' cried Nancy. 'Galoots we are. Bobtailed galoots and gummocks. Come on. He may be there now.'

Susan was just beginning to wipe the grease off the plates

271

with handfuls of dry moss, dropping the moss into the fire, where the grease sizzled and spat.

'No more meals tonight,' she said. 'But there'll be hot cocoa last thing. We've a lot of milk to spare with drinking grog instead of tea, and we've got that cocoa to use up. I emptied it into a paper bag to make room for the gold.'

'Who's coming?' said John.

'We all are,' said Titty.

'Peggy and I have got to wash up,' said Susan. 'And Roger's done enough for one day. No point in his making two journeys to the gulch. Unless he'll do without his cocoa . . .'

'Oh, I say,' said Roger.

'Or sleep in his tent for a change . . .'

'No, no,' said Roger.

'Right,' said Susan. 'Then you stay here now and help scrub Mrs Tyson's saucepan.'

'Whoever's coming had better come,' said John. 'There's been no one on guard since we stopped work and started looking for the others.'

'I saw him going home,' said Titty.

'A hundred years ago,' said Nancy. 'Come on, John.'

And the two captains, followed by Titty, Dorothea and the much-worried geologist, hurried off to Golden Gulch.

*

'Gosh,' said John, as he stooped and crawled into the mine. 'I went and left the lantern burning. If he's been in here and spotted that, he's discovered the whole thing.'

'It's all right,' said Nancy. 'If anybody'd been in who didn't know, they'd have gone ker-wallop over the crushing mill. I left it just inside the doorway and it's still there.'

'No blood on it?' said Titty.

'Not a drop, and it's just where I left it, anyway.'

'Where's the gold?' said Dorothea.

'Here,' said Nancy. 'He can't have been here or he'd have swiped it. I had the whole lot in the frying-pan when Susan came stewing along to say you idiots had disappeared.'

In the dim light of the lantern she was carefully raking the gold dust together and working it over the edge of the pan into the cocoa-tin.

'I say,' said Titty, 'you've done a jolly good lot.'

'We'd have done a lot more if you people hadn't got lost. The tin's only a bit more than half full.'

'How big ought an ingot to be?' asked Dorothea.

'It can't be too big,' said Titty. 'How big an ingot do you think we'll be able to make out of that?'

Dick was looking doubtfully at the cocoa-tin and at the damp glittering dust that was still sticking to the bottom of the frying-pan.

'It's sure to get a good deal smaller when it's all melted,' he said.

'You'll be able to do it all right, won't you?' said Dorothea.

'I wish you'd let me go and ask him about it first.'

'Who? Squashy?' said Nancy.

'Slater Bob,' said Dick. 'If he hasn't been here, perhaps they're not in league after all.'

Just for a moment even Nancy seemed a little doubtful. She was thinking, perhaps, if they could not find some way of asking Slater Bob about the making of ingots without giving away the secret that they had already found the gold out of which an ingot was to be made. After all, Slater Bob himself had told them where to look. Squashy Hat had been messing about on the hillside above them making his splashes of white paint all in a line, a sinister pointer, coming daily nearer and nearer to their mine. But, if Squashy Hat knew all that Slater Bob had told them, it was certainly funny that he had been content to spy from far away and had not taken his chance of

273

coming down into the gulch when they had left it unguarded for so long.

'Well, I don't know,' said Nancy.

Nobody had ever heard her say anything like that before.

John turned out the lantern, and they went out into the August evening, standing up in the gulch after stooping through the opening.

And then, suddenly, their doubts were settled for them.

Dorothea trod on a match-box.

It crunched under her foot, and, as she stooped to pick it up, she saw that there was something very queer about it.

Every day they had been most careful to leave nothing in the gulch that might betray the entry to the old working. The notice warning jumpers to beware had been planted in the middle of the little valley so that anybody might find it and read it and be warned off without discovering just where was the hidden vein of quartz and gold. Today, when Susan, full of native worry, had called them to look for the four who had vanished into the mountain, John and Nancy had not left the gulch before tidying everything away, stowing even the crushing mill out of sight inside the mine. For one moment she thought that, after all, they had overlooked one of the camp match-boxes. There were plenty of them. Even Roger had a match-box for lighting the little lantern in his tent. And John or Nancy might have dropped a match-box after lighting the lantern in the mine. But one glance at it, as it lay at her feet in the dusk, showed Dorothea that this was something else.

She was startled into making a sort of sighing gulp.

The others turned to look at her.

'You haven't gone and sprained your ankle?' said Titty, remembering Roger's squeak when he had twisted his.

'Look!' said Dorothea.

'He's been here,' cried Nancy, almost as if she was pleased. She picked up the match-box and looked at it. The others crowded round. Anybody could see it was not one of their own. For one thing, it was a different shape, not so deep. For another, instead of the familiar picture of Noah's Ark, there was a red triangle with an eye in the middle of it and red rays going in all directions.

'I say,' said Nancy. 'Giminy. It isn't English at all. What's this? "Phosphoros de Seguranca. ... Marca Registrada. Compannia Fiat Lux ...!"'

'It's a bit like Latin,' said John.

The match-box was squashed flat. Nancy pinched it into shape again.

'Well,' she said. 'He hasn't been in the mine but he's been jolly near.'

'What are we going to do about it,' said John.

'Go and leave it at Atkinson's,' said Nancy. 'So that he'll see we know what he's been up to. That ought to warn him off.'

They climbed the side of the gulch and looked out over the Topps. No one was in sight.

'Come on,' said Nancy. 'We've just time before dark. We'll go and leave it in the porch at Atkinson's, and then you can pick up Roger on the way back. They'll be having that cocoa ready, too. Come on.'

Tired though they were after that long day, Titty, Dick and Dorothea hurried after them as John and Nancy set off for the Dundale road. All the time they kept looking about them, but saw nothing moving.

'He'll be at home, I bet you anything,' said Nancy. 'Well, who thinks now he isn't after our gold? Bob must have told him everything.'

Nobody wanted to wait as sentinel at the edge of the Topps. All five of them ran down the road, and, led by John and Nancy, snaked along through the trees beside the cart track going down to Atkinson's.

It was falling dusk and there was already a light in one of the downstairs windows of the farm, looking out into the little garden.

''Sh,' said Nancy. 'Wait. . . .' She slipped off alone along under the garden wall. For a moment they saw her stooping in the porch. A minute later she was with them again.

'Listen,' she whispered. 'The Atkinsons are all at the other side of the house. That's his window. Let's just make sure he's at home. Keep close to the wall. If we get across to that holly bush we'll be able to see in.'

The first bats were swinging overhead against a still pale sky as they crept round the garden and reached the holly bush.

'He's there,' said John.

'What about that?' gasped Nancy. 'Look at the table . . .'

They could see through the window, open in the summer evening. Squashy Hat in his shirt-sleeves was sitting in an armchair, with his feet, in bedroom slippers, cocked up on another. On the table were the remains of a supper, but it was not at this that they were all looking. The white cloth covered only half the table. On the other half were some books, with a map thrown loosely on the top of them. And beside these books, gleaming in the light of an oil lamp, were half a dozen large bits of white quartz.

'Let's just charge,' said Titty.

'Quiet,' said John. 'Don't go and tread on a twig. We know now for certain. That's enough. Let's get out.'

Not another word was said until they were back once more on the Dundale road.

'Well,' said Nancy, 'that means it isn't safe to say a word to anybody. We've simply got to do the whole thing ourselves.'

'Dick'll manage, all right,' said Dorothea.

'We'll want a lot of charcoal,' said Dick.

'We know how to make charcoal,' said Nancy. 'We've watched the Billies often enough.'

SCOUTS AT DUSK

'And a proper blast furnace,' said Dick. 'You can't get a hot enough fire any other way.'

'What's it like?' said Nancy.

'It needs a bellows,' said Dick.

'Mother's got a beauty,' said Nancy, 'in the drawing-room. Come on and tell the others. Even Susan'll see it's serious now.'

*

They came back to the camp to find Susan stirring the cocoa rather grimly, and Roger, oddly silent, watching her. She had heard, at last, the whole dreadful story of how the tunnel had fallen in on the heels of the explorers. You would have thought that by this time it was too late for even a native to be much upset, seeing that everybody was alive and well, but Susan could not stop herself from thinking of what so easily might have been.

They told her of the finding of the match-box in the gulch and of how they had actually seen Squashy in his room at Atkinson's with lumps of quartz on the table beside him.

'So it's all settled,' said Nancy. 'We've got to manage without getting any help at all. Someone's got to go to Beck-foot tomorrow to get hold of the drawing-room bellows. And Dick wants a crucible and a blowpipe.'

'I don't care what we do,' said Susan, 'so long as there is no more going into tunnels.'

'There won't be,' said Nancy.

John and Titty looked at each other, and looked away again. What would Susan be saying if she had actually seen what John had seen, the string going into the hill and ending under a huge fall of rock and rotten timbers?

'Three more days'll do it,' said Nancy. 'We can fend off Squashy for that long. But we mustn't give him another chance of hunting about in the gulch.'

They sat round the camp fire, sipped the scalding cocoa and held council. By the time John and Roger went off to grope their way back to the gulch for the night, plans for the morrow had been made. Roger and Dorothea were to be trusted with the scouting. John, Susan and Nancy were to have a last go at the crushing and panning, and then begin gathering wood for the charcoal. Peggy, Titty and Dick were to go down to Beckfoot to do some shopping and borrowing. At least, it was not to be exactly borrowing, because, with things as they were, it had been decided that even at Beckfoot nothing more was to be said about the finding of the gold. That was why Peggy was to be one of the party. Neither Titty nor Dick had quite liked the idea of raiding Beckfoot and getting away with the bellows. They did not mind taking Captain Flint's things, because it was for his sake they were wanted. But the burgling of Mrs Blackett's bellows had to be done by one of Mrs Blackett's daughters.

'Anyway, Susan,' said Nancy, as she came down into the camp after watching the will-o'-the-wisp of John's torch flickering its way across the Topps, 'it's a jolly good thing the able-seamen *did* go through. It would have been pretty awful if we'd gone across tomorrow with the gold dust and given the whole show away.'

CHAPTER 27

A RUN ON BLOWPIPES

Two dusty dromedaries turned in at the Beckfoot gate. Peggy was riding her own, standing on the pedals, with Titty sitting on the seat behind her. Dick was riding Nancy's and finding it rather big in the bone, even after the seat had been let down as far as it would go. Two or three times he had nearly come off, though that was mostly because he had been thinking of something else. It was all very well, Nancy labelling him Professor and expecting him to know everything. He had made a sketch of a furnace, partly copied from the book, but he had not yet thought out how to hold a crucible steady in the middle of the red-hot charcoal.

Squashy or no Squashy, he would very much have liked to have a talk with Slater Bob.

They stopped in the stableyard.

'We'll shove the droms against the wall,' said Peggy to Dick. 'They'll be all right here. . . . Hullo, Cook!'

'Well, Miss Peggy, and you're a stranger. . . . And how's Miss Ruth . . . ?'

'Nancy's all right,' said Peggy. 'And how are you? We've brought nothing to eat . . .'

'I thought Cook couldn't be talking to anybody else. . . .' Mrs Blackett was leaning from an upstairs window. 'Tired of prospecting? And how are you, Titty? And you, Dick? There are letters for both of you. Any more miners about? No? Did you say we had anything for them to eat, Cook?'

'There's always dry bread, ma'am.'

'We'll give them just that,' said Mrs Blackett. 'Oh yes, and Dick, it's a good thing you've come. . . . That bell of yours isn't what it was. Yesterday it only gave a tinkle and stopped. If I hadn't happened to be in the passage, your pigeon might have come home and nobody the wiser. He was very late, too . . .'

'We didn't send him off till pretty late,' said Dick. 'You see . . .' And then he caught Peggy's eye, and remembered. After all, as Nancy had said, everybody had got back out of the hill all right, and there was no point in stirring people up about it afterwards.

They went through the kitchen door and the back passage into a house that still looked rather as if tornadoes and hurricanes had been chasing each other from room to room. Mrs Blackett came running down the carpetless stairs, kissed Peggy and Titty and shook hands with Dick.

'Here are your letters,' she said. 'One for Dick, one for Dorothea, one for Titty. . . . Oh yes, and two coloured post-cards of the River Plate for a pair of wild nieces.'

'From Uncle Jim!' said Peggy, who, like Dick, had something on her mind, and was, indeed, already working round towards the drawing-room door. She took her postcard and looked at it as if she had nothing else to think of. 'Nothing about Timothy?' she said. 'And nothing's come?'

'Only the crates,' said Mrs Blackett. Dick, with his letter half-opened, saw the big printed labels on the two huge crates that were standing in the hall. 'International Mining Equipment Corporation.' He wished he could have seen inside. 'I rang up the station again only yesterday,' Mrs Blackett went on. 'But they had nothing and there isn't even a word on your postcards. I do wish your uncle would write letters . . .'

'He's drawn his elephant flag at the masthead of one of the ships in the river,' said Peggy.

'It wouldn't have taken him half so long just to say what ship he was sailing in and when she would arrive,' said her mother.

'Mother sends her love,' said Titty, 'and so does Bridget. And mother hopes we aren't being too much of a nuisance. We aren't, are we, being right away. . . . I mean until now, of course.'

'Not yet, anyway,' said Mrs Blackett. 'As good as gold. You'll deserve all you find. . . . Come out of the drawing-room, Peggy. We've just begun getting it straight.'

Peggy had dodged through the door only for a moment, but it had been long enough. She was out again in the hall, and, without turning round, slipped away with a quick crab-like motion, and disappeared through the door into the passage.

Dick, reading slowly through his letter, saw nothing of what had happened, but Titty, who had darted through hers, caught a glimpse of what Peggy was hiding behind her. 'Good as gold?' Her cheeks went hot. Oh well, nobody would be likely to want to light the drawing-room fire right in the middle of the summer.

'And what are your plans?' Mrs Blackett was saying.

'We've got to go across to Rio,' said Titty. 'We've used up all our torch batteries.'

'And there may be other things, too,' said Dick. 'We've got to look in Captain Flint's room first.'

Peggy was back in the hall. 'You're not spring-cleaning the study, are you?' she said.

'He likes that left just as it is,' said her mother. 'Something always seems to get lost if we even go over things with a duster. But I'm glad you're going across to the village. It'll save me going round. I'll make out a list for you. . . . I'll just see what Cook wants. And you'd better have lunch before going.'

Peggy looked at Dick.

'Several things to look up,' he said. 'And the bell to put right.'

Mrs Blackett was gone. 'Well, Cook, isn't that lucky? What about our grocery list? Castor sugar running short. . . . And what's this? Cinnamon?' They could hear her chattering cheerfully in the kitchen as they went into Captain Flint's deserted study.

*

'Got the bellows, anyway,' said Peggy.
  'I saw,' said Titty.

*

Ten days had passed since they had last seen the study. There was a smell of long-dead marigolds. Dick did not notice it. He went straight to the glass-fronted shelf where Captain Flint kept all kinds of apparatus, weighing-scales, bottles, filters, spirit-lamps, and test-tubes in rows of six.

'Good,' he said. 'He's got some splendid crucibles. I thought I'd seen them . . .'

But Titty and Peggy hardly heard him. They were looking at the faded garlands that decorated the armadillo's sleeping-hutch.

'Oh,' said Titty, 'everything's dead. It's really lucky he hasn't come.'

'Those postcards only came yesterday,' said Peggy. 'Timothy may turn up any time if Uncle Jim sent him by the same boat. They always get the mails off first.'

'"Welcome Home" still looks all right,' said Titty, 'but we must put some fresh flowers.'

'If we put them in water, they'd keep fresher than garlands,' said Peggy.

'I'll tell you what,' said Titty. 'He'd probably feel more at home with tropical plants . . .'

'There's a cactus we could borrow for him,' said Peggy.

'He'll love it,' said Titty. 'And isn't there a palm in the drawing-room? ... and some ferns ... do you think if we asked? ...'

'Jolly good to get them in here out of the dust,' said Peggy. 'Mother'll be delighted.'

'We'll make him a forest glade,' said Titty.

And so, while Dick was looking up blast furnaces in the Encyclopaedia and comparing the pictures with the sketch he made, the faded garlands were thrown away, and Timothy's hutch, with its 'Welcome Home' in red and blue cardboard letters, began to look altogether different, standing in the shade of a palm tree, with a prickly cactus by the front door and half a dozen spreading ferns to make a background of tropical greenery.

'I think we ought to take the biggest of the crucibles,' said Dick.

'Take the lot,' said Peggy, standing at a little distance to get a better view of the armadillo's forest home.

'Even the biggest's rather small,' said Dick. 'But I think it'll do. ... But I can't find a blowpipe anywhere.'

'What does it look like?'

'Just a pipe to blow through,' said Dick. 'Big at one end, with a very small jet at the other ...'

'He's probably got it with him,' said Peggy, after poking about in the shelf, and startling Dick by nearly dropping the whole nest of crucibles on the floor.

'I'll buy one in Rio,' said Dick. 'It'll always come in useful.'

Mrs Blackett stood in the doorway, looking at the forest.

'Oh, Peggy!' she said, and then laughed in spite of herself.

'It won't hurt them,' said Peggy.

'I must say,' said Mrs Blackett, 'it looks lovely. It'll really be a pity if the wretched animal's died on the voyage. ...

How are you getting on, Dick? What about the pigeon-bell?
Lunch in another half-hour.'

*

Dick hurried out to the pigeon-loft. One of his wires must
have slipped. Nothing much else could have gone wrong. He
would put it right at once. He hurried out, with his mind
still full of what the Encyclopaedia had said about blast
furnaces. He climbed the ladder up to the loft and opened the
door.

'Hullo, Sophocles,' he said, thinking really of something
else. 'Hullo, Homer! . . .' and stopped. Sophocles. . . .
Homer. . . . Two pigeons were fluttering about his head as he
bent to look at his wires. . . . Two. . . . But. . . . Surely. . . .
Oh, well, Titty would know. . . . He went back to the outer
door at the top of the ladder.

'Titty,' he called.

'Hey!'

They were both just crossing the yard. Peggy had a handful
of peas as a treat for Sophocles.

'How many pigeons ought there to be?' said Dick.

'One,' said Titty. 'We've got two at home.'

'But there's two here.'

Peggy hurled herself up the ladder.

'It's Homer,' she said.

'He must have escaped,' said Dick.

'Look at his leg,' cried Titty.

'Shut the slide,' shouted Peggy. 'Quick, Dick, you gummock. Don't let him out. He's got a message. Phiu. . . .
Phiu. . . . Phiu. . . .' She called to the pigeons, and they
quietened down, and came nearer to look at the peas. In
another moment she had caught Homer and pulled a
rolled slip of thin paper from under the elastic band on his
leg.

Trembling fingers unrolled it.

On it was the usual skull and two short sentences:

ENEMY IN FULL RETREAT. SCOUTS SAW HIM DRIVING AWAY.

'If he's gone,' said Dick, with great relief, 'we'll be able to get Slater Bob to help.'

Ten minutes later the wires had been put right. Homer, taken outside and bustling in again for more peas, rang the bell in the kitchen passage so loudly that cook nearly dropped yet another pile of plates. Dick, his work done, went into lunch with a very happy smile. Mrs Blackett noticed it.

'Hullo, Dick,' she said. 'What's happened? Ought we to be wishing you "Many Happy Returns of the Day"?'

'It's jolly good news,' said Peggy. 'Nancy's sent Homer to let us know the enemy's gone.'

Mrs Blackett seemed pleased, too. 'I'm glad he's gone before he met Nancy,' she said.

*

But they did not enjoy the good news for long. After a lunch that was not dry bread after all, during which Mrs Blackett told them just what shops to go to and what to get – 'Don't get oranges, if they look dried up. . . . I haven't put down what brand of chocolate. . . . Isn't there a special kind that Roger likes? . . . Titty knows it . . . the kind that breaks into squares. . . .' – they rowed across to Rio in the hot, windless afternoon. Peggy and Titty went off with two baskets apiece, leaving Dick at the door of the chemist's shop to buy batteries and blowpipe.

The chemist's shop was rather crowded. Visitors were buying things to save their skins from sunburn, and things to save their throats from hay fever. But for Dick, chemist's shops were always interesting, and he did not mind having to wait his turn. He found a place where he could see behind the piles of patent medicines on the counter to a laboratory bench where a man was making up a prescription. Dick watched him juggling with test-tubes and glass-stoppered bottles. After a minute or two he thought it might be his turn, but the man who was selling things was still busy and there seemed to be more people in the shop than ever. A lot of new people had come in. Close to Dick were some very long and very baggy flannel trousers. Money was being nervously jingled in a pocket. 'Er. . . . Er. . . .' Twice the man who owned those trousers had made a shy beginning of asking for what he wanted. Dick looked up above the trousers. . . . A grey flannel coat hanging very loosely . . . an old brown hat. . . . Dick looked anxiously towards the door. . . . What would the others think he ought to do? And then, before Dick could do anything at all, the man behind the counter dabbed some red sealing-wax on a pill-box, done up in white paper, handed it to another customer, and turned to Squashy Hat . . .

'Are you being attended to, sir?'

'Er. . . . Er . . .' said Squashy Hat. 'I wonder if you have such a thing as a small blowpipe . . .'

Dick's mouth fell open. He shut it again. He took off his spectacles and wiped them. His fingers shook so that he nearly dropped his spectacles.

The man behind the counter had offered Squashy Hat a handful of blowpipes to choose from.

'They're all a little dusty,' he was saying. 'It isn't often we're asked for them.'

'This'll do very well,' said Squashy Hat. 'How much did you say? Oh no. No need to wrap it up. . . .' He slipped the blowpipe into his breast pocket, paid for it and worked his way nervously out between customers and narrow counters hung with sponge bags and hot-water bottles, and piled with thermos flasks and tooth-brushes and patent medicines.

'And what can I do for you?'

Dick pulled himself together.

'I want a blowpipe, please,' he said.

'Well, that is a funny thing,' said the man behind the counter. 'We don't get asked for them, not once in a blue moon. And I've just sold one this minute, and now another. And what are you wanting a blowpipe for? Egg-collecting?'

'No,' said Dick, flushing red. But the man could hardly know that he was interested in birds and hated egg-collectors.

'It isn't the time of year, is it?' said the man. 'Now I wonder what that gentleman ...' But there were other customers waiting, and he gave Dick his blowpipe and took his shilling, and, before Dick had had time to answer his question, was telling an old lady with a bad cold that there was nothing like Sims' Smelling Salts for hay fever.

Dick stumbled out of the shop and ran straight into the others who were staggering along the pavement with baskets crammed to the brims.

'I say, Dick,' said Peggy. 'We've got to look out. Squashy's not gone. He's here, in Rio. We've just seen him.'

'I know,' said Dick. 'He was in the chemist's shop. He was buying a blowpipe. He's taken it away in his pocket ...'

'The beast. The awful beast,' said Peggy. 'That means he's got something to use it on.'

'Our gold,' said Titty.

'Come on,' said Peggy. 'Let's hurry up. We ought to let them know about Squashy. We've done our shopping, all but the ginger beer. Where are the batteries?'

But Dick had forgotten everything except the blowpipe. They went back into the shop. There was no waiting this time. Peggy caught the eye of the man, picked up the eight little batteries they wanted, handed over the money and was out again on the pavement in a moment.

They looked up and down the street and along the front by
the boat-piers. There was no sign of Squashy Hat. They went
to the little shop where, two years before, Captain John and
Susan had bought grog for the crew of the *Swallow*. Peggy
ticked off the last thing on her list. 'Two doz. pop.' And the
man very kindly helped to stow the bottles, a dozen each, in
Dick's and Titty's knapsacks. Peggy's had been left behind
with the dromedaries at Beckfoot, because there was something in it already. The two knapsacks, full of bottles, were
just about as much as Dick could manage, one in each hand.
The other two, laden with groceries, had no hands to spare.
All three rejoiced in a breath of wind from the south that
rippled the water by the boat-pier and allowed them to sail
Amazon back to Beckfoot without having to use the oars
except at the mouth of the river.

*

When they landed their cargo in the boat-house, and carried
it across the lawn to the house, they learnt that most of the
things they had been buying were for their own camp. Mrs
Blackett offered to run them up the valley to Tyson's in old
Rattletrap. For a moment they hesitated, but, as Peggy said,
the dromedaries would have to be loaded anyway to get the
stuff up to the camp.

'Just as you like,' said her mother. 'And now there'll be
tea ready in half an hour. You'd better wait.'

'Squashy hasn't gone,' said Peggy. 'And we've got to let
them know.'

'It'll be ready as soon as you are,' said her mother.

They went into the stableyard and loaded up the dromedaries. There could be no riding this time for anyone. The
two knapsacks full of ginger beer bottles were slung on each
side of the saddle of Nancy's lanky beast. The travelling
basket, with Homer and Sophocles as inside passengers, was

strapped on the carrier. A basket of mixed stores was roped to the handlebars. Peggy's dromedary carried four dozen eggs in cardboard boxes, a basket of oranges, and a basket with bread, biscuits and a huge tinned tongue for a special occasion, besides some smaller parcels and Peggy's knapsack with the bellows in it. The bellows were pretty well hidden, but they were an awkward shape, and, no matter what she did, the brass nozzle showed out of the top. There was a moment's difficulty about this . . .

All afternoon Mrs Blackett had, as Peggy said, been whirlwinding in the drawing-room, and, by bad luck, though it was the hottest day of the summer, she had missed the drawing-room bellows from their nail on the wall when fender and fire-irons had been put back and she was taking a general look at the room. She was still lamenting when, after ringing the gong, she came out into the yard to admire the caravan and to suggest that with all that weight to carry, the dromedaries had really better put off starting until the cool of the evening . . .

'One thing after another,' she was saying. 'You'd almost think the furniture did it for fun, the way things manage to get lost. . . . Those old bellows now. . . . I'm almost sure I saw them only yesterday . . .'

She saw Peggy's face and stopped. 'Why,' she said. 'Do you know something about them? . . . I might have guessed . . . where have you hidden them? . . . And then, following Peggy's eyes, she looked at Peggy's dromedary leaning up against the wall. She saw the basket of oranges, the knapsack, and then the tip of the brass nozzle of the bellows poking out of the top of the knapsack and glinting in the sun. . . . 'Peggy, you awful child!'

'We've simply got to have them,' said Peggy. 'And they won't be wanted in the drawing-room till winter. And we'll only keep them a few days . . .'

'Don't you know how to start a camp-fire without bellows?' said her mother.

'It isn't a camp-fire,' said Dick. 'And it's no good without bellows. . . .' He stopped short. In another moment he would have blurted all their plans.

Titty put in a helpful word.

'We'll take great care of it,' she said. 'Susan knows we're bringing it.'

'Oh well,' said Mrs Blackett, 'if Susan knows. . . . But if you get a lot of smoke on that beautiful brass nozzle. . .'

'We'll make Roger polish it. Or I will. We haven't had any brass-work to polish up for ages.'

Mrs Blackett gave it up. 'Come along and have your tea,' she said, and the grateful camel-drivers agreed that they would probably travel all the faster if they had a hasty cup.

*

The journey home was one long trudge. There was little talking. They rested one at a time, walking free, while the other two pushed the laden dromedaries. Going up hills, whoever was resting helped to push. Going down, whoever was resting helped to hold back the dromedary that seemed most inclined to run away. At the worst places the only thing to do was to move one dromedary at a time.

They were nearly half-way to Tyson's when a horn sounded in the road behind them. A motor-car rushed past and left them choking with dust. But they had all seen who was in it.

'That was Dick Elleray driving,' said Peggy. 'Squashy must have hired him for the day.'

'Well, he hasn't bolted,' said Titty. 'He's come back.'

'With a blowpipe,' said Dick.

All three rested at the foot of the wood, after going through the farmyard at Tyson's. They left one dromedary there, and found that, laden like this, one was just about as much as they could manage, pushing and pulling, stumbling and slipping, up that steep, winding track under the trees.

They were very tired.

Up and up they climbed, propping the dromedary first on one side and then on the other. Sweat filled their eyes and ran down their noses.

They had heard the noise up in the top of the wood for some time before they really noticed it. Plunk, plunk, plunk, and the rhythmic scrawk of a saw. . . . Plunk. . . . Plunk. . . . Plunk . . .

'Charcoal-burners,' exclaimed Titty. 'It's just their noise.'

'Charcoal-burners it jolly well is,' said Peggy.

Suddenly less tired, they hurried on.

They came at last through the trees into the camp. It looked a different place. All afternoon the others had been at work there. A big round patch of the old pitstead had been swept clear of dead leaves. It was black with the old ashes of the real charcoal-burners of other years. Beside it was a huge pile of green branches. John, swinging the axe, plunk, plunk, plunk, was chopping the thinner branches all to the same length. Nancy, with the saw, was cutting up the thicker bits. Dorothea and Roger were stacking them ready for use.

'Good men,' shouted Nancy. 'They've brought the pigeons. Have you got the bellows? Did you get our message? Where's the other drom?'

'Down at the bottom of the wood,' said Peggy. 'It's jolly well laden.'

'Back nearly broken,' said Titty. 'Like ours.'

'All right. We'll go down for it. What do you think of this?'

'Squashy hasn't bolted,' said Peggy. 'He passed us just now coming back. We saw him in Rio.'

'He was in the chemist's shop with Dick,' said Titty. 'And the awful thing is . . .'

'What? What?' said Nancy.

'He was buying a blowpipe, too.'

CHAPTER 28

CHARCOAL-BURNERS

BREAKFAST was over. Work had begun again. Susan was by the well, washing up. Roger was looking out from the top of the ash tree. Dick was alone in the camp. If he had not been so intent on what he was doing, he could have heard the noise of the wood-cutters. They needed a little more wood to finish the charcoal mound, which looked just now like a cake made of sticks all pointing towards the middle, a cake with a slice cut out of it. The others were busy getting wood to fill in that missing slice.

But Dick heard nothing. He was lying on his stomach on the ground using his new blowpipe to drive the flame of a candle into a tiny hole he had scraped in a bit of charcoal left on the pitstead by the real charcoal-burners of long ago. The edges of the hole turned first red and then white with heat. He stopped to take breath. Dipping the blade of his knife into the cocoa-tin of gold dust, he lifted a little on the tip and put it in the hole in the charcoal.

'It ought to do now,' he said to himself, aloud, though he had not known he had spoken at all.

A shadow fell across his hands. Titty and Dorothea had dumped a load of wood by the mound and were watching him.

He looked up with eyes that hardly saw them.

'Shall I go and fetch Nancy?' said Dorothea.

'Not till there's a bubble of gold,' said Dick.

He took a long breath and started again. His cheeks were blown out to hold as much air as he could and let him keep up a steady blast through the pipe even while he was breathing in through his nose. The flame made a hissing noise. Again the charcoal round the hole turned red, then glowing white. The little pile of gold dust darkened.

'It's all running together,' said Dorothea.

'Melting,' said Titty.

The dust was gone. In its place was a tiny red-hot drop.

Dick blew on and on. The glowing drop moved in the hole, driven round it by the jet of candle-flame.

'He's done it,' cried Dorothea.

'It's a baby nugget,' cried Titty. 'Come and look.'

John and Nancy threw down their armfuls of sticks and crossed the camp on the run.

'Giminy,' said Nancy.

Dick stopped blowing. The sweat was standing on his forehead. He put blowpipe and charcoal carefully down, rolled over, sat up, took off his spectacles and wiped them and put them on again. The charcoal was cooling. The little glowing drop turned darker and darker.

The others looked at him with a question. What had happened? They had all thought that as it cooled it would be a tiny nugget of shining gold. It was dull, dark, almost black.

'Something's gone wrong,' said Dick.

'Perhaps it's just the dirt on the outside of it,' said John.

Dick burnt the tip of his finger, and then used the tip of his knife instead, in getting the little dark drop out of its nest in the charcoal.

'It's too small to scrape,' said Nancy. 'What about cutting it in half to see the inside?'

Dick worked the little dark drop off the charcoal on a flat stone. It was so small that it was not easy to use the knife on it. Twice it nearly rolled off the stone to be lost altogether. Then it stuck in a crack and Dick got the edge of his knife across it and pressed. It broke up into dark powder.

'Funny,' he said. 'It melted all right.'

'I bet it got mixed up with the charcoal,' said Nancy. 'You said yourself it ought to be in a crucible.'

'Of course, it wasn't a very clean bit of charcoal,' said Dick, but he said it very doubtfully.

'Anyway, it's not much good trying with just a pinch,' said Nancy. 'You'll see, it'll be quite all right when we do it properly.'

'The book does say a crucible.'

'Let's get on with the charcoal-burning,' said Nancy. 'And there's the furnace to build, too. We'll be smelting the whole lot tomorrow and have a nugget as big as my fist. Golly, Roger, you did give me a start.'

'Ahoy!' Roger's shrill yell sounded again from the top of the ash tree. 'Ahoy! He's just coming out of the farm.'

'Two scouts to the gulch,' ordered Nancy. 'Roger can go. And Titty. Head him off if he looks like jumping. Signal if you need help. We'll keep a look-out. Skip along and get there first.'

*

'Where's he going?'

'He isn't coming here.'

The scouts whispered to each other, their bodies in the gulch, their heads just high enough to see out over the edge.

Squashy Hat, after a short visit to the lowest of his white spots, was walking across the Topps in the direction of Ling Scar. For a long time they watched him, walking on and on, till he came to the foot of the ridge.

'He's going through the tunnel to see Slater Bob,' said Titty.

'He can't,' said Roger.

'He doesn't know that yet,' said Titty.

'I wonder if he knows which hole to go in at.'

Squashy Hat seemed to have no doubts about the hole. Up

he went, and then, just where he had startled the watchers of two days before by suddenly appearing, he was gone.

'Not for long,' said Roger. 'This time he'll be more like a Jack-in-the-box than ever.'

They could not from the gulch see the hole in the hillside, but they could see the rocks round it and knew exactly where it was. They watched. Minute after minute went by.

'He can't be digging his way through,' said Titty.

'Another good dollop may have come down on the top of him,' said Roger hopefully.

'Oh no, no,' said Titty, pushing away the horrible idea. Squashy Hat might be a rival. He might be in league with Slater Bob. He might be a possible jumper of claims. But, no matter, Titty was content to let him go in peace. 'Oh, it's all right,' she said. 'There he is.'

'Pretty mad, I bet,' said Roger.

Squashy Hat seemed to have got his clothes very dirty. They saw him take his coat off and shake it and do his best to clean it with a handkerchief. Then they saw him trying to tidy up the knees of his trousers.

'Fallen down in the tunnel,' said Roger, with a note of satisfaction rather than of pity.

'What'll he do now,' said Titty.

He was not long in making up his mind. Flinging his jacket across his shoulder, Squashy Hat turned to the ridge and began climbing up it just where, two days ago, four able-seamen had come racing down.

'He's got something to say to Slater Bob,' said Titty. 'I wonder what he's found out. I expect he was blowpiping all night.'

'He'll be pretty hot by the time he gets to the top,' said Roger.

Squashy Hat went slowly up the steep side of the ridge. The watchers at the edge of the gulch had no need of the telescope.

His shirt made a white speck that was easy to follow. Up and up it went, stopping a moment while the climber rested, going on again, up and up, disappearing in gullies of rock and heather, showing again on the further side of them, always higher and higher, until at last it reached the skyline and was gone.

For a minute or two they watched the empty hillside. Then Titty jumped up.

'Come on, Roger,' she said. 'Let's go and report.'

*

'Good,' said Nancy, whom they found with Dick, busy with spades at the top of the Great Wall. 'Probably his blowpiping went wrong, too, and he's gone over to ask Slater Bob about it.'

'I wish *we* could,' said Dick.

'What *are* you doing,' said Roger. 'Gardening?'

A long wide strip of rock at the top of the Great Wall had been cleared of turf. The earth was thin there, and easy to lift with a spade. They watched Nancy slide her spade under the turf, turn it over, and cut it into square clods. A pile were already waiting.

'Crust for the charcoal pudding,' said Nancy. 'Go on. Take as many as you can. Carry them down and you'll see.'

Dick helped to load them and they staggered off down the gully to the camp, meeting Peggy and Susan coming up for another lot.

The charcoal mound was looking altogether different. The missing slice had been filled in, leaving only a small tunnel along the ground leading to the middle of the mound. The top of the mound was already covered with turfs like those they were carrying. John, stretched full length, was reaching through the tunnel.

'It's all right this time,' he said, pulling his arm out and getting up. 'The tunnel fell in twice.'

'Shall we put these bits of crust on, too?' said Roger.

'Get them damped first,' said John. 'Put them down with the others.'

At the side of the charcoal cake which had thus turned into a charcoal pudding were rows and rows of clods ready for use. Dorothea came out of the trees from the well with the kettle.

'Oh good,' she said, pouring water on the clods. 'But the well's getting rather muddy with me dipping so often.'

'Can't be helped,' said John. 'We're nearly ready for lighting. Look out, Roger, don't kick those sticks away. They're waiting to be crammed into the tunnel after we've got it going.'

Susan, Peggy, Dick and Nancy came down into the camp, each with as many of the cut turfs as they could manage.

'Got about enough, haven't we?' said Nancy. 'How's the tunnel now?'

'All clear,' said John.

Nancy pulled out a box of matches.

'Go on, John,' she said. 'You've got the longest arm.'

John lay down again, lit a match and worked his arm into the tunnel.

'It's gone out,' he said.

He tried another.

'Why won't it light anywhere?' asked Roger.

'Green wood,' said Dick. 'He's got dry leaves and sticks right in the middle.'

A third match went out.

'We'll have to open it out to start it,' said Nancy.

'It'll go like a bonfire if we do,' said John.

Dick was watching. Nancy saw his earnest face.

'Spit it out, Professor,' she said.

'Couldn't we make a torch at the end of a stick? What about dry moss?'

'I know where there is some,' said Roger.

He was back in a moment with a couple of handfuls. John tied the bundle to the end of a stick. He lay down again.

'You light it, Nancy, and I'll shove it in.'

The moss flared up. John plunged it into the tunnel. There was a sudden loud crackling from the middle of the mound. John reached for the green sticks, all cut to length, that were to fill up the tunnel. He jammed them in.

Smoke began to pour out through holes in the crust. The crackling grew louder.

'Quick. Quick. . . . Slap them on,' said Nancy.

'It's off,' said Titty. 'It's off. It's going to blaze in a minute.'

'It jolly well mustn't,' said Nancy. 'Quick. Damp turfs, not dry ones.'

Thick smoke was pouring from the mound. For a few desperate minutes it almost seemed that it would beat them. But with eight people stopping the leaks, the fire had but a poor chance. They closed up hole after hole until, at last, the charcoal-mound under its crust of turfs, all with the grassy side inwards, looked like a dead heap of earth.

'Have we put it out?'

'I can still hear it,' said Titty, listening with her head close to it.

'Better open a hole or two,' said Nancy. 'They never shut it up altogether till the smoke changes colour.'

Here and there they lifted a clod, and the smoke poured out, tawny, greenish, choking.

'It's all right,' said Nancy. 'Getting hold properly inside. So long as we don't let the whole pile flare up.'

'What time is it now?' said Peggy.

'How long does it have to stay lit?' asked Dick, pulling out his watch. 'It's nearly three o'clock . . .'

'Then it's all right for anybody to be hungry,' said Roger.

'And I've got no dinner,' said Susan. 'Sardines, it'll have to be.'

'The charcoal-burners keep their mounds burning for weeks and weeks,' said Peggy.

'But we can't,' said Titty.

'Not with all our natives coming,' said Dorothea.

'We can't, anyway,' said Nancy. 'Uncle Jim – Captain Flint may be back at any minute. He may be back now. He may be just strolling up here to say howdy and us without an ingot to show him. There's no need for more than a day either. Their mounds are big enough to cover the whole camp, and ours is tiny. . . . Ours ought to be properly cooked by tomorrow evening. All right, Susan. Trot out the sardines . . .'

'Swim them out,' Titty heard Roger murmur to himself. 'Or trot them, whichever's quickest.'

Peggy had gone to the store under the elderberry bush where all the tinned things were kept in a hole in the ground for the sake of coolness.

'Nine tins,' she said.

'It's no good keeping just one,' said Roger. 'There are sixteen sardines in each tin, so there'll be a tin for each of us, and then two extra sardines each to finish off.'

'All right,' said Susan. 'We'll give you hot minced pemmican for supper and boiled potatoes. I'm awfully sorry about dinner.'

Nobody really minded. The charcoal mound, smoking like a gigantic pudding, was itself a kind of cooking. Nobody had had time to think of cooking dinners as well. People wandered round it, using spoons to eat sardines out of the tins, and licking up the last drops of the oil. It was no good thinking of making tea until the water in Titty's well had settled down again. The quick dipping up of water for the damping of the turfs had made it very muddy.

'I ought to have put a kettleful aside,' said Susan. 'We could have managed with the saucepan for watering the crust.'

'We needed the kettle as well,' said Dorothea.

'And lots of miners die from hunger and thirst,' said Titty. 'It's perfectly all right to go without tea for one day.'

'Plenty of grog,' said Roger.

'We'll share out what's left of the milk,' said Susan. 'And somebody'll have to go down for a fresh lot this evening.'

'Let me,' said Dorothea.

'We'll both go,' said Titty.

Meanwhile the charcoal pudding could not be left for a moment. They had to let the moisture escape, and at the same time not to give the fire too much air. It was late in the afternoon before the smoke changed colour, and the greenish, tawny fumes drifting from the holes in the crust turned to the clear blue smoke that comes from dry wood.

'It's begun to cook,' said Peggy.

'Been cooking all the time,' said Nancy. 'Nothing to do now but to keep it well under. Let's have some more water on the clods.'

'Use the saucepan this time,' said Susan. 'And half a minute while I fill the kettle. We must have tea for supper. And the water is fairly clear again.'

Now and then somebody went to the Great Wall, or up the tree, to look out, but there was no sign of Squashy Hat either on the Topps or at Atkinson's.

They sent off Homer with a cheerful message:

EVERYTHING GOING VERY WELL INDEED.

It was not until evening that they had news of the enemy. Titty and Dorothea had gone down to Tyson's with the milk-

CHARCOAL PUDDING

can, and had run on as far as the little bridge to cool their feet in what was left of the river. They were sitting on stones with their feet in the water when steps sounded on the road above them.

'Lurk! Lurk!' whispered Dorothea.

But it was too late for lurking. And Squashy Hat, with his coat over his arm, came up the road and went by.

'He's been with Slater Bob all day,' said Titty.

They hurried up the wood to the camp and told what they had seen.

'Who cares?' said Nancy. 'The more they chatter the better. We're well ahead of him now. Dick's got a grand lot of stones for the blast furnace. And we'll have charcoal tomorrow and an ingot the day after.'

Susan was making up for their sardine dinner by cooking a tremendous supper. Potatoes were simmering in the pot. Pemmican had been put through the mincing machine and was hotting in the frying-pan that was no longer needed for gold. And, in the middle of the old pitstead, the mound was quietly steaming. They put their hands on its earthy crust to feel the warmth coming through.

'Who's going to stop up all night with it?' asked Roger after supper.

'Not you,' said Susan. 'Aren't you going to the gulch?'

'No one's going to the gulch,' said John. 'We'll have to watch the fire all night. Squashy won't try anything in the dark, and we'll be on the look out again as soon as it's light.

'The able-seamen will have to go to bed at the proper time,' said Susan.

'What if I keep awake,' said Roger.

But as dusk fell and darkness closed in on the camp, and owls called far below, and the churr of the nightjar sounded in the wood, Roger, like the other able-seamen, found his eyes closing. They went to bed, though not at once to sleep. For some time they lay in their tents, watching the glow of the camp-fire. John and Nancy, Susan and Peggy, were taking turns with the charcoal-burning. The able-seamen lay there listening as now and then a clod of turf was thumped into place to stop a leak in the mound where the smoke was coming out. They slept, but even while asleep, knew that people were stirring in the camp. Titty half waked as the flash of a torch passed across her tent. She heard John whisper, 'Where's that thermos flask?' She heard Nancy whisper back, 'I've poured it out. Don't step on the mug. What's the time?' The torch flashed again, and she heard John's voice. . . . 'Another hour before we wake Susan.' Titty pulled her sleeping-bag over her ears. All was well.

CHAPTER 29

BLAST FURNACE

TITTY woke with the smell of wood smoke tickling her nostrils.

Was that Dorothea whispering at the door of her tent?

'Don't wake Nancy. Let Titty see them first . . .'

'Captains and mates, indeed!' That was Roger's voice.

'Hullo, Dot!' said Titty.

''Sh!' said Dorothea and beckoned.

Titty crawled out into the camp. Charcoal-burning was still going on, but what had happened to the charcoal-burners? Dick and Roger, of all unlikely people, were sprinkling water and quietly patting down clods of earth on the smoking mound, and Dorothea pointed silently at the tent that was shared by Nancy and Peggy. There, with her head on her arm, lay Captain Nancy as fast asleep as anyone could be. Peggy was asleep, too, and so were John and Susan.

'Lucky we woke,' said Roger.

'Dick heard the fire crackle,' said Dorothea.

'We were just in time,' said Roger. 'One small flame had licked its way through, but we soon stopped it. They're all four sleeping like logs. It just shows. They ought to have let us sit up.'

'Let's put the kettle on,' said Dorothea.

'Let's.'

'What about dressing?'

'Afterwards,' said Titty. 'Let them wake and find everything ready.'

But just then Nancy's head moved with a sudden jerk. Her

eyes opened. She began to yawn, and in the middle of her yawn, remembered.

'Bobstays and jib-booms,' she cried. 'Hey! Susan. Your watch. Yours and Peggy's.' She tugged hard at one of Peggy's feet, sleeping-bag and all. 'Wake up. I've given you longer than I ought to have done. I must have been asleep the last few minutes.'

'Ho, ho,' laughed Roger.

'What are you doing out of bed?' said Nancy, blinking, and then, seeing Dorothea and Titty looking at her, and the bright sunlight, she laughed.

'Barbecued billygoats,' she exclaimed. 'All asleep. Well done the able-seamen! You haven't let the charcoal burn?'

'It wanted to,' said Dorothea.

John and Susan came sleepily out of their tents.

'This is awful,' said Nancy. 'I ought to have routed Susan out hours ago. It was only just beginning to get light. . . . Look here, you'll have to brew a lot of tea to keep us awake tonight . . .'

'Tonight?' said Susan.

'Blast furnace,' said Nancy.

John stretched himself.

'I'm off for the milk, anyway,' he said, and a moment later was running down the path through the wood.

*

By the time the others had done as much washing as they could afford, and breakfast was ready, he came panting back again.

'Your hair's all wet,' said Susan.

'I just had an in and out while she was filling the milk-can,' said John.

'Lucky beast,' said Roger.

'One more day,' said Nancy. 'We must hang on dirty till

tomorrow. Then we'll take the ingot to mother and have a swim in the lake. Some in the morning and some in the afternoon. We'll have nothing more to do then except to keep watch and see that Squashy does no jumping. By the way, he isn't on the prowl yet?'

'Not yet,' said Titty, who had already had a look out over the Topps.

'When are we going to cut the pudding?' said Roger, looking at the brown earth-covered mound from which little wisps of blue smoke trickled here and there.

'Not till the last minute,' said Nancy. 'We'll give it as long as we can. The furnace isn't built yet . . .'

'The stones are all ready,' said Dick.

'Let's have a look at that plan.'

Dick pulled out his pocket-book and showed a drawing to Nancy.

'It's a section really. Not awfully clear. There ought to be a plan as well. It'll be round, not square. And I haven't put in any sizes. There ought to be just room to have the crucible in the middle, with charcoal all round it, and the bellows coming in at the side and underneath the crucible.'

No one would have thought, to listen to Dick, that he was an able-seaman telling captains and mates just what they ought to do.

'We can't have a door to open and shut,' he was saying. 'But that won't matter. We'll have to build the crucible in at the last minute, and pour the bits of charcoal in at the top. I don't see how we can manage a chimney, but with the bellows going all the time, we ought to get a good enough draught without, don't you think?'

'Can't make head or tail of it, Professor,' said Captain Nancy. 'But I expect it's all right.' She passed the notebook to John.

'How are you going to fix the bellows?' asked John.

'They won't really have to be fixed, will they?' said Dick. 'Just a hole for the nose of the bellows. The rest of the bellows will all be outside. Of course it isn't like the ones in the book, but the principle is the same.'

'It looks the right shape,' said Nancy.

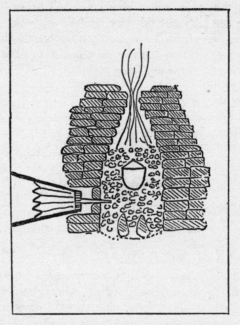

PAGE FROM DICK'S POCKET-BOOK

The building of the furnace began even before the breakfast things were washed up. It took a good deal longer than anyone had expected. In one way only was it different from the furnace of Dick's sketch. They found that there was no good way of holding the crucible in the middle of the fire if they tried to balance it on stones. Crucibles are an awkward shape, like teacups with lids but no handles, and narrower at the bottom than at the top. What was wanted was iron bars, and Peggy remembered a bit of old railing rusting away behind the Tysons' orchard wall. John galloped down the wood for the second time and brought it back. He filed three deep nicks in it with the file that was one of the most useful tools in the knife he had been given at Christmas. Then, bending the rusty rail this way and that he broke it at the nicks into four pieces. These four iron bars were built into the furnace, two one way and two the other, so that the crucible would be held in the middle.

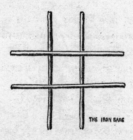

THE IRON BARS

The furnace was only half done when Susan, who had opened the tinned tongue to save cooking ('This *is* a special occasion,' Peggy had said), called builders and charcoal-burners to their dinner. Even while they ate, people had to be getting up every other minute to pat a clod on the charcoal mound, and to do a little watering of places on the crust that looked too dry. The furnace-builders went back to their work after eating their share of the tongue, and put stones in place with one hand while holding plum cake with the other.

All was going well when Roger, who had taken his cake up the look-out tree, came slithering down in a hurry to say that Squashy Hat was on the Topps below Grey Screes and not very far from the gulch.

'Oh, bother him,' said Nancy. 'Just when everybody's busy.'

'Dick and I could go,' said Roger, who thought scouting was more important than fitting stones together and damping clods of earth.

'Not the Professor, anyhow,' said Nancy.

'Let me go,' said Dorothea. 'Dick's got to be here.'

'There'd better be two of you,' said John.

With a telescope and *The Outlaw of the Broads*, Roger and Dorothea went off together.

*

A couple of hours later, or maybe three, Dorothea, wide-eyed and white-faced, came breathlessly into camp.

'What's happened?' cried Titty.

'It's the heat,' cried Susan. 'You'd better lie down.'

'He tried to jump,' said Dorothea.

John almost dropped the stone that he was fitting into place. Nancy started up.

'Where is he now?' she cried.

'Gone,' said Dorothea. 'Roger's snaking after him.'

'What happened?' said Titty.

'We were in the gulch,' said Dorothea, 'and I was reading to Roger and all of a sudden I looked up and there he was, looking down over the edge.'

'What did he say?' asked Nancy.

'He said, "I beg your pardon. I didn't know anyone was here."'

'I bet he didn't,' said Nancy, 'or he wouldn't have been trying to jump. Gosh, it's a good thing we didn't show our gold to Slater Bob. What did you say?'

'I didn't say anything,' said Dorothea, 'and Roger didn't either. And Squashy turned round and went away. He didn't go back to his white spots. He went straight home.'

'Foiled,' said Titty. 'I wish I'd been there.' She looked at Nancy. Surely she would call the whole camp to arms and march down to Atkinson's at once.

But Nancy did nothing of the sort. She looked at the charcoal mound, steaming all over because Peggy and Susan had just been sprinkling water on it. She looked at the furnace, now all but finished, a round stone pillar, hollow inside and tapering towards the top. She looked at the mouth of her tent where the cocoa tin, full to the brim with gold dust, was waiting to be emptied into the crucible.

'Oh well,' she said, 'we can't do everything at once. Making the ingot matters most of all, and we're just ready to start. So long as he doesn't actually jump. ... Come on, Dick, where's the crucible? We'd better have everything right before we open up the charcoal.'

Dick brought the crucible from his tent, where it had been put for safety's sake, with so many charcoal-burners and miners stamping about the camp. Solemnly Nancy poured in the gold dust. Dick put the lid on.

'What'll it look like when we see it again?' said Titty.

'All scummy on the top,' said Dick. 'The pure gold'll be underneath.'

'Put it in your tent till we get the furnace lit. Now for the charcoal. Come on. All hands to cut the pudding. Slosh some more water on it first and get another lot of wet clods ready.'

'And the fire-brooms,' said John. He unstacked them and laid them handy in case of need.

'Slosh some more water on it first,' said Nancy again.

'We'd better wet the ground all round it,' said Susan.

The charcoal pile was no longer the round smooth pudding it had been. Here and there it had fallen in. Here and there it was swollen with clods of turf that had been plastered on it to stop a leak of smoke. Susan with the kettle, John with the saucepan, sprinkled water over the crust, and a great mass of steam poured up above the camp. Kettle and saucepan were filled again. Everybody had a damp clod ready.

'Here goes,' cried Nancy. She pulled a big clod of earth from the side of the pile and dumped it on the top. 'That's the way,' she said, 'it'll be hottest in the middle, and the earth'll keep it under.'

Unburnt ends of sticks showed. There was a sudden crackling inside the mound. Nancy pulled out a stick. The end of it was red hot and dripping sparks. She put it on the wet ground and dumped a clod on it. The stick broke into bits.

'It's charcoal all right,' said Dick.

'Three cheers,' said Titty.

'Three million,' said Nancy, pulling out another bit. 'Ouch! my fingers!'

The crackling inside grew louder, and smoke began to pour out and mingle with the steam.

'Look out! It'll flare up in a minute,' said Susan.

'It shan't,' said Nancy. 'More water! Stand by. Don't get too near. John and I'll open it up.'

John and Nancy, working round the mound, pulled away clods of earth, dumped them in the middle, and hauled out stick after stick, letting each lie separately on the wetted ground. Peggy and Dick pressed wet clods on the red-hot ends. Titty and Dorothea raced backwards and forwards between the camp and the well, damping clods that had gone dry. Susan, with kettle and saucepan, poured water over any bits that looked like flaring. In a very few minutes there was nothing left of the charcoal mound but a small heap of violently steaming clods of earth.

'It hasn't all turned into charcoal,' said Dick, looking at the blackened sticks lying all round it.

'We've got a whacking good lot,' said Nancy. 'Giminy, I was afraid it was going to blaze up after all.'

'It's still red hot in the middle under that earth,' said Susan.

'We'll want that,' said John.

Roger came into the camp while they were still busy watering the charcoal to cool it and breaking it into bits small enough for use.

'Why didn't anybody come?' he said. 'Didn't Dot tell you? Oh, I say, what pigs, opening the pudding without waiting for me.'

'You're just in time for the furnace,' said Nancy. 'What's Squashy doing?'

'Eating bread and cheese,' said Roger. 'And he's got some bits of quartz on the table and some candles, and he's blow-piping, just like Dick. I got a good view from behind the hollybush.'

'Good,' said Nancy. 'That'll keep him busy. Look here, John, what on earth can we use for a shovel?'

'There's only the frying-pan,' said John.

'Oh no,' said Susan.

'It's the very thing,' said Nancy.

A minute later John was clearing away the clods that covered what had once been the burning middle of the mound. Nancy scooped a frying-pan full of red-hot charcoal from under them and carried it carefully across to the furnace. Some handfuls of dry twigs had already been put in there to give the fire a start. Using her knife, Nancy worked the red hot embers from the frying-pan through the bars. The twigs blazed up beneath them.

'Quick. More charcoal,' she cried. 'Come on, Dick. Shove in the crucible.'

Handfuls of black charcoal were put in. Dick brought the precious crucible and, regardless of the heat, balanced it in the middle of the bars as gently as if it had been an egg.

'May I start the bellows?' said Roger.

'One second. We've got to get the crucible walled in first. And then fill up with charcoal from the top.'

John and Nancy worked feverishly together, blocking up the hole through which the crucible had been put in. First the big stone that was lying ready. Then small ones. Then earth. The others dropped bits of black charcoal down the chimney. Dick leaned over and looked in but could see nothing for bitter smoke.

'The fuller the better,' he said. 'We've got to keep it full and red hot.'

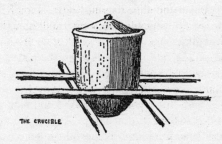

THE CRUCIBLE

'It'll go out in a minute,' said Susan.

'Go ahead with the bellows, Roger,' said Nancy. 'And keep it up while we get all the holes properly caulked. That's right, Titty. Shove a bit of earth in everywhere you see smoke coming out between the stones.'

Roger had already poked the nose of the bellows through the hole that had been left for it at the bottom of the furnace. He began pumping. 'Wough. . . . Wough. . . . Wough.'

'It makes the right sort of noise,' said Titty, as Roger quickened the time of his blowing and the hiss of the air into the fire turned to a regular snoring roar.

'How much more charcoal must we put in, Dick?' asked Dorothea, wiping her hot face with charcoal-covered hands.

Peggy, seeing her, suddenly burst into laughter. But Dorothea broke into laughter also, for Peggy had wiped her own face a moment before.

'Oh well,' said Susan, looking at both of them, 'it can't be helped.'

'Look here,' said Roger. 'Somebody else's turn.'

These bellows were worse than the crushing mill. They were so near the ground that even Roger had to crouch to be able to work them.

Nancy took over. She, too, started at a racing stroke, but slowed down after the first minute. She tried one way and then another of squatting and stooping at the side of the furnace, so as to be able to work the bellows without breaking her back at the same time.

'Giminy,' she said, 'this is lots worse than the charcoal-burning. And we've got to keep it up all night.'

'All night?' said Titty.

'Proper blast-furnaces never go out,' said Nancy, who was all the time working the bellows. 'And we've got to get it boiling and keep it boiling, so that all the gold will go to the bottom and all the rubbish come up to the top. Twenty-four hours at least, Dick says.'

'Not you four,' said Susan. 'You'll go to bed after supper as usual. Last night was bad enough. I don't believe any of you slept right through. Tonight all able-seamen go to bed at half past eight . . .'

'You have a turn,' panted Nancy, and John took her place.

'Don't start too fast,' said Nancy. 'It's much worse than you'd think.'

This John found for himself, and Peggy after him. Keeping the bellows going steadily was no sort of a joke, and none of the captains and mates seemed at all unwilling when Titty, Dick and Dorothea asked to be allowed to work the bellows in their turn.

'Jolly hard work, isn't it?' said Roger, watching them with his hands in his pockets.

'Twenty-four hours of it,' said Nancy. 'Suffering alligators! What time is it now?'

'Oh,' said Susan. 'I ought to have been thinking about supper. It'll have to be only potted meat. This is an awful day . . .'

'And the pigeon's not gone,' said Dorothea.

'Giminy,' said Nancy.

'Sappho's turn,' said Titty.

'Better send Sophocles,' said Nancy. 'It's late already and you can't depend on Sappho. We don't want the natives charging in tonight. And they will if the pigeon doesn't turn up. Tomorrow it won't matter. We'll be there ourselves. We'll take the ingot down to show mother.'

Nancy scrawled the message: TRIUMPH IN SIGHT. LOVE FROM ALL. S.A.D.M.C.

'That'll puzzle her,' she said. She took a bit of charcoal and scratched a skull on the back of the paper. . . . 'Just to let her know there's nothing to worry about.'

'Dot's turn to let fly,' said Titty.

*

'Wough. . . . Wough. . . . Wough.' The bellows never stopped for a moment. As fast as one of them tired, another took over. Charcoal was poured in at the top of the furnace. Susan was busy with the supper. Everybody was startled by a sudden native voice.

'Whatever are you doing?'

Mrs Tyson was standing in the camp, looking at the steaming remains of the charcoal-mound, and at the blast furnace. Anybody could see she was both frightened and angry.

'You'll have the wood on fire for sure. And after all I tell you. With the smoke blowing I thought it was alight already.

MRS TYSON VISITS THE CAMP

Nay, I can't have this. There's nowt to stop it if a spark catches hold ... Miss Nancy! MISS NANCY!'

The miners blinked at her with eyes reddened by the smoke. Hands, faces, clothes were black with charcoal.

'It's quite safe,' said Nancy. 'It wasn't smoke you saw. Only steam. Go on, Peggy. Don't stop blowing.'

'Wough. ... Wough. ... Wough.' The regular noise of the bellows, that had slackened for a moment, went on.

Dick dropped another handful of charcoal in at the top.

'Nay, but stop it!' said Mrs Tyson. 'If you've owt to cook, you can come down and use the kitchen range.'

'We can't stop now,' said Nancy.

John and Susan looked at each other.

'We're taking great care,' said John.

'Care!' snorted Mrs Tyson. 'And making fires like yon. They've had fires and enough on yon side of the lake, where they've plenty folk to put them out. But here, with none to help us, we'll be burnt like a handful of tow. Put it out, Miss Nancy. I can't do with you here, and I must tell Mrs Blackett. You'll go home to Beckfoot tomorrow, and if you don't like it you mun lump it. Put it out, Miss Nancy. Put it out and no more said.'

'We'll be done by tomorrow,' said Nancy.

'You'll be home tomorrow and away out of here,' said Mrs Tyson. 'Have you all gone daft?'

And she went off down the wood, muttering to herself.

'I say,' said John, 'what can we do?'

'Nothing,' said Nancy. 'Keep it up, Peg. ... Oh, all right. I'll take a turn. ... We'll have the ingot made by tomorrow. She'll calm down when she sees nothing's happened. It's too late for her to go and talk to mother tonight ...'

'If only she was like Mrs Dixon,' said Dorothea.

'Mr Dixon would be helping if he was here,' said Dick.

'It's no good talking about it,' said Nancy. 'We can't throw it all up now, just because Mrs Tyson's in a stew.'

Titty and Roger looked at Susan and John. What would mother say to such handling of a difficulty with the natives? But it was no good saying anything to Nancy. They were in for it now. Mrs Tyson was gone. Susan with a sigh went on spreading potted meat, looking rather native herself. John beat out a few red embers left from the charcoal-burning, and put another double handful of charcoal into the top of the furnace.

Work never stopped for a moment. People ate their suppers in turn, when they could be spared. There was very little talking . . . only the noise of the flames inside the furnace, and the 'Wough wough, wough' of the bellows.

'You'll simply have to let us stay up tonight,' said Roger, who was watching Susan work the bellows while he munched an apple to round off his supper.

Susan said nothing, but looked more native than ever.

'Eight's better than four,' said Roger. 'And even Captain Nancy snored this morning.'

'Snored!' said Captain Nancy. 'Shiver my timbers!' But she looked at Susan and then at John and added, 'The more hands the better all the same.'

'It can't be helped,' said John. 'Somebody'll have to keep blowing all the time. And somebody'll have to keep on feeding in the charcoal.'

And gradually even Susan's stern intentions weakened. Facts were too strong. The whole result of all their mining was in the crucible inside the grey stone furnace. At all costs the draught had to be kept up and the fire fed. And this business of pumping away at the bellows tired anybody out in no time. The more there were at it the better for everybody, to let the turns be as short as might be and the rests between the turns as long. Finally, Dick was the only one who really knew about blast furnaces and crucibles. If Dick was to be awake, and they could not do without him, how could the others be expected to go to sleep? In the end the thing just happened. Supper was never washed up. The kettle was boiled again and again. People ate hunks of chocolate and bread and butter when they felt hungry. Parched throats were wetted with hot weak tea at all sorts of hours. When one miner was tired of working the bellows another took over. Miners not busy feeding the furnace lay by the camp fire, or squatted on their heels looking with hot eyes into the flames. The night darkened about the camp. The fire gave just enough light to make the sky seem black as pitch. Talk died away. Work went on. With eight of them to take their turns there was time for each of them to get a little rested, but not to settle down to sleep. Before the sky began to pale overhead, and trees showed grey against it, they felt they had been tending blast furnaces all their lives. Charcoal-smeared faces made no one laugh, for all alike were grimed.

CHAPTER 30

DISASTER

THE sun climbed over the hills to the north-east and lit the tops of the trees. The leaves that had been grey were green once more. The camp-fire, fed with the unburnt ends of the sticks that had been used for charcoal-making, no longer threw wild shadows of the prospectors as they moved about their work. They looked a wild lot, with eyes sore from smoke and want of sleep, and faces smudged with charcoal.

For a long time now there had been no talking. The only noise was the steady murmur of the furnace and the regular snore and creak of the bellows, stopping only for a moment now and then when one tired pair of hands gave up the bellows to another.

'How much longer?' said Susan at last.

'As long as ever we can,' said Dick.

'It was pretty well evening when we st . . . arted,' said Nancy, using a black hand to cover a pink yawn in a piebald face. 'We'll have burnt all our charcoal by tonight. . . . Ow. . . . I'm not sleepy, really.'

So they were to go on all day. Well, why not? They had got beyond being tired. They had kept up the pumping so long that it was as if they had been working those bellows for weeks and were to go on working them until the end of time. Another eight hours to go. Roger was at the bellows at the moment. Dick had just filled up the furnace with fresh charcoal. Dorothea and Titty were stumbling about, gathering a fresh supply of good bits. John was stretching his arms after a long go of pumping. Peggy was stoking up the camp fire.

'I'm not sleepy either,' said Roger stoutly. 'Let's go on till the day after tomorrow to make sure of it.' And he put a little extra beef into his working of the bellows.

'Wough. . . . Wough. . . . Wough . . .'

The bellows had been steadily at work for a dozen hours.

'Wough. . . . Wough. . . . Wough . . .'

'Stick to it,' said Roger to himself.

And then, suddenly, the noise changed, and the bellows needed no strength at all to work them. It was as if he had been pushing at a closed door and the bolt had slipped out without his knowing it. There was a thin wheeze from the bellows, no more. He could open and shut them a hundred times in a minute if he wanted. No air at all was being driven into the furnace.

'Oh, Roger!' said Titty.

'What's gone with the bellows?' said Nancy.

'Bust,' said Roger. 'I don't know how they did it. There's the place.'

Anybody could see the place. Hour after hour of steady work had worn the leather through.

'It's gone all along the join,' said Nancy, poking her finger through it. 'Oh well, that settles it, anyhow.'

'What'll Mrs Blackett say?' said Susan.

'We'll put a patch in it,' said Nancy. 'I've got an old purse. We'll get it when we take the ingot home. But I say, Dick, will it matter not going on all day?'

Dick was fumbling with the red book. 'It doesn't say how long the smelting ought to take.'

'It isn't as if there was a tremendous lot of gold,' said Nancy.

'Won't it go on for a bit by itself?' said John.

'Not hot enough,' said Dick.

Already the murmur of the furnace was dying away.

'It's been at full blaze a very long time,' said Susan.

'It's probably done,' said Nancy.

'Let's open it and see the ingot,' said Roger.

'Just you try,' said Nancy, waving up and down a hand that had gone too near.

'We've got to let it cool,' said Dick. 'The gold'll all be melted. And we'll have to let it get solid again before we try turning it out.' He tried to look in at the top of the furnace to see if the last lot of charcoal had got red hot to the top before the busting of the bellows. He listened. The fire was quieting down.

The miners looked at each other and at the stone furnace that was far too hot to touch. They were suddenly tired. It was as if the string of a necklace had snapped and the beads were rolling all ways on the floor. The work that had kept them all awake was at an end. With no bellows to work or furnace to feed they were no longer a team, and each one separately was wondering how it had been possible to keep awake so long.

Susan, finding her eyes closing, pulled herself together.

'Will they have done the milking yet?' she said, and then, remembering Mrs Tyson, 'But perhaps she won't give us any milk.'

'I'll go,' said Nancy.

'Don't have a row,' said John.

Peggy took the milk can and, without meaning to, put a new smudge of black across her sleepy eyes.

'I'd better go,' she said. 'It's Nancy she feels like eating, not me.'

Everybody knew that she was right, and Peggy, swinging the milk can rather harder than she need, left the camp and set off down the path through the wood.

No one meant to go to sleep. Roger, squatting beside the furnace, fell over sideways and, somehow, did not feel like getting up again. John lugged him up and plumped him down at the doorway of his tent. Roger crawled half-way inside and dozed again, still hearing the 'wough, wough' of the bellows that had long since come to an end. Titty, as if in a dream, saw Nancy stagger across the camp. Her own eyes kept closing.

'Go and lie down for a bit,' said Susan. 'You, too, Dot. No need to keep awake while the thing's getting cool. . . .' She went off to the well, refilled the kettle and put it on the fire. John was in his tent already. Dorothea crawled into hers. Titty wriggled feet first into hers, and lay with her head in the doorway, and her chin in her hands, watching the camp-fire and the thin wisps of smoke that still rose from the embers of the charcoal mound. Susan was staring at the kettle. She leant sideways. She rested on an elbow. Only Dick seemed to be properly awake, looking up melting points of metals in the mineralogy book. But presently Titty opened her eyes again, a little surprised to find that she had closed them, and saw Dick's head drop on his book and stay there. 'Oh well,' she thought. 'Why not? . . .' This time she closed her eyes on purpose, but kept seeing the throbbing glow of red hot charcoal in the furnace. The blisters on her hands made her feel she was still working the bellows. She was not awake, but you could hardly say she was properly asleep.

*

This dozing of the tired and charcoal-smeared prospectors was brought to an end by a loud 'Hullo!' and the return of Peggy with the morning milk. Everybody started up. Even Roger was out of his tent in a moment. And then, as they looked at Peggy and at each other, they laughed, and Peggy laughed, too. For Peggy's hair was wet, and her face was scrubbed and shining. They saw each other's faces as if for the first time that day. It was as if Peggy were the only white in a crowded camp of Hottentots.

'Head under the pump,' said Peggy. 'Mrs Tyson made me look in a looking glass.'

'Has she calmed down?' said Susan.

'She gave me the milk all right. But she's still going to tell mother she can't do with us any more.'

'Oh well,' said Nancy, 'we've done the work now. We've made the ingot. And Captain Flint'll be back any minute. He'll manage her.'

*

Breakfast was over. It was Dick's moment. When it came to science, whether it was stars or stones, even John and Nancy, captains of their ships, were ready enough to leave everything to the professor. It was his job and the others had not even troubled to look into the red book except just to see a sentence or a diagram that Dick had wanted to show them. Even the furnace, slowly cooling in the middle of the camp, had been built from the drawing he had made. And now, minute by minute, the time was coming nearer when he would lift the little earthen lid from the crucible that he had put in there so many hours ago. Bother those bellows busting. With twenty-four hours of smelting he would have felt a good deal happier. But twelve was a good long time. Why couldn't the man who wrote that book have said how many hours of smelting ought to be given to how many pounds or ounces of the raw stuff?

'What about it now, Dick?' said Nancy at last. 'It's still pretty hot.'

'If it's under two thousand and sixty degrees,' said Dick, 'the gold won't be liquid any more.'

'It must be less than that by now,' said John.

'Better unbuild it from the top,' said Nancy.

'So long as none of the stones fall down inside,' said Dick, who would have been ready to wait till everything was cold.

Roger, gingerly, pushed a stone sideways off the top of the

furnace. John pushed one off. So did Nancy. So did Titty.

Dick stood watching them. Two thousand and sixty degrees. It seemed a tremendous lot. What if after all they had not got it hot enough even with the bellows? No. It must have been hot enough. Whose knife had a file on it? John's. They would want that to clean the scum off the ingot, to turn it into a shining lump of pure gold. Pure? Carats. How did people measure carats? Captain Flint would do that.

'Don't all try to help at once,' said Nancy.

One at a time the stones were pushed off. People pushed them off with lumps of earth or other stones, to save the burning of their fingers.

'They do keep hot a long time,' said Nancy.

'Poor conductors,' said Dick. 'If they were iron they'd be cold again by now.'

The furnace was growing lower and lower while a ring of stones grew wider round it.

'Can you see the top of the crucible?' asked Titty.

'Not yet.'

'We'd better open the side now,' said Dick, 'or that big stone'll fall in.'

Everybody pressed round. John and Nancy were pulling out the stones with which the opening at the side of the furnace had been closed after the crucible had been put in.

'Steady!' said Nancy.

Dick, as in all moments of great excitement, took off and wiped his spectacles.

John suddenly gasped.

'There's no crucible,' he said.

'Oh rot,' said Nancy.

'Well, here's where it was,' said John. 'And there's nothing but white ash.'

'It's slipped through the bars,' said Nancy.

'It couldn't,' said Dick.

'Oh hurry up,' said Nancy.

Stones flew from the furnace, pulled aside by tingling fingers. The furnace grew lower and lower. They had come to the four bent rusty bars on which the crucible had rested. It was not there. More stones were pulled aside.

'There's a bit of it,' said John grimly.

'Bust,' said Nancy.

With two sticks, John pulled a bit of blackened pottery from the ashes. Everybody knew what it was.

'Well, he's got lots of crucibles,' said Peggy.

'The gold can't have got away,' said Dick. 'It'll be in a lump at the bottom.'

'He won't mind what shape it is,' said Nancy. 'Come on, let's get at it.'

The last stones were pulled aside, and they began raking apart the heap of hot ash that was left. It rose in clouds into their faces.

'It'll be right underneath,' said Dick.

They found other bits of the crucible, the lid in two pieces, the bottom all in one, and curved fragments of the sides. But there was never a sign of an ingot. Worse. The gold dust had disappeared. There was nothing left but pale ash and a few small lumps of slag.

'But there must be *something*,' said Nancy, scraping frantically among the stones.

'There isn't,' said John.

Dick, with trembling fingers, fitted together two bits of the broken crucible.

'It can't just have gone,' he said.

'But it has,' said Nancy.

They looked at each other with despair. Two whole weeks had gone with the gold dust, and if Captain Flint were to come home now, they had nothing to show him. Crushing, panning, charcoal-burning and smelting . . . the result of all their labours was a little heap of hot stones and smoking ash.

'Oh, Dick!' said Dorothea, and in spite of all she could do tears trickled slowly down and made white channels on her still charcoaled face.

'We ought to have had a snake for luck,' said Titty. 'Like the real charcoal-burners.'

'We ought to have asked Slater Bob how to do it,' said Susan.

'We couldn't,' said Nancy, almost crossly. 'Do be sensible. Nice and useful it would have been . . . giving away secrets when he and Squashy were seeing each other almost every day.'

Dick, wiping his spectacles, blinked as he looked from face to face. He looked at them but hardly saw them. He knew mistily that they were all miserable. He was miserable himself. They had counted on him and everything had gone wrong, but his mind was not on their misery nor on his own. Everything had gone wrong. But why? How had it gone wrong?

'I must have made a mistake somewhere,' he said slowly. 'The same thing's happened that happened when I tried a little with the blow-pipe.' He took a half-burnt stick and raked among the ashes. 'It's my fault,' he said. 'I can't have read the book right. But if it wasn't hot enough nothing would have happened, and I don't believe we could have got it too hot.'

'I wonder why the crucible broke,' said John. 'We couldn't have done it dropping in the charcoal . . .'

'Hotter in one place than another,' said Dick. 'But it's the gold going I can't understand . . .'

'It probably wasn't gold at all,' said Susan. 'We ought to have made sure.'

Dick looked up suddenly.

'There is one way we could,' he said. 'Did we put all the gold dust in the crucible?'

'All but that pinch we got first,' said Nancy.

'But I put that in with the rest,' said Peggy. 'I thought it was being forgotten.'

'Then the whole lot's gone,' said Nancy.

'We could try it with *aqua regia*,' said Dick. 'You know, a chemical test. The book says gold dissolves in *aqua regia*. If it does, we'd know for certain. Captain Flint's got the acids and test-tubes. They're in the glass cupboard.'

Nancy suddenly thumped the breath out of him.

'Good for you, Dick,' she said. 'Are you sure you can do it?'

'He's got both the right acids,' said Dick.

'But there's no time,' said Susan. 'If Mrs Tyson's going to say we've got to leave.'

'Come on,' said Nancy. 'We'll get some more right away. Even if we don't have time to smelt an ingot, the main thing is to prove the stuff is gold.'

But Susan put her foot down.

'Not the able-seamen,' she said. 'If they don't have some proper sleep they'll all be dead.' And Nancy, looking round at their tired faces, agreed that she was right.

'Well, I'll go anyway,' she said.

'Come on,' said John.

'We'll all four go,' said Susan. 'But not the able-seamen. They ought to get to bed and sleep till tea-time.'

'Dinner-time,' said Roger.

'But what about Dick?' said Nancy.

Dick stared at her. 'I'll sleep when I come back,' he said. 'It's no good trying till I've made sure.'

Susan looked not at him but at Dorothea. Dot was Dick's sister and ought to know. Dorothea remembered her father sitting up all night over a scrap of papyrus covered with

Egyptian hieroglyphics, and her mother making hot coffee for him but not even trying to get him to go to bed. What was the good of going to bed if people could not sleep for thinking?

'He'll be all right,' said Dorothea.

'And the sooner he goes the better,' said Nancy. 'Where's that frying-pan? And we'd better take the bucket. The crushing mill's in the mine. We'll get a pinch of gold panned for him to take, and then get as much as we can done before he comes back. There's charcoal left, and we'll mend the bellows, and have another go at an ingot.'

'But Mrs Tyson . . .' began Susan.

'She isn't going all the way down to Beckfoot just to tell mother we've got to clear out,' said Nancy. 'We've got one more day, anyhow. Come on.'

'What about the pigeons?' said Peggy. 'We've only got Sappho here.'

Dick heard her. . . . Pigeons? . . . Bring back pigeons? . . . What had happened to everybody? Why was it that Peggy sounded almost cheerful? He never guessed for a moment that he himself had given them a new hope and plucked them out of their despair. What was that? Peggy was talking again to him . . .

'The basket goes on the handlebars all right. We must have Homer and Sophocles back. Sappho's no good. Whatever happens we mustn't have mother not getting a letter at the proper time and coming up here before Mrs Tyson's calmed down.'

'And we want a bit of leather for the bellows,' said Nancy. 'My old purse. Mother'll give it you. And good strong needles. And a box of tacks to nail the leather down when it's mended. Right-hand drawer in the table in the hall. Come on, John. And what about you, Susan? The sooner we get the stuff for him, the sooner he can start.'

'I'm coming. Go to bed, you three.'

Even Susan sounded hopeful. Dick gave up trying to understand.

*

Ten minutes later the camp was silent.

Roger, Titty and Dorothea slept in their tents, tired out.

Nancy, John, Susan and Peggy were hurrying across the Topps to Golden Gulch.

Dick strapped the pigeon-basket on the handlebars of Peggy's bicycle, tucked his blow-pipe into the handkerchief pocket of his shirt, put the red mineralogy book into his knapsack, pulled it out again, just to have another look at 'Tests for gold,' left the dromedary to lean against a tree, and hurried off after the others.

It was the hottest of a whole fortnight of hot days. The hot air over the Topps made everything seem to quiver in a haze. Away in the valley a motor-car was hooting through the woods. It roared up and along the Dundale road. Its noise stopped. Another of these picnic parties, Dick supposed. How awfully hot it was. Hullo. There was Squashy out on the Topps. On the far side of Golden Gulch. Very near it, too? And Dick thought of that other blow-pipe, and wondered whether Squashy had been more successful than himself. And with that he was thinking again of the opening of their own furnace. What really had happened? What had he done wrong? Had the gold just trickled away into the earth? Or had there been no gold? He would find out now, for certain.

He came to the gulch, and at the opening to the mine heard the thud, thud of the crushing mill inside.

'You don't want much panned, do you?' said Nancy, as he came in. 'We've got a bit nearly all gold.'

John had quarried out some splendid lumps of quartz, with yellow glinting in the cracks.

The panning took longer than the crushing, but it was done

FORLORN HOPE

at last, and the greeny gold sediment was poured into Dick's handkerchief. He brought the four corners together, and John, with a bit of string, put a lashing round the handkerchief so that the precious dust was as safe as if it was in a bag. Dick took two or three small lumps of quartz and put them in his pocket.

'I might want to try with a raw bit,' he said.

'We'll get all this lot crushed before you get back,' said Nancy. 'Good luck to you, Professor.'

Dick was off.

'Don't forget the pigeons,' Peggy called after him.

'Tacks,' shouted Nancy. 'And the old purse for the patch.'

He was out in the sunshine, racing across the narrow gulch, climbing the side of it, and hurrying across the Topps.

He had gone perhaps a hundred yards when he stopped short.

'Better write them down,' he said to himself. 'I'm sure to forget them if I don't.' He pulled out his pocket-book and wrote 'Pigeons, Nails in drawer in hall, Nancy's old purse.'

Then he ran on, stumbling and hot, over the uneven ground.

*

Squashy Hat, with problems of his own, was coming nearer to the gulch. He had noticed that boy, hurrying through the bracken. He looked back at the white spots up on the hillside behind him, and along the line they pointed out across the Topps. He must have another look in daylight. If only those children were playing somewhere else . . .

Susan, Nancy, Peggy and John were in the mine.

Dorothea, Titty and Roger slept in their tents.

Dick, his mind full of mineralogy, tiptoed through the camp, pushed off on Peggy's dromedary, found his balance on it after one frantic wobble and, braking fairly hard, began the steep descent down the old track, through Tyson's wood.

The motor-car that had stopped at the side of the Dundale road was gone. The visitors who had rested there, eaten their sandwiches by the roadside and admired the view over the hills, were already a dozen miles away. A thin wisp of blue smoke curled in the grass where they had been. No one saw it. This time there were no watchers on the Great Wall.

PESTLE·AND·MORTAR

CHAPTER 31

SMOKE OVER HIGH TOPPS

THE camp dozed in the sweltering heat. Titty, Roger and Dorothea slept their well-earned sleep. Even Sappho, alone in the big cage, was silent, and slept upon her perch, her bill buried in the feathers of her breast.

Hour after hour went by.

*

There came a change in the air. The pigeon was the first to notice it, stirring uneasily in her cage. A smell of burning found its way into the dreams of the three sleeping miners. Roger patted the ground in his sleep. He was closing a leak in the earthy crust of the charcoal pudding, where the smoke was coming through. Dorothea dreamed of singeing a handkerchief in taking off a kettle. Titty was the first to be actually waked by the strange new smell. She rolled over and sniffed and sniffed again. Was it Susan's cooking fire? Had the embers of the charcoal-burning somehow started again? As for the furnace, she remembered miserably how everything had gone wrong, and how the furnace had been pulled to pieces and the fire in it killed by anxious seekers for gold among its ashes. Susan must be making tea. Perhaps it was already late. How long had she slept? Titty did not know. Perhaps it was already next day.

'Susan,' said Titty quietly, so as not to wake the others. 'Is he back? Is it gold after all?'

There was no answer.

Instead there was the whirr of wings overhead and the

startled cry of frightened grouse. . . . 'Go back. Go back. Go back!' Several times during the last ten days the prospectors had put up grouse from among the heather, and Titty herself had once all but fallen backwards when an old cock grouse whirred up from under her feet with that sudden, loud, disturbing cry.

Why didn't Susan answer? Or was it one of the others at the fire? Titty sat up and flung herself round so that she could see out into the camp. There was no one there. The camp-fire, damped down by Susan, was dozing peaceably under its clods, from which little thin wisps of smoke were rising. All that smell of smoke could not be coming from there. It was a different smell, too. The ashes and ruins of the furnace were not smouldering. Nor were the remains of the charcoal. But how strong that smell was. And there was something funny about the camp. For the first time in daylight since they had been there, things were not casting shadows. No pattern of dappled leaves was dancing over the pale gold canvas of the tents. Something had happened to the sun.

More grouse whirred overhead.

Titty crawled out of the tent. On all fours at the mouth of it she sniffed again, and listened. A smell of burning, but not quite like the smell of wood smoke. And what was that noise? Sharp, sudden crackling. And the haze above the trees?

'Roger . . . Dot. . . . Get up . . . Get up at once.'

She reached into Roger's tent, caught him by a foot and pulled him out. Dorothea's face, startled, questioning, showed that she was at least awake.

'Come out,' said Titty. 'It's . . . At least I think it is. There's a fire somewhere . . .'

'Where,' said Roger. 'Anyway, you shouldn't pull me out like that. . . . It's *my* foot. . . .' But Titty was gone.

'There really *is* a fire,' said Dorothea.

Titty ran out of the camp by the little path that led to the well and so to the hedgehog's bramble thicket and the narrow gully that made a pathway for them up the Great Wall. If there was a fire someone ought to tell the others at once. They would know what to do. That crackling was quite near. And she knew now that the haze overhead was smoke. She raced up the gully.

A huge wall of smoke lay across High Topps. Dimly, above it she saw the summit of Kanchenjunga. Along the foot of it was a line of crackling flames, now thin and broken, now suddenly leaping upwards like the tossed crest of a wave. Everything beyond it, until, far away, the top of the mountain climbed into the sky, was hidden by the rolling smoke. Somewhere over there was the gulch, but Titty knew at once that it was no use trying to get there. It never came into her head that the elders might be themselves in danger. They were cut off from the camp by this wall of smoke and the fire that made it. It would take them a long time to come to the rescue. Meanwhile she had to do the best she could. What would Susan be doing if she were here? Or John? And anyway, what was there to be done? Minute after minute passed and she still stood there looking at the smoke and the line of fire along the foot of it.

Dorothea and Roger climbed up and stood beside her.

'Golly,' said Roger. 'Mrs Tyson'll be saying "I told you so".'

'Dick'll be safe at Beckfoot by now, won't he?' said Dorothea.

'Ages ago,' said Titty.

What little wind there was had been blowing from the south. There was a sudden change. The smoke rolled towards them as if Kanchenjunga had puffed at it. A moment later it rolled back again and they saw that in a dozen places the flames beneath it had leapt nearer.

'It's coming this way,' said Roger.

'Yes it is,' said Dorothea.

'We've got to save the camp,' said Titty. 'Once it gets to the trees nothing'll stop it. Come on. Get the tents down.'

There was another sudden hot breath from Kanchenjunga across the Topps, another loud crackling as the fire leapt forward over the dry bent, and some patches of bracken flared up into the smoke.

The three of them rushed down the gully and back into the camp.

'Roll up your sleeping-bag, Roger, and get your tent down. You, too, Dot. We'll have to do everybody's. And then we'll have to get them down somehow. We'll never be able to manage the handcart by ourselves. Oh dear, and there's the pigeons' cage. . . . And Sappho.'

'Let her fly,' said Roger. 'She'll be able to look after herself.'

Titty checked herself.

'Well done, Rogie. We'll send her for help. An SOS. Oh, if only she was Homer or Sophocles. . . . You can't count on Sappho. But we'll try. Anyway she'll be all right. She'll get home some time or other. What are you doing, Dot?'

Dorothea was pushing *The Outlaw of the Broads* into her knapsack.

'I must save the *Outlaw*,' she said.

'Let's have a bit of paper,' said Titty, and Dorothea, without hesitating a moment, tore off half the title-page of her precious novel.

'And here's a pencil,' she said.

Titty wrote three words only:

FIRE HELP QUICK.

She tore off the strip of paper on which she had written them and rolled it into a thin slip. Roger, who was on very good terms with Sappho, caught her without difficulty. He croodled to her to keep her calm. Dorothea was telling her to

339

fly straight. 'Keep out of the smoke and you'll be all right. And you'll find Dick at Beckfoot. Only do fly straight, just this once.'

Titty slipped the message under the rubber ring on Sappho's left leg.

'Shall I let her go?' said Roger.

'Not in the trees,' said Titty.

They hurried back to the edge of the Topps. A wave of smoke rolled towards them.

'Now,' said Titty. 'Quick!'

Roger threw the pigeon into the air.

'You simply mustn't hang about,' said Titty. 'Go home. Quick. Quick.'

And Sappho rose high above the smoke, and was gone.

'She may not get home till tomorrow,' said Dorothea. 'You can't count on Sappho.'

'Come on and pack the tents,' said Titty, and then, running down the gully, she remembered something else. Below the Great Wall was the bramble thicket. And in the bramble thicket was the hedgehog. What about it? It was no good calling to the hedgepig to come out. And if the fire came leaping down from the Topps, the bramble thicket would roar up in flames and the hedgepig would be cooked in the middle of them.

'Never mind the tents,' she said. 'We've got to save the hedgepig.' This was dreadful. First one thing and then another. No settled plan. Nancy or John would have thought of everything at once and there would have been none of this dithering.

'We've got fire-brooms,' suggested Roger.

'If it gets to the edge of the Topps, we're done,' said Titty.

'It's blowing the other way now,' said Dorothea, who had her knapsack on her back, empty except for the *Outlaw*.

At that moment the wind veered again. A hot breath blew

in their faces and the smoke rolled towards them. It was only for a moment, but as the smoke rolled back and lifted, they saw that the fire had taken hold of a new wide strip of withered bent and bracken.

Titty looked about her. They were standing on the top of the long ridge of rock that made the Great Wall. There was very little grass there for the flames to catch, none at all, except in the cracks of the stone and in the gully that made a path down into the wood. Then, beyond the Great Wall, Nancy's turf-cutting had made another obstacle for the fire, in the wide strip of ground from which the grassy clods had been lifted and used for the damping of the charcoal fire. If only the wind did not help the flames to leap across it, or send flying sparks to light the brambles and grass below the rock. Yes, there was just a chance . . . if the wind did not change.

'We'll want the fire-brooms,' said Titty. 'But first we must wet all the grass along the top of the Wall . . .'

'A chain of buckets going from hand to hand,' said Dorothea.

'We've only got one bucket,' said Titty. 'If they didn't take it to the gulch. But there's the kettle. If only we hadn't used such a lot of water yesterday . . .'

Roger was already in the camp and lugging a couple of the fire-brooms along the ground.

'There's lots of water in the well,' Titty shouted. 'Kettle, Dot!'

'The kettle's full,' called Dorothea. 'Susan filled it.'

'Oh good,' said Titty, looking quickly round the camp. 'But they've taken the saucepan. And they've got the bucket, too . . .'

'There's a biscuit-tin,' said Roger. 'We can eat the biscuits or put them in our pockets.'

'Come on, then. Damping first. Fire-brooms later.' She took the big sugar-tin and emptied all the lump sugar out on the ground. Susan herself would not have tried to save it. If only they had thought of anything like this happening, they would never have taken the bucket. Titty filled the sugar-tin and raced after Dorothea, who had run on with the kettle.

'What am I to do with it?' said Dorothea.

'Wet the grass at the top of the gully,' said Titty. 'Wet all the grass along the top of the rock, on this side of Nancy's digging. The fire'll go out if it has nothing to burn but stone.'

Titty slopped the water out of the sugar-tin. Dorothea used the kettle as a watering-can, pouring the water on the dry ground, that was so dry that the water did not sink into it but lay in sparkling drops. They raced down the gully to the well, and met Roger coming carefully up with a biscuit-tin full to the brim.

'What *have* you been doing?' said Titty.

'I hadn't got room in my pockets for all the biscuits,' said Roger. 'So I piled the rest in the store tent.'

'Buck up,' said Titty. 'There ought to be fifty of us instead of three.'

The fire was nearer each time they came back to the top of the rock. It checked for some minutes at one of the ridges of stone that pushed up out of the heather. They began almost to think it had been stopped, and then they saw little flames trickling over the ridge, following the moss and grass that had found foothold between the rocks. It flared up again on the near side of the ridge as the flames caught a wide patch of bracken.

Backwards and forwards they ran, with kettle, biscuit-tin, sugar-tin, pudding-bowl and even washing-up basin, Titty and Dorothea managing two things at once. But after the first few journeys, the level of the water in the well began to fall. Good little spring though it was, they were taking water out faster than it was coming in.

'It wouldn't be much good if there were fifty of us,' said

Roger at last, out of breath with running to and fro. 'The well's empty. I've scooped the last mud with the lid of the tin. We've got to give it time to fill up again.'

'It'll be too late,' said Dorothea.

'John and Susan and the Amazons'll be here soon,' said Titty, looking desperately into the high wall of smoke that was rolling towards Ling Scar and now hid even the peak of Kanchenjunga. 'They'll be able to get round behind it . . .'

And then once more, when it had almost seemed that the fire was sweeping past them, the wind wavered, a line of fire raced across the ground under the smoke, and the sea of bracken, in which so often scouts had lurked, flared up with a crackling roar as if someone were wasting thousands of fireworks by lighting them all at once.

'It's coming,' said Roger. 'What ought we to do about the tents? . . .'

'Oh PLEASE rain. . . . PLEASE rain. . . .' Dorothea did not know that she was saying the words aloud.

'Beat it out,' cried Titty. 'Beat it out . . . wherever it starts. . . . Look out. There's a bit burning behind you. . . . On the rock.'

The fire was licking along the edge of the Topps. If the wind were to swing round to the west and stay there, nothing could save them. Even as it was, smoke filled their eyes, and sparks fluttered in the air like burning moths. They hurried this way and that along the Great Wall, stumbling, half-blind, flailing away with their fire-brooms at tufts of grass that caught fire, smouldered and flared at their very feet.

'I do wish they'd be quick,' said Titty to herself. 'Stick to it, Rogie! Well done, Dot!' and then, to herself again, 'We'll never do it alone . . .'

CHAPTER 32

IN THE GULCH

IN the gulch, once Dick had hurried away with his pinch of
dust in his handkerchief, nothing seemed worth doing any
more. While he was there, with his talk of *aqua regia* and tests
to prove that gold was gold, everybody had felt that there was
still hope. Now that he was gone, it was as if he had taken the
hope with him. They could think only of the broken crucible
and the worthless ashes among the ruins of the blast furnace.
'Triumph in sight' had been the last message sent to Beckfoot. Today they were to have carried home the ingot. And
there was no ingot. All their work had gone for nothing.
Even Nancy felt it was hardly worth while going on with
the quarrying and crushing until the professor came back.

They had taken some splendid lumps of quartz seamed all
over with glinting yellow out into the sunshine. It looked
good enough, but was it?

'I wonder if it is or it isn't?' said John, turning over the
best bits.

And Nancy did not feel like shivering timbers. She said,
flatly, 'I don't know.' A moment later she added, 'It's our
fault, really, not Dick's. We ought to have sweated up the
chemistry ourselves.'

'Dick nearly always *is* right,' said Peggy. 'About things
like that.'

'Not this time,' said Susan.

'Even if he is,' said John, 'we're not going to have time to
make an ingot . . .'

'We can't go on staying if Mrs Tyson wants us to go,'
said Susan.

They went dismally back into the mine.

In there, in the comfortable darkness, that was broken only by the dim light of the hurricane lantern hanging from the iron peg, all four miners felt more and more sleepy. After all, it was two days since anybody had had a proper night's rest. No one was in a hurry to get back to work. They did not feel even like talking. When somebody said something it just dropped dead like a stone.

'Dick can't be back till pretty late,' said Susan. The others heard her, but that was all.

'How long does it take to come from South America?' said John.

'Not long in a fast ship,' said Nancy dully. 'But ages in a tramp.' And John was too tired to ask her what was the use of an answer like that.

'Peggy, you're falling asleep,' said Nancy, a few minutes later.

'Well, why not?' Peggy yawned, leaning back against the wall. Nancy said nothing. She found her own eyes closing.

It was a long time before anybody spoke again.

*

Peggy opened her eyes and blinked hard. Who was asleep? Not she. And then she smiled at seeing that Nancy's eyes were shut. John's head had fallen forward, and Susan's was all on one side. The lantern burned dimly on the wall of rock. What time of day was it? Perhaps no need to wake them yet. Peggy stood up and went, on tiptoe, to the mouth of the cave. . . . What on earth was happening? What were those crackling noises? And the sky was full of smoke. For one moment she could not believe it. Then she knew. It had happened, the thing people had been dreading all the summer. This was the end of everything.

She darted back into the mine and pulled Nancy by the arm, and John.

'Wake up,' she cried. 'Nancy! John! Susan! Quick! Wake up! The fell's on fire.'

'What's the matter?' said Nancy, more than half asleep.

'Fire,' shouted Peggy. 'FIRE!'

'Don't be a galoot,' yawned Nancy.

'It's not time to get up yet,' said John, stretching an arm.

'FIRE,' yelled Peggy. 'It's a big one. Oh, Susan! Do wake *up*!'

Nancy staggered to her feet and went sleepily out of the mine, steadying herself with her hands against the rocky walls. The others, rubbing their eyes and yawning, were close behind her. They were not out of the tunnel before they heard that queer running crackle of fire in short grass and smelt the smoke in the air.

'Giminy,' said Nancy. 'She's right. Some wretched idiot's set the fell on fire. . . . I say, and all the fire-brooms are in the camp . . .'

'What about Titty and Roger?' cried Susan.

'And Dorothea,' said John.

They came out into the gulch. Thick clouds of smoke were rolling high overhead. The sun showed through them like a red-hot penny, disappearing as the smoke thickened and showing again as it thinned.

They were just bolting across the gulch when they saw that they were not alone.

Only a few yards from the secret entry to their mine a man was lying full length on the ground, pillowed on a clump of heather. His feet were what they noticed first, large feet in heavily nailed climbing-boots. His face was hidden. He had been using a map, and had spread it over his face like a tent to keep off the sun. He was lying on his back, and his left hand rested on the pile of good lumps of quartz that John had brought out from the mine that morning. The sight of that hand, half-closed over the quartz, turned it to gold again, at least for Nancy.

'It's Squashy Hat,' she said, almost in a whisper. 'And he's got his paw on our gold . . .'

'Gosh!' said Peggy.

'Come on,' said John. 'We've got to get across . . .'

Susan was already climbing the other side of the gulch. The fell was on fire, and for gold and Squashy Hat she had not a thought to spare. . . . Roger, and Titty, left alone . . .

'He's asleep,' said Peggy.

'Serve him right if we let him roast,' said Nancy, but she could hardly do that. Instead she poked him with a foot.

'Wake up,' she said. 'FIRE! Come on, Peggy!' and leaving Squashy Hat to do what he thought best, she and Peggy raced after the others.

Bracken flared in their faces and a cloud of thick smoke rolled down to meet them over the edge of the gulch. They dropped back choking.

'It's between us and the camp,' shouted John. 'We'll have to get round.'

'It'll be in the gulch in another minute,' said Nancy.

'Prairie fire,' said a quiet voice below them. 'No time to be lost. We've got to run for it. All right if we get away up on the Screes.'

They looked down. Squashy Hat, whose guilty conscience had always made him bolt at the sight of them, had a voice that was somehow steadying.

'We can't,' said Nancy.

'We've got to get back to the camp,' said Susan, desperately looking this way and that at the smoke that seemed to be coming from all sides at once.

Squashy Hat ran up the steep slope, and stood there in the smoke.

347

'You're right,' he said, 'we can't get to the Screes. But we've a chance yet,' he went on, in that same steadying voice. 'There's a bit of a gap to the norrard.'

They raced together, the four prospectors and the rival they had caught with a clutching hand actually resting on their gold. They raced along the bottom of the gulch. They came up out of the gulch at its northern end just in time to see the flames meet again beyond them. The gulch was an island in the middle of the fire.

The island was growing quickly smaller as the fire came licking through the stones from grass patch to grass patch, blazing noisily through heather and bracken.

Squashy Hat looked anxiously round. They could see he was wondering what best to do. He spoke again, rather gravely. 'The whole place'll be ablaze in another two minutes,' he said. 'Our best chance will be among those stones ...'

'But Titty and Roger....' Susan stared hopelessly into the smoke.

'We must get back,' shouted Nancy. 'Come on, you!'

They ran back. Squashy Hat stopped on a bit of stony ground where there was not much grass to feed the fire.

'What are you waiting for?' shouted Nancy. He might be a rival, a robber and jumper of claims, but she could not leave him to burn.

Squashy Hat was taking off his coat. 'You'd better get your heads under this,' he was saying. 'But I'm afraid we're fairly trapped.'

'Come on,' said Nancy. 'Get back into the mine ...'

'What mine?' said Squashy Hat.

'Ours,' said Nancy. And even in that dreadful moment a note of triumph came into her voice. He had not found it. 'Our mine,' she said again. 'We'll let you in, but no jumping!'

'What do you mean?' said Squashy Hat.

There was a sudden wide leaping flame and a roar as the fire caught the dry grass at the southern end of the gulch. There were sparks flying red in the smoke above their heads. On the farther side of the gulch a patch of bracken blazed up like a bundle of fireworks.

'Look here,' said John. 'I've got to get across to the camp.'

'You can't,' said Nancy. 'Get into the mine. It's the only hope. Your getting burnt won't help anybody. Come on. Get in, Peggy. Quick.'

Peggy was waiting by the mouth of the old working. She stooped and was gone.

'Well, I never saw that,' said Squashy Hat.

'Hurry up, Susan!'

'Go in yourself!' said John.

'Of all the turnipheads!' said Nancy, and bolted in after Susan.

The heather flared close above them.

'After you,' said Squashy Hat.

'It's not your mine,' said John.

'I beg your pardon,' said Squashy Hat. He stooped and bent his long legs and worked his way through the tunnel with John close behind him.

They were not a moment too soon. They were hardly inside the mine, where the lantern still burnt and lit their startled faces, before thick smoke closed the entry.

'We've just got to wait till it's over,' said Nancy, and sat down comfortably on the floor of the cave, to show Peggy that there was really nothing to worry about. John and Susan stared at her. 'Nothing to worry about!' And then, suddenly, there was a glow of red in the mouth of the mine. Then leaping flames as the fire roared past. Then, again, nothing but smoke.

'I'm very much obliged to you,' said Squashy Hat gravely. 'I shouldn't have stood much of a chance outside.'

'You oughtn't to have been there,' said Nancy. 'Didn't you see our notice? It'll be burnt now, but you must have seen it.'

'Well, yes, I did,' said Squashy Hat. 'But I was busy looking for something, and I didn't think any of you were about . . .'

Nancy jumped to her feet. 'All the worse,' she said. 'What were you looking for?'

'It wouldn't interest you,' said Squashy Hat mildly. 'Not really. Mining, you know. It's my job. I was following up a vein . . .'

'What?' Nancy's indignation was almost more than she could bear.

'Funny I never noticed this,' he said. 'I was thinking there might be something of the sort.'

'It's ours,' said Nancy. 'Couldn't you read that notice?'

'Something about some game,' said Squashy Hat. 'Something about riding or leaping wasn't it? And a picture of a death's head?'

'Telling people not to jump claims,' said Nancy. 'You must have known . . .'

But there was no more on that subject, for the noise of the fire was farther away, and the smoke was clearing outside, and John and Susan were already starting out of the mine.

'Take care,' said Squashy Hat suddenly. 'Give it time to cool underfoot.'

'We've got to go,' said John.

'The others won't know what to do,' said Susan, and followed John.

'What others?' said Squashy Hat.

'Three more of us,' said Peggy. 'Younger than us. In the camp at the top of the wood.'

Squashy Hat hurried after John and Susan. Nancy and Peggy hurried after Squashy Hat.

Even in the mine the air had been bitter with smoke. It was far worse outside. The fire was raging at the northern end of the gulch. It had swept through, burning everything but earth and rock. Clumps of heather were still flickering like torches dropped and forgotten by a procession on the march. The ground smoked under their feet. They burned their hands when they touched the rocks in scrambling up the steep side of the little valley. The fire had poured northwards over the Topps, which were black and smoking as far as they could see. Stretches of grass and bracken were still blazing between the gulch and Tyson's wood. A high curtain of smoke hid the Great Wall and the trees beyond it, and along the foot of that curtain they could see little spurts of flame.

'The wood itself may be on fire,' said John, as he dashed forward with the ashes smoking about his feet.

'They may be asleep in their tents,' cried Susan.

'Oh, no. . . . No . . .' shouted Nancy fiercely. 'They aren't utter galoots . . .'

'Not that way,' shouted Squashy Hat. 'You follow me. We've got to cut round that lot.'

His long arms were working like a windmill. He was leaping rocks that came in his way, dodging others he could not leap.

The four prospectors raced after their rival. They were not prospectors now. There was only one thought in all their minds as they skirted a stretch of blazing bracken and ran splashing through the hot ash, towards that wall of smoke. Somewhere behind that smoke was the camp.

'If only they've had the sense to run away,' panted Susan.

'They'll be all right,' said Nancy, and choked with the fine ash in her mouth.

And then a puff of wind blew the smoke towards them. It lifted and for a moment cleared. Dimly beneath it they saw figures, small, dim, beating frantically at the ground.

351

THE FLAMES ROARED PAST OUTSIDE

'Titty. . . . Dorothea . . .'

'There's old Roger,' shouted Nancy.

The smoke rolled down again thicker than before. But Squashy Hat had seen them, too. A moment later, racing straight for them, he, too, had disappeared.

'Come on,' John shouted over his shoulder. 'They're all right. This way!'

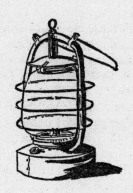

CHAPTER 33

AT BECKFOOT

DICK braked carefully, feeling first in one pocket and then in another to make sure that he had forgotten nothing. Blowpipe in handkerchief pocket with fountain pen. *Phillips on Metals* bumping in the knapsack on his back . . . no forgetting that. Lumps of quartz in one side pocket of his shorts. . . . Charcoal in paper in the other. . . . Pinch of precious dust in handkerchief. . . . Notebook with knife in hip pocket. . . . Bump. . . . Bump. His hand flew back to the jerking handlebar. Nearly off that time. He must not let himself think of anything but the steering of his dromedary. . . . Oh. . . . The dromedary skidded on the loose stones as the path suddenly turned a corner, and Dick got a foot to the ground only just in time to save himself.

He pushed off again and found his pedal. . . . Woa. . . . Don't let the beast get going too fast. And don't go jamming the brake on so that the wheels lock. . . . If only they had not put all the gold dust into the furnace. Quantity did not count. Nancy had said at the beginning that all that mattered was to prove that the gold was there. . . . Just a blob. . . . One golden blob would be enough. With the blowpipe and a proper spirit-lamp he ought to be able to manage that, try it with *aqua regia* to make sure, and then everything would be all right after all. Meanwhile the dromedary was jolting him almost to pieces as it slipped and jumped and jibbed and skidded and bucked over the loose stones in the old path down the wood. You never would have thought it was possible to get so hot going down-hill. He came at last to the bottom, bumped across the bobbles of the farmyard, was glad not to see

Mrs Tyson, crossed the bridge and came out on the valley road which, dusty as it was, was much better travelling for dromedaries. He pedalled away down the valley as fast as anybody could on a girl's bicycle at least two sizes too big for him.

*

Beckfoot looked quite different. Paperers and painters and plasterers were gone. The carpets were down even on the stairs, and chairs and tables were all back in their places. He met Mrs Blackett in the hall.

'Hullo, Dick,' she said. 'You're just in time for lunch. Have you come to have a look at your pigeon-bell? I've just pushed the slide across to set it. It's been working beautifully since you put it right the other day. Nearly deafens us with every pigeon . . .'

'There won't be one today,' said Dick, 'because of me coming.'

'I'm glad one of you has come. I've got news for all of you. Your father and mother are going to be at Dixon's farm the day after tomorrow. And Mrs Walker and Bridget are coming here for a day or two before moving across to Holly Howe. And then I suppose you'll all be shifting camp to Wild Cat Island. My brother's in England, too. This postcard came today with a London postmark. A picture of the Tower Bridge and not a word on it except "Give my love to Timothy".'

'But has Timothy come?'

'No, he hasn't,' said Mrs Blackett. 'But what can I do about it? I don't even know my silly brother's address in town. Just like him . . .'

'Timothy must have died on the voyage,' said Dick. 'Not enough green food probably. Captain Flint'll be dreadfully disappointed.'

'Well I do wish he'd stop dashing off here and there about the world and sending home heaven knows what. It was bad enough with monkeys and parrots. But when it comes to dead lizards . . .'

'Armadillos aren't exactly lizards,' said Dick.

'Well, crocodiles,' said Mrs Blackett. Dick did not put her right. Zoology meant nothing to some people.

'Can I work in Captain Flint's room?' said Dick. 'It's something I've got to do before he comes back . . .'

'After lunch,' said Mrs Blackett. 'Come along, we'll find an extra plate for you.'

And Dick found himself somehow in the dining-room eating cold beef and salad. Dreadful, with the test still to be made and the acids waiting in their bottles in the little room on the other side of the hall. But it could not be helped, and Dick found himself very hungry, though two or three times he nearly fell asleep. Although at Dorothea's suggestion, he had done his best to clear the charcoal off his face, there must have been some smudges left. 'I expect you'll all be glad to get back from the desert and to have proper baths again,' said Mrs Blackett. Dick told her something about the charcoal-burning and the smelting, but not very much. She inquired after the bellows, and he said they had been very useful and that Nancy wanted her old purse to get a bit of leather for a patch, and some tacks. . . . And he pulled out his notebook to make sure. 'In drawer in hall,' he read. Mrs Blackett laughed. 'I suppose I ought to be glad the bellows survive at all,' she said, and then she kept asking him how he liked the new paper, and a lot of questions like that which were hard to answer when he was so sleepy and could think only of gold and *aqua regia*.

Luncheon was over at last and she took him to the study door.

'Here you are,' she said. 'You'll find me somewhere about

if there's anything you want. It seems to me you'll be glad to get back to school, Nancy's kept you so hard at work these holidays. What is it this time? Encyclopaedia?'

'Only partly,' said Dick. 'It's . . .' But he had no time to explain. Mrs Blackett was too busy to listen, and was talking to Cook in the hall even before she had shut the study door.

*

Dick knew exactly what he wanted and where it was. Lucky that in the general redecoration of Beckfoot, Captain Flint's study had been left alone. The glass door of the instrument cupboard was not locked. There was the little spirit-lamp he had seen, and, yes, there was some spirit in the blue bottle labelled 'Meth'. He filled the little lamp and left it for the wick to soak, while he had just one more look at the article on gold in the Encyclopaedia. Then, sitting at the table, he lit the lamp, opened his handkerchief with the gold dust, took out his blowpipe, put a pinch of dust in a hole in a bit of charcoal, and began. The spirit-lamp was much better than a candle, and he was able to keep a fine jet of flame playing on the dust. But everything happened just as it had in the camp. The dust seemed to gather together into a red-hot blob just as he had hoped, and then, when he let it cool, the blob turned dark and crumbled into powder when he pressed it with a knife. He tried again. No better. Bother the blob. He would have to make the acid test on the gold dust itself. Why not? If it was going to work, it would be easy to see if the gold disappeared.

In the cupboard was a stand with a row of test-tubes. Dick brought it to the table and chose the smallest. He put some of the gold dust on a scrap of paper and tilted it into the tube. Then he put the test-tube back in the stand and set about making the *aqua regia*. 'Nitric acid and hydrochloric acid.

. . . Equal parts.' It was not too easy to stir the glass stopper of the nitric acid bottle, and Dick was very much afraid of letting even a drop of the acid spurt out on Captain Flint's table. He managed in the end by wrapping his handkerchief round the stopper and so getting a better grip on it. He did not take the stopper right out, but, even so, the choking fumes of the acid seemed to fill the room. The bottle with hydrochloric acid opened easier. He poured a little into a test-tube, closed the bottle and put it aside. Then, doing his best not to breathe the fumes, he poured in the same amount of nitric acid. There. The *aqua regia* was ready. Dick might have been alone in a world empty except for two test-tubes, two bottles, *Phillips on Metals* and the *Encyclopaedia Britannica*. He did not hear the sudden stir in the house. . . . The opening and shutting of doors might have been in some other house a million miles away. Voices in the hall might just as well have been in Jupiter or Mars. Dick heard nothing, saw nothing, thought of nothing but the test that was at last to be made.

'Gold dissolves in *aqua regia*.'

That was the sentence in his mind. Well, would it? With a hand that trembled in spite of all he could do to keep it steady, he poured the *aqua regia* into the test-tube at the bottom of which lay that little pinch of glittering, golden dust.

It was as if the liquid suddenly boiled. Bubbles poured from the dust, which rose and fell in the acid as if it were trying to get away. The tube was hot to the touch. For a moment he was afraid it would crack and scatter acid in all directions. It was not boiling quite so hard. Sediment was settling at the bottom of the test-tube. The liquid above it was transparent, yellowish. Dick held it up to the light. Every glittering particle was gone, leaving only a dull sediment. The metallic dust had dissolved. A slow, happy grin spread over Dick's face. Gold after all.

And then, slowly, he came to know that the door of the study was open and that Captain Flint was standing in the doorway, Captain Flint, with a face burnt redder than ever, smiling at him and polishing a bald head with a green silk handkerchief. Captain Flint threw a felt hat on the table, brought a suitcase bright with steamer labels in from the hall, closed the door behind him and laughed.

'Well, Professor,' he said. 'What is it this time? It was astronomy when I found you in the cabin of the old house-boat. What's this? Chemistry?'

'Gold,' said Dick.

'Gold?' said Captain Flint. 'Don't you go and get interested in the wretched stuff. Gold or silver. I've sworn off both of them. Had quite enough of wasting time. . . . Hullo. What have you got in that test-tube?'

'*Aqua regia*,' said Dick. 'And gold dust. And it's gone all right.'

'What?' said Captain Flint. 'What's gone?'

'Dissolved,' said Dick. 'Gold in the *aqua regia*. I was just a bit afraid it might not be gold, after all.'

'But my dear chap,' said Captain Flint. '*Aqua regia* will dissolve almost anything. The point about gold is that it won't dissolve in anything else . . .'

Dick's face fell.

'I've messed it again,' he said. 'I ought to have tried with the nitric and hydrochloric separately first. I say, may I use a drop more of each of them?'

'Go ahead,' said Captain Flint. 'Got any more gold dust?'

'Only a little,' said Dick. 'Properly crushed and panned.'

Captain Flint rubbed his little finger in the dust still waiting on Dick's handkerchief. He pulled out a little magnifying-glass and held it close above those glittering particles.

'But this,' he said at last, 'looks to me like perfectly good copper pyrites. You haven't been crushing up some of my specimens, have you? Where did you get it?'

'High Topps,' said Dick. 'We had a tremendous lot ready panned, but there was an accident with our blast furnace . . .'

'Your what?'

'Blast furnace,' said Dick, 'and we lost it all mixed up with the ashes, and the crucible got broken. . . . Oh, I say, it was your crucible, you know. . . . We borrowed it. . . . There was only one that was big enough. Nancy said you wouldn't mind. You see, the gold was for you . . .'

'For me . . .? But what is all this? I couldn't make head or tail out of what my sister's been telling me.'

'She didn't know, really,' said Dick. 'At least not every-thing.'

Captain Flint had hauled up a chair and was sitting at the table. 'Let's have a look at that test-tube,' he said. 'What did you say was in it? Nitric acid, hydrochloric and some of this dust? . . . Just look along that shelf and fetch the bottle marked "Ammonia". . . . Good man. . . . Out with the cork. Let's have it. . . . Now . . .'

Drop by drop he let the ammonia trickle down the tube. There was some more fizzing. The clear liquid clouded thickly and then turned a brilliant blue.

'There you are,' said Captain Flint. 'Copper. . . . What on earth made you think it was gold?'

And Dick told of the plan and of Slater Bob's story.

Captain Flint interrupted. 'And the young man went to the war, and so his secret was lost. Why, I heard that story when I was a boy. Thirty years ago it was the South African war, and before that it was the Zulu or the Crimean, and I dare say a hundred years ago Slater Bob's grandfather was talking of the gold some young fellow would have mined if only he hadn't had to go off to fight Napoleon. But where did you get the copper? Nancy couldn't have had the slightest idea . . .'

Dick tried to explain, but he had hardly told Captain Flint about the old working in the gulch and the quartz before Captain Flint jumped up.

'Quartz. . . . Copper. . . . In one of the old workings. Got any here?'

Dick pulled a lump out of his pocket.

Captain Flint weighed it in his hand, looked at it closely, scratched with his knife at what Dick had thought was gold.

'Soft as butter,' he said eagerly. 'And is there much like that?'

'Lots,' said Dick. 'Susan wouldn't let us do any blasting. We had nothing to get it out with but hammers and a chisel. And I was sure it was gold. The others'll be dreadfully disappointed.'

'Do you know that's the richest copper ore I've ever seen?' said Captain Flint. 'If the rest's up to sample we're going to make our fortunes. . . . Gold. . . . Who wants it if there's enough of this about? I was sure it was up there somewhere. Now if only Timothy hadn't disappeared . . .'

Dick suddenly remembered that, if Nancy and the rest were to be disappointed about the gold, Captain Flint also had a dreadful misfortune to face.

'He's never arrived,' he said. 'And the worst of it is they would never know it was waste to bury him at sea instead of bringing him home to be stuffed for a museum.'

'What *do* you mean?' said Captain Flint.

'We had everything ready for him,' said Dick. 'We began as soon as your telegram came saying he was to be put in this room.'

Captain Flint's eyes, following Dick's, came to rest on the tropical grove, and the packing-case sleeping-hutch, with its

'Welcome Home' and its floral decorations. He looked closer and burst into a roar of laughter.

'Well, it's no good saying I wrote to explain. . . . I found the letter unposted in my pocket aboard ship. Poor old Timothy!' He slapped his knee and laughed again.

'Did you give him to a steward to look after?'

'But what did you think he was?'

'Armadillo,' said Dick, and gave his reasons.

'Skin not thick enough,' laughed Captain Flint. 'Well, we won't disturb the sleeping arrangements you've made for him. Hay? . . . Sawdust? . . . He ought to be very comfortable indeed. . . . Eh! Bless my soul! What's that? . . .'

Even Dick was startled by the suddenness of the noise.

'Br!r!r!r!r!r!r!r!r!r!r!r!r!r!r!r!r!r!!!! . . .'

There could be no possible doubt that the pigeons' bell was in splendid working order.

Captain Flint, old traveller as he was, admitted afterwards that he had jumped half out of his skin.

'Br!r!r!r!r!r!r!r!r!r!r!r!r!r!r!r!r!r!r!!!!! . . .'

Bell and tea-tray, with the kitchen passage as a sounding-box, made a noise almost deafening, urgent, threatening, like an alarm clock close to a sleeper's head.

'What on earth's that?'

'Br!r!r!r!r!r!r!r!r!r!r!r!r!r!r!r!r!r!r!r!!!! . . .'

'It's one of the pigeons,' said Dick. 'Funny their sending one today with me here . . .'

'Br!r!r!r!r!r!r!r!r!r!r!r!r!r!r!r!r!r!r!!!!! . . .'

'Can't we stop it?' said Captain Flint, with his hands to his ears.

Dick had already heard Mrs Blackett running downstairs. He was out in the hall in a moment.

'I'll stop it,' he said. 'It'll only be a message for me, something Nancy thought of after I'd started.' Mrs Blackett went upstairs again to get his room ready for Captain Flint.

Dick ran out of the back door, across the yard and up the steps to the pigeon loft. Out there in the yard the noise of the bell was not so bad. In the pigeon loft, Sappho could have had no idea of the dreadful din she had started in the house. She was talking quietly to Homer and Sophocles, and sipping a little water. Dick flicked back the contact wire. The ringing came to an end.

He had already seen the tiny roll of paper fastened by the rubber band to Sappho's leg. He had never had to take a message before. Always Peggy or Titty or Roger or Nancy had been there to handle the pigeon. His job had been with the wires and batteries and electric bells. But there was the message and he had to get it. He cooed and croodled to the pigeon as he had heard the others, and Sappho, after a little hesitation, let herself be caught. What could the message be? Something about the gold. What would they say when he brought the melancholy news that it was not gold at all? He pulled out the paper and unrolled it. Only three words. The first time he read it he hardly realized what it meant. He read it again.

FIRE HELP QUICK.

Joke? It couldn't be a joke. He was out of the pigeon loft in a moment, slammed the outer door on the startled pigeons, leapt the last eight steps, all but fell, picked himself up and dashed into the house.

'I'd like to see that bell contrivance of yours,' Captain Flint was saying as they met in the passage.

Dick held out the scrap of paper with Titty's desperate message.

'We've been afraid of it all the time,' he said.

'Where are they?' said Captain Flint shortly.

'At the corner of High Topps, above Mrs Tyson's farm. At least that's where the camp is . . .'

Captain Flint ran out into the garden and looked up the valley towards Kanchenjunga and that long spur of Ling Scar that held High Topps on its farther side.

Yes. The skyline up there was dim and blurred. Smoke was drifting over the top of the ridge.

Captain Flint was back in the house before Dick had had time to join him in the garden.

'Molly,' he called, in a voice that brought Mrs Blackett at once to the top of the stairs.

'What is it, Jim?'

'What's old Jolys' number? . . .'

'Seven something. . . . You'll see his fire-card on the telephone. What do you want him for?'

'Fire on High Topps. You be getting the car out while I telephone.'

Captain Flint ran to the telephone. There, pinned to the wall, was a card neatly type-written by Col. Jolys himself.

DROUGHT   FELL FIRES

IN CASE OF FIRE RING FELLSIDE 75

T. E. JOLYS (Lt.-Col.)

Captain Flint took off the receiver and violently joggled the bracket. Mrs Blackett, her face white, was gone. There was no time for Dick to make up his mind what he ought to do. The telephone had answered. Captain Flint was talking.

'Fellside, seven five. . . . No. . . . Not nine. . . . FIVE. . . . F for fool. I for idiot. . . . Yes. . . . SEVEN FIVE. . . . Hullo. . . . Hullo. . . . That Jolys. . . . Jim Turner speaking. . . . Oh

yes. Back today. . . . Listen! Fire on High Topps. . . . What?
. . . Yes. . . . Got a good hold by the look of it. . . . Blowing
from Dundale. . . . Southerly. . . . Right . . .'

There was a sudden roar in the yard, Mrs Blackett racing
Rattletrap's engine.

'Come on, Dick. Hop in.'

'What about the dromed . . . bicycle?' said Dick.

Captain Flint lifted it up and put it into the back of the car,
its handlebars and front wheel sticking up above the back seat.
The front wheel was still spinning. Dick scrambled in after it.
Mrs Blackett slipped out of the driver's seat to make room for
Captain Flint. 'Oh dear, oh dear,' she was saying, 'I ought
never to have let them camp up there in this drought.'

'It's all right, Molly,' said Captain Flint. 'Don't you
worry.' He clicked the gears in. Rattletrap, knowing her old
master, started off as if she meant it. They swung through the
gate and sharp right into the road. The gears changed,
second . . . third. . . . 'Hold tight, Dick,' said Captain Flint.
'She won't do forty except down-hill, but she's a bit of a
broncho round corners . . .'

The narrow road was all corners. Dick and the dromedary
were sometimes sharing a seat on one side of the car and
sometimes on the other. He held on as tightly as he could.
Rattletrap had never moved so fast. Even in the front seats
Mrs Blackett and Captain Flint were being tossed about as the
old car bounced across pot-holes and over loose stones. They
were not talking. Once Dick heard Captain Flint say 'Go it,
old girl,' but he was speaking to Rattletrap, not to his sister.
As they roared and rattled and clattered up the valley road
they could see dull, grey smoke drifting along above the
woods. What had happened up there? Where had the fire
started? Was the camp burnt? And Dick remembered how he
had tiptoed across it, leaving Dot and Titty and Roger sleeping in their tents. . . . And the gold wasn't gold. Every single

ABLE-SEAMEN FIGHTING THE FIRE

thing had gone wrong. And now this, worst of all. . . . What if they were too late?

And then, on two wheels, the car shot round, over the narrow bridge, scraping one mudguard, and into the Tysons' farmyard. It was deserted. Mrs Blackett jumped out of the car as it stopped, and ran across the yard to the path up into the wood.

'All up at the fire,' said Captain Flint. 'Hullo. Good. You'd better take one, too.'

The neat stack of fire-brooms was gone. But three or four of the fire-brooms were lying on the ground where the stack had been. Captain Flint took one and raced up the wood after his sister. Dick took another. He ran after Captain Flint, up and up the winding path. It had been bad enough riding down it on a dromedary. But now, with the fire-broom. . . . His heart thumped. His breath caught the back of his throat. On. On. His legs ached above the knees. He slipped and hurt his ankle, but in his hurry hardly felt the pain. There was Mrs Blackett. . . . He caught her up. . . . He passed her. . . . He caught just a glimpse of her face as he passed, climbing, climbing. . . . And now he could hear crackling. The acrid smell of burnt bracken filled his nose and throat at every gasping breath. He shifted the fire-broom to his shoulder. He let it drag behind him on the ground. He lifted it again. Nearly at the top. Gold dissolves in *aqua regia*. What a donkey he had been. Was Dot all right? Smoke drifted thickly through the trees. Somebody was shouting . . .

CHAPTER 34

THE NATIVES

'WE'LL never do it alone,' said Titty to herself. Here and there little snakes of fire ran along the cracks in the rock. As fast as one was trampled and beaten out, another showed itself. Dorothea, with the *Outlaw* safe in the knapsack on her back, was doing her best with one of the fire-brooms. Roger was doing his best with another. But again and again all three of them had to turn away from the blinding smoke, and Titty knew that the struggle could not last much longer. A shift of wind, even for a moment, and smoke and fire would come rolling down the gully, the dry leaves of the wood would catch, and, hedgehog or no hedgehog, she and Roger and Dorothea would have to run for their lives.

And at that moment help came from all sides.

A tall long-legged man in grey flannels came leaping through the smoke. He had lost his hat, but Titty knew who he was, and could never have believed she would have been so pleased to see him.

'We've got more fire-brooms,' said Roger.

'Give me yours,' said Squashy Hat, and set to work like a whirlwind.

And there were John, Nancy, Peggy and Susan.

'Are you all right?' panted Susan.

'I've burnt one hand a bit,' said Roger.

'You must butter it,' said Susan.

'They're all right, John,' said Nancy. 'Come on for the other brooms.' They dashed down into the camp and were back again in a moment.

Three men from Atkinson's farm came running along the

edge of the wood, each with a fire-broom of his own.

Squashy Hat looked round and saw them. Whatever might be said against him, he seemed to know what to do with a fire. The men from Atkinson's knew him, and in a few moments farmers and prospectors alike were working like a trained team.

'Don't let it get a hold this side of the rock,' shouted Squashy Hat, and the men shouted back, 'Aye, that's the way. . . . Keep him yonder!'

Then came Robin Tyson and the farm-hand from Tyson's with their brooms, and they, too, joined the line of the defenders, beating down every flame that showed itself in the dry grass that clung along the cracks in the rock.

And then came Mrs Tyson.

'You've done it this time, Miss Nancy. And nowt to stop it. I should have sent you packing yesterday.' And before Nancy could say a word in answer, she was gone to use her fire-broom by the side of Robin Tyson.

Roger, his scorched hand duly buttered, his face red with heat and indignation, came up to Titty. Mrs Tyson had passed through the camp.

'She thinks we started it,' he said.

'But we didn't,' said Titty. 'You told her . . .'

And then she saw Susan. A moment before, Susan's face had been all thankfulness that nobody was burnt. But now she too had heard what Mrs Tyson had said. Titty felt tears starting in her own eyes. Nothing ought ever to happen to make Susan like that.

The smoke had cleared a little from before them.

Squashy Hat was giving orders.

'You children stay here and don't let it get going again. Come on, men. Along the edge of the wood. . . . Will there be anybody fighting it from the other side?'

'There's Low Farm at Watersmeet,' said one of the men

from Atkinson's. 'But they've nobbut the old man and a li'l lad.'

'We'll keep it out of the wood if the wind doesn't shift,' shouted Squashy. 'But along there where the rock ends it'd take a hundred men to stop it. . . . Hullo, we must down that one.' And he raced off along the edge of the rock to meet a rolling mass of dark brown smoke.

Titty was startled by a sudden yell from Nancy.

'Uncle Jim!'

She turned round. There he was, with a fire-broom in his hands, hurriedly counting the prospectors.

'Nancy . . . Peggy . . . Titty . . . Susan . . . Dorothea . . . John . . . Roger. . . . That's all right.'

'Look here,' said Nancy. 'We didn't start it. They think we did.'

'All right,' said Captain Flint. 'I don't suppose . . .'

He broke off suddenly.

'What!' he cried. 'Hullo! Who's that? Well, I'm absolutely jiggered.'

'He's a jumper,' said Dorothea.

'He's after our gold,' said Titty.

'He's been spying on us, and plotting with Slater Bob. . . . We've been fending him off for all we were worth . . .'

But Captain Flint was not listening. He put his hand like a trumpet to his mouth and bellowed one word, one single word . . .

'TIMOTHY!'

And Squashy Hat turned round, waved a hand and went on beating in the smoke.

Captain Flint was gone to join him.

The weary, grimed prospectors stared open-mouthed at each other. Not one of them had said a word when Dick, dripping with sweat, came stumbling up the gully. . .

'Is Dot all right?' he gasped.

He dropped his fire-broom, and frantically tore off his

spectacles. He had got very hot indeed running up the wood, and could see nothing at all for the drops of sweat that had fallen on his glasses.

'Dick, Dick,' asked Dorothea urgently. 'Is it gold?'

In the excitement of the fire-fighting, and the dreadful discovery that Timothy, whom they had meant to welcome, and Squashy Hat, whom they had treated as an enemy, were one and the same, the others had forgotten everything else. Not Dorothea. How could she forget, when the success or failure of the whole expedition depended on Dick alone? Was it gold, or was it not?

'I was all wrong,' said Dick, panting. 'It's not gold at all. It's copper. Captain Flint showed me himself. It turned blue with ammonia . . .'

One blow after another.

And then came Mrs Blackett, who had not been able to keep up with Dick racing up the steep path through Tyson's wood. She, too, called a hurried roll of the prospectors . . .

'Nancy . . . Peggy . . . Titty . . . John . . . Susan. . . . Where's Dorothea? Oh there. And Roger? Not hurt? What have you done to your hand? . . . Oh, my dears, think what your parents would be saying to me if . . .'

'We're all right, mother. . . . Everybody is,' said Peggy.

'But Timothy's been here all the time,' said Nancy. 'He's just along there with Uncle Jim. . . . He jolly nearly got burnt, falling asleep in our gulch . . .'

'Look out, Susan,' shouted John. 'There's a bit smouldering right at your feet.'

'Help!' cried Dorothea, beating away frantically at the little flames that had been lurking in a tussock of dry bent and had suddenly flared up.

'Pouf, what smoke!' coughed Mrs Blackett. 'Haven't you a fire-broom to spare?'

'Have mine,' said Roger, who, with his buttered hand in a

bandage, found he could not do much good with the new fire-broom he had brought from the camp.

The main body of the fire was sweeping on along the rocky edge of the Topps. Captain Flint and Timothy and the farm men were moving with it, fighting hard to keep it from crossing the stony ground and getting down into the wood. Every now and then one or other of them showed in the drifting smoke, flailing away with a fire-broom, and then disappeared as the smoke rolled over him. The prospectors were hard at work beating out first one and then another spurt of fire along the edge of the ground already burnt, where red-hot sparks, creeping underfoot, were hard to see until unexpectedly they burst into flame. There was one dreadful moment when a little holly tree, on the low side of the rock and close to the wood and the bramble thicket blazed up suddenly like a firework, with a loud crackling noise. But John and Nancy were there in time to trample out the grass around it.

Mrs Tyson, in despair, came back out of the smoke.

'There's nowt'll stop it,' she said. 'Ye may fight it here along the rock, but when it comes to Greenbanks ye'll not hold it. Eh, Mrs Blackett, I didn't think it of them. I should have sent them packing yesterday. Never again. Never again . . .'

'But Colonel Jolys . . .' began Mrs Blackett.

'Colonel Jolys,' said Mrs Tyson bitterly. 'What's the good of Colonel Jolys? Who's to tell him? By the time they see the smoke over yonder the woods'll be ablaze, and the whole valley gone in ashes . . .'

She stopped short and listened.

'What's that?' said Roger.

The blast of a coach horn, the old blast on four notes that used to echo up and down these valleys thirty years ago, before the motors brought the coaches to an end, sounded not so very far away. It was answered by another, nearer.

'Tatarara-ta-ta. . . . Tatarara-ta-ta-ta. . . . Come to the cookhouse door, boys. Come to the cookhouse door.'

Dozens of motor horns sounded in the distance.

'It's the fire-fighters,' cried Nancy. 'It's Colonel Jolys. But how on earth have they come so quick? . . .

'We telephoned as soon as we got your message?'

'What message?'

'We sent Sappho,' said Roger . . .

'I wrote a letter,' said Titty, 'but we never thought she'd fly straight . . .'

Nancy jumped into the air with both feet.

'Well done!' she shouted. 'Well done the able-seamen! Good old Sappho! John! Susan! Peggy! *Do* you hear? They sent an S O S by pigeon post. And Sappho flew straight for once.'

'One o' them pigeons. . . .' said Mrs Tyson doubtingly.

There was a roar of cheering somewhere away along the top of the wood, answered by another. The horns sounded again.

'Nay, we've a chance yet,' cried Mrs Tyson, and was gone.

It was evening before they knew that the fire was beaten and the valley saved. Colonel Jolys and his men had been in time to burn a wide strip of ground in the path of the fire, so that the fire, when it came there, died for lack of fuel. High Topps was a black sea with wave crests of white ash. To the north the smoke was clearing, and Ling Scar showed clear above it.

'Slater Bob perhaps doesn't even know there's been a fire,' said Dorothea, thinking of the old miner working away alone in the middle of the hill.

Captain Flint, and Timothy, and the Atkinsons and Tysons came slowly back along the edge of the Topps with their fire-brooms over their shoulders.

Mrs Tyson came straight up to the prospectors where they were standing on the Great Wall looking out.

'Well,' she said, 'I was wrong that time, thinking you'd set the fell afire. I should have seen that if you'd done it, 'twould have been the wood to burn first. But you mun forgive me. When fire's afoot a body can't think. And if you'd not been here with they pigeons, we'd have had our farms burnt, and the hay in t' fields and all, before anybody could have gotten word. So I thank you, and yon pigeon of yours most of all. Eh, Mrs Blackett, they're welcome to camp where they like and when they like and how they like as long as they like. Now then, Robin. Nowt to stare at. We've the cows to milk, fire or no fire. And late it is and all.' And Mrs Tyson and Robin and the farm-hand went down into the wood.

'So that's all right,' said Mrs Blackett.

'You seem to have made a friend of Mrs Tyson,' said Captain Flint.

'Oh well,' said Nancy dismally, 'it doesn't matter now. The whole fortnight's wasted and we've failed . . .'

'Failed?' said Captain Flint. 'Failed? What do you mean?'

'It isn't gold,' said Nancy. 'Dick says it's only copper, after all.'

'But it's copper we've been trying for,' said Captain Flint.

PESTLE·AND·MORTAR

CHAPTER 35

THE END

AND then, at last, the prospectors heard the whole story of
what had happened. Captain Flint and Timothy had been
together in South America, looking for gold where there was
not any. High on a mountain-side they had talked of English
mining, and the old copper mines on the fells, and the copper
that must still be there where the old miners had failed to find
it. They had talked of the new ways of prospecting that the
old miners could never have tried. They had made up their
minds to have a look for themselves. 'There was something I
remembered seeing above High Topps. . . .' Timothy had been
going home first, and was to have brought with him a letter to
Mrs Blackett. 'And I wrote the letter,' said Captain Flint, 'and
found it still in my pocket when I'd been a week aboard ship
myself. But I didn't worry. I'd given him the Beckfoot address
and told him to go and talk to Slater Bob. And I'd telegraphed
besides. It never occurred to me that he'd be too shy to call.'

Timothy's blush could be seen even through his sunburn
and the black smears of smoke on his face.

'I wanted him to have the run of my room because of my
maps and things. Oh well, another prospector had the run of
them instead . . .'

'I'm awfully sorry about that crucible,' said Dick.

'Bother the crucible,' said Captain Flint, 'but I'd like to
see the place where you found that copper.'

'Come on,' said Nancy, looking across the black and
smoking Topps.

'When did anybody last have anything to eat?' said Mrs
Blackett.

'A hundred years ago,' said Roger.

'Let's make supper for everybody,' said Susan.

'Let's,' said Peggy.

'May I help?' said Mrs Blackett.

'Signal when you're ready,' said Nancy. 'We'll have time to get across there and back.'

*

Little wisps of smoke drifted from the blackened ground. The ash from burnt bent and bracken spurted from under their feet. Nothing was left of the purple heather but blackened stems that looked like tiny trees that had been struck by lightning.

'It's like walking about in a volcano,' said Titty.

Far away in the distance along the foot of Ling Scar they could see some of Colonel Jolys' volunteers.

'It isn't really fair,' said Roger. 'They don't give the fire a chance.'

'All jolly well,' said John. 'The fire wouldn't have given us much of a chance if we hadn't been able to get into the mine.'

'And think what would have happened if Sappho hadn't done her best,' said Dorothea.

'She didn't keep the natives away that time,' said Roger. 'She stirred up the whole crowd of them.'

Captain Flint and Squashy Hat were walking together talking copper, and Dick, stumbling along beside them, was doing his best to understand.

'I found the gosson all right,' Squashy Hat was saying, pointing across the Topps to the white spots he had painted on the slopes of Kanchenjunga.

'I beg your pardon,' said Dick. 'But what is gosson?'

'Decomposed ore,' said Captain Flint. 'No good in itself, but a sign of good stuff lower down . . .'

'I found the gosson all right ... red, porous muck, as promising as any I've seen anywhere. ... But, be hanged if I could find the vein once I followed it down. The gosson ended, and that was that. The only good ore I've seen was some loose bits I came on this morning ...'

'Ours,' interrupted Nancy.

'Yes,' said Captain Flint. 'From what Dick tells me, I think they beat you to it.'

They came to the edge of the gulch, where the rocks, except for their dark smoke stains, showed paler than the blackened ground.

Timothy pulled out a much-folded map.

'Look here, Jim,' he said. 'Here's the line of the gosson. ... Those white splashes mark my scratchings as I traced it down. ... I've picked it out in red on the map. ... It must come across this way, but never a sign of the vein ...'

'Come and look at it,' said Nancy, in something of her old manner. Gold it might not be, but if it was what Captain Flint wanted, it was good enough, and her spirits were going upstairs again three steps at a time. 'Come and look at it,' she said. 'Claim's staked, of course. The fire's burnt our notice, but the claim's staked all the same.'

They ran down the side of the gulch and crossed it and showed the way into the mine, not so well hidden now that the heather had been burnt round the opening.

'This way,' said Nancy, and dived into the mine. The others followed.

'Hullo,' said Captain Flint, as he straightened himself when well inside. 'Somebody's working here.'

'We forgot to put it out,' said John, looking at the hurricane lantern, still burning, hanging from the iron peg in the wall.

'And isn't that my old mortar?'

'Borrowed,' said Nancy.

'And where's the vein? ... Gosh, Timothy, do you see that? Let's have that lantern a bit nearer.' He picked up one of the hammers and started eagerly chipping at the quartz. 'Vein,' he said. 'It's better than I ever hoped.'

'It's the vein all right,' said Timothy. 'And I was in here this afternoon and never saw it even then.'

'You were looking the other way,' said Nancy. 'We all were, while the fire went roaring past.'

'But how did you find it, Nancy?' said Captain Flint.

'I found it,' said Roger.

'But how?'

'I just banged with a hammer and a bit of stone fell down, and there it was.'

'The old chaps must have stopped just an inch too soon,' said Captain Flint. 'Well, Timothy. We've missed the train. Roger and the rest are in before us and we may as well give up. Unless they'll float a company and let us join them ...'

Everybody looked at Nancy in the dim light of the lantern.

Was not that just what she had been wanting? The others expected her to jump at the chance. But Nancy set her lips firmly together, took all she could of the sparkle out of her eyes and looked doubtfully at Captain Flint.

'Um,' she said.

'Oh, look here, Nancy.'

'Conditions.'

'Out with them.'

'No more being away in the summer holidays,' said Nancy. 'Wild geese in South America and all that.'

'We can't work this properly without staying at home,' said Captain Flint. 'That's what I've come home for.'

'Oh is it?' said Nancy. 'What about us? You can work it in term-time. And, of course, a bit in the holidays. But what's the good of the houseboat if you're never there?'

'What do you want me to do?'

'We'll have two boats again when Mrs Walker comes, and Dick and Dorothea have never seen a battle.'

Captain Flint turned to Squashy Hat.

'Two against eight,' he said. 'Timothy, my lad, you don't know what you're in for. You wait till you walk the plank and step on nothingness and meet cold water and the sharks. All right, Nancy. It'll do him good. And, look here, Titty, will you help to make me a new flag? The old elephant's a bit moth-eaten and mildewed. What about something in the armadillo line? . . .'

There was a laugh from everybody except Squashy Hat, and even he smiled politely, as people do at some joke they do not understand.

And then, of course, Roger reminded them that Susan and Peggy and Mrs Blackett were probably already waiting for them. They started back.

Dick had said little, but now he had a question to put to Captain Nancy. 'Do you think it really didn't matter my being wrong about the gold?'

'Jolly good thing,' said Nancy. 'We might have just chucked it if we'd known before. Gold or copper, it's all the same if you have enough. Two hundred and forty pennies make a pound. Just look at them.' She pointed at Captain Flint and Squashy Hat, who were walking ahead comparing lumps of copper-laden quartz and talking eagerly together. 'Didn't you hear? They're going to get old Slater Bob to come and help them.'

'He said he'd like to give slates a rest and have another go at metal,' said Dorothea.

'And we can have a go too,' said Nancy, 'whenever we aren't too busy with something else.'

'Good,' said Roger. 'I thought so. There she is.'

Peggy was at the edge of the Topps, signalling with a handkerchief tied to a stick. There was no need for them to read more than the first two letters. Everybody knew that the word was 'GRUB'.

'Hurry up, Uncle Jim,' said Nancy. 'Everybody's starving.'

'All right. . . . Now, look here, Timothy. . . . It's just as we guessed up above Pernambuco. Those old miners knew nothing about gosson as a sign of good copper. They scratched what they saw, and if they couldn't see anything they gave up. Now this is just where it should be, on the line of the gosson higher up, and if we cut in there we'll be coming at richer ore than's ever been mined in these fells . . .'

'Greedy, greedy,' said Nancy.

Roger looked round indignantly.

'All right, Roger,' she said. 'I wasn't thinking of you.'

*

Supper was over.

Even people who had been too tired to be anything but silent began to talk.

Titty slipped off in the dusk.

The bramble thicket had been saved from the fire, but the little hedgepig, she thought, might have died from fright, with all that smoke, and the roaring of the flames, and the trampling of the fire-fighters. Something stirred by the well. She crept nearer. It was something small, thin, with a curved back . . . a weasel. It drank, lifted its little snakelike head, sniffed and was gone. . . . The water had risen in the well again, and there was some to spare even for weasels, but she wondered whether the coming of the weasel would frighten the hedgepig away. Behind her she could see the red glow of the camp-fire in the trees, and she could hear Mrs Blackett's voice saying how thankful she was that everybody was all right and how awful it would have been if somebody had got burnt just when the parents were coming. She heard Roger's voice. 'I did have to put some butter on my hand.' Would the talking keep the hedgepig away?

And then she heard the stirring of dry leaves, away under the brambles. She heard a sniff ... a grunt ... a sneeze. Perhaps some of the ash blown down from the Topps was tickling its nostrils. Then, in the dim light she saw it. With steady lumbering trot it was making for the well. She watched a little dark lump work itself down the steps. It was drinking. The water got into its nose, and she heard a small impatient snuffle. It climbed out again and trotted off. She lost sight of it in the shadows. But she had seen enough and slipped back to the camp.

The firelight threw everything outside the camp into darkness. Mrs Blackett and the two cooks were collecting the supper things, ready for washing-up. Titty looked round for Dick. He was lying on the ground, staring into the flames. She dropped between him and Nancy.

'It's all right about the hedgepig,' she said. 'He's just gone hunting, and I've seen him have a drink at the well.'

'Good,' said Dick.

Dorothea, lying on his other side, had heard. 'The animals and the birds will drink there for ever and ever,' she said, 'and if it wasn't for Titty there wouldn't be a well at all.'

'Captain Flint wouldn't believe you found water really,' said Nancy. 'Not till mother told him all about it.'

Meanwhile Roger was telling and re-telling his share in the fire-fighting, not because he wanted to boast, but because by telling it he somehow made sure of it for himself. At the time, things had been happening too fast.

'It wasn't very big flames at first,' he was saying. 'Just smoke and cracklings and spurtings of fire along the ground, and then the wind roared it up and it was all over everywhere. And the smell. . . . And we couldn't see anything. . . . And we sent off Sappho, just so she shouldn't get burnt. We never thought she'd be good and go straight home. . . . And then we thought of Titty's well. . . . And we were running with buckets . . . well, you know, tins. . . . We emptied out the sugar and biscuits. . . . And then there was no more water. . . . We were beating with the fire-brooms. . . . And Nancy and John and Susan and Peggy and Squashy Hat. . . . Oh well, you know who I mean. . . . They came bursting through the smoke and Susan was nearly crying. . . . Oh yes, you were, Susan. . . . Well, why not? . . . It would have been pretty awful if the wood had got burnt and all our tents . . .'

Captain Flint was talking too, with Squashy Hat.

They were lying by the camp-fire, smoking their pipes.

'Yes, my lad,' Captain Flint was saying. 'But why, why, didn't you go straight to Beckfoot? I'd telegraphed to let them know . . .'

Squashy Hat seemed to be turning shy again.

'My dear Jim, how could I? There were children popping up all over the place. It was like a school feast. . . . You wouldn't have gone in yourself. . . . How could I tell you hadn't bunged me into the middle of a holiday school? So I couldn't get at your maps, and that old chap up at the slate mine took a lot of thawing. He was all right the first day I saw him, but after that something seemed to have gone wrong with him, and he was like an oyster for days and days. I . . .'

Titty saw that Nancy was listening too. At this point Nancy rolled suddenly over so that the firelight no longer lit up her laughing face.

'But what business had you to be shy?' said Captain Flint, and, remembering something burst into a roar of laughter. 'Shy? Why, they were expecting you. They'd even built a special bedroom for you. I've seen it myself with, "Welcome Home" and your name on the door. A bit small, perhaps, but goodwill is what matters.'

Other Books by Arthur Ransome

SWALLOWS AND AMAZONS *
'Watch the effect of the first hundred pages on your own children. If they want no more, send for a doctor' – *Daily Telegraph*

SWALLOWDALE *
'If there is a nicer book this side of *Treasure Island* I have missed it' – *Observer*
'A perfect book for children of all ages, and better reading for the rest of us than are most novels' – *Spectator*

PETER DUCK *
'One of those rare books which come from time to time to enthral grown-up people and children at once with the spell of true romance. A book to buy, to read, to give away – and to keep' – *The Times*

COOT CLUB *
'There is a satisfactory realism about all that happens to the Coot Club, and the atmosphere and detail of the odd part of England where they navigate are conveyed with a charm and accuracy that only this author perhaps could bring to bear' – *Guardian*

WINTER HOLIDAY *
'One could hardly have a better book about children' – *The Times*

WE DIDN'T MEAN TO GO TO SEA
'This book is Ransome at the top of his form; and so needs no further recommendation from me' – *Observer*
'This is the seventh of the Arthur Ransome books about the Swallows, and I really think it is the best' – *Sunday Times*

SECRET WATER
'Once more the Swallows and Amazons have a magnificent exploring adventure, once more Mr Arthur Ransome has kept a complete record of their experiences, terrors, triumphs, and set it down with the cunning that casts a spell over new children and old' – *The Times Literary Supplement*

THE BIG SIX

'The setting is once more the Norfolk Broads, about which Mr Ransome obviously knows everything that can be known. As usual every single detail of the boatman's art and craft is meticulously explored. ... Mr Ransome once again equals or perhaps excels himself, and every boy who enjoys him – and every boy does – will vote this detective story super' – Rosamund Lehmann in the *New Statesman*

MISSEE LEE

'*Missee Lee*, by Arthur Ransome, seems to be his best yet. Not only are there pirates in it, but a super female pirate, Missee Lee herself, whose very surprising behaviour creates a situation far too good to be given away. This new Ransome like all the other Ransomes, is a book to buy, to read, and to read again, not once but many times' – *Observer*

THE PICTS AND THE MARTYRS

'*The Picts and the Martyrs* is quite up to the best standard of its predecessors, and to all old Ransome devotees the return to the lake of the first novels gives an added pleasure. It is impossible to finish it without wishing one did not have to leave when there are still "five more weeks of the holidays to go"' – *Glasgow Herald*

GREAT NORTHERN?

'What is that something possessed by Arthur Ransome that most of the others haven't got? I suppose really it is the old spell-binding stuff, the ability to weave and tell a story simply, directly, vividly and swiftly, and with that extra magic quality that raises the first-class story-teller so far above the rest. ... Here's the perfect boat and bird story for this Christmas, for any age and for those who like their books well produced and well illustrated too' – *Time and Tide*

All illustrated, and published by Jonathan Cape
* already available in Puffins